Wuthering Heights

The WILD and WANTON Edition

Annabella Bloom and Emily Brontë

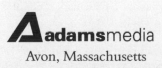adamsmedia

Avon, Massachusetts

Published by
Adams Media, a division of F+W Media, Inc.
57 Littlefield Street, Avon, MA 02322. U.S.A.
www.adamsmedia.com

ISBN 10: 1-4405-0659-0
ISBN 13: 978-1-4405-0659-8
eISBN 10: 1-4405-1130-6
eISBN 13: 978-1-4405-1130-1

Printed in the United States of America.

10 9 8 7 6 5 4 3 2 1

Library of Congress Cataloging-in-Publication Data
Bloom, Annabella.
Wuthering Heights : the wild and wanton edition / Emily Bronte and Annabella
Bloom.
p. cm.
ISBN-13: 978-1-4405-0659-8
ISBN-10: 1-4405-0659-0
ISBN-13: 978-1-4405-1130-1 (ebk.)
ISBN-10: 1-4405-1130-6 (ebk.)
1. Triangles (Interpersonal relations)—Fiction. 2. Revenge—Fiction. 3.
Yorkshire (England)—Fiction. I. Bront?, Emily, 1818-1848. Wuthering Heights.
II. Title.
PS3602.L657W87 2011
813'.6—dc22
2010041440

*This book is available at quantity discounts for bulk purchases.
For information, please call 1-800-289-0963.*

DEDICATION

To MY HUSBAND, my partner and lover in all things. May we continue to find happiness in the life we share, and joy in the everyday. We are two halves of the same coin, you and I, one dark and one light, forever joined.

PROLOGUE

March 15, 1780

I can feel the ghost of his hands on my skin, the roughness of his hands, the scratch of his rough beard on my cheek. My dreams are full of sensations of being with him. I can hardly bear the thought of waiting until later today to be with him again.

We came together as a man and a woman for the first time seven days ago. Since then I have thought of nothing else but being with him again. Each afternoon I go to the stables and wait behind the bales of hay until he arrives.

He smells of man and hard work, a concoction designed to drug my senses—mine and mine alone. When his arms surround me, I feel his body harden against me, his staff lengthen and press into my belly. I am lost in that moment, lost in the world we make together.

My body softens and readies itself for him. I shed my clothes and lie on the blanket, ready to receive my lover.

My Heathcliff.

CHAPTER 1

1801

I HAVE JUST RETURNED from a visit to my landlord—the solitary neighbor that I shall be troubled with. This is certainly a beautiful country! In all England, I do not believe that I could have fixed on a situation so completely removed from the stir of society.

A perfect misanthropist's heaven: and Mr. Heathcliff and I are such a suitable pair to divide the desolation between us. A capital fellow! He little imagined how my heart warmed towards him when I beheld his black eyes withdraw so suspiciously under their brows, as I rode up, and when his fingers sheltered themselves, with a jealous resolution, still further in his waistcoat, as I announced my name. **He was quite tall and thin but with broad shoulders needing no padding, as was the current custom amongst men in regular society. Mr. Heathcliff obviously cared nothing for fashion, however, judging by his clothing, which was as dark as his eyes.**

Yet there was something about him, a gypsy element that set him apart from most. He exuded sensuality from every pore, even his walk; his gestures and his speech were naturally of a carnal

nature. **The very air around him pulsed with it. This was something I had always aspired to, but never accomplished, not even when the opportunity to demonstrate my passion offered itself—**

Ah, but not to think of her now when confronted by the man who was the very epitome of what I wanted to be, but could never achieve. My ladylove had abandoned me likely for a gentleman such as my landlord. It was a painful wound not yet healed within me.

"Mr. Heathcliff?" I said. A nod was the answer. **The darkly intense gaze, however, never wavered from mine. What manner of welcome was this? His was a brutish nature, marked by the power of a beast.** "Mr. Lockwood, your new tenant, sir. I do myself the honor of calling as soon as possible after my arrival, to express the hope that I have not inconvenienced you by my perseverance in soliciting the occupation of Thrushcross Grange. I heard yesterday you had had some thoughts—"

"Thrushcross Grange is my own, sir," he interrupted with a swipe of one long-fingered hand in the air, wincing. "I should not allow anyone to inconvenience me, if I could hinder it—walk in!"

The "walk in" was uttered with closed teeth, and expressed the sentiment, "Go to the Deuce." Even the gate over which he leant manifested no sympathizing movement to the words; and I think that circumstance determined me to accept the invitation. I felt interested in a man who seemed more exaggeratedly reserved than myself.

When he saw my horse's breast fairly pushing the barrier, he did put out his hand to unchain it, and then sullenly preceded me up the causeway, calling, as we entered the court, "Joseph, take Mr. Lockwood's horse, and bring up some wine."

"Here we have the whole establishment of domestics, I suppose," was the reflection suggested by this compound order. "No wonder the grass grows up between the flags, and cattle are the only hedge-cutters."

Joseph was an elderly, nay, an old man, very old, perhaps, though hale and sinewy. "The Lord help us!" he soliloquized in an undertone of peevish displeasure, while relieving me of my horse. Looking, meantime, in my face so sourly that I charitably conjectured he must have need of divine aid to digest his dinner, and his pious ejaculation had no reference to my unexpected advent.

Wuthering Heights is the name of Mr. Heathcliff's dwelling. "Wuthering" being a significant provincial adjective, descriptive of the atmospheric tumult to which its station is exposed in stormy weather. Pure, bracing ventilation they must have up there at all times, indeed. One may guess the power of the north wind blowing over the edge, by the excessive slant of a few stunted firs at the end of the house, and by a range of gaunt thorns all stretching their limbs one way, as if craving alms of the sun. The house matched its master in its fierceness, and its brooding as well. There was perhaps a touch of the Wuthering house in his dark countenance as well. Happily, the architect had foresight to build it strong. The narrow windows are deeply set in the wall, and the corners defended with large jutting stones.

Before passing the threshold, I paused to admire a quantity of grotesque carving lavished over the front, and especially about the principal door, above which, among a wilderness of crumbling griffins and shameless little boys, I detected the date "1500," and the name "Hareton Earnshaw." I would have made a few comments, and requested a short history of the place from the surly owner, but his attitude at the door appeared to demand my speedy entrance, or complete departure, and I had no desire to aggravate his impatience previous to inspecting the penetralium. **He had an air about his person that put one in mind of barely controlled storm, waiting to unleash its fury on an unsuspecting man such as myself.**

One stop brought us into the family sitting room, without any introductory lobby or passage. They call it here "the house" preeminently. It includes kitchen and parlor, generally, but I believe at Wuthering Heights the kitchen is forced to retreat altogether into another quarter. At least I distinguished a chatter of tongues, and a clatter of culinary utensils, deep within, and I observed no signs of roasting, boiling, or baking, about the huge fireplace, nor any glitter of copper saucepans and tin cullenders on the walls. **Perhaps Mr. Heathcliff preferred the cacophony of the kitchen out of his range of hearing since by its very nature would cause all manner of noise. He did not appear to be the type of man to suffer without seeking out the offending clamor and using the force of his stare, force it into silence.**

One end, indeed, reflected splendidly both light and heat from ranks of immense pewter dishes, interspersed with silver jugs and tankards, towering row after row, on a vast oak dresser, to the very roof. The latter had never been under-drawn. Its entire anatomy lay bare to an inquiring eye, except where a frame of wood laden with oatcakes and clusters of legs of beef, mutton, and ham, concealed it. Above the chimney were sundry villainous old guns, and a couple of horse-pistols. And, by way of ornament, three gaudily painted canisters disposed along its ledge. The floor was of smooth, white stone, the chairs, high-backed, primitive structures, painted green. One or two heavy black ones lurking in the shade. In an arch under the dresser reposed a huge, liver-colored bitch pointer, surrounded by a swarm of squealing puppies, and other dogs haunted other recesses. **It appeared Mr. Healthcliff preferred the company of canines to humans.**

The apartment and furniture would have been nothing extraordinary as belonging to a homely, northern farmer, with a stubborn countenance, and stalwart limbs set out to advantage in knee-breeches and gaiters. Such an individual seated in his armchair, his mug of ale frothing on the round table before him, is to be seen in any circuit of five or six miles among these hills, if you go at the right time after dinner.

But Mr. Heathcliff forms a singular contrast to his abode and style of living. He is a dark-skinned gypsy in aspect, in dress and manners a gentleman. That is, as much a gentleman as many a country squire. Rather slovenly, perhaps, yet not looking amiss with his negligence, because he has an erect and handsome figure, and rather morose. Possibly, some people might suspect him of a degree of under-bred pride; I have a sympathetic chord within that tells me it is nothing of the sort. I know, by instinct, his reserve springs from an aversion to showy displays of feeling—to manifestations of mutual kindliness. He'll love and hate equally under cover, and esteem it a species of impertinence to be loved or hated again.

No, I'm running on too fast. I bestow my own attributes over-liberally on him. Mr. Heathcliff may have entirely dissimilar reasons for keeping his hand out of the way when he meets a would-be acquaintance, to those that actuate me. Let me hope my constitution is almost peculiar. My dear mother used to say I should never have a comfortable home, and only last summer I proved myself perfectly unworthy of one.

While enjoying a month of fine weather at the seacoast, I was thrown into the company of a most fascinating creature. A real goddess in my eyes, as long as she took no notice of me. I "never told my love" vocally, still, if looks have language, the merest idiot might have guessed I was over head and ears. She understood me at last, and looked a return—the sweetest of all imaginable looks. And what did I do? I confess it with shame—shrunk icily into myself, like a snail, unable to perform the feat which she inspired in me—until at her every glance I retired colder and farther, until finally the poor innocent was led to doubt her own senses, and, overwhelmed with confusion at her supposed mistake, persuaded her mamma to decamp. By this curious turn of disposition I have gained the reputation of deliberate heartlessness, how undeserved, I alone can appreciate.

I did not want to be too much similar to my host, yet I did wish to be as virile and passionate as he was. Fickle fate had lent me a bad hand in that manner. Curious that she did bestow those qualities on Mr. Heathcliff, who appeared to be averse to acceptable social behaviors.

I took a seat at the end of the hearthstone opposite that towards which my landlord advanced, and filled up an interval of silence by attempting to caress the canine mother, who had left her nursery, and was sneaking wolfishly to the back of my legs, her lip curled up, and her white teeth watering for a snatch. My caress provoked a long, guttural snarl.

"You'd better let the dog alone," growled Mr. Heathcliff in unison, checking fiercer demonstrations with a punch of his foot. **His tone and actions startled me into inaction—the man was nearly as frightening as the dog's maw.** "She's not accustomed to be spoiled—not kept for a pet." Then, striding to a side door, he shouted again, "Joseph!"

Joseph mumbled indistinctly in the depths of the cellar, but gave no intimation of ascending, so his master dived down to him, leaving me vis-à-vis the ruffianly bitch and a pair of grim shaggy sheep dogs, who shared with her a jealous guardianship over all my movements. Not anxious to come in contact with their fangs, I sat still, but, imagining they would scarcely understand tacit insults, I unfortunately indulged in winking and making faces at the trio, and some turn of my physiognomy so irritated madam, that she suddenly broke into a fury and leapt on my knees.

I flung her back, and hastened to interpose the table between us. This proceeding aroused the whole hive. Half-a-dozen four-footed fiends, of various sizes and ages, issued from hidden dens to the common center. I felt my heels and coat-laps peculiar subjects of assault, and parrying off the larger combatants as effectually as I could with the poker, I was constrained to demand, aloud, assistance from some of the household in reestablishing peace.

Mr. Heathcliff and his man climbed the cellar steps with vexatious phlegm. I don't think they moved one second faster than usual, though the hearth was an absolute tempest of worrying and yelping. Happily, an inhabitant of the kitchen made more dispatch. A lusty dame, with tucked-up gown, bare arms, and fire-flushed cheeks, rushed into the midst of us flourishing a frying pan. And used that weapon, and her tongue, to such purpose, that the storm subsided magically. **My gaze could not help but fall to her round breasts, at present heaving like a sea after a high wind. They were formed perfectly for a man's hand. The tips hardened and poked at her rough blouse from the effort of her exertions—an enticing invitation I had to forcibly restrain myself from accepting.**

A trickle of sweat had formed on the curve of skin rising from her bodice. I licked my lips, imagining the taste of the salty tang on my tongue. Visions of pushing her bodice aside and gazing upon her naked form filled my mind. My staff began to harden in my trousers and I allowed myself the liberty of wondering if the maiden were averse to servicing her master's guests in their beds. When finally I tore my gaze from the fruitfulness of her charms, I saw that she had raised one inquisitive brow in my direction. Did she appreciate my regard? Or was she annoyed—even repelled— by it? It was difficult to tell from her expression. I was about to speak to her when her master entered on the scene. The memory of being attacked by his canines returned with a rush, pushing aside all thoughts of a carnal nature.

"What the devil is the matter?" he asked, eyeing me in a manner that I could ill endure, after this inhospitable treatment. **There was a limit to the patience any visitor would reach when enduring a household and master as uncongenial as Wuthering Heights.**

"What the devil, indeed!" I muttered. "The herd of possessed swine could have had no worse spirits in them than those animals of yours, sir. You might as well leave a stranger with a brood of tigers!"

"They won't meddle with persons who touch nothing," he remarked, putting the bottle before me, and restoring the displaced table. "The dogs do right to be vigilant. Take a glass of wine?"

"No, thank you."

"Not bitten, are you?" **The words seemed pried from his mouth.**

"If I had been, I would have set my signet on the biter."

Heathcliff's countenance relaxed into a grin. "Come, come," he said, "you are flurried, Mr. Lockwood. Here, take a little wine. Guests are so exceedingly rare in this house that I and my dogs, I am willing to own, hardly know how to receive them. Your health, sir?"

I bowed and returned the pledge, beginning to perceive that it would be foolish to sit sulking for the misbehavior of a pack of curs; besides, I felt loath to yield the fellow further amusement at my expense, since his humor took that turn. He—probably swayed by prudential consideration of the folly of offending a good tenant— relaxed a little in the laconic style of chipping off his pronouns and auxiliary verbs, and introduced what he supposed would be a subject of interest to me—a discourse on the advantages and disadvantages of my present place of retirement. I found him very intelligent on the topics we touched, and before I went home, I was encouraged so far as to volunteer another visit tomorrow. He evidently wished no rep- etition of my intrusion. I was certain my host did not often have visi- tors nor was he inclined to welcome them for a repeat visit, perhaps for a sound reason. I shall go, notwithstanding. It is astonishing how sociable I feel myself compared with him.

CHAPTER 2

*Y*ESTERDAY AFTERNOON set in misty and cold. I had half a mind to spend it by my study fire, instead of wading through heath and mud to Wuthering Heights. I dine between twelve and one o'clock, the housekeeper, a matronly lady taken as a fixture along with the house, could not, or would not, comprehend my request that I might be served at five. On coming up from dinner, however, on mounting the stairs with this lazy intention, and stepping into the room, I saw a servant-girl on her knees surrounded by brushes and coalscuttles. **I paused a moment to admire the shape of her buttocks moving beneath her dress but she was raising an infernal dust as she extinguished the flames with heaps of cinders, so I did not linger.** I took my hat, and, after a four-miles' walk, arrived at Heathcliff's garden gate just in time to escape the first feathery flakes of a snow-shower.

On that bleak hilltop, the earth was hard with a black frost, and the air made me shiver through every limb. Wuthering Heights was as inhospitable as it had been my prior visit, yet I would not be deterred from my visit regardless. Being unable to remove the chain, I jumped over, and, running up the flagged causeway bordered with straggling gooseberry-bushes, knocked vainly for admittance, till my knuckles tingled and the dogs howled.

"Wretched inmates!" I ejaculated, mentally, "you deserve perpetual isolation from your species for your churlish inhospitality. At least, I would not keep my doors barred in the daytime. I don't care—I will get in!" So resolved, I grasped the latch and shook it vehemently. Vinegar-faced Joseph projected his head from a round window of the barn.

"What are ye for?" he shouted. "The master's down in the fold. Go round by th' end of the laith, if ye went to speak to him."

"Is there nobody inside to open the door?" I hallooed, responsively.

"There's nobody but the missus, and she'll not open to ye. You're making your fearsome noise for naught."

"Why? Cannot you tell her whom I am, eh, Joseph?"

"Not me! I'll have no hand in it," muttered the head, vanishing.

The snow began to drive thickly. **I peered into the nearest window, seeking assistance from an inmate when I beheld a sight that startled me greatly. Two figures stood near the fire, locked in a passionate embrace. From my vantage point, I could see a tall and broad-shouldered man towering over a slight, slender woman.**

The discomfort of the snow-storm no longer captured the focus of my attention. I watched, unable to avert my eyes, even were the sight sufficient to render me blind. The man kissed the woman roughly, devouring her lips with his. His big, work-roughened hands tugged at the buttons on her dress. My mouth opened to register my objection to his manhandling of the fair creature, but I stopped myself from forming the words when she pushed his hands away impatiently and unbuttoned the dress herself, her nimble, dainty fingers making quick work of the task. I swallowed the lump in my throat. If only the window were larger! Then I should be able to see more clearly.

The broad-shouldered man fair shook with impatience, watching with undisguised need as she bared her body to him. His chest heaved and those large hands trembled as he reached out to cup the perfect breasts once revealed. A tremor slipped through her body at his touch. My shaft thickened and throbbed at this stark reminder of what could pass between men and women, and my belly ached, empty with need. My own goddess had once allowed me to look upon her silken bare breasts, and to fit them to the palm of my hand—

He bent and took one breast into his mouth, suckling greedily. She gripped his shoulders, her small fingers like talons on the coarse fabric of his shirt, her body arched and her head tilted back, allowing him free rein as his mouth roved over her, leaving behind a wet trail that glistened in the firelight. The air around them shimmered with a heat that had nothing whatsoever to do with the fire behind them.

His hand crept beneath her skirt. I held my breath as I followed his painstaking progress up her leg until he found what he sought. She jerked as his fingers touched the most tender place between her thighs; I admit I made a small moan of pleasure myself.

Then, as I watched spellbound from my vantage point, insensate to the snow swirling about me, he lifted her skirts. I leaned nearer, my frantic breath fogging the glass of the window. Impatiently, I swiped at the pane with the sleeve of my coat. Once a clear view was restored, I could see that he had caused her undergarments to fall into a puddle at her ankles. She clutched her skirts in her hands, so he might have access to any part of her he desired. Her round thighs fair glowed in the firelight, naked and soft. My eyes flew to the juncture between her thighs, but I could not see what secret bounty she offered, for he was on his knees before her, lapping at her core. As I watched, she spread her legs wider to accommodate his hunger, and he nibbled and bit and sucked in the crudest way possible, probing her with his rough, demanding tongue, his big hands gripping her thighs in a most ungentlemanly manner that excited me in the extreme. Her hips moved against his mouth in a rhythm signifying her approbation of his efforts, and at her silent urging, he increased the roughness of his approach until her entire body stiffened and she exploded with pleasure. I could hear her small shriek through the glass of the window.

The release rendered her boneless, but he caught her before she fell to the floor. He kissed her on the mouth then, sharing with her her own essence, which she devoured as he had devoured her. When he lifted his head from hers, her small pink tongue reached out to taste it again, her naked and unconfined breasts spilling out of her dress, her dishevelment a mute testimony to what had gone before.

She began to button her dress. I must have made a noise then, because they stopped and both turned toward the window. Immediately, I ducked down and hid beneath the sill, my breath coming out in pants, a white cloud in the cool air. That was when I realized the snow was accumulating ever deeper and my exposed extremities had near to frozen solid. I had to find shelter inside soon, regardless of the young lovers.

I crept back to the door and seized the handle to essay another trial at catching someone's attention, when a young man without coat, and shouldering a pitchfork, appeared. His size led me to believe him to be the one I had seen through the window. In fact I was positive it was him, yet I said nothing. How could I voice my own pleasure at what I had seen? I was at my landlord's house uninvited and peering through windows.

He hailed me to follow him, and, after marching through a washhouse, and a paved area containing a coal-shed, pump, and pigeon-cot, we at length arrived in the huge, warm, cheerful apartment where I was formerly received. It glowed delightfully in the radiance of an immense

fire, compounded of coal, peat, and wood, and near the table, laid for a
plentiful evening meal, I observed the "missus."

**It was her. I was sure of it. This was the woman who had
displayed unbridled passion with the man who had escorted
me inside. Yet she was dressed in fine clothes, an obvious mistress of the house, not a serving girl. What obdurate perversity
had overtaken her, that she would pleasure herself with the farm
hand? What wicked impulse dared her to conduct an assignation
right beneath the master's nose? I had been right in assuming
Wuthering Heights was no ordinary domicile.**

**Hoping that my knowledge did not show on my face, I
bowed and waited, thinking she would bid me take a seat. She
looked at me, leaning back in her chair, and remained motionless
and mute.**

"Rough weather!" I remarked. "I'm afraid, Mrs. Heathcliff, the
door must bear the consequence of your servants' leisure attendance.
I had hard work to make them hear me."

She never opened her mouth. I stared—she stared also. At any
rate, she kept her eyes on me in a cool, regardless manner, exceedingly
embarrassing and disagreeable. **I felt my previous inadequacies rear
their ugly heads and I forcefully pushed them away.**

**The two of them shared a look, one I could not interpret,
but I suspected it was due to their coupling not five minutes earlier. The air was still perfumed with her scent, which I breathed in
deeply. It was fair intoxicating. Why would she prefer the rough,
muscled fellow who smelled of farm chores when she was so obviously a woman of quality, and could have a man of the same?**

"Sit down," said the young man, gruffly. "He'll be in soon."

I obeyed, and hemmed, and called the villain Juno, who deigned,
at this second interview, to move the extreme tip of her tail, in token
of owning my acquaintance.

"A beautiful animal!" I commenced again. "Do you intend parting with the little ones, madam?"

"They are not mine," said the amiable hostess, more repellingly than Heathcliff himself could have replied. **So the angel had the tongue of a devil. I wondered how sharp it was and whether it would rasp across a man's skin in the dark of night. A shiver danced up my spine at the thought.**

"Ah, your favorites are among these?" I continued, turning to an obscure cushion full of something like cats.

"A strange choice of favorites!" she observed scornfully.

Unluckily, it was a heap of dead rabbits. I hemmed once more, and drew closer to the hearth, repeating my comment on the wildness of the evening.

"You should not have come out," she said, rising and reaching from the chimneypiece two of the painted canisters. **Was her displeasure because I had come unannounced or because I had interrupted her afternoon assignation?**

Her position before was sheltered from the light, now, I had a distinct view of her whole figure and countenance. She was slender, and apparently scarcely past girlhood. An admirable form, and the most exquisite little face that I have ever had the pleasure of beholding, small features, very fair, flaxen ringlets, or rather golden, hanging loose on her delicate neck, and eyes, had they been agreeable in expression, that would have been irresistible. **She was an angel come to earth, sweet and innocent in appearance—yet I knew differently. She was in a word, perfect. I was resolved to leave behind my ineptness with the fairer sex and become more of a man, instead of a fool tripping over my own tongue.**

Fortunately for my susceptible heart, the only sentiment she evinced hovered between scorn and a kind of desperation, singularly unnatural to be detected there. The canisters were almost out of her reach. I made a motion to aid her, and she turned upon me as a miser might turn if any one attempted to assist him in counting his gold.

"I don't want your help," she snapped, "I can get them for myself."

"I beg your pardon!" I hastened to reply. **The kitten had claws, more's the better for the man who shared her bed.**

"Were you asked to tea?" she demanded, tying an apron over her neat black frock, and standing with a spoonful of the leaf poised over the pot.

"I shall be glad to have a cup," I answered.

"Were you asked?" she repeated.

"No," I said, half smiling. "You are the proper person to ask me."

She flung the tea back, spoon and all, and resumed her chair in a pet, her forehead corrugated, and her red under-lip pushed out, like a child's ready to cry. **The very idea that serving tea to a neighbor, her duty as mistress, would cause her to act so was astounding. This young creature was barely out of the schoolroom and it seemed she belonged right back inside—to learn proper etiquette and manners as a young woman should.**

Meanwhile, the young man had slung on to his person a decidedly shabby upper garment, and, erecting himself before the blaze, looked down on me from the corner of his eyes, for all the world as if there were some mortal feud unavenged between us. I began to doubt whether he were a servant or not.

His dress and speech were both rude, entirely devoid of the superiority observable in Mr. and Mrs. Heathcliff, his thick brown curls were rough and uncultivated, his whiskers encroached bearishly over his cheeks, and his hands were embrowned like those of a common laborer. **Those hands had recently been touching the perfect breasts now chastely concealed beneath Mrs. Heathcliff's dress; they had explored other more private areas as well. Shifting in my seat, I wondered if his fingers still carried her taste and her scent.**

His bearing was free, almost haughty, and he showed none of a domestic's assiduity in attending on the lady of the house. In the absence of clear proofs of his condition, I deemed it best to abstain from noticing his curious conduct, and, five minutes afterwards, the entrance of Heathcliff relieved me, in some measure, from my uncomfortable state. **Although his expression was as fierce as the rest of the strange family surrounding him, I was most heartily glad he was there.**

"You see, sir, I am come, according to promise!" I exclaimed, assuming the cheerful, "and I fear I shall be weather-bound for half an hour, if you can afford me shelter during that space."

"Half an hour?" he said, shaking the white flakes from his clothes, "I wonder you should select the thick of a snow-storm to ramble about in. Do you know that you run a risk of being lost in the marshes? People familiar with these moors often miss their road on such evenings, and I can tell you there is no chance of a change at present."

"Perhaps I can get a guide among your lads, and he might stay at the Grange till morning—could you spare me one?"

"No, I could not."

"Oh, indeed! Well, then, I must trust to my own devices to find my way."

"Umph!"

"Are you going to make the tea?" demanded he of the shabby coat, shifting his ferocious gaze from me to the young lady.

"Is he to have any?" she asked, appealing to Heathcliff.

"Get it ready, will you?" was the answer, uttered so savagely that I started. I no longer felt inclined to call Heathcliff a capital fellow if he flung such wickedness on such a young creature as his wife was. **Yet she had allowed the brutish young man such wanton liberties when her husband was not present that perhaps she had earned Mr. Heathcliff's censure. The tone in which the words were said revealed a darkly passionate man. I would not dare to cross him as Mrs. Heathcliff seemed bent on doing.**

When the preparations were finished, he invited me with— "Now, sir, bring forward your chair." And we all, including the rustic youth, drew round the table. An austere silence prevailed while we discussed our meal.

I thought, if I had caused the cloud between them all, it was my duty to make an effort to dispel it. They could not every day sit so grim and taciturn, and it was impossible, however ill tempered they might be, that the universal scowl they wore was their every-day countenance. **They were an odd lot of folks in expression, yet passion lurked just beneath the surface.**

"It is strange," I began, in the interval of swallowing one cup of tea and receiving another—"it is strange how custom can mould our tastes and ideas. Many could not imagine the existence of happiness in a life of such complete exile from the world as you spend, Mr. Heathcliff, yet, I'll venture to say, that, surrounded by your family, and with your amiable lady as the presiding genius over your home and heart—"

"My amiable lady!" he interrupted, with sheer surprise on his face, which quickly transformed into a scowl. "Where is she—my amiable lady?"

"Mrs. Heathcliff, your wife, I mean."

"Well, yes—oh, you would intimate that her spirit has taken the post of ministering angel, and guards the fortunes of Wuthering Heights, even when her body is gone. Is that it?"

Perceiving myself in a blunder, I attempted to correct it. I might have seen there was too great a disparity between the ages of the parties to make it likely that they were man and wife. One was about forty; a period of mental vigor at which men seldom cherish the delusion of being married for love, by girls. That dream is reserved for the solace of our declining years. The other did not look seventeen.

Then it flashed on me—"The clown at my elbow, who is drinking his tea out of a basin and eating his bread with unwashed hands, may be her husband. Heathcliff junior, of course. **This explained the sight I had witnessed earlier in this very room, but that begged an even more curious question. Why did she select this man to marry?** Here is the consequence of being buried alive. She has thrown herself away upon that boor from sheer ignorance that better individuals existed! A sad pity—I must beware how I cause her to regret her choice." The last reflection may seem conceited, but it was not. My young neighbor struck me as bordering on repulsive in looks I knew, through experience, that I was tolerably attractive.

"Mrs. Heathcliff is my daughter-in-law," said Heathcliff, corroborating my surmise. He turned, as he spoke, a peculiar look in her direction. Nearly a look of hatred, unless he has a most perverse set of facial muscles that will not, like those of other people, interpret the language of his soul.

"Ah, certainly—I see now. You are the favored possessor of the beneficent fairy," I remarked, turning to the gruff young man beside me.

This was worse than before. The youth grew crimson, and clenched his fist, with every appearance of a meditated assault. But he seemed to recollect himself presently, and smothered the storm in a brutal curse, muttered on my behalf. Which, however, I took care not to notice.

"Unhappy in your conjectures, sir," observed my host, "we neither of us have the privilege of owning your good fairy. Her mate is dead. I said she was my daughter-in-law. Therefore, she must have married my son."

"And this young man is—"

"Not my son, assuredly."

Heathcliff smiled again, as if it were rather too bold a jest to attribute the paternity of that bear to him.

"My name is Hareton Earnshaw," growled the other, "and I'd counsel you to respect it!"

"I've shown no disrespect," was my reply, laughing internally at the dignity with which he announced himself.

He fixed his eye on me longer than I cared to return the stare, for fear I might be tempted either to box his ears or render my hilarity audible. I began to feel unmistakably out of place in that not-so-pleasant family circle. The dismal spiritual atmosphere overcame, and more than neutralized, the glowing physical comforts round me, and I resolved to be cautious how I ventured under those rafters a third time.

The young widow obviously took her pleasure with the farm-hand, which many widows were wont to do. I could not judge her for finding solace in such a dismal place, but perhaps I could offer her a more refined indulgence. I would have to consider further how to approach the matter.

The business of eating being concluded, and no one uttering a word of sociable conversation, I approached a window to examine the weather. A sorrowful sight. Dark night had come down prematurely, and sky and hills mingled in one bitter whirl of wind and suffocating snow.

"I don't think it possible for me to get home now without a guide," I could not help exclaiming. "The roads will be buried already, and, if they were bare, I could scarcely distinguish a foot in advance."

"Hareton, drive those dozen sheep into the barn porch. They'll be covered if left in the fold all night. And put a plank before them," said Heathcliff.

"How must I do?" I continued, with rising irritation. **This family appeared to not have a shred of civility to their neighbors.**

There was no reply to my question. On looking round I saw only Joseph bringing in a pail of porridge for the dogs, and Mrs. Heathcliff leaning over the fire, diverting herself with burning a bundle of matches that had fallen from the chimneypiece as she restored the tea-canister to its place.

The former, when he had deposited his burden, took a critical survey of the room, and in cracked tones grated out—"I wonder how yah can fashion to stand there in idleness ! But you're nothing, and it's no use talking—you'll never mend your ill ways, but go straight to the devil, like yer mother afore ye!"

I imagined, for a moment, that this piece of eloquence was addressed to me, and, sufficiently enraged, stepped towards the aged rascal with an intention of kicking him out of the door. Mrs.

Heathcliff, however, checked me by her answer.

"You scandalous old hypocrite!" she replied. "Are you not afraid of being carried away bodily, whenever you mention the devil's name? I warn you to refrain from provoking me, or I'll ask your abduction as a special favor! Stop! Look here, Joseph," she continued, taking a long, dark book from a shelf, "I'll show you how far I've progressed in the Black Art. I shall soon be competent to make a clear house of it. The red cow didn't die by chance, and your rheumatism can hardly be reckoned among providential visitations!"

"Oh, wicked, wicked!" gasped the elder, "may the Lord deliver us from evil!"

"No, reprobate! You are a castaway—be off, or I'll hurt you seriously! I'll have you all modeled in wax and clay! And the first who passes the limits I fix shall—I'll not say what he shall be done to—but, you'll see! Go, I'm looking at you!"

The little witch put a mock malignity into her beautiful eyes, and Joseph, trembling with sincere horror, hurried out, praying, and ejaculating "wicked" as he went. **Clearly her passion ran through and through and I had a moment's hope that her wickedness could be turned to my benefit.** I thought her conduct must be prompted by a species of dreary fun, and, now that we were alone, I endeavored to interest her in my distress.

"Mrs. Heathcliff," I said earnestly, "you must excuse me for troubling you. I presume, because, with that face, I'm sure you cannot help being good-hearted. Do point out some landmarks by which I may know my way home. I have no more idea how to get there than you would have how to get to London!"

"Take the road you came," she answered, ensconcing herself in a chair, with a candle, and the long book open before her. "It is brief advice, but as sound as I can give."

"Then, if you hear of me being discovered dead in a bog or a pit full of snow, your conscience won't whisper that it is partly your fault?"

"How so? I cannot escort you. They wouldn't let me go to the end of the garden wall."

"You! I should be sorry to ask you to cross the threshold, for my convenience, on such a night," I cried. "I want you to tell me my way, not to show it. Or else to persuade Mr. Heathcliff to give me a guide."

"Who? There is himself, Earnshaw, Zillah, Joseph and I. Which would you have?"

"Are there no boys at the farm?"

"No, those are all."

"Then, it follows that I am compelled to stay."

"That you may settle with your host. I have nothing to do with it."

"I hope it will be a lesson to you to make no more rash journeys on these hills," cried Heathcliff's stern voice from the kitchen entrance. "As to staying here, I don't keep accommodations for visitors. You must share a bed with Hareton or Joseph, if you do."

"I can sleep on a chair in this room," I replied.

"No, no! A stranger is a stranger, be he rich or poor. It will not suit me to permit any one the range of the place while I am off guard!" said Heathcliff, the unmannerly wretch.

With this insult, my patience was at an end. I uttered an expression of disgust, and pushed past him into the yard, running against Earnshaw in my haste. It was so dark that I could not see the means of exit, and, as I wandered round, I heard another specimen of their civil behavior amongst each other. At first the young man appeared about to befriend me.

"I'll go with him as far as the park," he said.

"You'll go with him to hell!" exclaimed his master, or whatever relation he bore. "And who is to look after the horses, eh?"

"A man's life is of more consequence than one evening's neglect of the horses. Somebody must go," murmured Mrs. Heathcliff, more kindly than I expected.

"Not at your command!" retorted Hareton. "If you set store on him, you'd better be quiet." **Again the two young people shared a look of what appeared to be anger and intense dislike, but which I thought was passion—nay, even ferocious desire. They could not seem to be civil to one another, yet their bodies had been in perfect harmony. If I were not so distressed over my current situation, I might have examined that curiosity further.**

"Then I hope his ghost will haunt you, and I hope Mr. Heathcliff will never get another tenant till the Grange is a ruin," she answered, sharply.

"Hearken, hearken, she's cursing on 'em!" muttered Joseph, towards whom I had been steering.

He sat within earshot, milking the cows by the light of a lantern, which I seized unceremoniously, and, calling out that I would send it back on the morrow, rushed to the nearest postern.

"Master, master, he's stealing the lantern!" shouted the ancient, pursuing my retreat with his bones and joints creaking in the cold air. "Hey, Gnasher! Hey, dog! Hey Wolf, hold him, hold him!"

On opening the little door, two hairy monsters flew at my throat, bearing me down, and extinguishing the light, while a mingled guffaw from Heathcliff and Hareton put the copestone on my rage and humiliation. Fortunately, the beasts seemed more bent on stretching their paws, and yawning, and flourishing their tails, than devouring me alive, but they would suffer no resurrection, and I was forced to lie till their malignant masters pleased to deliver me. Then, hatless and trembling with wrath, I ordered the miscreants to let me out— on their peril to keep me one minute longer—with several incoherent threats of retaliation that, in their indefinite depth of virulence, smacked of King Lear.

The vehemence of my agitation brought on a copious bleeding at the nose, and still Heathcliff laughed, and still I scolded. I don't know what would have concluded the scene, had there not been one person at hand rather more rational than myself, and more benevolent than my entertainer. This was Zillah, the large-breasted housewife, who at length issued forth to inquire into the nature of the uproar. She thought that some of them had been laying violent hands on me, and, not daring to attack her master, she turned her vocal artillery against the younger scoundrel.

"Well, Mr. Earnshaw," she cried, "I wonder what you'll have again next? Are we going to murder folk on our very door-stones? I see this house will never do for me—look at t' poor lad, he's fair choking! Wisht, wisht, you mustn't go on so. Come in, and I'll cure that. There now, hold ye still."

With these words, she suddenly splashed a pint of icy water down my neck, and pulled me into the kitchen. Mr. Heathcliff followed, his accidental merriment expiring quickly in his habitual moroseness.

I was sick exceedingly, and dizzy, and faint, and thus compelled perforce to accept lodgings under his roof. He told Zillah to give me a glass of brandy, and then passed on to the inner room. While she condoled with me on my sorry predicament, and having obeyed his orders, whereby I was somewhat revived, ushered me to bed. **I was feeling so ill-used and out-of-sorts, that I didn't even wonder if Zillah could be persuaded to join me beneath the blankets.**

CHAPTER 3

WHILE LEADING THE WAY UPSTAIRS, she recommended that I should hide the candle, and not make a noise, for her master had an odd notion about the chamber she would put me in, and never let anybody lodge there willingly. I asked the reason. She did not know. Since she had only lived there a year or two, and they had so many queer goings on, she could not begin to be curious.

Too stupefied to be curious myself, I fastened my door and glanced round for the bed. The whole furniture consisted of a chair, a clothes press, and a large oak case, with squares cut out near the top resembling coach windows. Having approached this structure, I looked inside, and perceived it to be a singular sort of old-fashioned couch, very conveniently designed to obviate the necessity for every member of the family having a room to himself. In fact, it formed a little closet, and the ledge of a window, which it enclosed, served as a table. I slid back the paneled sides, got in with my light, pulled them together again, and felt secure against the vigilance of Heathcliff, and everyone else.

The ledge, where I placed my candle, had a few mildewed books piled up in one corner, and it was covered with writing scratched on the paint. This writing, however, was nothing but a name repeated in all kinds of characters, large and small—Catherine Earnshaw, here and there varied to Catherine Heathcliff, and then again to Catherine Linton.

In vapid listlessness I leant my head against the window, and continued spelling over Catherine Earnshaw—Heathcliff—Linton, till my eyes closed. They had not rested five minutes when a glare of white letters started from the dark, as vivid as specters—the air swarmed with Catherines. I, roused myself to dispel the obtrusive name when I discovered my candlewick reclining on one of the antique volumes, and perfuming the place with an odor of roasted calfskin.

I snuffed it off, and very ill at ease under the influence of cold and lingering nausea, sat up and spread open the injured tome on my knee. It was a Testament, in lean type, and smelling dreadfully musty. A flyleaf bore the inscription—"Catherine Earnshaw, her book," and a date some quarter of a century back. I shut it, and took up another and another, till I had examined all. Catherine's library was select, and its state of dilapidation proved it to have been well used, though not altogether for a legitimate purpose. Scarcely one chapter had escaped, a pen-and-ink commentary—at least the appearance of one—covering every morsel of blank that the printer had left. Some were detached sentences, other parts took the form of a regular diary, scrawled in an unformed, childish hand. At the top of an extra page (quite a treasure, probably, when first lighted on) I was greatly amused to behold an excellent caricature of my friend Joseph—rudely, yet powerfully sketched. An immediate interest kindled within me for the unknown Catherine, and I began forthwith to decipher her faded hieroglyphics.

"An awful Sunday," commenced the paragraph beneath. "I wish my father were back again. Hindley is a detestable substitute—his conduct to Heathcliff is atrocious—H. and I are going to rebel—we took our initiatory step this evening.

"All day had been flooding with rain, and we could not go to church. So Joseph must needs get up a congregation in the garret. While Hindley and his wife basked downstairs before a comfortable fire—doing anything but reading their Bibles, I'll answer for it—Heathcliff, myself, and the unhappy ploughboy were commanded to take our prayer books, and mount. We were ranged in a row, on a sack of corn, groaning and shivering, and hoping that Joseph would shiver too, so that he might give us a short homily for his own sake. A vain idea! The service lasted precisely three hours. Yet my brother had the face to exclaim, when he saw us descending,

"'What, done already?'

"On Sunday evenings we used to be permitted to play, if we did not make much noise. Now a mere titter is sufficient to send us into corners!

"'You forget you have a master here,' says the tyrant. 'I'll demolish the first who puts me out of temper! I insist on perfect sobriety and silence. Oh, boy! Was that you? Frances darling, pull his hair as you go by. I heard him snap his fingers.' Frances pulled Heathcliff's hair heartily, and then went and seated herself on her husband's knee. There they were, like two babies, kissing and talking nonsense by the hour—foolish palaver that we should be ashamed of.

"We spied on them once when they were naked and doing things to each other. It made me feel queer all over and Heathcliff's eyes grew wide as saucers. He tried to hide the front of his trousers from me but I saw it anyway. The sight of the awful couple touching each other had made his staff hard like a stallion. It made me wonder what it looked like up close, and perhaps one day I will find out.

"For now, we made ourselves as snug as our means allowed in the arch of the dresser. I had just fastened our pinafores together, and hung them up for a curtain, when in comes Joseph, on an errand from the stables. He tears down my handiwork, boxes my ears, and croaks—

"'The maister has just been buried, and Sabbath not over, the sounds of the gospel still in your lungs, and ye dare be lazing. Shame on ye! Sit ye down, ill children! There's good books enough if ye'll read 'em. Sit ye down, and think o' yer souls!'"

"Saying this, he compelled us so to square our positions that we might receive from the far-off fire a dull ray to show us the text of the lumber he thrust upon us. I could not bear the employment. I took my dingy volume by the binding, and hurled it into the dog-kennel, vowing I hated a good book. Heathcliff kicked his to the same place. Then there was a hubbub!

"'Maister Hindley!' shouted our chaplain. 'Maister, come hither! Miss Cathy's driven back off "The Helmet of Salvation," and Heathcliff's put his fist into "The Broad Way to Destruction!" It's fair frightful that ye let 'em go on this way. Ech! The old man would've laced 'em properly—but he's gone!'

"Hindley hurried up from his paradise on the hearth, and seizing one of us by the collar, and the other by the arm, hurled both into the back-kitchen where Joseph could throw more scripture at us. Old Nick would fetch us as sure as we were living, and so comforted, we each sought a separate nook to await his advent.

"I reached this book, and a pot of ink from a shelf, and pushed the house-door ajar to give me light. I have got the time on with writing for twenty minutes, but my companion is impatient, and proposes that we should appropriate the dairywoman's cloak, and have a scamper on the moors, under its shelter. A pleasant suggestion—and then, if the surly old man come in, he may believe his prophecy verified—we cannot be damper, or colder, in the rain than we are here."

I suppose Catherine fulfilled her project, for the next sentence took up another subject with much weeping, it seemed.

"How little did I dream that Hindley would ever make me cry so!" she wrote. "My head aches, till I cannot keep it on the pillow, and still I can't give over. Poor Heathcliff! Hindley calls him a vagabond, and won't let him sit with us, nor eat with us anymore, and, he says, he and I must not play together, and threatens to turn him out of the house if we break his orders. He has been blaming our father (how dared he?) for treating H. too liberally, and swears he will reduce him to his right place—"

I began to nod drowsily over the dim page. My eye wandered from manuscript to print. I saw a red ornamented title—"Seventy Times Seven, and the First of the Seventy-First. A Pious Discourse delivered by the Reverend Jabes Branderham, in the Chapel of Gimmerden Sough." And while I was, half-consciously, worrying my brain to guess what Jabes Branderham would make of his subject, I sank back in bed, and fell asleep.

Alas, for the effects of bad tea and bad temper! What else could it be that made me pass such a terrible night? I don't remember another that I can at all compare with it since I was capable of suffering.

I began to dream, almost before I ceased to be sensible of my locality. I thought it was morning, and I had set out on my way home, with Joseph for a guide. The snow lay yards deep in our road. As we floundered on, my companion wearied me with constant reproaches that I had not brought a pilgrim's staff. He told me that I could never get into the house without one, and boastfully flourished a heavy-headed cudgel, which I understood to be so denominated. For a moment, I considered it absurd that I should need such a weapon to gain admittance into my own residence. Then a new idea flashed across me. I was not going there. We were journeying to hear the famous Jabes Branderham preach, from the text—"Seventy Times Seven," and either Joseph, the preacher, or I had committed the "First of the Seventy-First," and were to be publicly exposed and excommunicated.

We came to the chapel. I have passed it really in my walks, twice or thrice. It lies in an elevated hollow, between two hills, near a swamp, whose peaty moisture is said to answer all the purposes of embalming on the few corpses deposited there. The roof has been kept whole hitherto. But as the clergyman's stipend is only twenty pounds per annum, and a house with two rooms threatening speedily to determine into one, no clergyman will undertake the duties of pastor. Especially as it is currently reported that his flock would rather let him starve than increase the living by one penny from their own pockets. However, in my dream, Jabes had a full and attentive congregation, and he preached. Good God! What a sermon, divided into four hundred and ninety parts, each fully equal to an ordinary address from the pulpit, and each discussing a separate sin! Where he searched for them, I cannot tell. He had his private manner of interpreting the phrase, and it seemed necessary the brother should sin different sins on every occasion. They were of the most curious character—odd. transgressions that I never imagined previously.

Oh, how weary I grew. How I writhed, and yawned, and nodded, and revived! How I pinched and pricked myself, and rubbed my eyes, and stood up, and sat down again, and nudged Joseph to inform me if he would ever have done. I was condemned to hear all out. Finally, he reached the "First of the Seventy-First." At that crisis, a sudden inspiration descended on me. I was moved to rise and denounce Jabes Branderham as the sinner of the sin that no Christian need pardon.

"Sir," I exclaimed, "sitting here within these four walls, at one stretch, I have endured and forgiven the four hundred and ninety heads of your discourse. Seventy times seven times have I plucked up my hat and been about to depart. Seventy times seven times have you preposterously forced me to resume my seat. The four hundred and ninety-first is too much. Fellow-martyrs, have at him! Drag him down, and crush him to atoms, that the place which knows him may know him no more!"

"Thou art the Man!" cried Jabes, after a solemn pause, leaning over his cushion. "Seventy times seven times didst thou gapingly contort thy visage. Seventy times seven did I take counsel with my soul.

Lo, this is human weakness. This also may be absolved! The First of the Seventy-First is come. Brethren, execute upon him the judgment written. Such honor have all His saints!"

With that concluding word, the whole assembly, exalting their pilgrim's staves, rushed round me in a body. I, having no weapon to raise in self-defense, commenced grappling with Joseph, my nearest and most ferocious assailant, for his. In the confluence of the multitude, several clubs crossed, blows, aimed at me, fell on other sconces. Presently the whole chapel resounded with rappings and counter-rappings. Every man's hand was against his neighbor. Branderham, unwilling to remain idle, poured forth his zeal in a shower of loud taps on the boards of the pulpit, which responded so smartly that, at last, to my unspeakable relief, they woke me.

I blinked and gazed around at the unfamiliar room, grateful for the rush of remembrance as to where I was. And what was it that had suggested the tremendous tumult? What had played Jabes's part in the row? Merely the branch of a fir-tree that touched my lattice as the blast wailed by, and rattled its dry cones against the panes! I listened doubtingly an instant, detected the disturber, then turned and dozed, and dreamt again. If possible, still more disagreeably than before.

This time, I remembered I was lying in the oak closet, and I heard distinctly the gusty wind, and the driving of the snow. I also heard the fir bough repeat its teasing sound, and ascribed it to the right cause. But it annoyed me so much, that I resolved to silence it, if possible. I rose and endeavored to unhasp the casement. The hook was soldered into the staple, a circumstance observed by me when awake, but forgotten.

"I must stop it, nevertheless!" I muttered, knocking my knuckles through the glass, and stretching an arm out to seize the importunate branch. Instead of which, my fingers closed on the fingers of a little, ice-cold hand! The intense horror of nightmare came over me.

I tried to draw back my arm, but the hand clung to it, and a most melancholy voice sobbed, "Let me in—let me in!"

"Who are you?" I asked, struggling, meanwhile, to disengage myself.

"Catherine Linton," it replied shiveringly. Why did I think of Linton? I had read Earnshaw twenty times for Linton.

"I'm come home. I'd lost my way on the moor!"

As it spoke, I discerned, obscurely, a young woman's face looking through the window. Terror made me cruel. Finding it useless to attempt shaking the creature off, I pulled its wrist on to the broken pane, and rubbed it to and fro till the blood ran down and soaked the bedclothes.

Still it wailed, "Let me in!" and maintained its tenacious grip, almost maddening me with fear.

"How can I!" I said at length. "Let me go, if you want me to let you in!" The fingers relaxed, I snatched mine through the hole, hurriedly piled the books up in a pyramid against it, and stopped my ears to exclude the lamentable prayer. I seemed to keep them closed above a quarter of an hour. Yet, the instant I listened again, there was the doleful cry moaning on!

"Begone!" I shouted. "I'll never let you in, not if you beg for twenty years."

"It is twenty years," mourned the voice. "Twenty years. I've been a waif for twenty years! Let me in! I know Heathcliff is there!"

Thereat began a feeble scratching outside, and the pile of books moved as if thrust forward. I tried to jump up, but could not stir a limb, and so yelled aloud, in a frenzy of fright. To my confusion, I discovered the yell was not ideal. Hasty footsteps approached my chamber door. Somebody pushed it open, with a vigorous hand, and a light glimmered through the squares at the top of the bed. I sat shuddering yet, and wiping the perspiration from my forehead. The intruder appeared to hesitate, and muttered to himself.

At last, he said, in a half-whisper, plainly not expecting an answer, "Is anyone here?"

I considered it best to confess my presence, for I knew Heathcliff's accents, and feared he might search further if I kept quiet. With this intention, I turned and opened the panels. I shall not soon forget the effect my action produced.

Heathcliff stood near the entrance, in his shirt and trousers, with a candle dripping over his fingers, and his face as white as the wall behind him, resembling more a specter than a man. **It was the first time I had seen my landlord looking so unguarded and unsure. He looked uneasily about the room, rooted to the spot, a curious sight to behold.**

Then a shaken whisper floated from his direction. "Is that you haunting me still? My love, why do you not show yourself to me?"

I nearly called out to him then, to spare him the humiliation of discovering too late my occupation of the room. Something stopped me from revealing my presence—an instinct that warned me to tread with special care where this man was concerned. I fell back against the pillows, praying he would leave the room upon hearing no response to his query. It was then I realized he was speaking to someone who was not present, addressing his words as a supplicant to a master. I had no idea my landlord was so inclined. I could not make a move or a sound as I watched him, transfixed by what I heard. Passion mixed with grief thickened his voice and stirred such pity in my heart that I had to constrain myself from calling out to him and offering my condolences.

"You made a shambles of my life and then abandoned me," he groaned. **"Each day when I walk the moors, I can hear you, smell you. I know you are there——but I never see you. How you torture me! I am lost, do you hear me? Lost." He made a noise that sounded more animal than human, low and deep in his throat.**

A mist of white appeared near him, less corporeal and more ethereal than the creature that had assailed me through the window, and yet something about Heathcliff's response made me think it appeared as perfectly formed to him as it had to me when it made its urgent entreaties through the broken window.

It floated about him, weaving through his arms and legs,

seeming even to caress him. I drew back at the sight, protected by my enclosure. Was this the specter of the lost Catherine? Perhaps what I saw and heard was truly that of a creature from the other world.

"Cathy," he moaned. "Touch me. My body aches for you as much as my heart does."

His hands fumbled at his trousers, pulling the buttons loose. Soon his shaft was freed from its confines, thick and engorged already.

He stumbled backwards onto a chair, as if propelled by the white mist. Whether it was attacking him or seducing him was not immediately clear, but whichever the case, Heathcliff was a more than willing participant.

A shiver raced up his skin, raising the small hairs as it went. His member pulsed with each beat of his heart. As I watched, the white mist twisted and turned, and he moaned his approval of whatever it was he thought she was doing. His eyes were tightly closed. As I watched, his hand wrapped around his member, and he gasped as if a woman of flesh and blood had just taken him into her mouth. Appalled, I stared, hardly able to breathe.

"Oh God, Cathy," he cried, arching into the ghostly mist, his hand gripping his length, each up-and-down movement thickening and distending him. "Let me touch you."

His entire body shook as he increased the pace of his stroking, the only sound in the room his low moan deep in his throat. The white mist slithered and slid about him, encouraging him, it seemed to me.

It was Heathcliff's undoing. He let loose a ferocious moan and lifted his hips from the chair as he exploded in orgasm with a roar. His seed found no purchase in the white mist of the specter and therefore landed on his clothing, as spent as its master.

He breathed heavily as the mist seemed to gather itself together, preparing to leave.

"No, Cathy, don't!" Heathcliff reached toward her. "Please

don't go. Stay with me, my love. Let me touch you, damn it!"

Yet the specter would have nothing to do with his orders. She vanished slowly until all that remained was a bit of white that was quickly swallowed by the darkness of the night.

Heathcliff breathed most unsteadily for several minutes, then found the strength and will to move from the chair. After using a handkerchief to clean up the remains of his pleasure, he adjusted his trousers, picked up the candle, and let out a frustrated sigh.

I was determined to let him believe himself alone, for I did not wish to admit that I had witnessed his private anguish and release. When he drew nearer my enclosure, my heart beat frantically, for he would surely come upon me at any moment. I leaned forward to ease the doors shut, in my haste forgetting that they did not move smoothly in their track.

The first creak of the oak startled him like an electric shock. The light leaped from his hold to a distance of some feet, and his agitation was so extreme, that he could hardly pick it up.

"It is only your guest, sir," I called out, knowing I could no longer hide my presence from him and must bear whatever consequences would ensue. "I had the misfortune to scream in my sleep, owing to a frightful nightmare. I'm sorry I disturbed you."

"Oh, God confound you, Mr. Lockwood! I wish you were at the—" commenced my host, setting the candle on a chair, because he found it impossible to hold it steady. **Were those tears on his cheeks?** "And who showed you up into this room?" he continued, crushing his nails into his palms, and grinding his teeth so hard his jaw made a popping sound. "Who was it? I've a good mind to turn them out of the house this moment?"

"It was your servant Zillah," I replied, flinging myself to the floor, and rapidly resuming my garments. "I should not care if you did, Mr. Heathcliff. She richly deserves it. I suppose that she wanted to get another proof that the place was haunted, at my expense. Well, it is—swarming with ghosts and goblins! You have reason in shutting it up, I assure you. No one will thank you for a doze in such a den!"

"What do you mean?" asked Heathcliff, "and what are you doing?"

Overwhelmed by all I had seen and experienced, and not a little frightened of Heathcliff, I cried, "I'm not going to endure the persecutions of your hospitable ancestors again. Was not the Reverend Jabes Branderham akin to you on the mother's side? And that minx, Catherine Linton, or Earnshaw, or however she was called—she must have been a changeling—wicked little soul! She told me she had been walking the earth these twenty years. A just punishment for her mortal transgressions, I've no doubt!"

Scarcely were these words uttered when I realized the folly it was to say such a thing to Heathcliff, who was still besotted by the creature. Charging forward, without showing further consciousness of the offense, I hastened to add, "The truth is, sir, I passed the first part of the night in—"

Here I stopped afresh—I was about to say "perusing those old volumes," then it would have revealed my knowledge of their written, as well as their printed, contents, so, correcting myself, I went on, "in spelling over the name scratched on that window-ledge. A monotonous occupation, calculated to set me asleep, like counting, or—"

"What can you mean by talking in this way to me!" thundered Heathcliff with savage vehemence. **The passion I had seen before came forward tenfold, this time with fury wrapped around it.** "How—how dare you, under my roof?—God! He's mad to speak so!" **He struck his forehead with rage, leaving me no doubt the man was a tortured soul in every respect.**

I did not know whether to resent this language or pursue my explanation. Yet, he seemed so powerfully affected that I took pity and proceeded with my dreams. I affirmed, I had never heard the appellation of "Catherine Linton" before, but reading it often over produced an impression which personified itself when I had no longer my imagination under control. **The specter I saw at the window would not be forgotten, by either of us.**

Heathcliff gradually fell back into the shelter of the bed, as I spoke, finally sitting down almost concealed behind it. I guessed, however, by his irregular and intercepted breathing, that he struggled to vanquish an excess of violent emotion. Not liking to show him that I had witnessed his private moment, I continued my toilette rather noisily, looked at my watch, and soliloquized on the length of the night. "Not three o'clock yet! I could have taken oath it had been six. Time stagnates here. We must surely have retired to rest at eight!"

"Always at nine in winter, and rise at four," said my host, suppressing a groan. And, as I fancied, by the motion of his arm's shadow, dashing a tear from his eyes. "Mr. Lockwood," he added, "you may go into my room. You'll only be in the way, coming downstairs so early. And your childish outcry has sent sleep to the devil for me."

I did not protest that the night had been disturbed by far more than my "childish outcry," instead deciding that the path of wisdom lay in keeping my mouth closed.

"And for me, too," I replied. "I'll walk in the yard till daylight, and then I'll be off. You need not dread a repetition of my intrusion. I'm now quite cured of seeking pleasure in society, be it country or town. A sensible man ought to find sufficient company in himself."

"Delightful company!" muttered Heathcliff. "Take the candle, and go where you please. I shall join you directly. Keep out of the yard, though, the dogs are unchained. And the house—Juno mounts sentinel there, and—nay, you can only ramble about the steps and passages. But, away with you! I'll come in two minutes!"

I obeyed, so far as to quit the chamber, when, ignorant where the narrow lobbies led, I stood still. **Unfortunately I was then witness, involuntarily, to a piece of superstition on the part of my landlord which belied his apparent sense yet reinforced the notion he was involved with the white mist specter.**

He got on to the bed, and wrenched open the lattice, bursting, as he pulled at it, into an uncontrollable passion of tears.

"Come in! come in!" he sobbed. "Cathy, do come. Oh, do— once more! Oh! My heart's darling! Hear me this time, Catherine, at last!" The specter showed a specter's ordinary caprice. It gave no sign of being, but the snow and wind whirled wildly through, even reaching my station, and blowing out the light.

There was such anguish in the gush of grief that accompanied this raving, that my compassion made me overlook its folly. I drew off, half-angry to have witnessed it at all, and vexed at having related my ridiculous nightmare, since it produced that agony, though why was beyond my comprehension.

I descended cautiously to the lower regions, and landed in the back kitchen, where a gleam of fire, raked compactly together, enabled me to rekindle my candle. Nothing was stirring except a brindled, grey cat, which crept from the ashes, and saluted me with a querulous mew.

Two benches, shaped in sections of a circle, nearly enclosed the hearth. I stretched myself on one, and Grimalkin mounted the other. We were both of us nodding ere any one invaded our retreat, and then it was Joseph, shuffling down a wooden ladder that vanished in the roof, through a trap. The ascent to his garret, I suppose. He cast a sinister look at the little flame which I had enticed to play between the ribs, swept the cat from its elevation, and bestowing himself in the vacancy, commenced the operation of stuffing a three-inch pipe with tobacco.

My presence in his sanctum was evidently esteemed a piece of impudence too shameful for remark. He silently applied the tube to his lips, folded his arms, and puffed away. I let him enjoy the luxury unannoyed. After sucking out his last wreath, and heaving a profound sigh, he got up, and departed as solemnly as he came.

A more elastic footstep entered next, and now I opened my mouth for a "good-morning," but closed it again, the salutation unachieved. Hareton Earnshaw was speaking sotto voce, in a series of curses directed against every object he touched, while he rummaged a corner for a spade or shovel to dig through the drifts. **His unhappy demeanor caused me to speculate if perhaps his lover had neglected him during the night. Wuthering Heights seemed to induce excesses of a sexual nature, albeit odd and nearly unbelievable at times.**

Hareton glanced over the back of the bench, dilating his nostrils, and thought as little of exchanging civilities with me as with my companion the cat. I guessed, by his preparations, that egress was allowed, and, leaving my hard couch, made a movement to follow him. He noticed this, and thrust at an inner door with the end of his spade, intimating by an inarticulate sound that there was the place where I must go, if I changed my locality.

It opened into the house, where the females were already astir. Zillah urged flakes of flame up the chimney with a colossal bellows. Mrs. Heathcliff knelt on the hearth, reading a book by the aid of the blaze. She held her hand interposed between the furnace heat and her eyes, and seemed absorbed in her occupation, desisting from it only to chide the servant for covering her with sparks, or to push away a dog, now and then, that snoozled its nose overforwardly into her face.

I was surprised to see Heathcliff there also. He stood by the fire, his back towards me, just finishing a stormy scene with poor Zillah, who ever and anon interrupted her labor to pluck up the corner of her apron, and heave an indignant groan.

"And you, you worthless—" he broke out as I entered, turning to his daughter-in-law, and employing an epithet as harmless as duck, or sheep, but generally represented by a dash—.

"There you are, at your idle tricks again! The rest of them do earn their bread—you live on my charity! Put your trash away, and find something to do. You shall pay me for the plague of having you eternally in my sight—do you hear, damnable jade?"

"I'll put my trash away, because you can make me if I refuse," answered the young lady, closing her book, and throwing it on a chair. "But I'll not do anything, though you should swear your tongue out, except what I please!"

Heathcliff lifted his hand, and the speaker sprang to a safer distance, obviously acquainted with its weight. Having no desire to be entertained by a cat-and-dog combat, I stepped forward briskly, as if eager to partake the warmth of the hearth, and innocent of any knowledge of the interrupted dispute. Each had enough decorum to suspend further hostilities. Heathcliff placed his fists, out of temptation, in his pockets. Mrs. Heathcliff curled her lip, and walked to a seat far off, where she kept her word by playing the part of a statue during the remainder of my stay.

That was not long. I declined joining their breakfast, and, at the first gleam of dawn, took an opportunity of escaping into the free air, now clear, and still, and cold as impalpable ice.

My landlord hallooed for me to stop ere I reached the bottom of the garden, and offered to accompany me across the moor. It was well he did, for the whole hill-back was one billowy, white ocean. The swells and falls did not indicate corresponding rises and depressions in the ground. Many pits, at least, were filled to a level, and entire ranges of mounds, the refuse of the quarries, blotted from the chart that my yesterday's walk left pictured in my mind.

I had remarked on one side of the road, at intervals of six or seven yards, a line of upright stones, continued through the whole length of the barren. These were erected and daubed with lime on purpose to serve as guides in the dark, and also when a fall, like the present, confounded the deep swamps on either hand with the firmer path. Excepting a dirty dot pointing up here and there, all traces of their existence had vanished. My companion found it necessary to warn me frequently to steer to the right or left, when I imagined I was following, correctly, the windings of the road.

We exchanged little conversation, and he halted at the entrance of Thrushcross park, saying, I could make no error there. Our adieux were limited to a hasty bow, and then I pushed forward, trusting to my own resources, for the porter's lodge is untenanted as yet.

The distance from the gate to the Grange is two miles. I believe I managed to make it four, what with losing myself among the trees, and sinking up to the neck in snow—a predicament that only those who have experienced it can appreciate. At any rate, whatever were my wanderings, the clock chimed twelve as I entered the house, and that gave exactly an hour for every mile of the usual way from Wuthering Heights.

My human fixture and her satellites rushed to welcome me, exclaiming, tumultuously, they had completely given me up. Everybody conjectured that I perished last night, and they were wondering how they must set about the search for my remains.

I bid them be quiet, now that they saw me returned, and, benumbed to my very heart, I dragged upstairs. After putting on dry clothes, and pacing to and fro thirty or forty minutes to restore the animal heat, I adjourned to my study, feeble as a kitten, almost too much so, to enjoy the cheerful fire and smoking coffee which the servant had prepared for my refreshment.

Yet the only way I could find peace, and enjoy my slumber, was to use my hand upon my shaft, picturing the fair Mrs. Heathcliff in my stead. Her hand brought me to a climax that left me gasping for more. I could not wait to see her again.

CHAPTER 4

HAT VAIN WEATHERCOCKS WE ARE! I, who had determined to hold myself independent of all social inter-course, and thanked my stars that, at length, I had lighted on a spot where it was next to impracticable. I, weak wretch, after maintaining till dusk a struggle with low spirits and solitude, was finally compelled to strike my colors. Under pretence of gaining information concern-ing the necessities of my establishment, I desired Mrs. Dean, when she brought in supper, to sit down while I ate it. I hoped, sincerely she would prove a regular gossip, and either rouse me to animation or lull me to sleep by her talk.

"You have lived here a considerable time," I commenced. "Did you not say sixteen years?"

"Eighteen, sir. I came when the mistress was married, to wait on her. After she died, the master retained me for his housekeeper."

"Indeed."

There ensued a pause. She was not a gossip, I feared, unless about her own affairs, and those could hardly interest me.

However, having studied for an interval, with a fist on either knee, and a cloud of meditation over her ruddy countenance, she ejaculated—

"Ah, times are greatly changed since then!"

"Yes," I remarked, "you've seen a good many alterations, I suppose?"

"I have. And troubles too," she said.

"Oh, I'll turn the talk on my landlord's family!" I thought to myself. "A good subject to start! And that pretty girl-widow, I should like to know her history. Whether she be a native of the country, or, as is more probable, an exotic that the surly indigenae will not recognize for kin. If so, I mean to try my hand at seducing the delectable creature."

With this intention I asked Mrs. Dean why Heathcliff let Thrushcross Grange, and preferred living in a situation and residence so much inferior. "Is he not rich enough to keep the estate in good order?" I inquired.

"Rich, sir!" she returned. "He has nobody knows what money, and every year it increases. Yes, yes, he's rich enough to live in a finer house than this, but he's very near—close-handed. And, if he had meant to flit to Thrushcross Grange, as soon as he heard of a good tenant he could not have borne to miss the chance of getting a few hundreds more. It is strange people should be so greedy, when they are alone in the world!"

"He had a son, it seems?"

"Yes, he had one—he is dead."

"And that young lady, Mrs. Heathcliff, is his widow?"

"Yes."

"Where did she come from originally?"

"Why, sir, she is my late master's daughter. Catherine Linton was her maiden name. I nursed her, poor thing! I did wish Mr. Heathcliff would remove here, and then we might have been together again." **I heard true affection in Mrs. Dean's voice, along with sadness and longing.**

"What! Catherine Linton?" I exclaimed, astonished. But a minute's reflection convinced me it was not the ghostly Catherine I had encountered. "Then," I continued, "my predecessor's name was Linton?"

"It was."

"And who is that Earnshaw? The Hareton Earnshaw who lives with Mr. Heathcliff? Are they relations?"

"No, he is the late Mrs. Linton's nephew."

"The young lady's cousin, then?"

"Yes, and her husband was her cousin also. One on the mother's, the other on the father's side. Heathcliff married Mr. Linton's sister."

The complexity of the relationships was nearly dizzying. Now that I knew better their history, I thought I understood the intensity of the carnal nature they shared, cold as they might be in outwardly appearance. A burning desire to explore the carnality of at least one of the inmates of the house made me even more anxious to visit Wuthering Heights again—and soon. "I see the house at Wuthering Heights has 'Earnshaw' carved over the front door. Are they an old family?"

"Very old, sir, and Hareton is the last of them, as our Miss Cathy is of us—I mean, of the Lintons. Have you been to Wuthering Heights? I beg pardon for asking, but I should like to hear how she is."

"Mrs. Heathcliff? She looked very well, and very handsome, yet, I think, not very happy." **I spoke honestly; despite having her sensual appetite fed, she had not appeared to be in the least happy or contented with her lot. I was determined to prove to Mrs. Heathcliff that I could make her happier than the roughneck who had pleasured her. Prudence, however, dictated that I not share this intention with Mrs. Dean.**

"Oh dear, I don't wonder! And how did you like the master?"

"A rough fellow, rather, Mrs. Dean. Is not that his character?" Again, prudence dictated that I not share with Mrs. Dean exactly how uncouth he was.

"Rough as a saw-edge, and hard as whinstone! The less you meddle with him the better."

"He must have had some ups and downs in life to make him such a churl. Do you know anything of his history?"

"It's a cuckoo's, sir—I know all about it, except where he was born, and who were his parents, and how he got his money at first. And Hareton has been cast out like an unfledged sparrow! The unfortunate lad is the only one in all this parish that does not guess how he has been cheated."

"Well, Mrs. Dean, it will be a charitable deed to tell me something of my neighbors. I feel I shall not rest if I go to bed, so be good enough to sit and chat an hour." **The more I knew about Heathcliff and the inmates of Wuthering Heights, the more likely I was to succeed in my aim of seducing Mrs. Heathcliff—and avoiding the wrath of Heathcliff while so doing.**

"Oh, certainly, sir! I'll just fetch a little sewing, and then I'll sit as long as you please. But you've caught cold. I saw you shivering, and you must have some gruel to drive it out."

The worthy woman bustled off, and I crouched nearer the fire. My head felt hot, and the rest of me chill. Moreover, I was excited, almost to a pitch of foolishness, through my nerves and brain. This caused me to feel, not uncomfortable, but rather fearful (as I am still) of serious effects from the incidents of today and yesterday. She returned presently, bringing a smoking basin and a basket of work. Having placed the former on the hob, drew in her seat, evidently pleased to find me so companionable.

Before I came to live here, she commenced—waiting no farther invitation to her story—I was almost always at Wuthering Heights, because my mother had nursed Mr. Hindley Earnshaw, that was Hareton's father, and I got used to playing with the children. I ran errands too, and helped to make hay, and hung about the farm ready for anything that anybody would set me to.

One fine summer morning—it was the beginning of harvest, I remember—Mr. Earnshaw, the old master, came downstairs, dressed for a journey. After he had told Joseph what was to be done during the day, he turned to Hindley, and Cathy, and me—for I sat eating my porridge with them—and he said, speaking to his son, "Now, my bonny man, I'm going to Liverpool today, what shall I bring you? You may choose what you like. Only let it be little, for I shall walk there and back. Sixty miles each way, that is a long spell!"

Hindley named a fiddle, and then he asked Miss Cathy. She was hardly six years old, but she could ride any horse in the stable, and she chose a whip. He did not forget me, for he had a kind heart, though he was rather severe sometimes. He promised to bring me a pocketful of apples and pears, and then he kissed his children, said good-bye, and set off.

It seemed a long while to us all—the three days of his absence—and often did little Cathy ask when he would be home. Mrs. Earnshaw expected him by suppertime on the third evening, and she put the meal off hour after hour. There were no signs of his coming, however, and at last the children got tired of running down to the gate to look. Then it grew dark and, she would have had them to bed, but they begged sadly to be allowed to stay up. And, just about eleven o'clock, the door-latch was raised quietly, and in stepped the master. He threw himself into a chair, laughing and groaning, and bid them all stand off, for he was nearly killed—he would not have such another walk for the three kingdoms.

"And at the end of it to be flighted to death!" he said, opening his greatcoat, which he held bundled up in his arms. "See here, wife! I was never so beaten with anything in my life; but you must even take it as a gift of God, though it's as dark almost as if it came from the devil."

We crowded round, and over Miss Cathy's head I had a peep at a dirty, ragged, black-haired child, big enough both to walk and talk. Indeed, its face looked older than Catherine's. Yet when it was set on its feet, it only stared round, and repeated over and over again some gibberish that nobody could understand.

I was frightened, and Mrs. Earnshaw was ready to fling it out of doors. She did fly up, asking how he could fashion to bring that gypsy brat into the house, when they had their own bairns to feed and fend for? What he meant to do with it, and whether he were mad?

The master tried to explain the matter, but he was really half-dead with fatigue. All that I could make out, amongst Mrs. Earnshaw's scolding, was his tale of his seeing it starving, and houseless, and as good as dumb, in the streets of Liverpool, where he picked it up and inquired for its owner. Not a soul knew to whom it belonged, he said.

His money and time being both limited, he thought it better to take it home with him at once, than run into vain expenses there, because he was determined he would not leave it as he found it. Well, the conclusion was, that my mistress grumbled herself calm, and Mr. Earnshaw told me to wash it, give it clean things, and let it sleep with the children.

Hindley and Cathy contented themselves with looking and listening till peace was restored. Then, both began searching their father's pockets for the presents he had promised them. The former was a boy of fourteen, but when he drew out what had been a fiddle, crushed to morsels in the greatcoat, he blubbered aloud. Cathy, when she learned the master had lost her whip in attending on the stranger, showed her humor by grinning and spitting at the stupid little thing, earning for her pains a sound blow from her father, to teach her cleaner manners.

They entirely refused to have it in bed with them, or even in their room. Being a young lady myself, I had no more sense, so I put it on the landing of the stairs, hoping it might be gone on the morrow. By chance, or else attracted by hearing his voice, it crept to Mr. Earnshaw's door, and there he found it on quitting his chamber. Inquiries were made as to how it got there. I was obliged to confess, and in recompense for my cowardice and inhumanity was sent out of the house.

This was Heathcliff's first introduction to the family. On coming back a few days afterwards (for I did not consider my banishment perpetual), I found they had christened him "Heathcliff"; it was the name of a son who died in childhood, and it has served him ever since, both for Christian and surname. Surprisingly in such a short time, Miss Cathy and he were now very thick, but Hindley hated him. To say the truth I did the same, and we plagued and went on with him shamefully. I wasn't reasonable enough to feel my injustice, and the mistress never put in a word on his behalf when she saw him wronged.

He seemed a sullen, patient child, perhaps hardened to ill-treatment. He would stand Hindley's blows without winking or shedding a tear. My pinches moved him only to draw in a breath and open his eyes, as if he had hurt himself by accident, and nobody was to blame.

This endurance made old Earnshaw furious, when he discovered his son persecuting the poor fatherless child, as he called him. He took to Heathcliff strangely, believing all he said (for that matter, the dark child said precious little, and generally the truth), and petting him up far above Cathy, who was too mischievous and wayward for a favorite.

So, from the very beginning, he bred bad feeling in the house. At Mrs. Earnshaw's death, which happened in less than two years after, the young master had learned to regard his father as an oppressor rather than a friend, and Heathcliff as a usurper of his parent's affections and his privileges. Hindley grew bitter with brooding over these injuries.

I sympathized a while, but when the children fell ill of the measles I had to tend them and take on me the cares of a woman at once, I changed my idea. Heathcliff was dangerously sick, and while he lay at the worst he would have me constantly by his pillow. I suppose he felt I did a good deal for him, and he hadn't wit to guess that I was compelled to do it. However, I will say this, he was the quietest child that ever nurse watched over.

The difference between him and the others forced me to be less partial. Cathy and her brother harassed me terribly, while Healthcliff was as uncomplaining as a lamb, though hardness, not gentleness, made him give little trouble.

He got through, and the doctor affirmed it was in a great measure owing to me, and praised me for my care. I was vain of his commendations, and softened towards the being by whose means I earned them, and thus Hindley lost his last ally. Still I couldn't dote on Heathcliff, and I wondered often what my master saw to admire so much in the sullen boy, who never, to my recollection, repaid his indulgence by any sign of gratitude. He was not insolent to his benefactor, he was simply indifferent, though knowing perfectly the hold he had on his heart, and conscious he had only to speak and all the house would be obliged to bend to his wishes.

As an instance, I remember Mr. Earnshaw once bought a couple of colts at the parish fair, and gave the lads each one. Heathcliff took the handsomest, but it soon fell lame, and when he discovered it, he said to Hindley, "You must exchange horses with me. I don't like mine, and if you won't I shall tell your father of the three thrashings you've given me this week, and show him my arm, which is black to the shoulder."

Hindley put out his tongue, and cuffed him over the ears.

"You'd better do it at once," Heathcliff persisted, escaping to the porch (they were in the stable). "You will have to. And if I speak of these blows, you'll get them again with interest."

"Off, dog!" cried Hindley, threatening him with an iron weight used for weighing potatoes and hay.

"Throw it," the younger boy replied, standing still, "and then I'll tell how you boasted that you would turn me out of doors as soon as he died, and see whether he will not turn you out directly."

Hindley threw it, hitting him on the breast, and down he fell, but staggered up immediately, breathless and white. Had not I prevented it, he would have gone just so to the master, and got full revenge by letting his condition plead for him, intimating who had caused it.

"Take my colt, Gypsy, then!" said young Earnshaw. "And I pray that he may break your neck. Take him, and he damned, you beggarly interloper! And wheedle my father out of all he has. Only afterwards show him what you are, imp of Satan. And take that, I hope he'll kick out your brains!"

Heathcliff had gone to loose the beast, and shift it to his own stall. He was passing behind it, when Hindley finished his speech by knocking him under its feet, and without stopping to examine whether his hopes were fulfilled, ran away as fast as he could. I was surprised to witness how coolly the child gathered himself up, and went on with his intention, exchanging saddles and all, and then sitting down on a bundle of hay to overcome the qualm, which the violent blow occasioned, before he entered the house. I persuaded him easily to let me lay the blame of his bruises on the horse. He minded little what tale was told since he had what he wanted. He complained so seldom, indeed, of such stirs as these, that I really thought him not vindictive. I was deceived completely, as you will hear.

CHAPTER 5

In the course of time, Mr. Earnshaw began to fail. He had been active and healthy, yet his strength left him suddenly, and when he was confined to the chimney corner, he grew grievously irritable. The slightest thing vexed him, and suspected slights of his authority nearly threw him into fits. This was especially to be remarked if any one attempted to impose upon, or domineer over, his favorite, Heathcliff.

Mr. Earnshaw was painfully jealous lest a word should be spoken amiss to the boy, seeming to have got into his head the notion that, because he liked Heathcliff, all hated, and longed to do him an ill turn. It was a disadvantage to the lad, for the kinder among us did not wish to fret the master, so we humored his partiality, and that humoring was rich nourishment to the child's pride and black tempers. Still it became in a manner necessary. Twice, or thrice, Hindley's manifestation of scorn, while his father was near, roused the old man to a fury. He seized his stick to strike his true son, and shook with rage that he could not do it.

At last, our curate (we had a curate then who made the living answer by teaching the little Lintons and Earnshaws, and farming his bit of land himself) advised that Hindley should be sent to college. Mr. Earnshaw agreed, though with a heavy spirit, for he said, "Hindley was nought, and would never thrive as where he wandered."

I hoped heartily we should have peace now. It hurt me to think the master should be made uncomfortable by his own good deed. I fancied the discontent of age and disease arose from his family disagreements, as he would have it that it did. Really, you know, sir, it was in his sinking frame. We might have got on tolerably, notwithstanding, but for two people—Miss Cathy, and Joseph, the servant. You saw him, I daresay, up yonder. He was, and is yet most likely, the wearisomest self-righteous Christian that ever ransacked a Bible to rake the promises to himself and fling the curses to his neighbors.

By his knack of sermonizing and pious discoursing, he contrived to make a great impression on Mr. Earnshaw. The more feeble the master became, the more influence Joseph gained. He was relentless in worrying his master about his soul's concerns, and about ruling his children rigidly. He encouraged him to regard Hindley as a reprobate. Night after night, Joseph regularly grumbled out a long string of tales against Heathcliff and Catherine, always minding to flatter Earnshaw's weakness by heaping the heaviest blame on the latter.

Certainly, she had ways with her such as I never saw a child take up before, and she put all of us past our patience fifty times and oftener in a day. From the hour she came downstairs till the hour she went to bed, we had not a minute's security that she wouldn't be in mischief. Her spirits were always at the high-water mark, her tongue always going—singing, laughing, and plaguing everybody who would not do the same.

A wild, wicked slip she was—but she had the bonniest eye, the sweetest smile, and lightest foot in the parish. After all, I believe she meant no harm, for when once she made you cry in good earnest, it seldom happened that she would not keep you company, and oblige you to be quiet that you might comfort her. She was much too fond of Heathcliff. **The two were thick as thieves, together almost**

constantly, running the moors and whispering to each other in a language it seemed only they understood.

The greatest punishment we could invent for her was to keep her separate from him. Yet she got chided more than any of us on his account. In play, she liked exceedingly to act the little mistress, using her words freely, and commanding her companions. She did so to me, but I would not bear ordering, and so I let her know.

Now, Mr. Earnshaw did not understand jokes from his children. He had always been strict and grave with them, and Catherine, on her part, had no idea why her father should be crosser and less patient in his ailing condition than he was in his prime. His peevish reproofs wakened in her a naughty delight to provoke him.

She was never so happy as when we were all scolding her at once, and she defying us with her bold, saucy look, and her ready words. Her behavior turned Joseph's religious curses into ridicule, baited me, and did just what her father hated most. Her pretended insolence, which he thought real, had more power over Heathcliff than his kindness. The boy would do her bidding in anything, and his only when it suited his own inclination. After behaving as badly as possible all day, she sometimes to his side to make it up at night.

"Nay, Cathy," the old man would say, "I cannot love thee, thou art worse than thy brother. Go, say thy prayers, child, and ask God's pardon. I doubt thy mother and I must rue that we ever reared thee!"

That made her cry, at first, and then being repulsed continually hardened her, and she laughed if I told her to say she was sorry for her faults, and beg to be forgiven.

I surmise this is one of the reasons the bond between Catherine and Heathcliff grew stronger with each passing day. He became the one who loved her above all else, without judgment or reproach. It filled the gap left by her father's disappointment, and her brother's wicked taunting. They were made to fit together as if God Himself had taken a coin and split it in two to create them—one dark and one light. Sometimes it was difficult

to tell them apart when I would see them running on the moors.

But the hour came, at last, that ended Mr. Earnshaw's troubles on earth. He died quietly in his chair one October evening, seated by the fireside. A high wind blustered round the house, and roared in the chimney. It sounded wild and stormy, yet it was not cold, and we were all together—I, a little removed from the hearth, busy at my knitting, and Joseph reading his Bible near the table (for the servants generally sat in the house then, after their work was done). Miss Cathy had been sick, and that made her still, she leant against her father's knee, and Heathcliff was lying on the floor with his head in her lap.

I remember the master, before he fell into a doze, stroking her bonny hair—it pleased him rarely to see her gentle—and saying, "Why canst thou not always be a good lass, Cathy?" And she turned her face up to his, and laughed, and answered, "Why cannot you always be a good man, father?" But as soon as she saw him vexed again, she kissed his hand, and said she would sing him to sleep.

She began singing very low, till his fingers dropped from hers, and his head sank on his breast. Then I told her to hush, and not stir, for fear she should wake him. We all kept as mute as mice a full half-hour, and should have done so longer, only Joseph, having finished his chapter, got up and said that he must rouse the master for prayers and bed. He stepped forward, and called him by name, and touched his shoulder, but he would not move. So he took the candle and looked at him. I thought there was something wrong as he set down the light, and seizing the children each by an arm, whispered them to "frame upstairs, and make little din—they might pray alone that evening—he had summut to do."

"I shall bid father good-night first," said Catherine, putting her arms round his neck, before we could hinder her. The poor thing discovered her loss directly and screamed out. "Oh, he's dead, Heathcliff! He's dead!" And they both set up a heart-breaking cry. **They fell into each other's arms and wept with heart-wrenching sobs. It was the truest grief I had ever seen, and I had no idea I would see it again one day, but I did.**

I joined my wail to theirs, loud and bitter, but Joseph asked what we could be thinking of to roar in that way over a saint in heaven. He told me to put on my cloak and run to Gimmerton for the doctor and the parson. I could not guess the use that either would be of, then. However, I went, through wind and rain, and brought one, the doctor, back with me, the other said he would come in the morning.

Leaving Joseph to explain matters, I ran to the children's room. Their door was ajar and I saw they had never lain down, though it was past midnight. They were calmer, and did not need me to console them. **Side by side on the bed, with their backs to the wall, arms round their small shoulders. I was struck again by how perfectly they were fitted to each other.** The little souls were comforting one another with better thoughts than I could have hit on, imagining Mr. Earnshaw's soul in its Lord's presence. No parson in the world ever pictured heaven so beautifully as they did, in their innocent talk, and, while I sobbed and listened, I could not help wishing we were all there safe together.

CHAPTER 6

*M*R. HINDLEY CAME HOME to the funeral, and—a thing
that amazed us, and set the neighbors gossiping right and
left—he brought a wife with him. What she was, and where she was
born, he never informed us. Probably, she had neither money nor
name to recommend her, or he would scarcely have kept the union
from his father.

She was not one that would have disturbed the house much on
her own account. The moment she crossed the threshold, every object
she saw and every circumstance that took place about her appeared to
delight her. Except the preparing for the burial, and the presence of
the mourners.

I thought she was half-silly, from her behavior while that went
on. She ran into her chamber, and made me come with her, though I
should have been dressing the children. There she sat shivering and
clasping her hands, and asking repeatedly, "Are they gone yet?"

Then she began describing with hysterical emotion the effect
it produced on her to see black, and started, and trembled, and, at
last, fell a-weeping. When I asked what was the matter, answered, she

didn't know, but she felt so afraid of dying! I imagined her as little likely to die as myself.

She was rather thin, but young, and fresh complexioned, and her eyes sparkled as bright as diamonds. I did remark, to be sure, that mounting the stairs made her breathe very quick, that the least sudden noise set her all in a quiver, and that she coughed troublesomely sometimes. But I knew nothing of what these symptoms portended, and had no impulse to sympathize with her. We don't in general take to foreigners here, Mr. Lockwood, unless they take to us first. **Heathcliff was no exception to that rule, except of course, to Catherine. He was no foreigner to my girl, but rather, an extension of her own self. It sounds odd, that it does, but it's the truth.**

Young Earnshaw was altered considerably in the three years of his absence. He had grown sparer, and lost his color, and spoke and dressed quite differently. On the very day of his return, he told Joseph and me we must thenceforth quarter ourselves in the back-kitchen, and leave the house for him. Indeed, he would have carpeted and papered a small spare room for a parlor, but his wife expressed such pleasure at the white floor, the huge glowing fireplace, the pewter dishes and delftcase and dog kennel, and the wide space there was to move about in where they usually sat. He thought it unnecessary to her comfort, and so dropped the intention.

She expressed pleasure, too, at finding a sister among her new acquaintance. She prattled to Catherine, and kissed her, and ran about with her, and gave her quantities of presents, at the beginning. Her affection tired very soon, however, and when she grew peevish, Hindley became tyrannical. A few words from her, evincing a dislike to Heathcliff, were enough to rouse in him all his old hatred of the boy. Hareton drove him from their company to the servants, deprived him of the instructions of the curate, and insisted that he should labor out of doors instead, compelling him to do so as hard as any other lad on the farm.

Heathcliff bore his degradation pretty well at first, because Cathy taught him what she learnt, and worked or played with him in the fields. They both promised fair to grow up as rude as savages, the young master being entirely negligent how they behaved, and what they did, so they kept clear of him. He would not even have seen after their going to church on Sundays, only Joseph and the curate reprimanded his carelessness when they absented themselves. That reminded him to order a flogging for Heathcliff, and a fast from dinner or supper for Catherine.

It was one of their chief amusements to run away to the moors in the morning and remain there all day, and the after punishment grew a mere thing to laugh at. The curate might set as many chapters as he pleased for Catherine to get by heart, and Joseph might thrash Heathcliff till his arm ached; they forgot everything the minute they were together again——at least the minute they had contrived some naughty plan of revenge. Many a time I've cried to myself to watch them growing more reckless daily, and I not daring to speak a syllable, for fear of losing the small power I still retained over the unfriended creatures.

I happened upon them once quite by accident. They sat beneath an ancient oak tree near the boundary that runs between Wuthering Heights and Thrushcross Grange, sitting so near to each other you could not make out where the one ended and the other began. They did not see or hear me, and I kept quiet, standing in the shadows of the fence, watching and listening as long as I dared—not because of idle curiosity, but because I hoped to learn how to increase that small store of power I retained over them by understanding what would induce them to behave in a manner more fitting to the household.

He stroked her hair as they talked, their voices low and hushed. In their repose, they were more calm than was their general behavior, individually or together, as if touching relaxed the demons that jumped and ran about inside them. They were not evil—no matter what denunciations Joseph thundered over their heads—but they had a wildness about them. They were exceedingly well-matched in that.

"It's so horribly unfair of Hareton to make you labor like an animal, Heathcliff." Cathy snuggled her face into the crook of his neck, not seeming to mind the smell of honest work on Heathcliff's skin.

His hand paused only momentarily and a shudder passed through him. I could tell that new feelings were awakening inside them. It shocked me, I will admit as much. They appeared so young, always dirty and running about barefoot, that it had scarcely occurred to me that they would recognize each other as man and woman instead of companions in mischief. I knew that Hareton's determination to keep them apart would not be easily accomplished now, as their bond, previously sealed by the likenesses of their natures, became something else altogether.

I know I should have stopped them, or left them to their own devices; I could do neither. I watched as Heathcliff tilted her chin up until their gazes met. For a long moment they stared into each other's eyes, unmindful of the world around them, as if the birds had stopped singing and the wind ceased blowing.

He pressed his lips to hers once, lighter than a butterfly's touch. She reached up and traced the shape of his mouth, her fingernails gritty with dirt from the moors. It didn't seem to matter.

"Do it again."

Although they were still very young, the passion between them seemed ancient and familiar. He obliged her request by pulling her tighter against his chest and seeking her mouth once more. This kiss was fiercer than the first, expressive of the new feelings they were exploring. The awkwardness of their movements betrayed their naïveté. I could tell, Mr. Lockwood, that they had not the slightest idea of the power of what they were dabbling in.

This time when he pulled back, Cathy touched her own lips, red and glistening from their kiss. Her eyes were wide with wonderment and, God help them both, love.

CHAPTER 7

ERE MRS. DEAN STOPPED HER TALE and, jumping up from the table, busied herself with taking my empty gruel dish to the sideboard, then prodding at the fire with the poker, though the fire appeared to be drawing perfectly well without her intervention. Her actions surprised me, for she had seem quite companionable as she told her tale, and I was intrigued as to what sudden unhappy memory had stopped her from completing the story.

Leaning back in my chair, watching her bustle about the room, I considered how I might induce her to continue her tale. It would require a delicacy of approach, for I might, without intending to, offend her, and in so doing seal her mouth closed. I knew I must not let her think I judged her actions, or criticized her for not taking a stronger hand with the young Heathcliff and Cathy.

I said, in an off-hand manner meant to convey a lack of interest that was the distinct opposite of what I actually felt, "I suppose their explorations became more fervent then? Come, Mrs. Dean, you need not fear that I'll repeat anything—"

"It wasn't them," she said, and poked the fire more vigorously. Her voice was muffled as she leaned nearer the fire, but I heard her say, "Not then, at any rate."

My curiosity piqued beyond bearing, I restrained myself from uttering an ejaculation that would make her ears burn. I prompted her with as much restraint as I could muster, "Ah. The newlyweds?"

She withdrew her head from the fireplace and said, "It was that selfsame day. I had never seen such a game in my life."

Now she had me salivating to learn what kind of game had gone on between Hindley and his bride. But the details must be drawn out with care, or she would stop herself, appalled at what she was relating to a man who was, in many respects, an absolute stranger.

"I suppose they were very much in love," I commented. "And not loath to show their feelings."

Mrs. Dean made a sound of contempt and heaved herself to her feet. "You would have thought they were connected to each other by their private parts," she said, and immediately the whole of my attention was engaged, though I had not thought it had previously flagged in the slightest. "I cannot count the number of times I came upon one or another of their many displays of affection."

I forced myself not to take her by the shoulders and shake her; she was not being deliberately coy. I gritted my teeth against the demand that she tell me every sordid detail. I leaned back in my chair again, the picture of indifference, and said, "I suppose you felt they were not the best models of propriety for Heathcliff and Cathy to follow."

"That's just so," she said, nodding vigorously, and coming round to sit at the table again. I noticed that she was breathing more heavily formerly, and I guessed that it was not her exertions that made her do so. She was flushed, as from the fire, but I was convinced the fire had naught to do with her physical appearance. She was remembering some extremely affecting scene, and I wanted—needed—to know what it was.

"On the selfsame day," I prompted her, "you came upon— Hindley and his wife? What was her given name?" I thought to lull her into believing my curiosity was directed elsewhere.

"Frances," she said promptly.

"Frances," I repeated, tasting the name on my lips. "And you came in from seeing the affection between Heathcliff and Cathy, and saw them—"

"And saw Frances teasing Hindley," she nodded vigorously, and a vast disappointment swept through me. Frances teasing Hindley was not what I had hoped to hear about.

"How so?" I asked, and this time my indifference was less feigned.

"Why, she kept kissing Hindley between bites of his dinner, much to his consternation. His face grew ruddier with each stolen kiss, and he kept darting glances at Cathy and the servants, then asking her to leave off, yet she continued."

It sounded like the silly game of a besotted bride, and not the sort of thing that Mrs. Dean would be loath to tell about. "And so?" I asked, not really interested anymore. "Did she push him too far?" It was not unheard of for a man to strike his wife for silliness, but I did not think the memory of some violent incident would be so difficult for Mrs. Dean to talk about.

"She did," Mrs. Dean concurred. "Not realizing the consequence of pushing him past his level of patience."

"Was he angry? Or excited?" I asked, keeping my voice even.

"I couldn't tell at first," Mrs. Dean admitted. "He said she was no better than Cathy and Heathcliff, always pushing him and never listening to him, nor yielding to his authority. I was a little shaken by his vehemence until I saw in his eyes that he wasn't furious, he was lustful."

That was much better. I relaxed a little in my chair. "So then what happened?"

She leaned forward a little, and told me the story.

CHAPTER 8

*H*INDLEY KNOCKED OVER HIS CHAIR and seized his wife by the wrist, much to the astonished surprise of Cathy and myself. Frances seemed to understand what her husband needed and wanted, for she smiled widely and didn't try to stop him as he growled in his throat and pulled her into their bedchamber, his tented trousers evidence of arousal from his wife's game.

I was concerned for Frances, because for all she was a silly girl, she was quite kind and a little frail, and I thought he might be too vigorous in his marital demands, so I crept after them, intending to intervene if he became unreasonable with her.

I eased open the door a little to watch, and found them so caught up in their game that they didn't hear me and probably wouldn't have heard ten Josephs thundering Bible verses at them.

She stood in the center of the room, her chest heaving with excitement. He stalked around her, watching her, a predator circling his prey.

"You've been naughty, Frances."

Her grin was quite coquettish. "Can I help it that I like to kiss you?"

He stopped pacing and stared at her, his hands opening and closing. "You are a wanton, disobedient woman."

"I have always done what you wished," Frances said. And that was true, he had had her every night from their wedding, and she never uttered a word against him, not in my hearing. I thought she must enjoy his attentions immensely to be so resigned to them.

"Not tonight."

He was still a little angry about that, and she must have been able to tell, because she drew near to him and said softly, "Then you must tell me what you want," she said, "so that I can show you that I do listen to you, and that I am your obedient wife."

"Tell you what I want?" he grunted. "And then?"

"Then I will give it to you."

"And what else?" he asked. "Then I must do as you demand, or bring you a gift of appreciation afterwards?"

"Nothing else. No other rules."

He stroked the front of his trousers as he regarded her. "I suppose you have a devious purpose that will be revealed to me in time."

"Perhaps."

"Very well." He took a step closer and cupped her breast in his hand.

"Oh," she said, taking a step back.

I could see his shaft throb against the confines of his trousers and I wondered if the lady knew how dangerous a game she played. He was capable of throwing her down on the bed and rutting with her like a stallion at his mare.

"I thought there were no other rules?"

"There are not. But you must tell me what you want."

"Well, I want to touch your breast," he said impatiently. She nodded encouragingly. He cleared his throat. "I want to touch your breast." His voice sounded harsh in the quiet of the room. This time when he reached to cup her, she did not move away.

Immediately he grasped the nature of the game. "I want to stroke your nipple," he said, and suited the action to the word. Her nipple tautened beneath his thumb. He reached with his other hand, then told her what he wanted. "I want to touch your other breast."

"Oh, Hindley," she whispered, saying his name like a blessing.

His hand closed over her breast. They stood like that for a moment, not touching or saying anything, and I could see the evidence of Hindley's desire, and I could smell the evidence of Frances's desire.

"Show me your breasts," he said. Her hands shook as they unlaced and parted the bodice of her dress, then pushed it off her shoulders. She caught the gown at her waist, baring her pretty breasts to him, ivory and rose. She was quite full and soft, for someone so delicate as she.

He bent, then recalled himself and whispered in her ear. "I want your breast in my mouth." He took her breast, suckling the nipple, flicking it with his tongue, teasing it with his teeth, partaking of her as a man might eat a particularly luscious dessert. She moaned and clutched her dress tighter.

"Frances," he said. "Put your arms around me."

She snaked her arms around his neck, arching her body to him, offering herself to him, showing him he was her master, and she embraced the requirements of her submission.

"Kiss me," he said, and crushed his mouth to hers. "Open your mouth to me," he said raggedly, a moment later, and she did. With a groan, he plundered her mouth with his hard demands.

"I want to see you naked," he said, breaking the kiss.

She stepped away from him and let the dress fall, pushing it over her hips and letting it puddle on the floor. She stood before him, naked and ready.

"Turn around," he said, his voice sounding rough.

She did as he instructed, obedient as a lamb, just as she promised him.

"I am going to touch you," he said. "I am going to touch your back"—he stroked her silky smooth back—"and your buttocks. Bend over, Frances." She bent, bracing herself on the table in anticipation, but I knew he had no intention of plunging into her yet. He would play the game longer, and she would see who won.

He cupped her soft buttocks, squeezing them gently, lifting and separating them, teasing her cleft with his finger. She made a mewling sound of pleasure that said she liked his hands on her, she liked his handling, welcomed it—

"I am going to stroke your thighs," he said, sliding his hands down the backs of her legs. His breath was coming in hard, labored gasps.

"Stand up," he demanded. "I am going to wrap my arms around you." He pulled her to him so her back rested against his chest. Her head fit by his shoulder. Her plump bottom perched against his hardness. If he wanted to let his hands roam all over her body, she would let him . . . he only had to tell her.

"Put your arms around my neck," he said. She reached up and linked her hands behind his neck, arching her back a little, exposing her body to his touch. He snuggled his shaft closer to her bottom. "I am going to touch your breasts," he said, then trailed his hands up her body to close over her breasts. He stroked and plucked them until her nipples stood straight out, and then he smiled and teased the nipples with the pads of his forefingers. She moaned at the touch, shifting against him.

"Do not move," he said. I knew he did not want to take her now, he wanted to play the game longer, but if she moved, he would not last.

She stilled, waiting for him. He bit back a chuckle. I could tell how much he liked the game and I knew he would make her play it again, over and over, and that she would do it happily, will-ingly—anything to please him.

Her hands were still linked around his neck. He lowered his head to whisper in her ear. "I am going to touch your body." He stroked his hands down her ribs. She shivered at his touch. He caressed her hips, then slid his hands across her belly. With one hand on her belly, he anchored her firmly against him, his shaft against her buttocks. He slid the other hand down until he barely touched the top of her curls between her legs. She waited, vibrat-ing, for his touch. He did not touch her.

"Oh, Hindley," she said, his name a moan on her lips. His name had never sounded so enticing to me before. He closed his eyes and his body shuddered but he mastered himself.

"Yes, my dear?"

"Touch me," she said in a voice that whimpered.

"That is not the game, Frances." He was so sure, so in com-mand, his shaft straining hard against his trousers.

She shifted restlessly against him. "Please, Hindley—"

"Do not move," he whispered in her ear, his hips pushing against her, a shadow of what I knew he wanted to do with her, to bend her over the table and take her, plunging and driving inside her hot wetness. His hands were very still and I could only imag-ine he was battling himself, trying to cool his lust, knowing what it felt like to be inside of her, so hot and wet, sheathing him tightly like a glove.

"Spread your legs," he growled. Everything he told her, she must do—

She spread her legs.

He exhaled heavily. "I am going to touch you between your legs," he said.

"Yes," she breathed.

He cupped her and she arched against his hand with a sharp cry of pleasure.

"Do not move," he said. "My God, I will explode if you move, I am that hot for you."

"Take me," she whispered, and I was surprised he did not do it right then, slamming into her the whole force of his lust.

"That is not how the game is played," he reminded her, though he had to say it through his teeth. He would win this battle with her if it killed him, and it appeared it might very well do so.

He held hard to his self control. Then he told her what he wanted from her. "I want you wet, Frances," he said, low in her ear.

"Yes."

"Are you wet for me?"

"Oh, yes."

"You play the game so well," he said. Then he announced his next move, gripping her hard against him. "I am going to stroke you, Frances."

He moved his hand over her mound, sliding his fingers back and forth against her softness. Teasing her mound, stroking her folds, he found her pleasure-knot and worked it with the pad of his forefinger. Her breath came in enticing, excited pants now.

"I am going to put my finger in you," he promised next, and then he slid it inside her sweet center.

"Oh," she gasped, rocking her hips against his hand.

"Do not move," he grated out, clutching her hips to his. "You must not move, Frances, I cannot take it." He plundered her with his finger as she held very still, so very obedient to his commands. His shaft. She would take it in her hot wet center. He would tell her to take it and she would, that was the rule of the game.

"I am going to put another finger inside you," he said, and she must let him because he had told her. He plunged another finger inside her, stroking more wetness from her. He wanted her dripping wet for his shaft——a man's shaft loves a woman's hot, wet place.

He withdrew his fingers. "I am going to stroke you now," he

said and using her own wetness stroked her pleasure-knot. She stiffened and cried out but did not move against his hand.

"Oh, yes," he approved. "Just feel my touch." Slowly he drew his finger away from her pleasure-knot.

"I want you to touch yourself," he said. He guided her small hand between her legs. "Like that. Stroke yourself, Frances. It gives me so much pleasure to watch you." She swallowed hard and began stroking herself.

"Keep your legs spread wide," he said hoarsely. "I am going to put my fingers inside you while you stroke yourself."

"Oh my God," she said, as he worked her opening wider with his hand and plunged his fingers inside her tight slick passage. The more he pumped and the more she stroked, the wetter she became.

"Do not move," he said, holding her tight against him, rocking his fingers in and out. She stiffened, every muscle clenching as she tried not to move.

"Oh, Hindley," she whispered. He must have known his demand that made the heat flare even hotter for her. His breath came hard as her fingers stroked her pleasure-knot and he thrust his fingers in and out of her opening. Then he decided to make another demand as her body bowed and tightened beneath his hands.

"I want you to come, Frances," he told her, thrusting faster and faster with his fingers and he said, "Oh, yes. Oh, yes." Then she screamed as the climax hit her, crying out his name over and over, and suddenly she was limp, her knees buckling. He lifted her and carried her to the bed.

"We are not through, Frances," he warned her, stripping off his shirt.

"I know," she said, gazing up at him with eyes dark with desire, moistening her lips with her pretty pink tongue. "Oh, Hindley, I thought I would die if I had to keep holding still."

"You did not die," he said, stripping off his trousers, a smug smile of satisfaction at his efforts, for he appeared to be winning her game.

His shaft sprang free, and I had to bite back a gasp. It was huge, engorged, red and thick, and I couldn't imagine how he expected it to fit into Frances.

She reached for him and though his shaft jumped, eager for the feel of her hands, he turned away. "I did not ask for you to touch me," he chided.

She grinned at him. "Then what would you have me do?"

"I have not decided," he said. He joined her on the bed, and lay on his back, folding his arms comfortably behind his neck. His erection jutted in the air.

"I would not mind putting my hands on you," Frances said frankly. She had shifted so she was kneeling beside him now, looking down at him, her hair a tangle about her shoulders, pretty breasts peeping through the curls——his to command. His shaft surged.

"Would you like a ride?" he asked.

"It is very kind of you to ask," she teased.

"Would you like to kiss me?" he said.

Her smiled deepened. "There," she said. "You are considerate of me. I would like to kiss you."

"Then stop chattering and do so," he said severely.

She lowered her mouth to his and he closed his eyes as she threaded her hands through his hair and deepened the kiss. When she came up for air, her lips were wet from his mouth. She had stopped grinning and her eyes had an out of focus look.

"Kiss me again," he said. "Open your mouth and use your tongue."

She did not speak but came to him again, and opened her mouth against his, and gave him her tongue. He groaned in the back of his throat at the pleasure of her obeying his erotic demand.

This time he broke the kiss to say, "Straddle me, Frances."

She shifted and moved astride him, her soft mound barely touching his iron-hard shaft. They both knew she would feel the length of it soon.

"Kiss me again," he breathed, and she bent to kiss him. Now she was thrusting her tongue in his mouth, dueling with him, the heated contest making the very air thick with lust and heat. Then she pulled free to draw breath, her face so dazed and thunderstruck that I wanted to reassure her that everything would turn out right, he was just trying to win a game.

"Take me inside you," he said. "All the way. Now."

She impaled herself onto him with a sigh of pleasure, talking the entire length of his rock-hard shaft. His hips rose to meet her, a gasp of desire wrenching from his lips. She spread her thighs wider to take all of him. Then she stopped.

He bit off an oath and it took him a long moment to remember her game.

"Ride me, Frances," he said.

She rose above him, so beautiful in the firelight, a bead of sweat trickling between her breasts. Then she sank down and he thrust his hips up to meet her. That was not enough for him, and he said, "I want you on your back," and he rolled her under him.

"I am going to give it to you hard," he said and she gasped as he thrust his full hard length deep, deep inside her, a groan tearing from his throat as he did.

He thrust again and then she clamped her hands on his buttocks, holding him in place though he wanted to delve deeper and deeper, the muscles in his back clenching with effort—

Her wide eyes were innocent even when she said, "You forgot to tell me what you were going to do."

He grunted at her words. "Very well," he ground out. "I am going to take you, lovely Frances," and he withdrew nearly all the way out and then slammed deep inside her. "Spread your legs wider," he said. "I want you to take every inch of me. I will not hold back."

She parted her thighs wider, her gaze locked on his.

"Oh, yes," he said. "Oh, yes. Do not move, Frances."

"Oh, Hindley."

"Do not move. Just feel it. Feel everything. Take everything." Oh, it was a lovely game—

"Take it all," he said.

"Yes," she whispered.

"I am going to thrust again." Just telling her what he was going to do made him so wild, he could hardly even breathe.

He hammered deep again. He kept his gaze on hers, so open, so intimate.

"Do not move," he challenged her. I knew he wanted her mad with pleasure. He did not want her to assuage her desire, not yet, he wanted her to explode, screaming, like she had done earlier.

"Oh, Robert," she said, letting him see everything in her eyes.

"Take me again, Frances."

"Yes."

He thrust long and slow and deep, every inch driving his pleasure up a notch.

"Again," he said.

"Yes."

This time her hips met his in unthinking cadence but he did not stop her this time or chide her for breaking the rules.

"Again," he told her and thrust hard.

"Oh!" she said and he growled at the sound.

"I am going to thrust faster," he said, as her hips met his.

"Oh, Hindley." She clenched his arms, her eyes huge as she gazed up at him. But it was not enough for the man. He wanted more.

"Faster and harder," he warned her, his hips slamming against hers. "Take me, Frances. Take me all the way."

"Yes," she said, rocking her hips to meet his thrusts, taking him hard and deep.

"Again," he said. "Again. Oh, yes. Again. Again."

"Yes," she whispered, her fingers digging into his shoulders, her legs spread so wide for him.

"Once more, Frances," he said, driving into her and then she gasped and he ground out, "I want you to come."

She gasped her pleasure at his command.

"I am going to ride you hard when you come," he said, and then her lovely eyes went blank and her muscles clenched and contracted all around him and she cried out his name over and over. He rode her hard as he had promised, slamming into her again and again and then he ground out, "I am going to spill my seed for you, Frances."

"Oh, yes," she whispered.

And then the climax crashed down on him and he emptied himself into her, pouring until the last drop of his essence had been wrung from him. He collapsed, breathless, heart thundering, into her welcoming arms, and I could tell that no matter how they decided the matter between them, they had both won that game.

CHAPTER 9

*H*INDLEY AND HIS NEW WIFE **were indeed perfectly matched. As they continued their playing their
private games, the younger ones continued their mischief as well.**

One Sunday evening, it chanced that Heathcliff and Catherine
were banished from the sitting room, for making a noise, or a light
offense of the kind. When I went to call them to supper, I could discover them nowhere. We searched the house, above and below, and the
yard and stables. They were invisible. At last, Hindley in a passion told
us to bolt the doors, and swore nobody should let them in that night.

The household went to bed, and I, too anxious to lie down,
opened my lattice and put my head out to harken, though it rained.
I was determined to admit them in spite of the prohibition, should
they return.

In a while, I distinguished steps coming up the road, and the
light of a lantern glimmering through the gate. I threw a shawl over
my head and ran to prevent them from waking Mr. Earnshaw by
knocking. There was Heathcliff, by himself. It gave me a start to see
him alone.

"Where is Miss Catherine?" I cried hurriedly. "No accident, I hope?"

"At Thrushcross Grange," he answered, "and I would have been there too, but they had not the manners to ask me to stay."

"Well, you will catch it!" I said. "You'll never be content till you're sent about your business. What in the world led you wandering to Thrushcross Grange?"

"Let me get off my wet clothes, and I'll tell you all about it, Nelly," he replied.

I bid him beware of rousing the master, and while he undressed and I waited to put out the candle, he continued—

"Cathy and I escaped from the washhouse to have a ramble at liberty, and got a glimpse of the Grange lights. We thought we would just go and see whether the Lintons passed their Sunday evenings standing shivering in corners, while their father and mother sat eating and drinking, and singing and laughing, and burning their eyes out before the fire. Do you think they do? Or reading sermons, and being catechized by their manservant, and set to learn a column of Scripture names, if they don't answer properly?"

"Probably not," I responded. "They are good children, no doubt, and don't deserve the treatment you receive, for your bad conduct."

"Don't cant, Nelly," he said. "Nonsense! We ran from the top of the Heights to the park, without stopping—Catherine completely beaten in the race, because she was barefoot. You'll have to seek for her shoes in the bog tomorrow. We crept through a broken hedge, groped our way up the path, and planted ourselves on a flower-plot under the drawing-room window. The light came from thence. They had not put up the shutters, and the curtains were only half closed. Both of us were able to look in by standing on the basement, and clinging to the ledge, and we saw—ah! it was beautiful—a splendid place carpeted with crimson, and crimson-covered chairs and tables, and a pure white ceiling bordered by gold, a shower of glass-drops hanging in silver chains from the center, and shimmering with little soft tapers." **He stopped to sigh softly.**

"Old Mr. and Mrs. Linton were not there, Edgar and his sisters had it entirely to themselves. Shouldn't they have been happy? We should have thought ourselves in heaven! And now, guess what your good children were doing? Isabella—I believe she is eleven, a year younger than Cathy—lay screaming at the farther end of the room, shrieking as if witches were running red-hot needles into her. Edgar stood on the hearth weeping silently, and in the middle of the table sat a little dog, shaking its paw and yelping, which, from their mutual accusations, we understood they had nearly pulled in two between them. The idiots! That was their pleasure! To quarrel who should hold a heap of warm hair, and each begin to cry because both, after struggling to get it, refused to take it. We laughed outright at the petted things. We did despise them! When would you catch me wishing to have what Catherine wanted? Or find us by ourselves, seeking entertainment in yelling, and sobbing, and rolling on the ground, divided by the whole room? I'd not exchange, for a thousand lives, my condition here, for Edgar Linton's at Thrushcross Grange—not if I might have the privilege of flinging Joseph off the highest gable, and painting the house-front with Hindley's blood!"

"Hush, hush!" I interrupted. "Still you have not told me, Heathcliff, how Catherine is left behind?"

"I told you we laughed," he answered. "The Lintons heard us, and with one accord they shot like arrows to the door, there was silence, and then a cry, 'Oh, Mamma, Mamma! Oh, Papa! Oh, Mamma, come here. Oh, Papa, oh!' They really did howl out something in that way. We made frightful noises to terrify them still more, and then we dropped off the ledge, because somebody was drawing the bars, and we felt we had better flee. I had Cathy by the hand, and was urging her on, when all at once she fell down.

"'Run, Heathcliff, run!' she whispered. 'They have let the bull-dog loose, and he holds me!'

"The devil had seized her ankle, Nelly; I heard his abominable snorting. She did not yell out—no! She would have scorned to do it, if she had been spitted on the horns of a mad cow. I did, though. I vociferated curses enough to annihilate any fiend in Christendom. I got a stone and thrust it between his jaws, and tried with all my might to cram it down his throat. A beast of a servant came up with a lantern, at last, shouting—'Keep fast, Skulker, keep fast!'"

"He changed his note, however, when he saw Skulker's game. The dog was throttled off, his huge, purple tongue hanging half a foot out of his mouth, and his pendent lips streaming with bloody slaver.

"The man took Cathy up. She was sick, not from fear, I'm certain, but from pain. He carried her in, and I followed, grumbling execrations and vengeance.

"'What prey, Robert?' hallooed Linton from the entrance.

"'Skulker has caught a little girl, sir,' he replied, 'and there's a lad here,' he added, making a clutch at me, 'who looks an out-and-outer! Very like the robbers were for putting them through the window to open the doors to the gang after all were asleep, that they might murder us at their ease. Hold your tongue, you foul-mouthed thief, you! You shall go to the gallows for this. Mr. Linton, sir, don't lay by your gun.'

"'No, no, Robert,' said the old fool. 'The rascals knew that yesterday was my rent day. They thought to have me cleverly. Come in. I'll furnish them a reception. There, John, fasten the chain. Give Skulker some water, Jenny. To beard a magistrate in his stronghold, and on the Sabbath, too! Where will their insolence stop? Oh, my dear Mary, look here! Don't be afraid, it is but a boy—yet the villain scowls so plainly in his face, would it not be a kindness to the country to hang him at once, before he shows his nature in acts as well as features?'

"He pulled me under the chandelier, and Mrs. Linton placed her spectacles on her nose and raised her hands in horror. The cowardly children crept nearer also, Isabella lisping—

"'Frightful thing! Put him in the cellar, papa. He's exactly like the son of the fortune-teller that stole my tame pheasant. Isn't he, Edgar?'"

"While they examined me, Cathy came round, she heard the last speech, and laughed. Edgar Linton, after an inquisitive stare, collected sufficient wit to recognize her. They see us at church, you know, though we seldom meet them elsewhere.

"'That's Miss Earnshaw,' he whispered to his mother, 'and look how Skulker has bitten her—how her foot bleeds!'

"'Miss Earnshaw? Nonsense!' cried the dame, 'Miss Earnshaw scouring the country with a gypsy! And yet, my dear, the child is in mourning—surely it is—and she may be lamed for life!'

"'What culpable carelessness in her brother!' exclaimed Mr. Linton, turning from me to Catherine. 'I've understood from Shielders' (that was the curate, sir) 'that he lets her grow up in absolute heathenism. But who is this? Where did she pick up this companion? Oho! I declare he is that strange acquisition my late neighbor made, in his journey to Liverpool—a little Lascar, or an American or Spanish castaway.'

"'A wicked boy, at all events,' remarked the old lady, 'and quite unfit for a decent house! Did you notice his language, Linton? I'm shocked that my children should have heard it.'

"I recommenced cursing—don't be angry, Nelly—and so Robert was ordered to take me off. I refused to go without Cathy. He dragged me into the garden, pushed the lantern into my hand, assured me that Mr. Earnshaw should be informed of my behavior, and, bidding me march directly, secured the door again.

"The curtains were still looped up at one corner, and I resumed my station as spy, because, if Catherine had wished to return, I intended shattering their great glass panes to a million of fragments, unless they let her out.

"She sat on the sofa quietly. Mrs. Linton took off the grey cloak of the dairymaid, which we had borrowed for our excursion, shaking her head and expostulating with her, I suppose. She was a young lady, and they made a distinction between her treatment and mine. Then the woman-servant brought a basin of warm water and washed her feet, Mr. Linton mixed a tumbler of spiced wine, Isabella emptied a plateful of cakes into her lap, and Edgar stood gaping at a distance. Afterwards, they dried and combed her beautiful hair, and gave her a pair of enormous slippers, and wheeled her to the fire. I left her, as merry as she could be, dividing her food between the little dog and Skulker, whose nose she pinched as he ate, and kindling a spark of spirit in the vacant blue eyes of the Lintons—a dim reflection from her own enchanting face. I saw they were full of stupid admiration. She is so immeasurably superior to them—to everybody on earth, is she not, Nelly?"

"There will more come of this business than you reckon on," I answered, covering him up and extinguishing the light. "You are incurable, Heathcliff, and Mr. Hindley will have to proceed to extremities, see if he won't."

My words came truer than I desired. The luckless adventure made Earnshaw furious. And then Mr. Linton, to mend matters, paid us a visit himself on the morrow, and read the young master such a lecture on the road he guided his family, that he was stirred to look about him, in earnest.

Heathcliff received no flogging, but he was told that the first word he spoke to Miss Catherine should ensure a dismissal. Mrs. Earnshaw undertook to keep her sister-in-law in due restraint when she returned home, employing art, not force. With force she would have found it impossible.

CHAPTER 10

ATHY STAYED AT THRUSHCROSS GRANGE five weeks, till Christmas. By that time her ankle was thoroughly cured, and her manners much improved. The mistress visited her often in the interval, and commenced her plan of reform by trying to raise her self-respect with fine clothes and flattery, which she took readily. Instead of a wild, hatless little savage jumping into the house, and rushing to squeeze us all breathless, there lighted from a handsome black pony a very dignified person, with brown ringlets falling from the cover of a feathered beaver, and a long cloth habit, which she was obliged to hold up with both hands that she might sail in.

Hindley lifted her from her horse, exclaiming delightedly, "Why, Cathy, you are quite a beauty! I should scarcely have known you. You look like a lady now. Isabella Linton is not to be compared with her, is she, Frances?"

"Isabella has not her natural advantages," replied his wife. "But she must mind and not grow wild again here. Ellen, help Miss Catherine off with her things. Stay, dear, you will disarrange your curls—let me untie your hat."

I removed the habit, and there shone forth beneath a grand plaid silk frock, white trousers, and burnished shoes. While her eyes sparkled joyfully when the dogs came bounding up to welcome her, she dared hardly touch them lest they should fawn upon her splendid garments. She kissed me gently. I was all flour making the Christmas cake, and it would not have done to give me a hug. Then she looked round for Heathcliff. Mr. and Mrs. Earnshaw watched anxiously their meeting, thinking it would enable them to judge, in some measure, what grounds they had for hoping to succeed in separating the two friends.

Heathcliff was hard to discover, at first. If he were careless, and uncared for, before Catherine's absence, he had been ten times more so since.

Nobody but I even did him the kindness to call him a dirty boy, and bid him wash himself, once a week. Young people of his age seldom have a natural pleasure in soap and water. Therefore, not to mention his clothes, which had seen three months' service in mire and dust, and his thick uncombed hair, the surface of his face and hands was dismally beclouded. He might well skulk behind the settle, on beholding such a bright, graceful damsel enter the house, instead of a rough-headed counterpart of himself, as he expected.

"Is Heathcliff not here?" she demanded, pulling off her gloves, and displaying fingers wonderfully whitened with doing nothing and staying indoors.

"Heathcliff, you may come forward," cried Mr. Hindley, enjoying his discomfiture, and gratified to see what a forbidding young blackguard he would be compelled to present himself. "You may come and wish Miss Catherine welcome, like the other servants."

Cathy, catching a glimpse of her friend in his concealment, flew to embrace him. She bestowed seven or eight kisses on his cheek within the second, and then stopped, and drawing back, burst into a laugh, exclaiming, "Why, how very black and cross you look! And how—how funny and grim! But that's because I'm used to Edgar and

Isabella Linton. Well, Heathcliff, have you forgotten me?"

She had some reason to put the question, for shame and pride threw double gloom over his countenance, and kept him immovable.

"Shake hands, Heathcliff," said Mr. Earnshaw, condescendingly, "once in a way, that is permitted."

"I shall not," replied the boy, finding his tongue at last, "I shall not stand to be laughed at. I shall not bear it!" He would have broken from the circle, but Miss Cathy seized him again.

"I did not mean to laugh at you," she said, "I could not hinder myself. Heathcliff, shake hands at least! What are you sulky for? It was only that you looked odd. If you wash your face and brush your hair, it will be all right, but you are so dirty!"

She gazed concernedly at the dusky fingers she held in her own, and also at her dress, which she feared had gained no embellishment from its contact with his.

"You needn't have touched me!" he answered, following her eye and snatching away his hand. "I shall be as dirty as I please. And I like to be dirty, and I will be dirty."

With that he dashed headforemost out of the room, amid the merriment of the master and mistress, and to the serious disturbance of Catherine, who could not comprehend how her remarks should have produced such an exhibition of bad temper.

After playing lady's maid to the newcomer, and putting my cakes in the oven, I made the house and kitchen cheerful with great fires, befitting Christmas Eve. I prepared to sit down and amuse myself by singing carols, all alone, regardless of Joseph's affirmations that he considered the merry tunes I chose as next door to songs.

He had retired to private prayer in his chamber, and Mr. and Mrs. Earnshaw were engaging Missy's attention by sundry gay trifles bought for her to present to the little Lintons, as an acknowledgment of their kindness. They had invited them to spend the morrow at Wuthering Heights, and the invitation had been accepted, on one condition. Mrs. Linton begged that her darlings might be kept carefully apart from that "naughty swearing boy."

Under these circumstances I remained solitary. I smelt the rich scent of the heating spices, and admired the shining kitchen utensils, the polished clock, decked in holly, the silver mugs ranged on a tray ready to be filled with mulled ale for supper, and above all, the speckless purity of my particular care—the scoured and well-swept floor.

I gave due inward applause to every object, and then I remembered how old Earnshaw used to come in when all was tidied, and call me a cant lass, and slip a shilling into my hand as a Christmas box. From that I went on to think of his fondness for Heathcliff, and his dread lest he should suffer neglect after death had removed him. And that naturally led me to consider the poor lad's situation now, and from singing I changed my mind to crying. No doubt he thought his Cathy had forgotten him and all they shared together.

It struck me soon, however, there would be more sense in endeavoring to repair some of his wrongs than shedding tears over them. I got up and walked into the court to seek him. He was not far; I found him smoothing the glossy coat of the new pony in the stable, and feeding the other beasts, according to custom.

"Make haste, Heathcliff!" I said. "The kitchen is so comfortable, and Joseph is upstairs. Make haste, and let me dress you smart before Miss Cathy comes out, and then you can sit together, with the whole hearth to yourselves, and have a long chatter till bedtime."

He proceeded with his task, and never turned his head towards me.

"Come—are you coming?" I continued. "There's a little cake for each of you, nearly enough; and you'll need half-an-hour's donning."

I waited five minutes, but getting no answer left him to brood. Catherine supped with her brother and sister-in-law. Joseph and I joined at an unsociable meal, seasoned with reproofs on one side and sauciness on the other. His cake and cheese remained on the table all night for the fairies. He managed to continue work till nine o'clock, and then marched dumb and dour to his chamber.

Cathy sat up late, having a world of things to order for the reception of her new friends from Thrushcross Grange. She came into the kitchen once to speak to her old one, but he was gone, and she only stayed to ask what was the matter with him, and then went back.

In the morning he rose early, and, as it was a holiday, carried his ill humor onto the moors, not reappearing till the family were departed for church. Fasting and reflection seemed to have brought him to a better spirit. He hung about me for a while, and having screwed up his courage, exclaimed abruptly, "Nelly, make me decent, I'm going to be good."

"High time, Heathcliff," I said, "you have grieved Catherine. She's sorry she ever came home, I daresay! It looks as if you envied her, because she is more thought of than you."

The notion of envying Catherine was incomprehensible to him, but the notion of grieving her he understood clearly enough.

"Did she say she was grieved?" he inquired, looking very serious.

"She cried when I told her you were off again this morning."

"Well, I cried last night," he returned, "and I had more reason to cry than she."

"Yes, you had the reason of going to bed with a proud heart and an empty stomach," said I. "Proud people breed sad sorrows for themselves. But, if you be ashamed of your touchiness, you must ask pardon, mind, when she comes in. You must go up and offer to kiss her, and say—you know best what to say. Only do it heartily, and not as if you thought her converted into a stranger by her grand dress. And now, though I have dinner to get ready, I'll steal time to arrange you so that Edgar Linton shall look quite a doll beside you, and that he does. You are younger, and yet, I'll be bound, you are taller and twice as broad across the shoulders. You could knock him down in a twinkling. Don't you feel that you could?"

Heathcliff's face brightened a moment, then it was overcast afresh, and he sighed.

"But, Nelly, if I knocked him down twenty times, that wouldn't make him less handsome or me more so. I wish I had light hair and a fair skin, and was dressed and behaved as well, and had a chance of being as rich as he will be!"

"And cried for mamma at every turn," I added, "and trembled if a country lad heaved his fist against you, and sat at home all day for a shower of rain. Oh, Heathcliff, you are showing a poor spirit! Come to the glass, and I'll let you see what you should wish. Do you mark those two lines between your eyes. And those thick brows, that, instead of rising arched, sink in the middle, and that couple of black fiends, so deeply buried, who never open their windows boldly, but lurk glinting under them, like devil's spies? Wish and learn to smooth away the surly wrinkles, to raise your lids frankly, and change the fiends to confident, innocent angels, suspecting and doubting nothing, and always seeing friends where they are not sure of foes. Don't get the expression of a vicious cur that appears to know the kicks it gets are its desert, and yet hates all the world, as well as the kicker, for what it suffers."

"In other words, I must wish for Edgar Linton's great blue eyes and even forehead," he replied. "I do—and that won't help me to them."

"A good heart will help you to a bonny face, my lad," I continued, "if you were a regular black, and a bad one will turn the bonniest into something worse than ugly. And now that we've done washing, and combing, and sulking—tell me whether you don't think yourself rather handsome? I'll tell you, I do. You're fit for a prince in disguise. Who knows but your father was Emperor of China, and your mother an Indian queen, each of them able to buy up, with one week's income, Wuthering Heights and Thrushcross Grange together? And you were kidnapped by wicked sailors and brought to England. Were I in your place, I would frame high notions of my birth. The thoughts of what

I was should give me courage and dignity to support the oppressions of a little farmer!"

So I chattered on, and Heathcliff gradually lost his frown and began to look quite pleasant, when all at once our conversation was interrupted by a rumbling sound moving up the road and entering the court. He ran to the window and I to the door, just in time to behold the two Lintons descend from the family carriage, smothered in cloaks and furs, and the Earnshaws dismount from their horses; they often rode to church in winter. Catherine took a hand of each of the children, and brought them into the house and set them before the fire, which quickly put color into their white faces.

I urged my companion to hasten now and show his amiable humor, and he willingly obeyed. But ill luck would have it that, as he opened the door leading from the kitchen on one side, Hindley opened it on the other. They met, and the master, irritated at seeing him clean and cheerful, or, perhaps, eager to keep his promise to Mrs. Linton, shoved him back with a sudden thrust.

He angrily bade Joseph "keep the fellow out of the room—send him into the garret till dinner is over. He'll be cramming his fingers in the tarts and stealing the fruit, if left alone with them a minute."

"Nay, sir," I could not avoid answering. "He'll touch nothing, not he. And I suppose he must have his share of the dainties as well as we."

"He shall have his share of my hand, if I catch him downstairs till dark," cried Hindley. "Begone, you vagabond! What! You are attempting the coxcomb, are you? Wait till I get hold of those elegant locks—see if I won't pull them a bit longer!"

"They are long enough already," observed Master Linton, peeping from the doorway, "I wonder they don't make his head ache. It's like a colt's mane over his eyes!"

He ventured this remark without any intention to insult, but Heathcliff's violent nature was not prepared to endure the appearance of impertinence from one whom he seemed to hate, even then, as a rival. He seized a tureen of hot applesauce (the first thing that came under his grip) and dashed it full against the speaker's face and neck, who instantly commenced a lament that brought Isabella and Catherine hurrying to the place.

Mr. Earnshaw snatched up the culprit directly and conveyed him to his chamber, where, doubtless, he administered a rough remedy to cool the fit of passion, for he appeared red and breathless. I got the dishcloth, and rather spitefully scrubbed Edgar's nose and mouth, affirming it served him right for meddling. His sister began weeping to go home, and Cathy stood by confounded, blushing for all.

"You should not have spoken to him thusly!" She expostulated with Master Linton. "He was in a bad temper, and now you've spoilt your visit. He'll be flogged. I hate him to be flogged! I can't eat my dinner. Why did you speak to him, Edgar?"

"I didn't," sobbed the youth, escaping from my hands, and finishing the remainder of the purification with his cambric pocket-handkerchief. "I promised mamma that I wouldn't say one word to him, and I didn't."

"Well, don't cry," replied Catherine, contemptuously. "You're not killed. Don't make more mischief. My brother is coming. Be quiet! Hush, Isabella! Has anybody hurt you?"

"There, there, children—to your seats!" cried Hindley, bustling in. "That brute of a lad has warmed me nicely. Next time, Master Edgar, take the law into your own fists—it will give you an appetite!"

The little party recovered its equanimity at sight of the fragrant feast. They were hungry after their ride, and easily consoled, since no real harm had befallen them.

Mr. Earnshaw carved bountiful platefuls, and the mistress made them merry with lively talk. I waited behind her chair, and was pained to behold Catherine, with dry eyes and an indifferent air, commence cutting up the wing of a goose before her.

"An unfeeling child," I thought to myself, "how lightly she dismisses her old playmate's troubles. I could not have imagined her to be so selfish."

She lifted a mouthful to her lips, then she set it down again. Her cheeks flushed, and the tears gushed over them. She slipped her fork to the floor, and hastily dived under the cloth to conceal her emotion. I did not call her unfeeling long, for I perceived she was in purgatory throughout the day, and wearying to find an opportunity of getting by herself, or paying a visit to Heathcliff, who had been locked up by the master. As I discovered, on endeavoring to introduce to him a private mess of victuals.

In the evening, we had a dance. Cathy begged that he might be liberated then, as Isabella Linton had no partner. Her entreaties were vain, and I was appointed to supply the deficiency. We got rid of all gloom in the excitement of the exercise. Our pleasure was increased by the arrival of the Gimmerton band, mustering fifteen strong, including a trumpet, a trombone, clarionets, bassoons, French horns, and a bass viol, besides singers. They go the rounds of all the respectable houses, and receive contributions every Christmas, and we esteemed it a first-rate treat to hear them.

After the usual carols had been sung, we set them to songs and glees. Mrs. Earnshaw loved the music, and so they gave us plenty.

Catherine loved it too, but she said it sounded sweetest at the top of the steps, and she went up in the dark. I followed, knowing there would be consequences if I did not. They shut the house door below, never noting our absence, it was so full of people. She made no stay at the stairs head, but mounted farther, to the garret where Heathcliff was confined, and called him.

He stubbornly declined answering for a while. She persevered, and finally persuaded him to hold communion with her through the boards. I let the poor things converse unmolested, till I supposed the songs were going to cease, and the singers to get some refreshment. Then I clambered up the ladder to warn her.

Instead of finding her outside, I heard her voice within. The little monkey had crept by the skylight of one garret, along the roof, into the skylight of the other, and it was with the utmost difficulty I could coax her out again.

When she did come, Heathcliff came with her, hand in hand, nigh inseparable. She insisted that I should take him into the kitchen, as my fellow servant had gone to a neighbor's, to be removed from the sound of our "devil's psalmody," as it pleased him to call it. I told them I intended by no means to encourage their tricks, but as the prisoner had never broken his fast since yesterday's dinner, I would wink at his cheating Mr. Hindley that once.

He went down. I set him a stool by the fire, and offered him a quantity of good things, but he was sick and could eat little, and my attempts to entertain him were thrown away. He leant his two elbows on his knees, and his chin on his hands and remained rapt in silent meditation.

On my inquiring the subject of his thoughts, he answered gravely. "I'm trying to settle how I shall pay Hindley back. I don't care how long I wait, if I can only do it at last. I hope he will not die before I do!"

"For shame, Heathcliff!" said I. "It is for God to punish wicked people. We should learn to forgive."

"No, God won't have the satisfaction that I shall," he returned, his eyes burning like coals in the fire. "I only wish I knew the best way! Let me alone, and I'll plan it out. While I'm thinking of that I don't feel pain."

But, Mr. Lockwood, I forget these tales cannot divert you. I'm annoyed how I should dream of chattering on at such a rate, and you nodding for bed! I could have told Heathcliff's history, all that you need hear, in half a dozen words.

Thus interrupting herself, the housekeeper rose, and proceeded to lay aside her sewing, but I felt incapable of moving from the hearth, and I was very far from nodding.

"Sit still, Mrs. Dean," I cried, "do sit still another half-hour. You've done just right to tell the story leisurely. That is the method I like, and you must finish it in the same style. I am interested in every character you have mentioned, more or less."

"The clock is on the stroke of eleven, sir."

"No matter—I'm not accustomed to go to bed in the long hours. One or two is early enough for a person who lies till ten."

"You shouldn't lie till ten. There's the very prime of the morning gone long before that time. A person who has not done one-half his day's work by ten o'clock, runs a chance of leaving the other half undone."

"Nevertheless, Mrs. Dean, resume your chair, because tomorrow I intend lengthening the night till afternoon. I prognosticate for myself an obstinate cold, at least."

"I hope not, sir. Well, you must allow me to leap over some three years; during that space Mrs. Earnshaw—"

"No, no, I'll allow nothing of the sort! Are you acquainted with the mood of mind in which, if you were seated alone, and the cat licking its kitten on the rug before you, you would watch the operation so intently that puss's neglect of one ear would put you seriously out of temper?"

"A terribly lazy mood, I should say."

"On the contrary, a tiresomely active one. It is mine, at present, and, therefore, continue minutely. I perceive that people in these regions acquire over people in towns the value that a spider in a dungeon does over a spider in a cottage, to their various occupants, and yet the deepened attraction is not entirely owing to the situation of the looker-on.

"They do live more in earnest, more in themselves, and less in surface, change, and frivolous external things. I could fancy a love for life here almost possible, and I was a fixed unbeliever in any love of a year's standing. One state resembles setting a hungry man down to a single dish, on which he may concentrate his entire appetite and do it justice. The other, introducing him to a table laid out by French cooks. He can perhaps extract as much enjoyment from the whole, but each part is a mere atom in his regard and remembrance."

"Oh! Here we are the same as anywhere else, when you get to know us," observed Mrs. Dean, somewhat puzzled at my speech.

"Excuse me," I responded. "You, my good friend, are striking evidence against that assertion. Excepting a few provincialisms of slight consequence, you have no marks of the manners I am habituated to consider as peculiar to your class. I am sure you have thought a great deal more than the generality of servants think. You have been compelled to cultivate your reflective faculties for want of occasions for frittering your life away in silly trifles."

Mrs. Dean laughed. "I certainly esteem myself a steady, reasonable kind of body," she said. "Not exactly from living among the hills and seeing one set of faces, and one series of actions, from year's end to year's end. I have undergone sharp discipline, which has taught me wisdom, and then, I have read more than you would fancy, Mr. Lockwood. You could not open a book in this library that I have not looked into, and got something out of also. Unless it be that range of Greek and Latin, and that of French. Those I know one from another. It is as much as you can expect of a poor man's daughter. However, if I am to follow my story in true gossip's fashion, I had better go on. Instead of leaping three years, I will be content to pass to the next summer—the summer of 1778, that is nearly twenty-three years ago."

CHAPTER 11

*O*N THE MORNING of a fine June day my first bonny little nursling, and the last of the ancient Earnshaw stock, was born. We were busy with the hay in a faraway field, when the girl that usually brought our breakfasts came running an hour too soon across the meadow and up the lane, calling me as she ran.

"Oh, such a grand bairn!" she panted out. "The finest lad that ever breathed! But the doctor says missus must go. He says she's been in a consumption these many months. I heard him tell Mr. Hindley. And now she has nothing to keep her, and she'll be dead before winter. You must come home directly. You're to nurse it, Nelly. To feed it with sugar and milk, and take care of it day and night. I wish I were you, because it will be all yours when there is no missis!"

"But is she very ill?" I asked, flinging down my rake and tying my bonnet.

"I guess she is, yet she looks bravely," replied the girl, "and she talks as if she thought of living to see it grow a man. She's out of her head for joy, it's such a beauty! If I were she, I'm certain I should not die. I should get better at the bare sight of it, in spite of Kenneth. I was fairly mad at him. Dame Archer brought the cherub down to master, in the house. His face just began to light up, when the old croaker steps forward, and says he, 'Earnshaw, it's a blessing your wife has been spared to leave you this son. When she came, I felt convinced we shouldn't keep her long. Now, I must tell you, the winter will probably finish her. Don't take on, and fret about it too much. It can't be helped. And besides, you should have known better than to choose such a rush of a lass!'"

"And what did the master answer?" I inquired.

"I think he swore, but I didn't mind him, I was straining to see the bairn," and she began again to describe it rapturously. I, as zealous as herself, hurried eagerly home to admire, on my part, though I was very sad for Hindley's sake. He had room in his heart only for two idols—his wife and himself. He doted on both, and adored one, and I couldn't conceive how he would bear the loss.

When we got to Wuthering Heights, there he stood at the front door, and, as I passed in, I asked, "How was the baby?"

"Nearly ready to run about, Nell!" he replied, putting on a cheerful smile.

"And the mistress?" I ventured to inquire. "The doctor says she's—"

"Damn the doctor!" he interrupted, reddening. "Frances is quite right. She'll be perfectly well by this time next week. Are you going upstairs? Will you tell her that I'll come, if she'll promise not to talk. I left her because she would not hold her tongue, and she must—tell her Mr. Kenneth says she must be quiet."

I delivered this message to Mrs. Earnshaw. She seemed in flighty spirits, and replied merrily, "I hardly spoke a word, Ellen, and there he has gone out twice, crying. Well, say I promise I won't speak, but that does not bind me not to laugh at him!"

Poor soul! Till within a week of her death that gay heart never failed her, and her husband persisted doggedly, nay, furiously, in affirming her health improved every day. When Kenneth warned him that his medicines were useless at that stage of the malady, and he needn't put him to further expense by attending her, Hindley retorted, "I know you need not—she's well—she does not want any more attendance from you! She never was in a consumption. It was a fever, and it is gone. Her pulse is as slow as mine now, and her cheek as cool."

He told his wife the same story, and she seemed to believe him. But one night, while leaning on his shoulder, in the act of saying she thought she should be able to get up tomorrow, a fit of coughing took her—a very slight one. He raised her in his arms, she put her two hands about his neck, her face changed, and she was dead.

He rocked her back and forth, weeping into her neck at the loss of his mate, and I grieved along with him. It was a sad time for the Earnshaw family.

The only bright spot was the wee lad. As the girl had anticipated, the child Hareton fell wholly into my hands. Mr. Earnshaw, provided he saw him healthy and never heard him cry, was contented, as far as regarded him. For himself, he grew desperate. His sorrow was of that kind that will not lament. He neither wept nor prayed. He cursed and defied, execrated God and man, and gave himself up to reckless dissipation.

The servants could not bear his tyrannical and evil conduct long. Joseph and I were the only two that would stay. I had not the heart to leave my charge, and besides, you know, I had been his foster-sister, and excused his behavior more readily than a stranger would. Joseph remained to hector over tenants and laborers, and because it was his vocation to be where he had plenty of wickedness to reprove.

The master's bad ways and bad companions formed a pretty example for Catherine and Heathcliff. His treatment of the latter was enough to make a fiend of a saint. And, truly, it appeared as if the lad were possessed of something diabolical at that period. He delighted to witness Hindley degrading himself past redemption, and became daily more notable for savage sullenness and ferocity.

I could not half tell what an infernal house we had. The curate dropped calling, and nobody decent came near us, at last, unless Edgar Linton's visits to Miss Cathy might be an exception.

At fifteen she was the queen of the countryside. She had no peer, and she did turn out a haughty, headstrong creature! I own I did not like her, after infancy was past, and I vexed her frequently by trying to bring down her arrogance. She never took an aversion to me, though. Cathy had a wondrous constancy to old attachments. Even Heathcliff kept his hold on her affections unalterably. And young Linton, with all his superiority, found it difficult to make an equally deep impression.

It was as I had predicted upon seeing them together beneath the ancient oak those several years before. Heathcliff and Catherine were forever joined in their hearts and no other could take their place, no matter how rich or sweet they might be. They spent many hours together, out of Hindley's grasp and view. I knew there was trouble ahead for them. No longer children experimenting with new feelings, they were nearly grown and therein lay the path of pain and suffering.

I saw them experimenting with kisses and touches many times. Once I even found them nearly undressed in the stable together. If I had not stopped them then, there may have been no turning back.

Despite her feelings for Heathcliff, and the Lintons' disapproval of him, Catherine had kept up her acquaintance with them since her five-weeks' residence among them. As she had no temptation to show her rough side in their company, and had the sense to be ashamed of being rude where she experienced such invariable courtesy, she imposed unwittingly on the old lady and gentleman by her ingenious cordiality. She gained the admiration of Isabella, and the heart and soul of her brother. Acquisitions that flattered her from the first—for she was full of ambition—and led her to adopt a double character without exactly intending to deceive anyone.

In the place where she heard Heathcliff termed a "vulgar young ruffian," and "worse than a brute," she took care not to act like him.

But at home she had small inclination to practice politeness that would only be laughed at, and restrain an unruly nature when it would bring her neither credit nor praise.

Mr. Edgar seldom mustered courage to visit Wuthering Heights openly. He had a terror of Earnshaw's reputation, and shrunk from encountering him. Yet he was always received with our best attempts at civility. The master himself avoided offending him, knowing why he came, and if he could not be gracious, kept out of the way.

I rather think Edgar's appearance there was distasteful to Catherine. She was not artful, never played the coquette, and had evidently an objection to her two friends meeting at all. For when Heathcliff expressed contempt of Linton in his presence, she could not half coincide, as she did in his absence. When Linton evinced disgust and antipathy to Heathcliff, she dared not treat his sentiments with indifference, as if depreciation of her playmate were of scarcely any consequence to her.

I've had many a laugh at her perplexities and untold troubles, which she vainly strove to hide from my mockery. That sounds ill natured. But she was so proud it became really impossible to pity her distresses, till she should be chastened into more humility. She did bring herself, finally, to confess, and to confide in me. There was not a soul else that she might fashion into an adviser. **She was playing a dangerous game with two young men, one as bright as the sun, the other as dark as the night.**

Mr. Hindley had gone from home one afternoon, and Heathcliff presumed to give himself a holiday on the strength of it. He had reached the age of sixteen then, I think, and without having bad features, or being deficient in intellect, he contrived to convey an impression of inward and outward repulsiveness that his present aspect retains no traces of.

In the first place, he had by that time lost the benefit of his early education. Continual hard work, begun soon and concluded late, had extinguished any curiosity he once possessed in pursuit of knowledge, and any love for books or learning. His childhood's sense of superiority, instilled into him by the favors of old Mr. Earnshaw, had faded away. He had struggled long to keep up an equality with Catherine in her studies, and yielded with poignant though silent regret, but he yielded completely. There was no prevailing on him to take a step in the way of moving upward, when he found he must, necessarily, sink beneath his former level. Then personal appearance sympathized with mental deterioration. He acquired a slouching gait and ignoble look. His naturally reserved disposition was exaggerated into an almost excessive unsociable moroseness. He took a grim pleasure, apparently, in exciting the aversion rather than the esteem of his few acquaintances.

I know, however, he did it with deliberateness only Heathcliff would endeavor to do. He wanted others to keep their distance while he kept his secrets. The only moments when he would rise from his darkened demeanor was when Catherine was in his presence. She alone would bring him into the sunshine, if only briefly and not forever.

CHAPTER 12

*T*HIS TIME WHEN MRS. DEAN STOPPED in her tale, I was not surprised, only disappointed with her pertinacious refusal to share the earthy details. She sighed, and rose to her feet, and cast about the room, as if her thoughts were trying to find a place to light.

"I suppose," I said gently, "that there came a time when you did not intervene with Cathy and Heathcliff. A time when you were too late?"

She sighed again, and said, "I was so taken up with caring for Hareton."

I rose and came around to where she stood, putting a hand on her shoulder. "You, of all people, are the most blameless in this affair!" I assured her. "No one could fault you for what you did, and tried to do."

She sniffed a little at that, as though not quite ready to believe it, but I could tell she appreciated my words. Then she said, her voice a little unsteady, "It's in her diary."

My thoughts flew immediately to the enclosure where I had

passed the previous night, with the knocking at the window, and the distraught Heathcliff—I had no intention of venturing to that domicile any time soon, not even to read Cathy's diary.

But Mrs. Dean surprised me. She opened a cupboard, and rummaged around inside for a moment, then produced a cloth-bound book that I immediately understood to have belong to Cathy.

She offered it to me, and I accepted it with alacrity, my eagerness perhaps somewhat unattractive, for Mrs. Dean drew back a little from me. It was then I realized that she could see the evidence of my arousal. The thought of Heathcliff and Cathy exploring the heights—and depths—of their carnal natures excited me, for I would have given a great deal to be as bold and lustful a man as Heathcliff was.

I retreated hastily to my seat at the table, hiding the evidence of my own carnal nature. When I glanced up, Mrs. Dean's expression was thoughtful, not repelled, and when she came over to the table again, she sat next to me, drawing her chair near enough that our thighs must occasionally brush together as we moved.

She indicated the diary in my hand. I handed it over, and she turned to the page she knew I wanted.

March 8, 1780

It happened tonight, as I have always known it would. Heathcliff has made me his own.

It commenced no differently from usual. I was trying to avoid Hindley, and had gone to the stable to find Heathcliff, hoping we might complain of Hindley's treatment together. It was still early and the dust motes floated in the sunshine as it streamed through the slats in the barn.

I saw him, hard at work already, and when he turned to me, his eyes were dark as pitch and his breathing labored. He had removed his shirt, and I could see the sheen of perspiration on his chest. Unthinking, I reached out to brush it away, and that was enough to set him off. He pulled me into his arms, roughly, this time, and I knew what he wanted, and it made me dizzy.

He kissed me, hard and deep, not as sweet and questioning as some of our kisses have been, but still a little clumsy and uncertain for all of that. I knew he had never been with another woman the way he wanted to be with me, and that if we took this step, it would be the first time for both of us.

I think he wanted to do it because he believed it could change something, anything. But at the time he kissed me, I couldn't think of what it would mean or what he meant by it, or what he would expect after it. When he kissed me like that, it sparked something deep inside me, a matching flame to his, a knowledge that had always been there.

I should have left but I didn't. I kissed him back. That seemed to ignite a frenzy in him, and then his hands were all over me, and I could feel the hardness between his legs as he thrust his hips against me, blunt and masculine.

I knew what he wanted, and I determined to give it to him. We were soul mates; we would consummate our connection; it was as simple and as logical as that.

I took him by the hand and walked to the back of the barn into the stall that held the hay. I placed a horse blanket over bales, then turned to Heathcliff. His gaze of adoration and love nearly broke my heart. My hands shook as I held out my arms to him. I will never forget the rightness of the moment when he came into my arms.

This time his kiss was less desperate. He knew he could take his time with me, and I would allow him all the liberties he desired. I stroked my hands across his bare back, marked with scars on top of muscle and sinew. This gypsy child had endured much.

I pressed my face into his chest, tasting the salt of his sweat. With gentle hands, he set me a little away from him. He tugged at the bodice of my dress, and my breasts tingled with the touch of his hands.

"Cathy," he said.

I turned around so that he could see the row of buttons that marched up the back of my dress. He was impatient of the petty task, and I warned him not to yank the buttons loose. I could feel his hands shake, and heard his muttered oath, as he undid my dress slowly and painstakingly. Then he had it done, and he shoved it from my shoulders, roughly spinning me around so he could take a look.

A shock of embarrassment coursed through me. Did I really mean to allow him to look at me, naked?

"Uncross your arms, Cathy," he pleaded. "I want to see you."

I took my time stepping away from the dress, then, with more care than I usually showed for my belongings, folded it neatly aside, keeping my back turned to him.

"Cathy," he said again. He had come up behind me, and he stroked my bare bottom, which made me jump, and then he laughed, and that made me mad, so I rounded on him, and he grabbed me up in his arms, crushing me to his chest. He buried his face in my neck, and said, "You feel so good against me."

And with that every bit of anger and embarrassment fled. His chest was strong and warm against the bareness of my body, and his hands, wandering at will, felt capable and solid. When he bore me back against the blanket, I made no attempt to stop him.

His gaze raked over me, full of fear, wonder and desire. "Oh, Cathy," he whispered, dipping his head to my bare neck and kissing me. His body was dark, a stark contrast to the lightness of mine. When he touched my breasts with his callused hands, cupping them tentatively, I clenched my fingers into the blanket. I could not help the moan that emanated from my throat.

I trembled with wanting him, but not knowing what to do, I had to trust my instincts to guide me. I shifted on the blanket, and let my thighs fall open to accommodate the breadth of his hips, my body soft and yielding beneath his lean and muscled strength.

"Yes," I whispered, and that seemed to ignite him.

"You are mine, Cathy," he said, his voice a fierce groan. "Mine."

He nipped at my shoulder, neck and ears, like a stallion worrying his mare, but I liked it, and tilted my head back so he could take his liberties. The heat of his mouth made my breasts feel heavy, and the nubs poked against his palms.

He licked the top of my breasts, then pressed his mouth between them. With a guttural grunt, he pulled one pink peak into his mouth and sucked. It was clumsy at first, but I gloried in the sensation. Then he nipped at my breast with his teeth, not so gentle now, and in moments I was mindless with the new, sharp waves of pleasure coursing through me. I had loved running wild and free on the moors; and this was that experience, heightened to a degree I had never believed possible.

I moaned and arched against him, wanting to be as close to him as possible, wanting to be in him and him in me.

He slowly sucked the nipple into the depths of his mouth, his lips moving against the ivory skin. His arms trembled with the force of his restraint. I sensed his caged power and shuddered against the sensual assault.

"Heathcliff," I whispered, hardly daring to believe we were doing this.

He leaned down and captured my mouth and I melted against him, my body curving into his as a key to a lock. His hand slid between my legs, his fingers seeking, then finding, the juncture between my thighs. I hissed a breath out at his blunt intrusion, but he did not remove his hand.

"You're so soft," he said, amazed, and touched and probed my mound with thick and inexperienced fingers.

"Stop that," I said, and then he found the tiny nub buried like a treasure between the folds of my body, and I sucked a breath in, and stopped wanting him to take his hand away. He stroked me there in a way that made my belly clench, and my breath come in labored gasps. My thighs spread even wider for him, as if moving of their own volition, and not mine, and his stroke came faster and firmer, until wetness gathered between my legs and I cried out for more of his touch.

At the scent of my arousal, he lifted his head and stared at me, his gaze dark and certain, but I knew he was asking a question. I swallowed hard and said what he wanted to hear: "Yes, Heathcliff. Yes."

He unbuttoned his trousers, sliding them down with his drawers until his erection sprang free. It was long and hard, nestled in a thatch of dark hair, pulsing with droplets of moisture at the tip. It sprang away from his body, enormous and demanding. My stomach somersaulted at the sheer size of him. Excitement warred with nervousness and I thought I might faint.

Heathcliff held the base of his member and squeezed, showing me what he liked, exactly the kind of rude lesson he would be inclined to teach.

"Touch me, Cathy."

I shook my head yet my hand reached out to him. I gripped him, satin on steel beneath my questing fingers. He groaned my name and closed his eyes, his hand closing over mine, teaching me how to stroke him. For a few moments I thought that would be the culmination of our efforts, but then he surged forward, pushing my hand away and roughly parting my legs with his thighs. His member nestled between my legs, his arms trembling with restraint as he held his body poised above mine but his restraint lasted only moments and then he plunged inside of me.

I cried out again for he broke my maidenhead in a single fierce thrust, with not a thought of gentleness in him, heeding only his eagerness to be inside me. He paused for barely long enough to let me catch my breath and then he was at it again, withdrawing and plunging, again and again, and finally the discomfort passed, and my body adjusted to his size and his wild need.

"Mine," he growled. "Oh, Cathy, you're finally mine."

That excited something deep within me, and my body moved against his, arching and bowing, our rhythm catching and matching, and with one final wild thrust, he buried himself deep inside of me, shouting my name and spewing his seed inside me, and I came to my completion at just that moment, his name a supplication on my lips.

In a little while, he rolled off of me. The only sound was our ragged breathing filled the air. I grew uneasy at the thought of what we had done, and what it might mean. Silently I dressed, and let him do up the buttons in the back of my dress, his hands not so clumsy or impatient this time.

Bits and pieces of the moor clung to our clothing, a sprig of heather and a touch of peat, as if the moor itself was a part of who we were, who we had become.

CHAPTER 13

I SET THE DIARY ASIDE, **somewhat troubled in my mind by what I had read. Cathy and Heathcliff loved each other, that was abundantly clear from their actions, but what had kept them from declaring it to all others? Who would stop them from doing as they pleased, even marrying? Surely not Hindley, drowned in his grief.**

I asked Mrs. Dean this, and she continued her story.

Catherine and he were constant companions still at his seasons of respite from labor, but he had ceased to express his fondness for her in words, and recoiled with angry suspicion from her girlish caresses, as if conscious there could be no gratification in lavishing such marks of affection on him. **I wondered, however, if they continued their passionate encounters in the barn, about which I would never tell Mr. Hindley or Heathcliff would surely be dead. I suspected they were lovers still, and Miss Cathy was torn between the man who held her heart and the man who could give her everything she wanted.**

While Hindley was away, Heathcliff came into the house to announce his intention of doing nothing, while I was assisting Miss

Cathy to arrange her dress. She had not reckoned on his taking it into his head to be idle, and imagining she would have the whole place to herself, she managed, by some means, to inform Mr. Edgar of her brother's absence, and was then preparing to receive him.

"Cathy, are you busy this afternoon?" asked Heathcliff. "Are you going anywhere?"

"No, it is raining," she answered.

"Why have you that silk frock on, then?" he said. His brows drew down with suspicion. "Nobody coming here, I hope?"

"Not that I know of," stammered Miss. "But you should be in the field now, Heathcliff. It is an hour past dinnertime. I thought you were gone."

"Hindley does not often free us from his accursed presence," observed the young man. "I'll not work anymore today. I'll stay with you."

"Oh, but Joseph will tell," she suggested. "You'd better go!"

"Joseph is loading lime on the further side of Peniston Crags. It will take him till dark, and he'll never know."

So, saying, he lounged to the fire, and sat down. Catherine reflected an instant, with knitted brows—she found it needful to smooth the way for an intrusion.

"Isabella and Edgar Linton talked of calling this afternoon," she said, at the conclusion of a minute's silence. "As it rains, I hardly expect them, but they may come, and if they do, you run the risk of being scolded for no good."

"Order Ellen to say you are engaged, Cathy," he persisted. "Don't turn me out for those pitiful, silly friends of yours! I'm on the point, sometimes, of complaining that they—but I'll not—"

"That they what?" cried Catherine, gazing at him with a troubled countenance. **He did not answer her, but put his passion into actions, not words. He jumped to his feet and took hold of her face and kissed her. His intemperate behavior shocked me so that I couldn't even draw breath to scold him. Cathy tried to push him** away at first, but he held her to him and continued plundering her mouth. Then she yielded, and a moan escaped from her throat.

I finally found my voice and called out, "Heathcliff!"

Heathcliff did not heed me, but Catherine seemed to collect herself and she pulled away from him, stumbling backwards. As always, the sparks that flew between them were made up of anger as much as any other emotion. She drew herself up in all of her haughty pride and said to him, "You cannot kiss me whenever you like. I am not a sow to be mishandled."

Heathcliff's face darkened. "I can kiss you whenever I like. You are mine, Cathy."

She didn't deign to respond to that, but turned away from him, coldly. Then she caught sight of her own reflection in the looking glass on the wall. "Oh, Nelly!" she said petulantly, jerking away from both of us. "You've combed my hair quite out of curl! That's enough. Let me alone. Why are you here, Heathcliff? What are you on the point of complaining about?"

"Nothing—only look at the almanac on that wall," he pointed to a framed sheet hanging near the window, his hand shaking. "The crosses are for the evenings you have spent with the Lintons, the dots for those spent with me. Do you see? I've marked every day."

"Yes—very foolish. As if I took notice!" replied Catherine. **From her peevish tone, I could tell that the lady she wished to be won out over the hellion she was, who loved Heathcliff.** "And where is the sense of that?"

"To show that I do take notice," said Heathcliff.

"And should I always be sitting with you?" she demanded, growing more irritated. **I could have told Heathcliff that he would not win Cathy over by confronting her.** "What good do I get? What do you talk about? You might be dumb, or a baby, for anything you say to amuse me, or for anything you do, either!"

"You never told me before that I talked too little, or that you disliked my company, Cathy!" **Heathcliff growled, much like a beast** of the moors.

"It's no company at all, when people know nothing and say nothing," she muttered, not meeting his eyes.

"You seem to like it well enough when I touch you."

At that she whirled and turned on him and I was half-afraid she would do worse than throw words at him. "I do not know what you're talking about!" she exclaimed. "If I endure your handling, it is only out of pity for you."

That got Heathcliff to come around, grabbing her shoulders and giving her a little shake. I would have stopped him but I wasn't entirely certain she hadn't earned the full brunt of his censure.

"You would discard me?" he fair spat at her. "I am no plaything to toss aside when you've no use for me."

"I have not discarded you, Heathcliff," she said, flouncing away from him. "But you have become cross and unpleasant to be around."

"Oh, I have been unpleasant? What about you?" He tried to grab her hand but she danced out of his way.

"Heathcliff, I cannot turn my back on everyone for you." She pressed her fist to her chest. "I cannot."

Her companion stepped towards her, but he hadn't time to express his feelings further, for a horse's feet were heard on the flags, and having knocked gently, young Linton entered, his face brilliant with delight at the unexpected summons he had received. **He did not sense the heavy currents in the room, or the nature of the relationship between Heathcliff and Catherine.**

Doubtless Catherine marked the difference between her friends, as one came in and the other went out. The contrast resembled what you see in exchanging a bleak, hilly, coal country for a beautiful fertile valley, and his voice and greeting were as opposite as his aspect. He had a sweet, low manner of speaking, and pronounced his words as you do. That's less gruff than we talk here, and softer.

"I'm not come too soon, am I?" he said, casting a look at me. I had begun to wipe the plate, and tidy some drawers at the far end in the dresser.

"No," answered Catherine. "What are you doing there, Nelly?"

"My work, Miss," I replied. (Mr. Hindley had given me directions to make a third party in any private visits Linton chose to pay.)

She stepped behind me and whispered crossly, "Take yourself and your dusters off. When company are in the house, servants don't commence scouring and cleaning in the room where they are!"

"It's a good opportunity, now that master is away," I answered aloud. "He hates me to be fidgeting over these things in his presence. I'm sure Mr. Edgar will excuse me."

"I hate you to be fidgeting in my presence," exclaimed the young lady imperiously, not allowing her guest time to speak. She had failed to recover her equanimity since the dispute with Heathcliff. She never had power to conceal her passion. It always set her whole complexion in a blaze.

"I'm sorry for it, Miss Catherine," was my response, and I proceeded assiduously with my occupation.

She, supposing Edgar could not see her, snatched the cloth from my hand, and pinched me, with a prolonged wrench, very spitefully on the arm. I've said I did not love her, and rather relished mortifying her vanity now and then. Besides, she hurt me extremely, so I started up from my knees, and screamed out, "Oh, Miss, that's a nasty trick! You have no right to nip me, and I'm not going to bear it."

"I didn't touch you, you lying creature!" cried she, her fingers tingling to repeat the act, and her ears red with rage.

"What's that, then?" I retorted, showing a decided purple witness to refute her.

She stamped her foot, wavered a moment, and then, irresistibly impelled by the naughty spirit within her, slapped me on the cheek, a stinging blow that filled both eyes with water.

"Catherine, love! Catherine!" interposed Linton, greatly shocked at the double fault of falsehood and violence his idol had committed.

"Leave the room, Ellen!" she repeated, trembling all over.

Little Hareton, who followed me everywhere, and was sitting near me on the floor, at seeing my tears commenced crying himself, and sobbed out complaints against "wicked aunt Cathy." It drew her fury on to his unlucky head. She seized his shoulders, and shook him till the poor child waxed livid, and Edgar thoughtlessly laid hold of her hands to deliver him.

In an instant one hand was wrung free, and the astonished young man felt it applied over his own ear in a way that could not be mistaken for jest. He drew back in consternation. I lifted Hareton in my arms, and walked off to the kitchen with him, leaving the door of communication open, for I was curious to watch how they would settle their disagreement.

The insulted visitor moved to the spot where he had laid his hat, pale and with a quivering lip.

"That's right!" I said to myself. "Take warning and begone! It's a kindness to let you have a glimpse of her genuine disposition."

"Where are you going?" demanded Catherine, advancing to the door.

He swerved aside, and attempted to pass.

"You must not go!" she exclaimed, desperation evident in her voice.

"I must and shall!" he replied in a subdued voice.

"No," she persisted, grasping the handle. "Not yet, Edgar Linton. Sit down please. You shall not leave me in that temper. I should be miserable all night, and I won't be miserable for you!"

"Can I stay after you have struck me?" asked Linton.

Catherine was mute. **She must have known her passions had taken control of her better sense, sending her into the wildness she was trying to escape. Edgar was the key to that escape and she had struck him.**

"You've made me afraid and ashamed of you," he continued. "I'll not come here again!"

Her eyes began to glisten and her lids to twinkle.

"And you told a deliberate untruth!" he said.

"I didn't!" she cried, recovering her speech. "I did nothing deliberately. Well, go, if you please—get away! And now I'll cry—I'll cry myself sick!"

She dropped down on her knees by a chair, and set to weeping in serious earnest. Edgar persevered in his resolution as far as the court. There he lingered. I resolved to encourage him.

"Miss is dreadfully wayward, sir," I called out. "As bad as any marred child. You'd better be riding home, or else she will be sick, only to grieve us."

The soft thing looked askance through the window. He possessed the power to depart as much as a cat possesses the power to leave a mouse half killed, or a bird half eaten. Ah, I thought, there will be no saving him. He's doomed, and flies to his fate!

And so it was. He turned abruptly, hastened into the house again, shut the door behind him. When I went in a while after to inform them that Earnshaw had come home rabid drunk, ready to pull the whole place about our ears (his ordinary frame of mind in that condition), I saw the quarrel had merely effected a closer intimacy. It had broken the outworks of youthful timidity, and enabled them to forsake the disguise of friendship, and confess themselves lovers.

I dreaded Heathcliff's reaction to this new development. But what could I do? Catherine was never one to be dissuaded once she had chosen a path.

Intelligence of Mr. Hindley's arrival drove Linton speedily to his horse, and Catherine to her chamber. I went to hide little Hareton, and to take the shot out of the master's fowling-piece, which he was fond of playing with in his insane excitement, to the hazard of the lives of any who provoked, or even attracted his notice too much. I had hit upon the plan of removing it, that he might do less mischief if he did go the length of firing the gun.

My mind, however, strayed quite a bit to the memory of seeing Edgar Linton's soft hand holding Catherine's. Fate had put her fickle hand in and stirred the soup of our lives yet again.

CHAPTER 14

*H*INDLEY ENTERED, spewing oaths dreadful to hear, and caught me in the act of stowing his son away in the kitchen cupboard. Hareton was impressed with a wholesome terror of encountering either his wild beast's fondness or his madman's rage. For in one he ran a chance of being squeezed and kissed to death, and in the other of being flung into the fire, or dashed against the wall, and the poor thing remained perfectly quiet wherever I chose to put him.

"There, I've found it out at last!" cried Hindley, pulling me back by the skin of my neck, like a dog. "By heaven and hell, you've sworn between you to murder that child! I know how it is, now, that he is always out of my way. But, with the help of Satan, I shall make you swallow the carving knife, Nelly! You needn't laugh, for I've just crammed Kenneth, head-downmost, in the Black-horse marsh, and two is the same as one—and I want to kill some of you. I shall have no rest till I do!"

"But I don't like the carving-knife, Mr. Hindley," I answered. "It has been cutting red herrings. I'd rather be shot, if you please."

"You'd rather be damned!" he said, "And so you shall. No law in

England can hinder a man from keeping his house decent, and mine's abominable! Open your mouth." He held the knife in his hand, and pushed its point between my teeth. For my part, I was never much afraid of his vagaries, or at least I never thought he would actually hurt me. I spat out, and affirmed it tasted detestably—I would not take it on any account.

"Oh!" said he, releasing me. "I see that hideous little villain is not Hareton. I beg your pardon, Nell. If it be, he deserves flaying alive for not running to welcome me, and for screaming as if I were a goblin. Unnatural cub, come hither! I'll teach thee to impose on a good-hearted, deluded father. Now, don't you think the lad would be handsomer cropped? It makes a dog fiercer, and I love something fierce—get me a scissors—something fierce and trim! Besides, it's infernal affectation—devilish conceit it is, to cherish our ears—we're asses enough without them. Hush, child, hush! Well then, it is my darling! Wisht, dry thy eyes—there's a joy, kiss me. What! It won't? Kiss me, Hareton! Damn thee, kiss me! By God, as if I would rear such a monster! As sure as I'm living, I'll break the brat's neck."

Poor Hareton was squalling and kicking in his father's arms with all his might, and redoubled his yells when he carried him upstairs and lifted him over the banister. I cried out that he would frighten the child into fits, and ran to rescue him. As I reached them, Hindley leant forward on the rails to listen to a noise below, almost forgetting what he had in his hands.

"Who is that?" he asked, hearing someone approaching the stairs.

I leant forward also, for the purpose of signing to Heathcliff, whose step I recognized, not to come further, and, at the instant when my eye quitted Hareton, he gave a sudden spring, delivered himself from the careless grasp that held him, and fell.

There was scarcely time to experience a thrill of horror before we saw that the little wretch was safe. Heathcliff arrived under-neath just at the critical moment. By a natural impulse he arrested his descent, and setting him on his feet, looked up to discover the author of the accident. A miser who has parted with a lucky lottery ticket for five shillings, and finds next day he has lost in the bargain five thousand pounds, could not show a blanker countenance than he did on beholding the figure of Mr. Earnshaw above. It expressed, plainer than words could do, the most intense anguish at having made himself the instrument of thwarting his own revenge. Had it been dark, I daresay he may have tried to remedy the mistake by smashing Hareton's skull on the steps. But, we witnessed his salvation, and I was presently below with my precious charge pressed to my heart. Hindley descended more leisurely, sobered and abashed.

"It is your fault, Ellen," he said. "You should have kept him out of sight. You should have taken him from me! Is he injured anywhere?"

"Injured!" I cried angrily. "If he is not killed, he'll be an idiot! Oh! I wonder his mother does not rise from her grave to see how you use him. You're worse than a heathen—treating your own flesh and blood in that manner!"

He attempted to touch the child, who, on finding himself with me, sobbed off his terror directly. At the first finger his father laid on him, however, he shrieked again louder than before, and struggled as if he would go into convulsions.

"You shall not meddle with him!" I continued. "He hates you— they all hate you—that's the truth! A happy family you have, and a pretty state you're come to!"

"I shall come to a prettier, yet, Nelly," laughed the misguided man, recovering his hardness. "At present, convey yourself and him away. And hark you, Heathcliff! Clear you too quite from my reach and hearing. I wouldn't murder you tonight, unless, perhaps, I set the house on fire, but that's as my fancy goes."

While saying this he took a pint bottle of brandy from the dresser, and poured some into a tumbler.

"Nay, don't!" I entreated. "Mr. Hindley, do take warning. Have mercy on this unfortunate boy, if you care nothing for yourself!"

"Any one will do better for him than I shall," he answered.

"Have mercy on your own soul!" I said, endeavoring to snatch the glass from his hand.

"Not I! On the contrary, I shall have great pleasure in sending it to perdition to punish its Maker," exclaimed the blasphemer. "Here's to its hearty damnation!"

He drank the spirits and impatiently bade us go, terminating his command with a sequel of horrid imprecations too bad to repeat or remember.

"It's a pity he cannot kill himself with drink," observed Heathcliff, muttering an echo of curses back after the door shut. "He's doing his very utmost, but his constitution defies him. Mr. Kenneth says he would wager his mare that he'll outlive any man on this side Gimmerton, and go to the grave a hoary sinner, unless some happy chance out of the common course befall him."

CHAPTER 15

ERE MRS. DEAN let her tale end, and worked at her sewing for a few moments without saying anything. Idly, I picked up Catherine's diary, where I had set it aside, and leafed through the pages until the words we met at the stable again caught my eye.

I sat up, and noted that the date on the entry was a year almost to the day after their first fumbling experience. I could tell that the stable had become their sanctuary, where they could shed their pretenses and discover all there was to know about each other.

"It is always late in the day, nearly evening, when we find these moments to steal together," the diary entry began.

I wait for him in the stall, my heart pounding in anticipation of his arrival, and my whole body softens at the thought of being with him again.

I know it's wrong, and knowing Heathcliff, even dangerous, but I cannot seem to give either of them up. Edgar is the one who can give me the life I want to live, while Heathcliff—

It must be possible to have both.

Tonight, when he finally arrived in the stall, his dark curls damp from a dunking, I had already removed my dress and wore only my shift, and the moment he saw me, he pulled me into his arms and I went willingly. This bond between us is unbreakable and permanent.

"You've been with him today." Heathcliff pressed his nose into my hair. There was no need to ask who "him" was—Edgar Linton—as if Edgar could be Heathcliff's rival!

"I don't wish to speak of anyone," I told him. "In fact, I don't wish to speak at all." When I touched his face, I felt the rasp of his whiskers on my hands. It was only a year ago when he had not a single one on his chin, and now they were a constant dark shadow on his chiseled face.

He gazed down at me for a moment and then without a word, he kissed me, his mouth hard and ferocious on mine.

"Does he kiss you like that?" Heathcliff demanded, lifting his head. "Does he?"

I could hardly catch a breath to tell him anything, but it didn't matter. His hands covered my breasts, and he said, "Do you like the feel of his hands on you?" He rubbed his hips against me. "And his cock, is it as hard as mine?"

He was ruining everything. "Heathcliff!" I pushed him away.

"You are the one who started this, Cathy," he said.

There was only one way I knew to assuage his jealous anger and make him stop thinking of Edgar. I moved closer to him, put my hand on the front of his trousers. "No," I said softly. "He's not as hard as you." I unbuttoned his trousers, but he shoved my hands out of the way and had his clothing off in a moment. He knew what I intended, and his breath came in hard fits of anticipation.

I dropped to my knees in front of him and took him in my hands, his shaft already thick and engorged; he was always ready in my presence. A breath hissed through his teeth as his entire body tightened like a bow string. Then I drew a long lick of my tongue down his length, and he cried out my name. He tasted a little of soap, of man and of Heathcliff.

I took him in my mouth and he fisted his fingers in my hair, thrusting himself deeper inside, his belly trembling as he gave an inarticulate moan of approval. I sucked him, his hips moving in the ancient rhythm we had experienced so many times together.

He shoved a little too hard, gagging me, and I drew back and nipped at him, and before I knew it, he had me on my back, shoving my shift up. He entered me in one fierce thrust. The perfection of that moment stole my breath. It was as if we were joined at an elemental level, beyond the mere physical. He had become one with me in body and soul.

He didn't say anything, or ask me if Edgar ever entered me like this. He moved, slowly at first, and I knew he was savoring the smooth slide of his shaft within me. Then his pace increased. With each thrust, I grew closer and closer to reaching the peak of fulfillment. He grunted, and for a moment we were rutting animals and I exploded, waves of bliss rolling over me, bucking up against him, hardly realizing he had reached his peak as well and buried himself deep within me.

"I love you." It was barely a whisper, but I heard it anyway.

CHAPTER 16

I THUMPED THE DIARY DOWN **on the table and Mrs. Dean started and looked round at me. "If Heathcliff loved her," I demanded, "and she him, how did she come to marry Mr. Linton?"**

Mrs. Dean nodded. "That's the very question, isn't it? Shall I tell you how it came to pass?"

I indicated that she should continue, and she did.

I was in the kitchen, and sat down to lull my little lamb to sleep. I thought Heathcliff walked through to the barn. I was wrong. It turned out afterwards that he only got as far as the other side the settle, when he flung himself on a bench by the wall, removed from the fire and remained silent.

I was rocking Hareton on my knee, and humming a song that began,—

"It was far in the night, and the bairnies grat,
The mither beneath the mools heard that,"

When Miss Cathy put her head in, and whispered, "Are you alone, Nelly?"

"Yes, Miss," I replied.

She entered and approached the hearth. I, supposing she was going to say something, looked up. The expression of her face seemed disturbed and anxious. Her lips were half asunder, as if she meant to speak, and she drew a breath, but it escaped in a sigh instead of a sentence.

I resumed my song, not having forgotten her recent behavior.

"Where's Heathcliff?" she said, interrupting me.

"About his work in the stable," was my answer.

He did not contradict me; perhaps he had fallen into a doze. There followed another long pause, during which I perceived a drop or two trickle from Catherine's cheek to the flags.

Is she sorry for her shameful conduct and so weeps for forgiveness?—I asked myself. That will be a novelty; but she may come to the point—as she will—I shan't help her! No, she felt small trouble regarding any subject, save her own concerns.

"Oh, dear!" she cried at last. "I'm very unhappy!"

"A pity," observed I. "You're hard to please: so many friends and so few cares, and can't make yourself content!"

"Nelly, will you keep a secret for me?" she pursued, kneeling down by me, and lifting her winsome eyes to my face with that sort of look which turns off bad temper, even when one has all the right in the world to indulge it.

"Is it worth keeping?" I inquired, less sulkily.

"Yes, and it worries me, and I must let it out! I want to know what I should do. Today, Edgar Linton has asked me to marry him, and I've given him an answer. Now, before I tell you whether it was a consent or denial, you tell me which it ought to have been."

"Really, Miss Catherine, how can I know?" I replied. "To be

sure, considering the exhibition you performed in his presence this afternoon, I might say it would be wise to refuse him. Since he asked you after that, he must either be hopelessly stupid or a venturesome fool."

"If you talk so, I won't tell you anymore," she returned, peevishly rising to her feet, her hands twisting together to and fro before she blurted. "I accepted him, Nelly. Be quick, and say whether I was wrong!"

"You accepted him! Then what good is it discussing the matter? You have pledged your word, and cannot retract."

"But say whether I should have done so—do!" she exclaimed in an irritated tone, chafing her hands together even harder, and frowning.

"There are many things to be considered before that question can be answered properly," I said, sententiously. "First and foremost, do you love Mr. Edgar?"

"Who can help it? Of course I do," she answered.

Then I put her through the following catechism. For a girl of twenty-two it was not injudicious.

"Why do you love him, Miss Cathy?"

"Nonsense, I do—that's sufficient."

"By no means, you must say why?"

"Well, because he is handsome, and pleasant to be with."

"Bad!" was my commentary.

"And because he is young and cheerful."

"Bad, still."

"And because he loves me."

"Indifferent, coming there."

"And he will be rich, and I shall like to be the greatest woman of the neighborhood, and I shall be proud of having such a husband."

"Worst of all. And now, say how you love him?"

"As everybody loves—You're silly, Nelly."

"Not at all—Answer."

"I love the ground under his feet, and the air over his head, and everything he touches, and every word he says. I love all his looks, and all his actions, and him entirely and altogether. There now!"

"And why?"

"Nay, you are making a jest of it. It is exceedingly ill natured! It's no jest to me!" said the young lady, scowling, and turning her face to the fire.

"I'm very far from jesting, Miss Catherine," I replied. "You love Mr. Edgar because he is handsome, and young, and cheerful, and rich, and loves you. The last, however, goes for nothing. You would love him without that, probably, and with it you wouldn't, unless he possessed the four former attractions."

"No, to be sure not. I should only pity him—hate him, perhaps, if he were ugly, and a clown."

"But there are several other handsome, rich young men in the world. Handsomer, possibly, and richer than he is. What should hinder you from loving them?"

"If there be any, they are out of my way. I've seen none like Edgar."

"You may see some, and he won't always be handsome, and young, and may not always be rich."

"He is now, and I have only to do with the present. I wish you would speak rationally."

"Well, that settles it. If you have only to do with the present, marry Mr. Linton."

"I don't want your permission for that—I shall marry him. And yet you have not told me whether I'm right."

"Perfectly right, if people be right to marry only for the present. And now, let us hear what you are unhappy about. Your brother will be pleased. The old lady and gentleman will not object, I think. You will escape from a disorderly, comfortless home into a wealthy, respectable one, and you love Edgar, and Edgar loves you. All seems smooth and easy. Where is the obstacle?"

"Here! and here!" replied Catherine, striking one hand on her forehead, and the other on her breast. "In whichever place the soul lives. In my soul and in my heart, I'm convinced I'm wrong!"

"That's very strange! I cannot make it out."

"It's my secret. But if you will not mock at me, I'll explain it. I can't do it distinctly, but I'll give you a feeling of how I feel."

She seated herself by me again. Her countenance grew sadder and graver, and her clasped hands trembled.

"Nelly, do you never dream queer dreams?" she said, suddenly, after some minutes' reflection.

"Yes, now and then," I answered.

"And so do I. I've dreamt in my life dreams that have stayed with me ever after, and changed my ideas. They've gone through and through me, like wine through water, and altered the color of my mind. And this is one. I'm going to tell it—but take care not to smile at any part of it."

"Oh! Don't, Miss Catherine!" I cried. "We're dismal enough without conjuring up ghosts and visions to perplex us. Come, come, be merry and like yourself! Look at little Hareton! He's dreaming nothing dreary. How sweetly he smiles in his sleep!"

"Yes, and how sweetly his father curses in his solitude! You remember him, I daresay, when he was just such another as that chubby thing, nearly as young and innocent. However, Nelly, I shall oblige you to listen. It's not long, and I've no power to be merry tonight."

"I won't hear it, I won't hear it!" I repeated, hastily. **I knew she would tell me something of Heathcliff, and I did not want to be witness to the words.**

I was superstitious about dreams then, and am still, and Catherine had an unusual gloom in her aspect, that made me dread something from which I might shape a prophecy, and foresee a fearful catastrophe. She was vexed, but she did not proceed. Apparently taking up another subject, she recommenced in a short time.

"If I were in heaven, Nelly, I should be extremely miserable."

"Because you are not fit to go there," I answered. "All sinners would be miserable in heaven."

"But it is not for that. I dreamt once that I was there."

"I tell you I won't harken to your dreams, Miss Catherine! I'll go to bed," I interrupted again.

She laughed, and held me down, for I made a motion to leave my chair.

"This is nothing," cried she. "I was only going to say that heaven did not seem to be my home, and I broke my heart with weeping to come back to earth, and the angels were so angry that they flung me out into the middle of the heath on the top of Wuthering Heights, where I woke sobbing for joy. That will do to explain my secret, as well as the other. I've no more business to marry Edgar Linton than I have to be in heaven, and if the wicked man in there had not brought Heathcliff so low, I shouldn't have thought of it. It would degrade me to marry Heathcliff now, so he shall never know how I love him. And that, not because he's handsome, Nelly, but because he's more myself than I am. Whatever our souls are made of, his and mine are the same, and Linton's is as different as a moonbeam from lightning, or frost from fire."

Ere this speech ended I became sensible of Heathcliff's presence. Having noticed a slight movement, I turned my head, and saw him rise from the bench, and steal out noiselessly. He had listened till he heard Catherine say it would degrade her to marry him, and then he stayed to hear no further. My companion, sitting on the ground, was prevented by the back of the settle from remarking his presence or departure, but I started, and bade her hush! The daggers of her words had no doubt drawn blood from their unintended victim.

"Why?" she asked, gazing nervously round.

"Joseph is here," I answered, catching opportunely the roll of his cartwheels up the road, "and Heathcliff will come in with him. I'm not sure whether he was not at the door this moment."

"Oh, he couldn't overhear me at the door!" said she. "Give me Hareton, while you get the supper, and when it is ready ask me to sup with you. I want to cheat my uncomfortable conscience, and be convinced that Heathcliff has no notion of these things. He has not, has he?" **Her gaze was locked on the door, waiting it seemed for the man she truly did love to appear, just so she could prove to herself they were ill suited to marry.**

"I see no reason that he should not know, as well as you," I returned, "and if you are his choice, he'll be the most unfortunate creature that ever was born! As soon as you become Mrs. Linton, he loses friend, and love, and all! Have you considered how you'll bear the separation, and how he'll bear to be quite deserted in the world? Because, Miss Catherine—"

"He quite deserted! We separated!" she exclaimed, with an accent of indignation. "Who is to separate us, pray? They'll meet the fate of Milo! Not as long as I live, Ellen, for no mortal creature. Every Linton on the face of the earth might melt into nothing before I could consent to forsake Heathcliff. Oh, that's not what I intend—that's not what I mean! I shouldn't be Mrs. Linton were such a price demanded! He'll be as much to me as he has been all his lifetime. Edgar must shake off his antipathy, and tolerate him, at least. He will, when he learns my true feelings towards him. Nelly, I see now you think me a selfish wretch, but did it never strike you that if Heathcliff and I married, we should be beggars? Whereas, if I marry Linton I can aid Heathcliff to rise, and place him out of my brother's power."

"With your husband's money, Miss Catherine?" I asked. "You'll find him not so pliable as you calculate upon. And, though I'm hardly a judge, I think that's the worst motive you've given yet for being the wife of young Linton."

"It is not," retorted she, "it is the best! The others were the satisfaction of my whims, and for Edgar's sake, too, to satisfy him. This is for the sake of one who comprehends in his person my feelings to Edgar and myself. I cannot express it, but surely you and everybody have a notion that there is or should be an existence of yours beyond you. What were the use of my creation, if I were entirely contained here? My great miseries in this world have been Heathcliff's miseries, and I watched and felt each from the beginning. My great thought in living is himself. If all else perished, and he remained, I should still continue to be, and if all else remained, and he were annihilated, the universe would turn to a mighty stranger. I should not seem a part of it. My love for Linton is like the foliage in the woods. Time will change it, I'm well aware, as winter changes the trees. My love for Heathcliff resembles the eternal rocks beneath—a source of little visible delight, but necessary. Nelly, I *am* Heathcliff! He's always, always in my mind. Not as a pleasure, any more than I am always a pleasure to myself, but as my own being. So don't talk of our separation again. It is impracticable, and—"

She paused, and hid her face in the folds of my gown, but I jerked it forcibly away. I was out of patience with her folly!

"If I can make any sense of your nonsense, Miss," I said, "it only goes to convince me that you are ignorant of the duties you undertake in marrying, or else that you are a wicked, unprincipled girl. But trouble me with no more secrets. I'll not promise to keep them."

"You'll keep that?" she asked, eagerly.

"No, I'll not promise," I repeated.

She was about to insist, when the entrance of Joseph finished our conversation, and Catherine removed her seat to a corner, and nursed Hareton, while I made the supper.

After it was cooked, my fellow servant and I began to quarrel who should carry some to Mr. Hindley, and we didn't settle it till all was nearly cold. Then we came to the agreement that we would let him ask, if he wanted any, for we feared particularly to go into his presence when he had been some time alone.

"And how isn't that ox come in from the field, be this time? What is he about? Great idle beast!" demanded the old man, looking round for Heathcliff.

"I'll call him," I replied. "He's in the barn, I've no doubt."

I went and called, but got no answer. On returning, I whispered to Catherine that he had heard a good part of what she said, I was sure, and told how I saw him quit the kitchen just as she complained of her brother's conduct regarding him.

She jumped up in a fine fright, flung Hareton on to the settle, and ran to seek for her friend herself, not taking leisure to consider why she was so flurried, or how her talk would have affected him.

I took after her, afraid of what I had started. The rain had begun in earnest by that time, but I didn't need to see her to know she was headed for the stable, where she and Heathcliff had been stealing their time together for some months.

He stood with his back to the door, hands up against the wall fisted so hard his skin was nearly white. His clothes were dry, so he had been there long enough to avoid the rain, yet his body shook, whether from cold or tears, I didn't know.

"Heathcliff—"

"Begone. I have no wish to speak to you."

"You heard what I told Nelly." She didn't ask a question, merely stated a truth.

"Go! Your wealthy husband will take good care of you. Now get out before I make you leave." He did not turn around to look at her.

Catherine stepped forward and placed her hand in the center of his back. He arched forward with a hiss, out of her reach.

"Do not think I will let you touch me."

Catherine swallowed a sob. "I cannot marry you, Heathcliff."

"I know that now, which is why you cannot be here, you cannot be in my arms any longer. Get away from me." He finally turned to face her.

"I love you."

"Don't you dare!" He held up a fist to her face. "Don't you ever utter those words to me again."

"Please! Heathcliff—"

"Nay. I'll not listen to you." He pushed past her, shoving her toward the hay bales as he ran from the stable.

Catherine picked herself up and went after him. She brushed past me, but did not register my presence. I went after them, knowing anything could happen, and even though I might not be able to prevent it, I could not stay behind.

Heathcliff loped across the moors like the beast some accused him of being. The rain pelted him as lightning lit up the night sky. As I hurried after the pair, I saw Heathcliff reach the ancient oak where he and Cathy had spent countless hours together. There he stopped, as if he knew better than to think, after all, that he could flee from her.

A primal howl rose from his throat, echoing across the deserted moors.

Catherine was there in a moment. She did not hesitate, but rather threw herself into his arms. This time, he did not push her away. Instead he captured her lips in a ferocious kiss, one rivaled only by the tempestuous storm that raged above them.

He backed her against the tree, and she didn't try to stop him. Thunder rolled across the moors, and I stood there, gaping. She yanked up her skirt and nearly tore her underthings off to make herself open to him. He shoved his own trousers down. Then he braced her against the tree and entered her in one wicked thrust.

Another bolt of lightning silhouetted their faces, for just one perfect moment, then darkness overtook them again.

They were like animals, moaning and biting each other as they surged together. The tempest around them matched their primal joining.

"Heathcliff." I could hardly recognize her voice as she cried out his name.

His only reply was a tightening of his hands on her hips as he thrust up into her, each stroke deeper and harder than the last. The rain beat down, but none of us seemed to notice. It did nothing to alter Heathcliff's ferocious hammering at her; and from the cries of pleasure she gave, she liked his handling well enough.

His pace increased and then he said, "Now." His command was so rough and low, I barely heard him make it, yet Catherine's body obeyed.

Their bodies moved as one being, two became one. The ecstasy ripped through them and this time, there were two howls echoing across the moors.

Then Heathcliff withdrew and set her on her feet, the two of them beautiful creatures of the moors, nothing like ordinary folk.

"Heathcliff," she began.

He shook her off with an angry swipe of his hand and I realized with a shock that the whole point of what had gone before was to degrade Catherine, as she had degraded him.

"Heathcliff, I love you——"

Without a word, he turned and left her at the tree.

Catherine sank to her knees and wrapped her arms around herself. She began to cry, her tears mixing with the rain, and though I didn't love her, I had enough heart to go to her, and lift her to her feet, my arms around her shoulders. She clung to my neck and wept incoherently, and then she demanded, "We must find him! He cannot leave like that!"

I persuaded her that it was no night for us to be prowling in search of Heathcliff, and that if she must see him, then we would send a servant after him. It seemed the perfect task for Joseph.

As soon as we returned to the house, Catherine issued a hurried command to Joseph that he must run down the road, and, wherever Heathcliff had rambled, find and make him re-enter directly! "I want to speak to him, and I must, before I go upstairs," she said. "And the gate is open. He is somewhere out of hearing, for he would not reply, though I shouted at the top of the fold as loud as I could." And that was true enough, and I had chastised her for it, and she had pinched me for my chastisement.

Joseph objected at first; she was too much in earnest, however, to suffer contradiction, and at last he placed his hat on his head, and walked grumbling forth. Meantime, Catherine paced up and down the floor, exclaiming, "I wonder where he is—I wonder where he can be! I do wish he'd come. I do wish he would!"

"What a noise for nothing!" I cried, though rather uneasy myself. "What a trifle scares you! It's surely no great cause of alarm that Heathcliff should take a moonlight saunter on the moors even if it rained on his dark head, or even lie too sulky to speak to us in the hayloft. I'll engage he's lurking there. See if I don't ferret him out!"

As the rain had ceased, I departed to renew my search, its result was disappointment, and Joseph's quest ended in the same.

"Yon lad gets worse and worse!" Joseph grumbled as he reentered the room. "He's left the gate at the full swing, and Miss's pony has trodden down two rows o' corn, and stomped through, right over into t' meadow! The master will play the devil tomorrow morning and he'll do well. He's patience itself with such careless, dark creatures—patience itself he is! But he'll not be so always—you'll see, all on ye! You mustn't drive him out of his head for now!"

"Have you found Heathcliff, you ass?" interrupted Catherine. "Have you been looking for him, as I ordered?"

"I should more likely look for th' horse," he replied. "It would be to more sense. But I cannot look for neither horse nor man of a night like this—as black as t' chimney! And Heathcliff's not a chap to come at my whistle—happen he'll be less hard o' hearing wi' *ye*!"

It was a very dark evening for summer. The clouds appeared inclined to thunder again, and I said we had better all sit down, the rain would be certain to bring him home without further trouble. However, Catherine would not be persuaded into tranquility, nor would she change her wet garments.

She kept wandering to and fro, from the gate to the door, in a state of agitation, which permitted no repose. At length she took up a permanent situation on one side of the wall, near the road. Where, heedless of my expostulations and the growling thunder, and the great drops that splashed around her, she remained, calling at intervals, and then listening, and then crying outright. She beat Hareton, or any child, at a good passionate fit of crying.

"Heathcliff, please come home. Please." For all the times I accused her of being selfish or silly, there was genuine pain in her voice. She shivered so hard her teeth clacked together, yet she did not give up her post, with her arms wrapped around her middle.

About midnight, while we still sat up, the storm came rattling over the Heights in full fury. There was a violent wind, as well as thunder, and either one or the other split a tree off at the corner of the building. A huge bough fell across the roof, and knocked down a portion of the east chimney stack, sending a clatter of stones and soot into the kitchen fire.

We thought a bolt had fallen in the middle of us, and Joseph swung on to his knees, beseeching the Lord to remember the patriarchs Noah and Lot, and, as in former times, spare the righteous, though he smote the ungodly.

I felt some sentiment that it must be a judgment on us also. The Jonah, in my mind, was Mr. Earnshaw, and I shook the handle of his den that I might ascertain if he were yet living. He replied audibly enough, in a fashion that made my companion vociferate, more clamorously than before, that a wide distinction might be drawn between saints like himself and sinners like his master. But the uproar passed away in twenty minutes, leaving us all unharmed, excepting Cathy, who got thoroughly drenched a second time for her obstinacy in refusing to take shelter, and standing bonnetless and shawl-less to catch as much water as she could with her hair and clothes.

She came in and lay down on the settle, all soaked as she was, turning her face to the back, and putting her hands before it.

"Well, Miss!" I exclaimed, touching her shoulder, "you are not bent on getting your death, are you? Do you know what o'clock it is? Half-past twelve. Come, come to bed! There's no use waiting any

longer on that foolish boy. He'll be gone to Gimmerton, and he'll stay
there now. He guesses we shouldn't wait for him till this late hour. At
least, he guesses that only Mr. Hindley would be up, and he'd rather
avoid having the door opened by the master."

"Nay, nay, he's not at Gimmerton," said Joseph. "It's a wonder he's not at the bottom of a bog hole. This visitation wasn't for
naught and I would have you to look out, Miss—you might be next.
Thank Heaven for all! All works together for good to them as is chosen and picked out from the rubbage. You know what the Scripture
says." And he began quoting several texts, referring us to chapters and
verses where we might find them.

I, having vainly begged the willful girl to rise and remove her
wet things, left him preaching and her shivering, and betook myself
to bed with little Hareton, who slept as fast as if everyone had been
sleeping round him. I heard Joseph read on a while afterwards, then I
distinguished his slow step on the ladder, and then I dropped asleep.

Coming down somewhat later than usual, I saw, by the sun-
beams piercing the chinks of the shutters, Miss Catherine still seated
near the fireplace. Her clothes were wrinkled and suffered the effects
of the double dousing from the night before. The house door was ajar,
too; light entered from its unclosed windows. Hindley had come out,
and stood on the kitchen hearth, haggard and drowsy.

"What ails you, Cathy?" he was saying when I entered. "You
look as dismal as a drowned whelp. Why are you so damp and pale,
child?"

"I've been wet," she answered reluctantly, "and I'm cold, that's
all." **The dark circles ringing her eyes told a different story.**

"Oh, she is naughty!" I cried, perceiving the master to be tolerably
sober. "She got steeped in the shower of yesterday evening, and there
she has sat the night through, and I couldn't prevail on her to stir."

Mr. Earnshaw stared at us in surprise. "The night through," he
repeated. "What kept her up? Not fear of the thunder, surely? That
was over hours since."

Neither of us wished to mention Heathcliff's absence, as long as we could conceal it, so I replied, I didn't know how she took it into her head to sit up, and she said nothing.

The morning was fresh and cool, I threw back the lattice, and presently the room filled with sweet scents from the garden, but Catherine called peevishly to me, "Ellen, shut the window. I'm starving!" And her teeth chattered as she shrank closer to the almost extinguished embers.

"She's ill," said Hindley, taking her wrist, "I suppose that's the reason she would not go to bed. Damn it! I don't want to be troubled with more sickness here. What took you into the rain?"

"Running after the lads, as usual!" croaked Joseph, catching an opportunity from our hesitation to thrust in his evil tongue. "If I were you, master, I'd just slam the boards in their faces all on 'em, gentle and simple! Never a day that you're off, but yon cat o' Linton comes sneaking hither, and Miss Nelly, she's a fine lass! She sits watching for ye i' t' kitchen, and as you're in at one door, he's out at t'other, and, then, the grand lady goes a-courting of her side! It's bonny behavior, lurking among t' fields, after twelve o' t' night, with that foul, flaysome devil of a gypsy, Heathcliff! They think I'm blind, but I'm nothing of the sort!—I seen young Linton both coming and going, and I seed yah" (directing his discourse to me), "you good for nothing, slatternly witch! Nip up and bolt into th' house, t' minute yah heard t' master's horse-fit clatter up t' road."

"Silence, eavesdropper!" cried Catherine, "none of your insolence, before me! Edgar Linton came yesterday by chance, Hindley, and it was I who told him to be off because I knew you would not like to have met him as you were."

"You lie, Cathy, no doubt," answered her brother, "and you are a confounded simpleton! But never mind Linton at present. Tell me, were you not with Heathcliff last night? Speak the truth, now. You need not be afraid of harming him. Though I hate him as much as ever, he did me a good turn a short time since that will make my conscience tender of breaking his neck. To prevent it, I shall send him about his business this very morning, and after he's gone, I'd advise you all to look sharp. I shall only have the more humor for you."

"I never saw Heathcliff last night," answered Catherine, beginning to sob bitterly. "And if you do turn him out of doors, I'll go with him. But, perhaps, you'll never have an opportunity; perhaps, he's gone." Here she burst into uncontrollable grief, and the remainder of her words was inarticulate.

Hindley lavished on her a torrent of scornful abuse, and bade her get to her room immediately, or she shouldn't cry for nothing! I obliged her to obey, and I shall never forget what a scene she acted when we reached her chamber. It terrified me. I thought she was going mad, and I begged Joseph to run for the doctor.

It proved the commencement of delirium. Mr. Kenneth, as soon as he saw her, pronounced her dangerously ill. She had a fever.

He bled her, and he told me to let her live on whey and water gruel, and take care she did not throw herself downstairs or out of the window, and then he left. He had enough to do in the parish, where two or three miles was the ordinary distance between cottage and cottage.

Though I cannot say I made a gentle nurse, and Joseph and the master were no better, and though our patient was as wearisome and headstrong as a patient could be, she weathered it through.

Old Mrs. Linton paid us several visits, to be sure, and set things to rights, and scolded and ordered us all. When Catherine was convalescent, she insisted on conveying her to Thrushcross Grange, for which deliverance we were very grateful. But the poor dame had reason to repent of her kindness. She and her husband both took the fever, and died within a few days of each other.

Our young lady returned to us saucier and more passionate, and haughtier than ever. Heathcliff had never been heard of since the evening of the thunderstorm, and, one day, I had the misfortune, when she had provoked me exceedingly, to lay the blame of his disappearance on her, where indeed it belonged, as she well knew. From that period, for several months, she ceased to hold any communication with me, save in the relation of a mere servant.

Joseph fell under a ban also. He would speak his mind, and lecture her all the same as if she were a little girl, and she esteemed herself a woman, and our mistress, and thought that her recent illness gave her a claim to be treated with consideration. Then the doctor had said that she would not bear crossing much, she ought to have her own way, and it was nothing less than murder in her eyes for anyone to presume to stand up and contradict her.

From Mr. Earnshaw and his companions she kept aloof, and tutored by Kenneth, and serious threats of a fit that often attended her rages, her brother allowed her whatever she pleased to demand, and generally avoided aggravating her fiery temper. He was rather too indulgent in humoring her caprices, not from affection, but from pride. He wished earnestly to see her bring honor to the family by an alliance with the Lintons, and as long as she let him alone she might trample on us like slaves, for aught he cared!

Edgar Linton, as multitudes have been before and will be after him, was infatuated, and believed himself the happiest man alive on the day he led her to Gimmerton Chapel, three years subsequent to his father's death.

Much against my inclination, I was persuaded to leave Wuthering Heights and accompany her here. Little Hareton was nearly five years old, and I had just begun to teach him his letters. We made a sad parting, but Catherine's tears were more powerful than ours. When I refused to go, and when she found her entreaties did not move me, she went lamenting to her husband and brother. The former offered me munificent wages, the latter ordered me to pack up. He wanted no women in the house, he said, now that there was no mistress, and as to Hareton, the curate should take him in hand, by-and-by. And so I had but one choice left: to do as I was ordered. I told the master he got rid of all decent people only to run to ruin a little faster, I kissed

Hareton, said good-bye, and since then he has been a stranger. It's very queer to think it, but I've no doubt he has completely forgotten all about Ellen Dean, and that he was ever more than all the world to her and she to him!

At this point of the housekeeper's story she chanced to glance towards the timepiece over the chimney, and was in amazement on seeing the minute-hand measure half-past one. She would not hear of staying a second longer. In truth, I felt rather disposed to defer the sequel of her narrative myself. **As I drowsed at the table, my mind turned toward the situation Catherine had gotten herself into, and wondered at Heathcliff's disappearance. How had Cathy fared with her husband? I imagined their wedding night, with Edgar such a meek and gentle contrast to Heathcliff. How had Cathy explained the loss of her maidenhead? For Edgar was the sort who would be shocked beyond belief to discover his idol was no virgin. She had probably claimed that she'd been thrown from a horse, or suffered some mysterious female ailment, and Edgar, all blushing, would not have dared pry further.**

I settled back against my chair, stroking the front of my trousers. With Edgar, was Catherine a meek and gentle lover? Did she banish the darker forces of carnality when she was in his bed? I imagined Edgar's furtive forays and gentle entreaties. The Catherine I had heard about would be impatient of them, but perhaps she had gained some maturity and level-headedness as the years passed.

I closed my eyes and pictured Cathy in her nightgown, leaning back in the bed, her hair dark against the pillows, Edgar, coming into the room, embarrassed and excited all at once. Would he have had any sexual experience? I assigned him a little, for most

men did find a willing maid or two in their lives before they took their wedding vows.

"Edgar, my love," she would whisper, and mean it, for he was handsome and young and rich. "Edgar, darling."

I sank back into my imaginings.

Edgar came across the carpet, and sat on the bed next to her. Lifting her hand to his lips, he said, "My dear, you have made me entirely happy this day."

She smiled up at him. "And you have made me the same, Edgar."

Leaning down, he kissed her gently, then gave a small chuckle and said, "I am ready to make you my wife in deed as well as in name."

"Oh, Edgar," she whispered, wrapping her arms around his neck, running her fingers through his blonde hair; the counter to Heathcliff's darkness. "Be gentle."

"I will," he promised. He kissed her again, still gentle, and she let her eyes drift closed. He divested himself of his clothing, and joined her on the bed. She turned to see him, his lithe body so different from Heathcliff's.

His hands fumbled a bit at the fastenings on her gown, but soon he had it off, and she was as naked as he.

His hands stroked down her sides, his fingers grazing the curves of her breasts. She shifted at his touch to give him easier access, but he did not put his hands on her breasts. Still, she did not complain. She melted into the bed, lazy and languid.

Then his hands cradled her hips. He held still for a moment and then his fingers began to caress the tops of her thighs. She let out a murmur of pleasure. When his fingers feathered lightly over her mound, she shifted against the mattress and bit her lip to keep the moan in.

He stroked her softness again, his touch a little firmer. When his fingers dipped further down, she sucked in her breath.

"Did that—"

"Do not stop, Edgar," she said.

He chuckled a little at her words. She quivered in anticipation but he moved his fingers from her mound and began stroking her thighs again, so soft and round, drawing a long moan of pleasure from her. She parted her legs for him, revealing her pink soft folds, but he did not take the silent invitation at first. He slid his fingers down her inner thighs, but while he came tantalizingly close to her soft mound, he did not touch it.

She moaned and shifted on the bed, not the wild thrashing of her couplings with Heathcliff, but exciting all the same. Wetness gathered between her legs. She wanted his hands on her, wanted his hard length inside her.

He touched her with gentle strokes, caressing her legs until she was weak with need, aching with desire, her mound swollen and heavy with anticipation, her arousal scenting the air as delightfully as any perfume. She wanted—needed—him inside of her.

"Edgar—"

She turned to look at him. His shaft, though not quite as big and thick as Heathcliff's, still jutted stiff and hard away from his belly. She reached for his hardness. He gathered her hands in his and pulled them over her head, settling them on the pillow. His muscled chest brushed her soft breasts when he moved.

"I will not last if you touch me," he said and lowered his mouth to hers, taking her lower lip between his teeth, then sliding his tongue inside her mouth. She opened herself to him, reveling in the pleasure of his demands.

"Touch me," she whispered. He straightened, still straddling her, and did her bidding, putting his hands on her, his palms teasing her nipples into stiff peaks, plucking them taut with his fingers. He kneaded and stroked and pinched until she cried out with pleasure, moaning his name over and over.

"Touch me, Edgar," she begged.

He stroked down her belly with deep, pleasing caresses. She gave a tiny whimper when his hands touched her thighs again. As his hands stroked, he urged her legs wider apart and his fingers teased her inner thighs, stroking higher and higher but not touching where she waited wet and swollen for him. She clenched her fingers into his shoulders.

"Touch me," she said again, moving restlessly on the bed, her hips thrusting, seeking his hands. He teased further, stroking her hips, sliding his fingers down her belly to the tangle of curls. Just not far enough to satisfy her.

"My dear, I am touching you," he said. Only his ragged breathing revealed that his play had sparked his desire as much as hers.

"Between my legs," she whispered. "Touch me between my legs."

He settled his palm lightly on her mound and she arched against him, gasping at the contact.

"Oh, yes. Stroke me," she said, her hips moving against his hand, her head thrown back and eyes closed. Her breath came in uneven gasps as he drew his fingers across her softness, her wetness dripping for him.

He slipped a finger in her opening and she jerked against it, gasping with pleasure. He glanced up at her face to be sure she was not hurt, then worked another finger inside, spreading her opening and drawing more wetness from her.

When she was entirely ready for him, he dipped his head and claimed her mouth, easing his member inside of her gently, and she sighed at their joining. It warmed her that he could be so gentle, his body a gift and not a demand. He nuzzled her neck as he moved deeper into her, stoking her desire with tender effort. She closed her eyes as the quiet pleasure swelled, his lazy rhythm spreading delicious warmth through her belly. She caught her breath as his rhythm increased but never demanded, only offered,

and then the slow deep pull of her climax, tumbling her from the
precipice, her release coming in languid, sweet waves.

"Oh," she whispered, holding him closer, the gentle release
so unexpected. With a final thrust, he took his own sweet pleasure
and afterwards fell asleep in her arms.

With a jerk, I realized I had let them reach their own completion without allowing myself the chance of reaching mine. I
sighed, and took the candle, and went up to bed.

CHAPTER 17

a CHARMING INTRODUCTION to a hermit's life! Four weeks' torture, tossing, and sickness! Oh, these bleak winds and bitter northern skies, and impassable roads, and dilatory country surgeons! And oh, this dearth of the human physiognomy! And, worse than all, the terrible intimation of Kenneth that I need not expect to be out of doors till spring!

Mr. Heathcliff has just honored me with a call. About seven days ago he sent me a brace of grouse—the last of the season. Scoundrel! He is not altogether guiltless in this illness of mine, and that I had a great mind to tell him. But, alas! How could I offend a man who was charitable enough to sit at my bedside a good hour, and talk on some other subject than pills and draughts, blisters and leeches? This is quite an easy interval. **If only Catherine would visit me. I am sure her fair beauty would heal me and perhaps the young widow might enjoy sharing my bed for an afternoon.**

Alas, she did not visit. And I am too weak to read, yet I feel as if I could enjoy something interesting. Why not have up Mrs. Dean to finish her tale? I can recollect its chief incidents, as far as she had gone.

Yes. I remember her hero had run off, and never been heard of for three years, and the heroine was married. I'll ring. She'll be delighted to find me capable of talking cheerfully.

Mrs. Dean came.

"It wants twenty minutes, sir, to taking the medicine," she commenced.

"Away, away with it!" I replied, "I desire to have—"

"The doctor says you must drop the powders."

"With all my heart! Don't interrupt me. Come and take your seat here. Keep your fingers from that bitter phalanx of vials. Draw your knitting out of your pocket—that will do—now continue the history of Mr. Heathcliff, from where you left off, to the present day. Did he finish his education on the Continent, and come back a gentleman? Or did he get a sizar's place at college, or escape to America, and earn honors by drawing blood from his foster-country? Or make a fortune more promptly on the English highways?"

"He may have done a little in all these vocations, Mr. Lockwood, but I couldn't give my word for any. I stated before that I didn't know how he gained his money, neither am I aware of the means he took to raise his mind from the savage ignorance into which it was sunk. But, with your leave, I'll proceed in my own fashion, if you think it will amuse and not weary you. Are you feeling better this morning?"

"Much."

"That's good news."

I got Miss Catherine and myself to Thrushcross Grange, and, to my agreeable disappointment, she behaved infinitely better than I dared to expect. She seemed almost overfond of Mr. Linton, and even to his sister she showed plenty of affection. They were both very attentive to her comfort, certainly. It was not the thorn bending to the honeysuckles, but the honeysuckles embracing the thorn. There were no mutual concessions. One stood erect, and the others yielded. Who can be ill natured and bad-tempered when they encounter neither opposition nor indifference?

I observed that Mr. Edgar had a deep-rooted fear of ruffling Catherine's humor. He concealed it from her, but if ever he heard me answer sharply, or saw any other servant grow cloudy at some imperious order of hers, he would show his trouble by a frown of displeasure that never darkened on his own account. He many a time spoke sternly to me about my pertness, and averred that the stab of a knife could not inflict a worse pang than he suffered at seeing his lady vexed.

Not to grieve a kind master, I learned to be less touchy, and, for the space of half a year, the gunpowder lay as harmless as sand, because no fire came near to explode it.

Catherine had seasons of gloom and silence now and then. They were respected with sympathizing silence by her husband, who ascribed them to an alteration in her constitution, produced by her perilous illness, as she was never subject to depression of spirits before. The return of sunshine was welcomed by answering sunshine from him. I believe I may assert that they were really in possession of deep and growing happiness.

It ended. Well, we must be for ourselves in the long run, the mild and generous are only more justly selfish than the domineering. It ended when circumstances caused each to feel that the one's interest was not the chief consideration in the other's thoughts.

On a mellow evening in September, I was coming from the garden with a heavy basket of apples I had been gathering. It had got dusk, and the moon looked over the high wall of the court, causing undefined shadows to lurk in the corners of the numerous projecting portions of the building. I set my burden on the house steps by the kitchen door, and lingered to rest, and drew in a few more breaths of the soft, sweet air. My eyes were on the moon, and my back to the entrance, when I heard a voice behind me.

"Nelly, is that you?"

It was a deep voice, and foreign in tone, yet there was something in the manner of pronouncing my name made it sound familiar. I turned about to discover who spoke, fearfully for the doors were shut, and I had seen nobody on approaching the steps. Something stirred in the porch, and, moving nearer, I distinguished a tall man dressed in dark clothes, with dark face and hair. He leant against the side, and held his fingers on the latch as if intending to open for himself. "Who can it be?" I thought. "Mr. Earnshaw? Oh, no! The voice has no resemblance to his."

"I have waited here an hour," he resumed, while I continued staring. "And the whole of that time all round has been as still as death. I dared not enter. You do not know me? Look, I'm not a stranger!"

A ray fell on his features, the cheeks were sallow, and half covered with black whiskers, the brows lowering, the eyes deep-set and singular. I remembered the eyes.

"What!" I cried, uncertain whether to regard him as a worldly visitor, and I raised my hands in amazement. "Heathcliff! You come back? Is it really you? Is it?"

"Yes, Heathcliff," he replied, glancing from me up to the windows, which reflected a score of glittering moons, but showed no lights from within. "Are they at home? Where is she? Nelly, you are not glad! You needn't be so disturbed. Is she here? Speak! I want to have one word with her—your mistress. Go, and say some person from Gimmerton desires to see her."

"How will she take it?" I exclaimed. "What will she do? The surprise bewilders me—it will put her out of her head! And you are Heathcliff! But altered! Nay, there's no comprehending it. Have you been for a soldier?"

"Go and carry my message," he interrupted, impatiently. "I'm in hell till you do!"

He lifted the latch, and I entered, but when I got to the parlor where Mr. and Mrs. Linton were, I could not persuade myself to proceed. At length I resolved on making an excuse to ask if they would have the candles lighted, and I opened the door.

They sat together in a window whose lattice lay back against the wall. From that window, a body could see beyond the garden trees, and the wild green park, the valley of Gimmerton, with a long line of mist winding nearly to its top. Very soon after you pass the chapel, as you may have noticed, the sough that runs from the marshes joins a beck that follows the bend of the glen. Wuthering Heights rose above this silvery vapor, but our old house was invisible, it rather dips down on the other side.

Both the room and its occupants, and the scene they gazed on, looked wondrously peaceful. I shrank reluctantly from performing my errand. I was actually going away leaving it unsaid, after having put my question about the candles, when a sense of my folly compelled me to return, and mutter, "A person from Gimmerton wishes to see you, ma'am."

"What does he want?" asked Mrs. Linton.

"I did not question him," I answered.

"Well, close the curtains, Nelly," she said, "and bring up tea. I'll be back again directly."

She quitted the apartment. Mr. Edgar inquired, carelessly, who it was.

"Someone mistress does not expect," I replied. "That Heathcliff— you recollect him, sir—who used to live at Mr. Earnshaw's."

"What! The gypsy—the ploughboy?" he cried. "Why did you not say so to Catherine?"

"Hush! You must not call him by those names, master," I said. "She'd be sadly grieved to hear you. She was nearly heartbroken when he ran off. I guess his return will make a jubilee to her."

Mr. Linton walked to a window on the other side of the room that overlooked the court. He unfastened it, and leant out. I suppose they were below, for he exclaimed quickly. "Don't stand there, love! Bring the person in, if it be anyone particular."

Ere long, I heard the click of the latch, and Catherine flew upstairs, breathless and wild, too excited to show gladness. Indeed, by her face, you would rather have surmised an awful calamity.

"Oh, Edgar, Edgar!" she panted, flinging her arms round his neck. "Oh, Edgar darling! Heathcliff's come back—he is!" And she tightened her embrace to a squeeze.

"Well, well," cried her husband, crossly. "Don't strangle me for that! He never struck me as such a marvelous treasure. There is no need to be frantic!"

"I know you didn't like him," she answered, repressing a little the intensity of her delight. "Yet, for my sake, you must be friends now. Shall I tell him to come up?"

"Here," he said, "into the parlor?"

"Where else?" she asked.

He looked vexed, and suggested the kitchen as a more suitable place for him. Mrs. Linton eyed him with a droll expression—half angry, half laughing at his fastidiousness.

"No," she added, after a while, "I cannot sit in the kitchen. Set two tables here, Ellen. One for your master and Miss Isabella, being gentry, the other for Heathcliff and myself, being of the lower orders. Will that please you, dear? Or must I have a fire lighted elsewhere? If so, give directions. I'll run down and secure my guest. I'm afraid the joy is too great to be real!"

She was about to dart off again, but Edgar arrested her.

"You bid him step up," he said, addressing me, "and, Catherine, try to be glad, without being absurd. The whole household need not witness the sight of your welcoming a runaway servant as a brother."

I descended, and found Heathcliff waiting under the porch, evidently anticipating an invitation to enter. He followed my guidance without waste of words, and I ushered him into the presence of the master and mistress, whose flushed cheeks betrayed signs of warm talking. But the lady's glowed with another feeling when her friend appeared at the door. She sprang forward, took both his hands, and led him to Linton, and then she seized Linton's reluctant fingers and crushed them into his.

Now, fully revealed by the fire and candlelight, I was amazed, more than ever, to behold the transformation of Heathcliff. He had grown a tall, athletic, well-formed man, beside whom my master seemed quite slender and youth-like. His upright carriage suggested the idea of his having been in the army. His countenance was much older in expression and decision of feature than Mr. Linton's, it looked intelligent, and retained no marks of former degradation. A half-civilized ferocity lurked yet in the depressed brows and eyes full of black fire, but it was subdued, and his manner was even dignified, quite divested of roughness, though stern for grace.

My master's surprise equaled or exceeded mine. He remained for a minute at a loss how to address the ploughboy, as he had called him. Heathcliff dropped his slight hand, and stood looking at him coolly till he chose to speak.

"Sit down, sir," Edgar said, at length. "Mrs. Linton, recalling old times, would have me give you a cordial reception, and, of course, I am gratified when anything occurs to please her."

"And I also," answered Heathcliff, "especially if it be anything in which I have a part. I shall stay an hour or two willingly."

He took a seat opposite Catherine, who kept her gaze fixed on him as if she feared he would vanish were she to remove it. He did not raise his to her often. A quick glance now and then sufficed, but it flashed back, each time more confidently, the undisguised delight he drank from hers.

They were too much absorbed in their mutual joy to suffer embarrassment. Not so Mr. Edgar. He grew pale with pure annoyance, a feeling that reached its climax when his lady rose, and stepping across the rug, seized Heathcliff's hands again, and laughed like one beside herself.

"I shall think it a dream tomorrow!" she cried. "I shall not be able to believe that I have seen, and touched, and spoken to you once more. And yet, cruel Heathcliff! You don't deserve this welcome. To be absent and silent for three years, and never to think of me!"

"A little more than you have thought of me," he murmured. "I heard of your marriage, Cathy, not long since. While waiting in the yard below, I meditated this plan—just to have one glimpse of your face, a stare of surprise, perhaps, and pretended pleasure, afterwards settle my score with Hindley, and then prevent the law by doing execution on myself. Your welcome has put these ideas out of my mind, but beware of meeting me with another aspect next time! Nay, you'll not drive me off again. You were really sorry for me, were you? Well, there was cause. I've fought through a bitter life since I last heard your voice, and you must forgive me, for I struggled only for you!"

"Catherine, unless we are to have cold tea, please to come to the table," interrupted Linton, striving to preserve his ordinary tone, and a due measure of politeness. "Mr. Heathcliff will have a long walk, wherever he may lodge tonight, and I'm thirsty."

Catherine took her post before the urn, and Miss Isabella came, summoned by the bell, then, having handed their chairs forward, I left the room.

The meal hardly endured ten minutes. Catherine's cup was never filled. She could neither eat nor drink. Edgar had made a slop in his saucer, and scarcely swallowed a mouthful. Their guest did not protract his stay that evening above an hour longer.

I asked, as he departed, if he went to Gimmerton.

"No, to Wuthering Heights," he answered. "Mr. Earnshaw invited me, when I called this morning."

Mr. Earnshaw invited him! And he called on Mr. Earnshaw! I pondered this sentence painfully, after he was gone. Is he turning out a bit of a hypocrite, and coming into the country to work mischief under a cloak? I mused. I had a presentiment in the bottom of my heart that he had better have remained away.

That night, I had reason to notice that for the first time since they had wed, Catherine did not excuse herself from the parlor ahead of her husband to prepare for his arrival in their bedchamber. After Heathcliff had quitted the premises, I went into the

parlor where I often spent an evening with my sewing, listening as Cathy and Mr. Edgar spoke of this and that, but that evening, Cathy could not seem to settle herself for a conversation. She kept leaping up from her chair and pacing from door to window, as if to catch a glimpse of her beloved.

Edgar in exasperation finally said, "Will you not retire for the evening, my dear?" His question was heavy with meaning, but she didn't seem to catch the sense of it, for she said, "What? Retire?" She scowled at him. "I'm not ready to sleep."

Edgar visibly controlled his temper. I believe I could hear him counting five through his teeth before he spoke again. "I bid you prepare for bed, Catherine."

She gave him the kind of abstracted look that would have driven a less temperate man into a frothing rage, and said what was possibly the worst thing she could have done. "Edgar, you must give me leave to regain my wits. It has been a trying day." She continued her pacing. "I find I am not myself."

"You're thinking about him, are you not?" he demanded. "When you should be thinking about me."

She must have sensed something of the danger she was in because she gave him a wide-eyed stare and said, "How can you think it? You are my husband."

"Do you love him?"

This time Cathy was able to meet his demand with a scornful look. "What a silly notion."

Edgar crossed the room in three short strides. He caught her up in his hands and shook her. "Do you wish he were your husband? That he were warming your bed each night? Do you?"

"Edgar!" she exclaimed, as if the very idea were beyond credibility. "Heathcliff may have been an important part of my past, but you are my present."

I remembered what she had said about marrying Edgar for the present, and I noted that she did not claim that he was her future.

"I wish I could believe you." He thrust her away from him.

She stumbled against the chair, then turned on him, her face red with anger, her lips twisted into a snarl. "I have done nothing to earn your disdain or your ill-treatment. I am your wife!"

I had never seen Edgar in such a temper, nor Cathy so put out with him before, and I should have realized what it would lead to. Cathy was too passionate not to give expression to her feelings, and Edgar was too in love with her to doubt her for long, and when he said, "Then show me!" I knew that she was not showing Edgar her love for him, but seeing in him a substitute for Heathcliff, a receptacle for the wild passions seeing Heathcliff had aroused in her, for all of the anger Edgar himself had sparked in her.

When they kissed, it was not with the gentle affection I had sometimes seen them share, but a passionate consummation, so single-minded and out-of-control that they took no notice that I was still in the room. I would have left them to it, but they were blocking the way to the door, and I did not want to interfere with them. There was no telling what Cathy would have done to me if I had, or Edgar for that matter. I had never seen him in such a state.

Cathy's hands flew to his trousers, and when his member sprang free, she began to undo her dress so that he could take her, but that was not what he wanted. In one movement, he turned her and bent her over the table. She braced her forearms on the surface, her bottom thrust in the air. Her eyes were closed, her face taut with pleasure, and her whole body quivered with excitement. It was as shameful a thing as I have ever seen, but I could not seem to avert my eyes.

With rough hands, Edgar shoved her dress up to her waist, and pulled her underclothes down, baring her round buttocks to him. He squeezed them, kneading them hard. She gasped at his touch, but did not bid him stop.

"Are you ready?" he demanded.

"Oh, yes," she whispered. He found her softness, his firm

fingers probing her slickness, touching her between her legs quite wickedly. His harsh breathing called answering gasps from her. She bit a knuckle to keep from crying out as he stroked her, but when he thrust a finger inside she gave a shaken cry.

He grunted his satisfaction and withdrew his finger. "Spread your legs wider," he said hoarsely. "I am enormous."

And he was, his member huge and red, quite nearly the size of Heathcliff's. She did as she was told, opening herself completely to him.

"Take your pleasure, my darling," she whispered and with a groan he plunged inside of her.

"So wet," he gasped and she moaned at his hard possession. He thrust, powerful and deep, his thick iron-hard shaft plunging again and again into her, his hands hard on her hips.

"Take me deeper, Catherine," he demanded. "I feel very wicked tonight." I could tell he cared nothing for Catherine's satisfaction and only looked after his own, abandoning his self-control, taking her with no more care than a wild stallion would cover a mare. She reveled in his heated possession, her body rocking in mindless cadence with his.

"Yes," he whispered, his fingers curling into her hips as he sank deeper and deeper with each thrust. "Oh, Catherine, yes."

She cried out helplessly as he plundered her over and over while and her muscles clenched and convulsed around him, the shocks of pleasure deepened by his powerful strokes. "Oh yes, oh yes," she cried out. "Oh yes!"

An exultant cry tore from his throat as his final thrust brought him hard and deep and home, spilling his hot essence inside of her.

And then Cathy made a mistake I knew she would regret, and she moaned, "Oh, Heathcliff," at the moment of culmination.

Edgar bent, panting over her for a time, his entire body shaking, slick with heat and spent desire. Then he withdrew, pulled his trousers up, and left the room without another word.

CHAPTER 18

*A*BOUT THE MIDDLE OF THE NIGHT, I was wakened from my first nap by Mrs. Linton gliding into my chamber, taking a seat on my bedside, and shaking my shoulder to rouse me.

"I cannot rest, Ellen," she said, by way of apology. "And I want some living creature to keep me company in my happiness! Edgar is sulky, because I'm glad of a thing that does not interest him. He refuses to open his mouth, except to utter pettish, silly speeches, and he affirmed I was cruel and selfish for being glad of Heathcliff's return. He always contrives to be sick at the least cross! I gave a few sentences of commendation to Heathcliff, and he, either for a head-ache or a pang of envy, began to cry, so I got up and left him."

I did not let on that I had seen exactly what had happened between them. I was not the least surprised that Mr. Linton's anger had carried over to their bedroom, nor did I for a moment doubt that Catherine had tried to laugh it off or fling it back on him.

"What use is it praising Heathcliff to him?" I answered. "As lads they had an aversion to each other, and Heathcliff would hate just as much to hear him praised. It's human nature. Let Mr. Linton alone about him, unless you would like an open quarrel between them."

"But does it not show great weakness?" pursued she. "I'm not envious. I never feel hurt at the brightness of Isabella's yellow hair and the whiteness of her skin, at her dainty elegance, and the fondness all the family exhibit for her. Even you, Nelly, if we have a dispute sometimes, you back Isabella at once, and I yield like a foolish mother. I call her a darling, and flatter her into a good temper. It pleases her brother to see us cordial, and that pleases me. But they are very much alike. They are spoiled children, and fancy the world was made for their accommodation, and though I humor both, I think a smart chastisement might improve them all the same."

"You're mistaken, Mrs. Linton," said I. "They humor you. I know what there would be to do if they did not. You can well afford to indulge their passing whims as long as their business is to anticipate all your desires. You may, however, fall out, at last, over something of equal consequence to both sides, and then those you term weak are very capable of being as obstinate as you."

"And then we shall fight to the death, shan't we, Nelly?" she returned, laughing. "No! I tell you, I have such faith in Linton's love, that I believe I could kill him, and he wouldn't wish to retaliate."

I advised her to value him the more for his affection.

"I do," she answered, "but he needn't resort to whining for trifles. It is childish and, instead of melting into tears because I said that Heathcliff was now worthy of anyone's regard, and it would honor the first gentleman in the country to be his friend. He ought to have said it for me, and been delighted from sympathy. He must get accustomed to him, and he may as well like him, considering how Heathcliff has reason to object to him, I'm sure he behaved excellently!"

"What do you think of his going to Wuthering Heights?" I inquired. "He is reformed in every respect, apparently. Quite a Christian offering the right hand of fellowship to his enemies all around!"

"He explained it," she replied. "I wonder as much as you. He said he called to gather information concerning me from you, supposing you resided there still, and Joseph told Hindley, who came out and fell to questioning him of what he had been doing, and how he had been living, and finally, desired him to walk in. There were some persons sitting at cards, Heathcliff joined them, my brother lost some money to him, and, finding him plentifully supplied, he requested that he would come again in the evening, to which he consented. Hindley is too reckless to select his acquaintance prudently. He doesn't trouble himself to reflect on the causes he might have for mistrusting one whom he has basely injured. But Heathcliff affirms his principal reason for resuming a connection with his ancient persecutor is a wish to install himself in quarters at walking distance from the Grange, and an attachment to the house where we lived together. Also a hope that I shall have more opportunities of seeing him there than I could have if he settled in Gimmerton. He means to offer liberal payment for permission to lodge at the Heights, and doubtless my brother's covetousness will prompt him to accept the terms. He was always greedy, though what he grasps with one hand he flings away with the other."

"**What of his desire to be close to the Grange?" I knew there was more to his motives than rekindling an old friendship.**

"**What of it? You know he is my friend, Nelly.**"

"**He was much more than that." I did not elaborate on what I insinuated. Her cheeks flushed in the candlelight and I knew she understood my words.**

"**I nearly died for wanting to see him while he was absent. I cannot bear him to go away again.**"

"**You have a husband.**"

"**I shall be faithful to my husband. There is no doubt I honor Edgar's name." She squared her shoulders as if the very idea of betraying her husband put her spine straighter.**

"**But he will be so close. At Wuthering Heights!** It's a nice place for a young man to fix his dwelling in!" said I. "Have you no fear of the consequences, Mrs. Linton?"

"None for my friend," she replied. "His strong head will keep him from danger, a little for Hindley, but he can't be made morally worse than he is. I stand between him and bodily harm. The event of this evening has reconciled me to God and humanity! I had risen in angry rebellion against Providence. Oh, I've endured very, very bitter misery, Nelly! If Heathcliff knew how bitter, he'd be ashamed to cloud its removal with idle petulance. It was kindness for him that induced me to bear it alone. Had I expressed the agony I frequently felt, he would have been taught to long for its alleviation as ardently as I. However, it's over, and I'll take no revenge on his folly, I can afford to suffer anything hereafter! Should the meanest thing alive slap me on the cheek, I'd not only turn the other, but I'd ask pardon for provoking it. And, as a proof, I'll go make my peace with Edgar instantly. Good night! I'm an angel!"

In this self-complacent conviction she departed, and the success of her fulfilled resolution was obvious on the morrow. Mr. Linton had not only abjured his peevishness (though his spirits seemed still subdued by Catherine's exuberance of vivacity), but he ventured no objection to her taking Isabella with her to Wuthering Heights in the afternoon. She rewarded him with such a summer of sweetness and affection in return as made the house a paradise for several days, both master and servants profiting from the perpetual sunshine.

Heathcliff—Mr. Heathcliff I should say in future—used the liberty of visiting at Thrushcross Grange cautiously, at first. He seemed estimating how far its owner would bear his intrusion. Catherine, also, deemed it judicious to moderate her expressions of pleasure in receiving him, and he gradually established his right to be expected. He retained a great deal of the reserve for which his boyhood was remarkable, and that served to repress all startling demonstrations of feeling. However, his eyes gave him away every time. I did not miss it, yet my master did. His uneasiness experienced a lull, and further circumstances diverted it into another channel for a space.

Edgar's new source of trouble sprang from the not-anticipated misfortune of Isabella Linton evincing a sudden and irresistible attraction towards the tolerated guest. She was at that time a charming young lady of eighteen, infantile in manners, though possessed of keen wit, keen feelings, and a keen temper, too, if irritated. Her brother, who loved her tenderly, was appalled at this fantastic preference for Mr. Heathcliff.

Leaving aside the degradation of an alliance with a nameless man, and the possible fact that his property, in default of heirs male, might pass into such a one's power, he had sense to comprehend Heathcliff's disposition. To know that, though his exterior was altered, his mind was unchangeable and unchanged. And he dreaded that mind. It revolted him. He shrank forebodingly from the idea of committing Isabella to its keeping.

He would have recoiled still more had he been aware that her attachment rose unsolicited, and was bestowed where it awakened no reciprocation of sentiment; for the minute he discovered its existence he laid the blame on Heathcliff's deliberate designing.

We had all remarked, during some time, that Miss Linton fretted and pined over something. She grew cross and wearisome, snapping at and teasing Catherine continually, at the imminent risk of exhausting her limited patience. We excused her, to a certain extent, on the plea of ill-health. She was dwindling and fading before our eyes. But one day, when she had been peculiarly wayward, rejecting her breakfast, complaining that the servants did not do what she told them, that the mistress would allow her to be nothing in the house, and Edgar neglected her, that she had caught a cold with the doors being left open, and we let the parlor fire go out on purpose to vex her, with a hundred yet more frivolous accusations. Mrs. Linton peremptorily insisted that Isabella should go to bed; and, having scolded her heartily, threatened to send for the doctor. Mention of Kenneth caused Isabella to exclaim, instantly, that her health was perfect, and it was only Catherine's harshness which made her unhappy.

"How can you say I am harsh, you naughty fondling?" cried the mistress, amazed at the unreasonable assertion. "You are surely losing your reason. When have I been harsh, tell me?"

"Yesterday," sobbed Isabella, "and now!"

"Yesterday!" said her sister-in-law. "On what occasion?"

"In our walk along the moor. You told me to ramble where I pleased, while you sauntered on with Mr. Heathcliff?"

"And that's your notion of harshness?" said Catherine, laughing. "It was no hint that your company was superfluous. We didn't care whether you kept with us or not. I merely thought Heathcliff's talk would have nothing entertaining for your ears."

"Oh, no," wept the young lady, "you wished me away, because you knew I liked to be there!"

"Is she sane?" asked Mrs. Linton, appealing to me. "I'll repeat our conversation, word for word, Isabella, and you point out any charm it could have had for you."

"I don't mind the conversation," she answered. "I wanted to be with—"

"Well?" said Catherine, perceiving her hesitate to complete the sentence.

"With him. And I won't be always sent off!" she continued, kindling up. "You are a dog in the manger, Cathy, and desire no one to be loved but yourself!"

"You are an impertinent little monkey!" exclaimed Mrs. Linton, in surprise. "But I'll not believe this idiocy! It is impossible that you can covet the admiration of Heathcliff—that you consider him an agreeable person, a match for you? I hope I have misunderstood you, Isabella?"

"No, you have not," said the infatuated girl. "I love him more than ever you loved Edgar, and he might love me, if you would let him!"

"I wouldn't be you for a kingdom, then!" Catherine declared, emphatically. She seemed to speak sincerely. "Nelly, help me to convince her of her madness. Tell her what Heathcliff is—an unreclaimed creature, without refinement, without cultivation, an arid wilderness of furze and whinstone. I'd as soon put that little canary into the park on a winter's day, as recommend you to bestow your heart on him! It is deplorable ignorance of his character, child, and nothing else, which makes that dream enter your head. Pray, don't imagine that he conceals depths of benevolence and affection beneath a stern exterior! He's not a rough diamond—a pearl-containing oyster of a rustic. He's a fierce, pitiless, wolfish man. I never say to him, 'Let this or that enemy alone, because it would be ungenerous or cruel to harm them,' I say, 'Let them alone, because I should hate them to be wronged.' He'd crush you like a sparrow's egg, Isabella, if he found you a troublesome charge. I know he couldn't love a Linton, and yet he'd be quite capable of marrying your fortune and expectations. Avarice is growing with him a besetting sin. There's my picture, and I'm his friend—so much so, that had he thought seriously to catch you, I should, perhaps, have held my tongue, and let you fall into his trap."

Miss Linton regarded her sister-in-law with indignation.

"For shame! For shame!" Isabella repeated, angrily. "You are worse than twenty foes, you poisonous friend!"

"Ah! You won't believe me, then?" said Catherine. "You think I speak from wicked selfishness?"

I had thought the same, truth be told. I wondered if she was protecting her sister-in-law or her own obsession with the dark-eyed man.

"I'm certain you do," retorted Isabella, "and I shudder at you!"

"Good!" cried the other. "Try for yourself, if that be your spirit. I have done, and yield the argument to your saucy insolence."

"And I must suffer for her egotism!" Isabella sobbed, as Mrs. Linton left the room. "All, all is against me. She has blighted my single consolation. But she uttered falsehoods, didn't she? Mr. Heathcliff is not a fiend. He has an honorable soul, and a true one, or how could he remember her?"

"Banish him from your thoughts, Miss," I said. "He's a bird of bad omen, no mate for you. Mrs. Linton spoke strongly, and yet I can't contradict her. She is better acquainted with his heart than I, or any one besides, and she never would represent him as worse than he is. Honest people don't hide their deeds. How has he been living? How has he got rich? Why is he staying at Wuthering Heights, the house of a man whom he abhors? They say Mr. Earnshaw is worse and worse since he came. They sit up all night together continually, and Hindley has been borrowing money on his land, and does nothing but play and drink. I heard only a week ago—it was Joseph who told me—I met him at Gimmerton. He told me they played cards and Mr. Earnshaw is handing over markers each day. Heathcliff laughs but it's a devil's jest. Drinking, cards all the night through until noon! They are loud and boisterous, not caring how they disturb good, clean folks. It's a nest of vipers at Wuthering Heights, and that's not Joseph speaking, it's what I know to be true. Now, Miss Linton, Joseph is an old rascal, but no liar, and, if his account of Heathcliff's conduct be true, you would never think of desiring such a husband, would you?"

"You are leagued with the rest, Ellen!" she replied. "I'll not listen to your slanders. What malevolence you must have to wish to convince me that there is no happiness in the world!"

Whether she would have got over this fancy if left to herself, or persevered in nursing it perpetually, I cannot say. She had little time to reflect. The day after, there was a justice-meeting at the next town; my master was obliged to attend, and Mr. Heathcliff, aware of his absence, called rather earlier than usual.

Catherine and Isabella were sitting in the library, on hostile terms, but silent. The latter was alarmed at her recent indiscretion, and the disclosure she had made of her secret feelings in a transient fit of passion; the former, on mature consideration, really offended with her companion; and, if she laughed again at her pertness, inclined to make it no laughing matter to her.

She did laugh as she saw Heathcliff pass the window. I was sweeping the hearth, and I noticed a mischievous smile on her lips. Isabella, absorbed in her meditations, or a book, remained till the door opened, and it was too late to attempt an escape, which she would gladly have done had it been practicable.

"Come in, that's right!" exclaimed the mistress, gaily, pulling a chair to the fire. "Here are two people sadly in need of a third to thaw the ice between them, and you are the very one we should both of us choose. Heathcliff, I'm proud to show you, at last, somebody that dotes on you more than myself. I expect you to feel flattered. Nay, it's not Nelly, don't look at her! My poor little sister-in-law is breaking her heart by mere contemplation of your physical and moral beauty. It lies in your own power to be Edgar's brother! No, no, Isabella, you shan't run off," she continued, arresting, with feigned playfulness, the confounded girl, who had risen indignantly. "We were quarrelling like cats about you, Heathcliff, and I was fairly beaten in protestations of devotion and admiration. Moreover, I was informed that if I would but have the manners to stand aside, my rival, as she will have herself to be, would shoot a shaft into your soul that would fix you forever, and send my image into eternal oblivion!"

"Catherine!" said Isabella, calling up her dignity, and disdaining to struggle from the tight grasp that held her. "I'd thank you to adhere to the truth and not slander me, even in joke! Mr. Heathcliff, be kind enough to bid this friend of yours release me. She forgets that you and I are not intimate acquaintances, and what amuses her is painful to me beyond expression."

As the guest answered nothing, but took his seat, and looked thoroughly indifferent what sentiments she cherished concerning him, she turned and whispered an earnest appeal for liberty to her tormentor.

"By no means!" cried Mrs. Linton in answer. "I won't be named a dog in the manger again. You shall stay. Now then! Heathcliff, why don't you evince satisfaction at my pleasant news? Isabella swears that the love Edgar has for me is nothing to that she entertains for you. I'm sure she made some speech of the kind, did she not, Ellen? And she has fasted ever since the day before yesterday's walk, from sorrow and rage that I dispatched her out of your society under the idea of its being unacceptable."

"I think you belie her," said Heathcliff, twisting his chair to face them. "She wishes to be out of my society now, at any rate!"

And he stared hard at the object of discourse, as one might do at a strange repulsive animal—a centipede from the Indies, for instance, which curiosity leads one to examine in spite of the aversion it raises.

The poor thing couldn't bear that. She grew white and red in rapid succession, and, while tears beaded her lashes, bent the strength of her small fingers to loosen the firm clutch of Catherine. After perceiving that as fast as she raised one finger off her arm another closed down, and she could not remove the whole together, she began to make use of her nails, and their sharpness presently ornamented the detainers with crescents of red.

"There's a tigress!" exclaimed Mrs. Linton, setting her free, and shaking her hand with pain. "Begone, for God's sake, and hide your vixen face! How foolish to reveal those talons to him. Can't you fancy the conclusions he'll draw? Look, Heathcliff! They are instruments that will do execution—you must beware of your eyes."

"I'd wrench them off her fingers, if they ever menaced me," he answered, brutally, when the door had closed after her. "But what did you mean by teasing the creature in that manner, Cathy? You were not speaking the truth, were you?"

"I assure you I was," she returned. "She has been dying for your sake several weeks, and raving about you this morning, and pouring forth a deluge of abuse, because I represented your failings in a plain light, for the purpose of mitigating her adoration. But don't notice it further. I wished to punish her sauciness, that's all. I like her too well, my dear Heathcliff, to let you absolutely seize and devour her up."

"And I like her too ill to attempt it," said he, "except in a very ghoulish fashion. You'd hear of odd things if I lived alone with that mawkish, waxen face. The most ordinary would be painting on its white the colors of the rainbow, and turning the blue eyes black, every day or two. They detestably resemble Linton's."

"Delectably!" observed Catherine. "They are dove's eyes—angel's!"

"She's her brother's heir, is she not?" he asked, after a brief silence.

"I should be sorry to think so," returned his companion. "Half a dozen nephews shall erase her title, please heaven! Abstract your mind from the subject at present. You are too prone to covet your neighbor's goods. Remember this neighbor's goods are mine."

"If they were mine, they would be none the less that," said Heathcliff, "but though Isabella Linton may be silly, she is scarcely mad, and, in short, we'll dismiss the matter, as you advise."

From their tongues they did dismiss it, and Catherine, probably, from her thoughts. The other, I felt certain, recalled it often in the course of the evening. I saw him smile to himself—grin rather—and lapse into ominous musing whenever Mrs. Linton had occasion to be absent from the apartment.

I determined to watch his movements. My heart invariably cleaved to the master's, in preference to Catherine's side. With reason I imagined, for he was kind, and trustful, and honorable, and she— she could not be called opposite, yet she seemed to allow herself such wide latitude, that I had little faith in her principles, and still less sympathy for her feelings. I wanted something to happen which might have the effect of freeing both Wuthering Heights and the Grange of Mr. Heathcliff, quietly, leaving us as we had been prior to his advent. His visits were a continual nightmare to me, and, I suspected, to my master also. His abode at the Heights was an oppression past explaining. I felt that God had forsaken the stray sheep there to its own wicked wanderings, and an evil beast prowled between it and the fold, waiting his time to spring and destroy.

CHAPTER 19

*S*OMETIMES, while meditating on these things in solitude, I've got up in a sudden terror, and put on my bonnet to go see how all was at the farm. I've persuaded my conscience that it was a duty to warn him how people talked regarding his ways, and then I've recollected his confirmed bad habits, and, hopeless of benefiting him, have flinched from re-entering the dismal house, doubting if I could bear to be taken at my word.

One time I passed the old gate, going out of my way, on a journey to Gimmerton. It was about the period that my narrative has reached. A bright frosty afternoon, the ground bare, and the road hard and dry.

I came to a stone where the highway branches off on to the moor at your left hand, a rough sand-pillar, with the letters W. H. cut on its north side, on the east, G., and on the south-west, T. G. It serves as a guide-post to the Grange, the Heights, and village.

The sun shone yellow on its grey head, reminding me of summer, and I cannot say why, but all at once a gush of child's sensations flowed into my heart. Hindley and I held it a favorite spot twenty years before.

I gazed long at the weather-worn block, and, stooping down, perceived a hole near the bottom still full of snail-shells and pebbles, which we were fond of storing there with more perishable things, and, as fresh as reality, it appeared that I beheld my early playmate seated on the withered turf. His dark, square head bent forward, and his little hand scooping out the earth with a piece of slate.

"Poor Hindley!" I exclaimed, involuntarily.

I started. My bodily eye was cheated into a momentary belief that the child lifted its face and stared straight into mine! It vanished in a twinkling, but immediately I felt an irresistible yearning to be at the Heights. Superstition urged me to comply with this impulse. Supposing he should be dead! I thought—or should die soon!—supposing it were a sign of death!

The nearer I got to the house the more agitated I grew, and on catching sight of it I trembled in every limb. The apparition had outstripped me. It stood looking through the gate. That was my first idea on observing an elf-locked, brown-eyed boy setting his ruddy countenance against the bars. Further reflection suggested this must be Hareton, my Hareton, not altered greatly since I left him, ten months since.

"God bless thee, darling!" I cried, forgetting instantaneously my foolish fears. "Hareton, it's Nelly! Nelly, thy nurse."

He retreated out of arm's length, and picked up a large flint.

"I am come to see thy father, Hareton," I added, guessing from the action that Nelly, if she lived in his memory at all, was not recognized as one with me.

He raised his missile to hurl it. I commenced a soothing speech, but could not stay his hand. The stone struck my bonnet, and then ensued, from the stammering lips of the little fellow, a string of curses, which, whether he comprehended them or not, were delivered with practiced emphasis, and distorted his baby features into a shocking expression of malignity. You may be certain this grieved more than angered me. Fit to cry, I took an orange from my pocket, and offered it to appease him. He hesitated, and then snatched it from my hold, as if he fancied I only intended to tempt and disappoint him. I showed another, keeping it out of his reach.

"Who has taught you those fine words, my bairn?" I inquired. "The curate?"

"Damn the curate, and thee! Give me that," he replied.

"Tell us where you got your lessons, and you shall have it," said I. "Who's your master?"

"Devil daddy," was his answer.

"And what do you learn from Daddy?" I continued.

He jumped at the fruit. I raised it higher. "What does he teach you?" I asked.

"Naught," said he, "but to keep out of his gait. Daddy cannot bide me, because I swear at him."

"Ah! And the devil teaches you to swear at Daddy?" I observed.

"Ay—nay," he drawled.

"Who, then?"

"Heathcliff."

I asked if he liked Mr. Heathcliff.

"Ay!" he answered again.

Desiring to have his reasons for liking him, I could only gather the sentences—"I known't. He pays Dad back what he gives to me—he curses Daddy for cursing me. He says I mun do as I will."

"And the curate does not teach you to read and write, then?" I pursued.

"No, I was told the curate should have his teeth dashed down his throat, if he stepped over the threshold Heathcliff had promised that!"

I put the orange in his hand, and bade him tell his father that a woman called Nelly Dean was waiting to speak with him, by the garden gate.

He went up the walk, and entered the house, but, instead of Hindley, Heathcliff appeared on the door stones. I turned directly and ran down the road as hard as ever I could race, making no halt till I gained the guide-post, and feeling as scared as if I had raised a goblin.

This is not much connected with Miss Isabella's affair, except that it urged me to resolve further on mounting vigilant guard, and doing my utmost to cheek the spread of such bad influence at the Grange, even though I should wake a domestic storm, by thwarting Mrs. Linton's pleasure.

The next time Heathcliff came, my young lady chanced to be feeding some pigeons in the court. She had never spoken a word to her sister-in-law for three days, but she had likewise dropped her fretful complaining, and we found it a great comfort.

Heathcliff had not the habit of bestowing a single unnecessary civility on Miss Linton, I knew. Now, as soon as he beheld her, his first precaution was to take a sweeping survey of the house-front. I was standing by the kitchen window, but I drew out of sight. He then stepped across the pavement to her, and said something. She seemed embarrassed, and desirous of getting away. To prevent it, he laid his hand on her arm. She averted her face. He apparently put some question that she had no mind to answer. There was another rapid glance at the house, and supposing himself unseen, the scoundrel had the impudence to embrace her.

CHAPTER 20

*T*HIS TIME I WAS NOT SURPRISED when Mrs. Dean stopped her story; her dogged refusal to share intimate details without prompting was well known to me by now. Many times previously had I cajoled her to continue, but this time, I fell back on my pillows and let her cluck about me for a moment, fluffing pillows and promising to fetch me a nourishing broth.

When she left the room, I contented myself with imagining what had taken place between Isabella and Heathcliff that fateful afternoon.

Heathcliff would have enticed her to follow him to the stable where he and Catherine had spent many passionate moments. I knew he would want—need—to despoil those memories. In my mind, they entered the shadows of the building, their steps muffled on the hay-strewn ground.

He stepped purposefully toward the opposite end from the hay stall where he and Catherine—he ground his teeth to stop that thought before it could be completed. Catherine had made her choice, and in making that choice had driven Heathcliff to make his. If she did not like the result, she had no one to blame but herself.

Isabella's hand trembled as he pulled her forward. Another way in which she was not Catherine. Catherine, afraid to experience the culmination of their passion? Hardly. Or perhaps he was giving her more credit than was due. Look at what she had done to avoid becoming his—

The stable was cool, the grayish light of morning barely penetrating the building. He led Isabella to the tack room, knowing that at this time of day, no one else would be about. That was as he planned. He closed the door, then, noting the lack of a lock, picked up the bench and wedged it against the door. No one would interrupt them now. The room was scarcely ideal, but it was private. An illicit tryst needed only that.

He turned to Isabella. In the dim light, she looked pale and frightened, her blue eyes wide as she watched his every movement. His lips tightened. She professed her love of him and still managed to be frightened by him. What did she know of love? Vain and shallow—but beautiful, he must admit that.

He let his gaze roam over her, and she withstood his scrutiny with pride enough; he didn't begrudge her that. Her blonde hair was neatly arranged. Catherine's would be falling around her neck by now—no, not anymore. Not since she had become the lady he despised. He made an impatient sound, and Isabella started as if he'd prodded her.

"Heathcliff?" she whispered, her heart in her eyes. Not the Earnshaw eyes, but Linton eyes.

Damn her.

He snared her roughly against him, kissing her harshly. She let out a sound—pleasure, dismay?—he didn't know, or care. A shiver raced through her body, igniting a sudden primal need in him. She was small, fragile in his arms, light and angelic. Everything Catherine was not.

He felt her pulse fluttering on her throat as he nibbled at it, nipping at the blood flow, giving her a surge with each bite. She gasped again and he smiled. He did not think she would try to stop him now. She had set upon her course, just as he had set upon his.

Isabella's light blue eyes were nearly consumed by the darkness of her pupils. Without speaking, he reached for the buttons of her dress, neatly done up to her neck.

She inhaled sharply, but said nothing as his hands worked the buttons free, kissing her exposed alabaster skin as it was exposed.

When he reached the end of the buttons, he slid the dress down her arms until it gathered around her waist. Then he pushed it to the floor. His fingers closed on her arms, the thin fabric of her shift the merest barrier between them. At the touch of his hands, she inhaled sharply and he saw her nipples harden, teasing him. He gazed at the sweet curve of her breasts beneath the linen. He could tell she wore nothing beneath the shift. His shaft swelled and throbbed at her near-nakedness.

Denying himself no longer, he took her breast gently in his hand, feeling its warm weight, delighting in the poke of the hard nub of her nipple through her thin shift. She whispered, "Oh!" and closed her eyes. Her heart surged beneath his hand, a mute testimony to her desire.

He dragged his hand up the column of her throat to cradle her face. Then he thrust his other hand into her golden hair and tilted her head back, her throat silky smooth and creamy in the dim light. Desire arced along his body as he nuzzled her exposed neck. The contrast of his male darkness with her female lightness stirred him.

He inhaled her scent, her arousal already apparent, and fought the urge to push her shift up and take her now to achieve the release he had needed since Catherine—

"Oh!" Isabella whispered again, the tiny sound whipping flames of heat through him. He wanted more soft murmurs, more cries of pleasure; he wanted her to moan her completion when he filled her. Could she take all of him? She was so small, would she be able to take him all the way, to the hilt? His stomach clenched. He stroked her flank with his hand, his erection already hard and enormous against her belly and he had barely touched her yet.

"Heathcliff," she whispered, moving her head, seeking his mouth. At the touch of her lips on his, he forgot control and crushed his mouth against hers, her soft sweetness inviting him to take what he wanted. The desire seared in his belly as he deepened the kiss, demanding that she open her mouth to accept him. She yielded gracefully and his breath grew ragged at the thought of her yielding her body to him the same way. He thrust his tongue deep inside her to say This is what I will do.

She moaned low in her throat, taking him as deep as he wanted. Her breath coming faster, she stroked his tongue with her own, the boldness of the movement stopping him for a shocked moment. He dragged his mouth from hers and stared deeply into her blue gaze, dark with heat and desire for him.

He slid her shift up with his hands and pulled it free. Then she was naked, her hair tumbling over her breasts, emphasizing the fact of her nudity, feminine, lovely.

Her hands rested lightly on his shoulders. She kept still, not looking at him, as he gazed at her, his eyes greedy, drinking in his fill of the sight of her. Beautiful, perfectly ripe, his. Fierce possessive desire rose in him, wholly unexpected, overwhelming. He would glory in those curves and soft places but no other man would have her, not until he was sated, not until he had taken all he wanted.

"Heathcliff?" she asked again.

"You are beautiful," he whispered and pulled her against him, hissing at the pleasure of her bare breasts against his hard muscled chest. She wrapped her arms around his neck, burying her face in his shoulder. His hands smoothed over her, stroking her bottom, lifting her against him. Through the fabric of his trousers, his shaft throbbed against her belly. Oh God, how soft and warm she was, how much he wanted her.

"You feel like heaven," he said, then lowered his mouth to claim hers. Her lips parted beneath his and he explored her mouth with a gentle tongue, stroking and teasing until she moaned and melted against his body. His heart slammed into his chest even as his arms tightened around her. He broke the kiss, trailing his mouth down her throat to her breast. She gasped at the touch of his lips on her skin and pulled his head down closer. He suckled at her nipple, using his teeth to nip and bite—he wanted to leave his mark on her somehow, his hot desire for her goading him—and her soft moans urged him on.

He lavished attention on her breast until the nipple was as hard as a pebble. Covering her breast with his hand, he stroked her nipple with his thumb while he turned his attention to her other breast. She lifted it to his mouth and caught her breath as he captured the nipple gently between his teeth. She arched her body urgently against his, rubbing the soft place between her legs against his thigh, more and more urgently as he suckled her.

He knew what she wanted, even if she did not. He released her for a moment, regretting the lost touch of their bodies, but he wanted so much more—and so did she. He stripped his trousers off, freeing his enormous shaft. He battled the urge to grab her, spread her wide and plunge inside her. He stood before her, not holding her, mere inches away from her. In the candlelight she was so beautiful, so desirable. Her nipples were hard and wet from the possession of his mouth. His belly clenched and he swallowed a groan. They were both naked, no barriers between them now. He could take her whenever he wanted. She would never stop him now.

He sucked a breath in between his teeth and slid his hand up her inner thigh. She jerked at his touch. Drawing in her own breath, she parted her legs for him, giving him access to the unbearably sweet mound between her legs. He took in another ragged breath as his fingers curled into her nest. Stroking the folds gently with his hand, he ignored the piercing heat in his shaft, the demand that he take her now. With a sharp, wordless sound, Isabella rubbed her hips against his hand.

"Oh," she said. The sound traveled directly to his shaft, which leapt in silent demand. His hand tightened on her hip. He swallowed hard and focused on letting his fingers explore her mound, feathering gently around the knot of pleasure and circling her center.

"Please," she whispered, clutching his shoulders. "Please."

"Please?" he asked, his breath uneven. He stroked a finger over her knot and she bucked. "Yes?" he asked, then set the pad of his finger firmly against the nub and worked it. Her belly clenched at his touch and her fingers dug into his shoulders. She pressed her face against his chest and moaned, her hips moving against him in an ancient rhythm. He did not think she realized it but she parted her legs wider to give him better access. Without thinking, he responded to the mute invitation.

She cried out in shocked surprise as his fingers eased her opening wide and slipped inside.

"My pet," he gasped. "How wet you are for me."

"Yes," she breathed, and then he bore her back onto the bench.

"Spread your legs for me," he groaned. He could not wait one moment longer. He would explode. His shaft was huge and hard for her and she must take him now and slake his hot, desperate need. "Now." And then he was inside her, plunging into her hot inviting wetness. Yes. Oh, yes. This. This. Her hips thrust against him as she gasped her pleasure at his hard, deep invasion. He drove harder and she matched him, her hips countering his every movement. He grunted his pleasure, holding her close as he plunged deeper and deeper into her, her body sweetly meeting every drive. Looking down at her, her body arched and wanting beneath him, he gloated at his victory.

"Yes," she moaned. His gut clenched. He buried his face in her neck, clutching her hips closer to him. "Oh, yes," she said, wrapping her legs around him. "Yes, Heathcliff. Yes."

He took a gasping breath as his control broke and he thrust hard and deep, taking his pleasure without regard to hers, hammering into her yielding flesh over and over. The heat and the desire slammed through him and the pleasure built and built in his body, his shaft now in total control, his mind blank, unable to form a coherent thought other than yes, yes. He was so nearly there and the knowledge drove him harder.

Then Isabella cried out as her climax broke over her, her sweet feminine center clenching around his hard shaft in a timeless rhythm that spurred him on even as it left him speechless. Her mewling sounds of delight whipped him to ride her harder, the sounds of her pleasure driving him towards his own end. With a final, perfect thrust, he spilled his seed hot and deep inside her.

"Heathcliff, my love," she cried out.

My love.

He closed his eyes against the pain.

CHAPTER 21

BY THE TIME NELLY RETURNED with the broth, I had managed to clean up the evidence of my imaginings and had crept back into bed, pulling the covers up to my chin.

Once she had helped me take my nourishment, she set the bowl aside and felt my brow. I informed her that I was feeling better, and wanted to listen to more of her tale.

"Did you confront Heathcliff about his action with Isabella?" I asked, to get her started.

"Did I!" she demanded, pulling herself up. "The moment he returned from the stable, on his way to the house as if nothing had happened, I confronted him, sir!"

And she continued her story.

"Judas! Traitor!" I ejaculated. "You are a hypocrite, too, are you? A deliberate deceiver."

"Who is, Nelly?" said Catherine's voice at my elbow. I had been over-intent on watching the pair outside to mark her entrance.

"Your worthless friend!" I answered, warmly. "The sneaking rascal yonder. Ah, he has caught a glimpse of us—he is coming in! I wonder will he have the heart to find a plausible excuse for making love to Miss, when he told you he hated her?"

Mrs. Linton saw Isabella tear herself free, and run into the garden, and a minute after, Heathcliff opened the door.

I couldn't withhold giving some loose to my indignation, but Catherine angrily insisted on silence, and threatened to order me out of the kitchen, if I dared to be so presumptuous as to put in my insolent tongue.

"To hear you, people might think you were the mistress!" she cried. "You want setting down in your right place! Heathcliff, what are you about, raising this stir? I said you must let Isabella alone!—I beg you will, unless you are tired of being received here, and wish Linton to draw the bolts against you!"

"God forbid that he should try!" answered the black villain. I detested him just then. "God keep him meek and patient! Every day I grow madder after sending him to heaven!"

"Hush!" said Catherine, shutting the inner door. "Don't vex me. Why have you disregarded my request? Did she come across you on purpose?"

"What is it to you?" he growled. "I have a right to kiss her, if she chooses, and you have no right to object. I am not your husband. You needn't be jealous of me!"

"I'm not jealous of you," replied the mistress. "I'm jealous for you. Clear your face. You shan't scowl at me! If you like Isabella, you shall marry her. But do you like her? Tell the truth, Heathcliff! There, you won't answer. I'm certain you don't."

"And would Mr. Linton approve of his sister marrying that man?" I inquired.

"Mr. Linton should approve," returned my lady, decisively.

"He might spare himself the trouble," said Heathcliff. "I could do as well without his approbation. And as to you, Catherine, I have a mind to speak a few words now, while we are at it. I want you to be aware that I know you have treated me infernally—infernally! Do you hear? And if you flatter yourself that I don't perceive it, you are a fool, and if you think I can be consoled by sweet words, you are an idiot. And if you fancy I'll suffer unrevenged, I'll convince you of the contrary, in a very little while! Meantime, thank you for telling me your sister-in-law's secret. I swear I'll make the most of it. And stand you aside!"

"What new phase of his character is this?" exclaimed Mrs. Linton, in amazement. "I've treated you infernally—and you'll take your revenge! How will you take it, ungrateful brute? How have I treated you infernally?"

"I seek no revenge on you," replied Heathcliff, less vehemently. "That's not the plan. The tyrant grinds down his slaves and they don't turn against him, they crush those beneath them. You are welcome to torture me to death for your amusement, only allow me to amuse myself a little in the same style, and refrain from insult as much as you are able. Having leveled my palace, don't erect a hovel and complacently admire your own charity in giving me that for a home. If I imagined you really wished me to marry Isabel, I'd cut my throat!"

"Oh, the evil is that I am not jealous, is it?" cried Catherine. "Well, I won't repeat my offer of a wife. It is as bad as offering Satan a lost soul. Your bliss lies, like his, in inflicting misery. You prove it. Edgar is restored from the ill-temper he gave way to at your coming, I begin to be secure and tranquil, and you, restless to know us at peace, appear resolved on exciting a quarrel. Quarrel with Edgar, if you please, Heathcliff, and deceive his sister. You'll hit on exactly the most efficient method of revenging yourself on me."

The conversation ceased. Mrs. Linton sat down by the fire, flushed and gloomy. The spirit that served her was growing intractable. She could neither lay nor control it. He stood on the hearth with folded arms, brooding on his evil thoughts.

In this position I left them to seek the master, who was wondering what kept Catherine below so long.

"Ellen," said he, when I entered, "have you seen your mistress?"

"Yes, she's in the kitchen, sir," I answered. "She's sadly put out by Mr. Heathcliff's behavior. Indeed, I do think it's time to arrange his visits on another footing. There's harm in being too soft, and now it's come to this."

I related the scene in the court, and, as near as I dared, the whole subsequent dispute. I fancied it could not be very prejudicial to Mrs. Linton, unless she made it so afterwards, by assuming the defensive for her guest.

Edgar Linton had difficulty in hearing me to the close. His first words revealed that he did not clear his wife of blame.

"This is insufferable!" he exclaimed. "It is disgraceful that she should own him for a friend, and force his company on me! Call me two men out of the hall, Ellen. Catherine shall linger no longer to argue with the low ruffian—I have humored her enough."

He descended, and bidding the servants wait in the passage, went, followed by me, to the kitchen.

Its occupants had recommenced their angry discussion. Mrs. Linton, at least, was scolding with renewed vigor, Heathcliff had moved to the window, and hung his head, somewhat cowed by her violent rating apparently. He saw the master first, and made a hasty motion that she should be silent, which she obeyed, abruptly, on discovering the reason of his intimation.

"How is this?" said Linton, addressing her, "what notion of propriety must you have to remain here, after the language which has been held to you by that blackguard? I suppose, because it is his ordinary talk you think nothing of it. You are habituated to his baseness, and, perhaps, imagine I can get used to it too!"

"Have you been listening at the door, Edgar?" asked the mistress, in a tone particularly calculated to provoke her husband, implying both carelessness and contempt of his irritation.

Heathcliff, who had raised his eyes at the former speech, gave a sneering laugh at the latter, on purpose, it seemed, to draw Mr. Linton's attention to him. He succeeded, but Edgar did not mean to entertain him with any high flights of passion.

"I've been so far forbearing with you, sir," he said quietly, "not that I was ignorant of your miserable, degraded character, but I felt you were only partly responsible for that, and Catherine wishing to keep up your acquaintance, I acquiesced—foolishly. Your presence is a moral poison that would contaminate the most virtuous. For that cause, and to prevent worse consequences, I shall deny you hereafter admission into this house, and give notice now that I require your instant departure. Three minutes' delay will render it involuntary and ignominious."

Heathcliff measured the height and breadth of the speaker with an eye full of derision. "Cathy, this lamb of yours threatens like a bull!" he said. "It is in danger of splitting its skull against my knuckles. By God! Mr. Linton, I'm mortally sorry that you are not worth knocking down!"

My master glanced towards the passage, and signed me to fetch the men. He had no intention of hazarding a personal encounter. I obeyed the hint, but Mrs. Linton, suspecting something, followed, and when I attempted to call them, she pulled me back, slammed the door to, and locked it.

"Fair means!" she said, in answer to her husband's look of angry surprise. "If you have not courage to attack him, make an apology, or allow yourself to be beaten. It will correct you of feigning more valor than you possess. No, I'll swallow the key before you shall get it! I'm delightfully rewarded for my kindness to each! After constant indulgence of one's weak nature, and the other's bad one, I earn for thanks two samples of blind ingratitude, stupid to absurdity! Edgar, I was defending you and yours. And I wish Heathcliff may flog you sick, for daring to think an evil thought of me!"

It did not need the medium of a flogging to produce that effect on the master. He tried to wrest the key from Catherine's grasp, and for safety she flung it into the hottest part of the fire, whereupon Mr. Edgar was taken with a nervous trembling, and his countenance grew deadly pale. For his life he could not avert that excess of emotion. Mingled anguish and humiliation overcame him completely. He leant on the back of a chair, and covered his face.

"Oh, heavens! In old days this would win you knighthood!" exclaimed Mrs. Linton. "We are vanquished! We are vanquished! Heathcliff would as soon lift a finger at you as the king would march his army against a colony of mice. Cheer up! You shan't be hurt! Your type is not a lamb, it's a sucking leveret."

"I wish you joy of the milk-blooded coward, Cathy!" said her friend. "I compliment you on your taste. And that is the slavering, shivering thing you preferred to me! I would not strike him with my fist, but I'd kick him with my foot, and experience considerable satis-faction. Is he weeping, or is he going to faint for fear?"

The fellow approached and gave the chair on which Linton rested a push. He'd better have kept his distance. My master quickly sprang erect, and struck him full on the throat a blow that would have leveled a slighter man.

It took his breath for a minute, and while he choked, Mr. Linton walked out by the back door into the yard, and from thence to the front entrance.

"There! You've done with coming here," cried Catherine. "Get away, now. He'll return with a brace of pistols and half-a-dozen assis-tants. If he did overhear us, of course he'd never forgive you. You've played me an ill turn, Heathcliff! But go—make haste! I'd rather see Edgar at bay than you."

"Do you suppose I'm going with that blow burning in my gullet?" he thundered. "By hell, no! I'll crush his ribs in like a rotten hazel-nut before I cross the threshold! If I don't floor him now, I shall murder him some time, so, as you value his existence, let me get at him!"

"He is not coming," I interposed, framing a bit of a lie. "There's the coachman and the two gardeners, you'll surely not wait to be thrust into the road by them! Each has a bludgeon, and master will, very likely, be watching from the parlor windows to see that they ful-fill his orders."

The gardeners and coachman were there, but Linton was with them. They had already entered the court. Heathcliff, on the second thoughts, resolved to avoid a struggle against three underlings. He seized the poker, smashed the lock from the inner door, and made his escape as they tramped in.

Mrs. Linton, who was very much excited, bade me accompany her upstairs. She did not know my share in contributing to the disturbance, and I was anxious to keep her in ignorance.

"I'm nearly distracted, Nelly!" she exclaimed, throwing herself on the sofa. "A thousand smiths' hammers are beating in my head! Tell Isabella to shun me, this uproar is owing to her, and should she or anyone else aggravate my anger at present, I shall get wild. And, Nelly, say to Edgar, if you see him again tonight, that I'm in danger of being seriously ill. I wish it may prove true. He has startled and distressed me shockingly! I want to frighten him. Besides, he might come and begin a string of abuse or complainings; I'm certain I should recriminate, and God knows where we should end! Will you do so, my good Nelly? You are aware that I am no way blamable in this matter. What possessed him to turn listener? Heathcliff's talk was outrageous, after you left us, but I could soon have diverted him from Isabella, and the rest meant nothing. Now all is dashed wrong, by the fool's craving to hear evil of self that haunts some people like a demon! Had Edgar never gathered our conversation, he would never have been the worse for it. Really, when he opened on me in that unreasonable tone of displeasure after I had scolded Heathcliff till I was hoarse for him, I did not care hardly what they did to each other, especially as I felt that, however the scene closed, we should all be driven asunder for nobody knows how long! Well, if I cannot keep Heathcliff for my friend—if Edgar will be mean and jealous, I'll try to break their hearts by breaking my own. That will be a prompt way of finishing all, when I am pushed to extremity! But it's a deed to be reserved for a forlorn hope; I'd not take Linton by surprise with it. To this point he has been discreet in dreading to provoke me; you must represent the peril of quitting that policy, and remind him of my passionate temper, verging, when kindled, on frenzy. I wish you could dismiss that apathy out of that countenance, and look rather more anxious about me!"

The stolidity with which I received these instructions was, no doubt, rather exasperating; for they were delivered in perfect sincerity, but I believed a person who could plan the turning of her fits of passion to account, beforehand, might, by exerting her will, manage to control herself tolerably, even while under their influence. I did not wish to "frighten" her husband, as she said, and multiply his annoyances for the purpose of serving her selfishness.

Therefore I said nothing when I met the master coming towards the parlor, but I took the liberty of turning back to listen whether they would resume their quarrel together. He began to speak first.

"Remain where you are, Catherine," he said, without any anger in his voice, but with much sorrowful despondency. "I shall not stay. I am neither come to wrangle nor be reconciled, but I wish just to learn whether, after this evening's events, you intend to continue your intimacy with—"

"Oh, for mercy's sake," interrupted the mistress, stamping her foot, "for mercy's sake, let us hear no more of it now! Your cold blood cannot be worked into a fever. Your veins are full of ice-water, but mine are boiling, and the sight of such chillness makes them dance."

"You know that to be untrue. However, to get rid of me, answer my question," persevered Mr. Linton. "You must answer it, and that violence does not alarm me. I have found that you can be as stoical as anyone, when you please. Will you give up Heathcliff hereafter, or will you give up me? It is impossible for you to be my friend and his at the same time, and I absolutely require to know which you choose."

"I require to be let alone?" exclaimed Catherine, furiously. "I demand it! Don't you see I can scarcely stand? Edgar, you—you leave me!"

She rang the bell till it broke with a twang, but I entered leisurely. It was enough to try the temper of a saint, such senseless, wicked rages! There she lay dashing her head against the arm of the sofa, and grinding her teeth, so that you might fancy she would crash them to splinters!

Mr. Linton stood looking at her in sudden compunction and fear. He told me to fetch some water. She had no breath for speaking.

I brought a glass full, and as she would not drink, I sprinkled it on her face. In a few seconds, she stretched herself out stiff, and turned up her eyes, while her cheeks, at once blanched and livid, assumed the aspect of death.

Linton looked terrified.

"There is nothing in the world the matter," I whispered. I did not want him to yield, though I could not help being afraid in my heart.

"She has blood on her lips!" he said, shuddering.

"Never mind!" I answered, tartly. And I told him how she had resolved, previous to his coming, on exhibiting a fit of frenzy.

I incautiously gave the account aloud, and she heard me, for she started up—her hair flying over her shoulders, her eyes flashing, the muscles of her neck and arms standing out preternaturally. I made up my mind for broken bones, at least, but she only glared about her for an instant, and then rushed from the room.

The master directed me to follow, I did, to her chamber-door. She hindered me from going further by securing it against me.

As she never offered to descend to breakfast next morning, I went to ask whether she would have some carried up. "No!" she replied, peremptorily.

The same question was repeated at dinner and tea, and again on the morrow after, and received the same answer.

Mr. Linton, on his part, spent his time in the library, and did not inquire concerning his wife's occupations. Isabella and he had had an hour's interview, during which he tried to elicit from her some sentiment of proper horror for Heathcliff's advances. But he could make nothing of her evasive replies, and was obliged to close the examination unsatisfactorily, adding, however, a solemn warning, that if she were so insane as to encourage that worthless suitor, it would dissolve all bonds of relationship between herself and him.

CHAPTER 22

WHILE MISS LINTON MOPED ABOUT the park and garden, always silent, and almost always in tears, and her brother shut himself up among books that he never opened—wearying, I guessed, with a continual vague expectation that Catherine, repenting her conduct, would come of her own accord to ask pardon, and seek reconciliation. She fasted pertinaciously, under the idea, probably, that at every meal Edgar was ready to choke for her absence, and pride alone held him from running to cast himself at her feet. I went about my household duties, convinced that the Grange had but one sensible soul in its walls, and that lodged in my body.

I wasted no condolences on Miss, nor any expostulations on my mistress, nor did I pay much attention to the sighs of my master, who yearned to hear his lady's name, since he might not hear her voice.

I determined they should come about as they pleased for me, and though it was a tiresomely slow process, I began to rejoice at length in a faint dawn of its progress—as I thought at first.

Mrs. Linton, on the third day, unbarred her door, and having finished the water in her pitcher and decanter, desired a renewed supply, and a basin of gruel, for she believed she was dying. That I set down as a speech meant for Edgar's ears; I believed no such thing, so I kept it to myself and brought her some tea and dry toast.

She ate and drank eagerly, and sank back on her pillow again, clenching her hands and groaning.

"Oh, I will die," she exclaimed, "since no one cares anything about me. I wish I had not taken that."

Then a good while after I heard her murmur, "No, I'll not die—he'd be glad—he does not love me at all—he would never miss me!"

"Did you want anything, ma'am?" I inquired, still preserving my external composure, in spite of her ghastly countenance and strange, exaggerated manner.

"What is that apathetic being doing?" she demanded, pushing the thick entangled locks from her wasted face. "Has he fallen into a lethargy, or is he dead?"

"Neither," replied I, "if you mean Mr. Linton. He's tolerably well, I think, though his studies occupy him rather more than they ought. He is continually among his books, since he has no other society."

I should not have spoken so if I had known her true condition, but I could not get rid of the notion that she acted a part of her disorder.

"Among his books!" she cried, confounded. "And I dying! I on the brink of the grave! My God! does he know how I'm altered?" continued she, staring at her reflection in a mirror hanging against the opposite wall. "Is that Catherine Linton? He imagines me in a pet—in play, perhaps. Cannot you inform him that it is frightful earnest? Nelly, if it be not too late, as soon as I learn how he feels, I'll choose between these two. Either to starve at once—that would be no punishment unless he had a heart—or to recover, and leave the country. Are you speaking the truth about him now? Take care. Is he actually so utterly indifferent for my life?"

"Why, ma'am," I answered, "the master has no idea of your

being deranged, and of course he does not fear that you will let yourself die of hunger."

"You think not? Cannot you tell him I will?" she returned.
"Persuade him! Speak of your own mind. Say you are certain I will!"

"No, you forget, Mrs. Linton," I suggested, "that you have eaten
some food with a relish this evening, and tomorrow you will perceive
its good effects."

"If I were only sure it would kill him," she interrupted, "I'd kill
myself directly! These three awful nights I've never closed my lids—
and oh, I've been tormented! I've been haunted, Nelly! But I begin to
fancy you don't like me. How strange! I thought, though everybody
hated and despised each other, they could not avoid loving me. And
they have all turned to enemies in a few hours. They have, I'm positive, the people here. How dreary to meet death, surrounded by their
cold faces! Isabella, terrified and repelled, afraid to enter the room,
it would be so dreadful to watch Catherine go. And Edgar standing
solemnly by to see it over, then offering prayers of thanks to God for
restoring peace to his house, and going back to his books! What in the
name of all that feels has he to do with books, when I am dying?"

She could not bear the notion that I had put into her head of Mr.
Linton's philosophical resignation. Tossing about, she increased her
feverish bewilderment to madness, and tore the pillow with her teeth,
then raising herself up all burning, desired that I would open the window. We were in the middle of winter, the wind blew strong from the
northeast, and I objected.

Both the expressions flitting over her face, and the changes of
her moods, began to alarm me terribly, and brought to my recollection her former illness, and the doctor's injunction that she should
not be crossed.

A minute previously she was violent, now, supported on one
arm, and not noticing my refusal to obey her, she seemed to find
childish diversion in pulling the feathers from the rents she had just
made, and ranging them on the sheet according to their different

species: her mind had strayed to other associations.

"That's a turkey's," she murmured to herself, "and this is a wild duck's, and this is a pigeon's. Ah, they put pigeons' feathers in the pillows—no wonder I couldn't die! Let me take care to throw it on the floor when I lie down. And here is a moor cock's, and this—I should know it among a thousand—it's a lapwing's. Bonny bird, wheeling over our heads in the middle of the moor. It wanted to get to its nest, for the clouds had touched the swells, and it felt rain coming. This feather was picked up from the heath, the bird was not shot. We saw its nest in the winter, full of little skeletons. Heathcliff set a trap over it, and the old ones dared not come. I made him promise he'd never shoot a lapwing after that, and he didn't. Yes, here are more! Did he shoot my lapwings, Nelly? Are they red, any of them? Let me look."

"Give over with that baby-work!" I interrupted, dragging the pillow away, and turning the holes towards the mattress, for she was removing its contents by handfuls. "Lie down and shut your eyes. You're wandering. There's a mess! The down is flying about like snow."

I went here and there collecting it.

"I see in you, Nelly," she continued dreamily, "an aged woman. You have grey hair and bent shoulders. This bed is the fairy cave under Peniston Crag, and you are gathering elf-bolts to hurt our heifers, pretending, while I am near, that they are only locks of wool. That's what you'll come to fifty years hence. I know you are not so now. I'm not wandering. You're mistaken, or else I should believe you really were that withered hag, and I should think I was under Peniston Crag, and I'm conscious it's night, and there are two candles on the table making the black press shine like jet."

"The black press? Where is that?" I asked. "You are talking in your sleep!"

"It's against the wall, as it always is," she replied. "It does appear odd—I see a face in it!"

"There's no press in the room, and never was," said I, resuming my seat, and looping up the curtain that I might watch her.

"Don't you see that face?" she inquired, gazing earnestly at the mirror.

And say what I could, I was incapable of making her comprehend it to be her own, so I rose and covered it with a shawl.

"It's behind there still!" she pursued, anxiously. "And it stirred. Who is it? I hope it will not come out when you are gone! Oh! Nelly, the room is haunted! I'm afraid of being alone!"

I took her hand in mine, and bid her be composed, for a succession of shudders convulsed her frame, and she would keep straining her gaze towards the glass.

"There's nobody here!" I insisted. "It was yourself, Mrs. Linton. You knew it a while since."

"Myself!" she gasped, "and the clock is striking twelve! It's true, then! That's dreadful!"

Her fingers clutched the clothes, and gathered them over her eyes. I attempted to steal to the door with an intention of calling her husband, but I was summoned back by a piercing shriek—the shawl had dropped from the frame.

"Why, what is the matter?" cried I. "Who is coward now? Wake up! That is the glass—the mirror, Mrs. Linton, and you see yourself in it, and there am I too by your side."

Trembling and bewildered, she held me fast, but the horror gradually passed from her countenance, its paleness gave place to a glow of shame.

"Oh, dear! I thought I was at home," she sighed. "I thought I was lying in my chamber at Wuthering Heights. Because I'm weak, my brain got confused, and I screamed unconsciously. Don't say anything, but stay with me. I dread sleeping. My dreams appall me."

"A sound sleep would do you good, ma'am," I answered. "And I hope this suffering will prevent your trying starving again."

"Oh, if I were but in my own bed in the old house!" she went on bitterly, wringing her hands. "And that wind sounding in the firs by the lattice. Do let me feel it—it comes straight down the moor—do let me have one breath!"

To pacify her I held the casement ajar a few seconds. A cold blast rushed through, I closed it, and returned to my post. She laid still now, her face bathed in tears. Exhaustion of body had entirely subdued her spirit. Our fiery Catherine was no better than a wailing child.

"How long is it since I shut myself in here?" she asked, suddenly reviving.

"It was Monday evening," I replied, "and this is Thursday night, or rather Friday morning, at present."

"What! Of the same week?" she exclaimed. "Only that brief time?"

"Long enough to live on nothing but cold water and ill-temper," observed I.

"Well, it seems a weary number of hours," she muttered doubtfully. "It must be more. I remember being in the parlor after they had quarreled, and Edgar being cruelly provoking, and me running into this room desperate. As soon as ever I had barred the door, utter blackness overwhelmed me, and I fell on the floor. I couldn't explain to Edgar how certain I felt of having a fit, or going raging mad, if he persisted in teasing me! I had no command of tongue, or brain, and he did not guess my agony, perhaps. It barely left me sense to try to escape from him and his voice." **Her body trembled upon the bed sheets as she spoke.**

"Before I recovered sufficiently to see and hear, it began to be dawn, and, Nelly, I'll tell you what I thought, and what has kept recurring and recurring till I feared for my reason. I thought as I lay there, with my head against that table leg, and my eyes dimly discerning the grey square of the window, that I was enclosed in the oak-paneled bed at home, and my heart ached with some great grief which, just waking, I could not recollect. I pondered, and worried myself to discover what it could be, and, most strangely, the whole last seven years of my life grew a blank! I did not recall that they had been at all.

"I was a child, my father was just buried, and my misery arose from the separation that Hindley had ordered between me and Heathcliff. I was laid alone, for the first time, and, rousing from a dismal doze after a night of weeping, I lifted my hand to push the panels aside. It struck the tabletop! I swept it along the carpet, and then memory burst in. My late anguish was swallowed in a paroxysm of despair. I cannot say why I felt so wildly wretched. It must have been temporary derangement, for there is scarcely cause. But, supposing at twelve years old I had been wrenched from the Heights, and every early association, and my all in all, as Heathcliff was at that time, and been converted at a stroke into Mrs. Linton, the lady of Thrushcross Grange, and the wife of a stranger. An exile, and outcast, thenceforth, from what had been my world. You may fancy a glimpse of the abyss where I groveled!

"Shake your head as you will, Nelly, you have helped to unsettle me! You should have spoken to Edgar, indeed you should, and compelled him to leave me quiet! Oh, I'm burning! I wish I were out of doors! I wish I were a girl again, half-savage and hardy, and free . . . and laughing at injuries, not maddening under them! Why am I so changed? Why does my blood rush into a hell of tumult at a few words? I'm sure I should be myself were I once among the heather on those hills. Open the window again wide. Fasten it open! Quick, why don't you move?"

"Because I won't give you your death of cold," I answered.

"You won't give me a chance of life, you mean," she said, sullenly. "However, I'm not helpless yet, I'll open it myself."

And sliding from the bed before I could hinder her, she crossed the room, walking very uncertainly, threw it back, and bent out, careless of the frosty air that cut about her shoulders as keen as a knife.

I entreated, and finally attempted to force her to retire. But I soon found her delirious strength much surpassed mine (she was delirious, I became convinced by her subsequent actions and ravings).

There was no moon, and everything beneath lay in misty

darkness. Not a light gleamed from any house, far or near all had been extinguished long ago; and those at Wuthering Heights were never visible—still she asserted she caught their shining.

"Look!" she cried eagerly, "that's my room with the candle in it, and the trees swaying before it, and the other candle is in Joseph's garret. Joseph sits up late, doesn't he? He's waiting till I come home that he may lock the gate. Well, he'll wait a while yet. It's a rough journey, and a sad heart to travel it, and we must pass by Gimmerton Kirk to go that journey! We've braved its ghosts often together, and dared each other to stand among the graves and ask them to come. . . . But, Heathcliff, if I dare you now, will you venture? If you do, I'll keep you. I'll not lie there by myself. They may bury me twelve feet deep, and throw the church down over me, but I won't rest till you are with me. I never will!"

She paused, and resumed with a strange smile. "He's considering—he'd rather I'd come to him! Find a way, then! Not through that kirkyard. You are slow! Be content, you always followed me!"

Perceiving it vain to argue against her insanity, I was planning how I could reach something to wrap about her, without quitting my hold of herself (for I could not trust her alone by the gaping lattice), when, to my consternation, I heard the rattle of the door-handle, and Mr. Linton entered. He had only then come from the library, and, in passing through the lobby, had noticed our talking and been attracted by curiosity, or fear, to examine what it signified, at that late hour.

"Oh, sir!" I cried, checking the exclamation risen to his lips at the sight that met him, and the bleak atmosphere of the chamber. "My poor mistress is ill, and she quite masters me. I cannot manage her at all. Pray, come and persuade her to go to bed. Forget your anger, for she's hard to guide any way but her own."

"Catherine ill?" he said, hastening to us. "Shut the window, Ellen! Catherine! why—"

He was silent. The haggardness of Mrs. Linton's appearance smote him speechless, and he could only glance from her to me in horrified astonishment.

"She's been fretting here," I continued, "and eating scarcely anything, and never complaining. She would admit none of us till this evening, and so we couldn't inform you of her state, as we were not aware of it ourselves, but it is nothing."

I felt I uttered my explanations awkwardly, the master frowned. "It is nothing, is it, Ellen Dean?" he said sternly. "You shall account more clearly for keeping me ignorant of this!" And he took his wife in his arms, and looked at her with anguish.

At first she gave him no glance of recognition. He was invisible to her abstracted gaze. The delirium was not fixed, however; having weaned her eyes from contemplating the outer darkness, by degrees she centered her attention on him, and discovered who it was that held her.

"Ah! You are come, are you, Edgar Linton?" she said, with angry animation. "You are one of those things that are ever found when least wanted, and when you are wanted, never! I suppose we shall have plenty of lamentations now—I see we shall—but they can't keep me from my narrow home out yonder. My resting-place, where I'm bound before spring is over! There it is, not among the Lintons, mind, under the chapel roof, but in the open air, with a head-stone, and you may please yourself whether you go to them or come to me!"

"Catherine, what have you done?" commenced the master. "Am I nothing to you anymore? Do you love that wretch Heath—"

"Hush!" cried Mrs. Linton. "Hush, this moment! You mention that name and I end the matter instantly by a spring from the window! What you touch at present you may have, but my soul will be on that hilltop before you lay hands on me again. I don't want you, Edgar. I'm past wanting you. Return to your books. I'm glad you possess a consolation, for all you had in me is gone."

"Her mind wanders, sir," I interposed. "She has been talking nonsense the whole evening, but let her have quiet, and proper attendance, and she'll rally. Hereafter, we must be cautious how we vex her."

"I desire no further advice from you," answered Mr. Linton. "You knew your mistress's nature, and you encouraged me to harass her. And not to give me one hint of how she has been these three days! It was heartless! Months of sickness could not cause such a change!"

I began to defend myself, thinking it too bad to be blamed for another's wicked waywardness. "I knew Mrs. Linton's nature to be headstrong and domineering," cried I. "But I didn't know that you wished to foster her fierce temper! I didn't know that, to humor her, I should wink at Mr. Heathcliff. I performed the duty of a faithful servant in telling you, and I have got a faithful servant's wages! Well, it will teach me to be careful next time. Next time you may gather intelligence for yourself!"

"The next time you bring a tale to me you shall quit my service, Ellen Dean," he replied.

"You'd rather hear nothing about it, I suppose, then, Mr. Linton?" said I. "Heathcliff has your permission to come a-courting to Miss, and to drop in at every opportunity your absence offers, on purpose to poison the mistress against you?"

Confused as Catherine was, her wits were alert at applying our conversation.

"Ah! Nelly has played traitor," she exclaimed, passionately. "Nelly is my hidden enemy. You witch! So you do seek elf-bolts to hurt us! Let me go, and I'll make her rue! I'll make her howl a recantation!"

A maniac's fury kindled under her brows, she struggled desperately to disengage herself from Linton's arms. I felt no inclination to tarry the event, and, resolving to seek medical aid on my own responsibility, I quitted the chamber.

In passing the garden to reach the road, at a place where a bridle hook is driven into the wall, I saw something white moved irregularly, evidently by another agent than the wind. Notwithstanding my hurry, I stayed to examine it, lest ever after I should have the conviction impressed on my imagination that it was a creature of the other world.

My surprise and perplexity were great on discovering, by touch more than vision, Miss Isabella's springer, Fanny, suspended by a handkerchief, and nearly at its last gasp.

I quickly released the animal, and lifted it into the garden. I had seen it follow its mistress upstairs when she went to bed, and wondered much how it could have got out there, and what mischievous person had treated it so.

While untying the knot round the hook, it seemed to me that I repeatedly caught the beat of horses' feet galloping at some distance, but there were such a number of things to occupy my reflections that I hardly gave the circumstance a thought, though it was a strange sound, in that place, at two o'clock in the morning.

Mr. Kenneth was fortunately just issuing from his house to see a patient in the village as I came up the street, and my account of Catherine Linton's malady induced him to accompany me back immediately.

He was a plain rough man, and he made no scruple to speak his doubts of her surviving this second attack, unless she were more submissive to his directions than she had shown herself before.

"Nelly Dean," said he, "I can't help fancying there's an extra cause for this. What has there been to do at the Grange? We've odd reports up here. A stout, hearty lass like Catherine does not fall ill for a trifle, and that sort of people should not either. It's hard work bringing them through fevers, and such things. How did it begin?"

"The master will inform you," I answered, "but you are acquainted with the Earnshaws' violent dispositions, and Mrs. Linton caps them all. I may say this, it commenced in a quarrel. She was struck during a tempest of passion with a kind of fit. That's her account, at least, for she flew off in the height of it, and locked herself up. Afterwards, she refused to eat, and now she alternately raves and remains in a half-dream, knowing those about her, but having her mind filled with all sorts of strange ideas and illusions."

"Mr. Linton will be sorry?" observed Kenneth, interrogatively.

"Sorry? He'll break his heart should anything happen!" I replied. "Don't alarm him more than necessary."

"Well, I told him to beware," said my companion, "and he must bide the consequences of neglecting my warning! Hasn't he been thick with Mr. Heathcliff lately?"

"Heathcliff frequently visits at the Grange," answered I, "though more on the strength of the mistress having known him when a boy, than because the master likes his company. At present he's discharged from the trouble of calling, owing to some presumptuous aspirations after Miss Linton that he manifested. I hardly think he'll be taken in again."

"And does Miss Linton turn a cold shoulder on him?" was the doctor's next question.

"I'm not in her confidence," returned I, reluctant to continue the subject.

"No, she's a sly one," he remarked, shaking his head. "She keeps her own counsel! But she's a real little fool. I have it from good authority that last night (and a pretty night it was!) she and Heathcliff were walking in the plantation at the back of your house above two hours, and he pressed her not to go in again, but just mount his horse and away with him! My informant said she could only put him off by pledging her word of honor to be prepared on their first meeting after that. When it was to be he didn't hear, but you urge Mr. Linton to look sharp!"

This news filled me with fresh fears, I outstripped Kenneth, and ran most of the way back. The little dog was yelping in the garden yet. I spared a minute to open the gate for it, but instead of going to the house door, it coursed up and down snuffing the grass, and would have escaped to the road, had I not seized it and conveyed it in with me.

On ascending to Isabella's room, my suspicions were confirmed. It was empty.

Had I been a few hours sooner Mrs. Linton's illness might have arrested her rash step. But what could be done now? There was a bare possibility of overtaking them if pursued instantly. I could not pursue them, however, and I dared not rouse the family, and fill the place with confusion, still less unfold the business to my master, absorbed as he was in his present calamity, and having no heart to spare for a second grief!

I saw nothing for it but to hold my tongue, and suffer matters to take their course. Kenneth arrived, and I went with a badly composed countenance to announce him.

Catherine lay in a troubled sleep. Her husband had succeeded in soothing the excess of frenzy; now he now hung over her pillow, watching every shade and every change of her painfully expressive features.

The doctor, on examining the case for himself, spoke hopefully to him of its having a favorable termination, if we could only preserve around her perfect and constant tranquility. To me, he signified the threatening danger was not so much death, as permanent alienation of intellect.

I did not close my eyes that night, nor did Mr. Linton. Indeed, we never went to bed, and the servants were all up long before the usual hour, moving through the house with stealthy tread, and exchanging whispers as they encountered each other in their vocations. Everyone was active but Miss Isabella, and they began to remark how sound she slept. Her brother, too, asked if she had risen, and seemed impatient for her presence, and hurt that she showed so little anxiety for her sister-in-law.

I trembled lest he should send me to call her, but I was spared the pain of being the first proclaimant of her flight. One of the maids, a thoughtless girl, who had been on an early errand to Gimmerton, came panting upstairs, open-mouthed, and dashed into the chamber, crying. "Oh, dear, dear! What mun we have next? Master, master, our young lady—"

"Hold your noise!" cried, I hastily, enraged at her clamorous manner.

"Speak lower, Mary. What is the matter?" said Mr. Linton. "What ails your young lady?"

"She's gone, she's gone! Yon' Heathcliff's run off w' her!" gasped the girl.

"That is not true!" exclaimed Linton, rising in agitation. "It cannot be. How has the idea entered your head? Ellen Dean, go and seek her. It is incredible. It cannot be."

As he spoke he took the servant to the door, and then repeated his demand to know her reasons for such an assertion.

"Why, I met on the road a lad that fetches milk here," she stammered, "and he asked whether we weren't in trouble at the Grange. I thought he meant for missis's sickness, so I answered, yes. Then says he, 'There's somebody gone after 'em, I guess?' I stared. He saw I knew naught about it, and he told how a gentleman and lady had stopped to have a horse's shoe fastened at a blacksmith's shop, two miles out of Gimmerton, not very long after midnight! And how the blacksmith's lass had got up to spy who they were. She knew them both directly. And she noticed the man—Heathcliff it was, she felt certain, nobody could mistake him, besides—put a sovereign in her father's hand for payment. The lady had a cloak about her face, but having desired a cup of water, while she drank, it fell back, and she saw her very plain. Heathcliff held both bridles as they rode on, and they set their faces from the village, and went as fast as the rough roads would let them. The lass said nothing to her father, but she told it all over Gimmerton this morning."

I ran and peeped, for form's sake, into Isabella's room, confirming, when I returned, the servant's statement. Mr. Linton had resumed his seat by the bed, on my reentrance, he raised his eyes, read the meaning of my blank aspect, and dropped them without giving an order, or uttering a word.

"Are we to try any measures for overtaking and bringing her back," I inquired. "How should we do?"

"She went of her own accord," answered the master. "She had a right to go if she pleased. Trouble me no more about her. Hereafter she is only my sister in name, not because I disown her, but because she has disowned me."

And that was all he said on the subject. He did not make single inquiry further, or mention her in any way, except directing me to send what property she had in the house to her fresh home, wherever it was, when I knew it.

CHAPTER 23

MRS. DEAN BROKE OFF HER TALE with a fresh round of pillow-plumping. She bent to straighten the bed-clothes, and I made an impatient sound that I supposed reminded her of Cathy, for she gave me a faint smile and patted my shoulder.

She picked up my empty bowl of broth, and inquired whether I should like another sup, which I declined. Then she left the room, promising to be back ere long, to continue her tale.

I moved restlessly on the sheets. Heathcliff and Isabella had run off together. I surmised that Heathcliff had married her to revenge himself on Catherine. I did not know where my sympathies lay; Heathcliff could hardly have expected Catherine to pine away for him when he left her without a word; but by the same token, she had scorned the very idea of marrying him, so what was he to do?

I settled back against the pillows. I had imagined Heathcliff's first passionate encounter with Isabella, and now I considered what it would have been like to be Isabella. After eloping, they would have stopped at an inn for rest. Heathcliff would hardly have treated her sensibilities delicately and would have expected to indulge his desire for marital relations. Isabella, no doubt, would have been pleased to oblige. She had abandoned her family for her lover, and could hardly withhold from him that to which he was entitled, having thrown her lot in with his.

She was married. Mrs. Heathcliff.

The room was somewhat gloomy, illuminated only by the meager light of the lantern. The door closed behind them with a thump that made her start.

"Nervous, Isabella?"

"Of course. What I meant to say was, of course not." Her hand fluttered at her throat. "I'm not nervous about what is to be between us." She gave a trembling smile that belied her words. "I am just thinking about how angry Edgar will be. He would never have allowed a marriage between us."

She looked up at her new husband, and started again. His countenance was always dark, but in the weak light of the room at the inn, his dark complexion gave him a sinister aspect. His black eyes bored into her soul. She struggled to take a breath.

"A little late for regrets and recriminations, my pet."

"It's not that," Isabella's heart thundered as loudly as a team of eight. Heathcliff stepped toward her, looking more like a predator than a man. She thought he might ask her to elucidate, but he was uninterested in conversation. He reached her, and swept her into his arms. His lips captured hers so quickly, she did not have time to react, only to feel. Every part of her body tingled as her husband took mastery over her. He was elemental, rough and so unlike anything else in her life. She knew she should be afraid— Catherine had been right about his character—but it was why she loved him, his willingness to unleash his passion, and hers, his desire to vanquish her and approve her submission to him.

The sound of fabric tearing met her ears as he tore her clothes asunder and she gloried in the act that so demonstrated his desire and ardor for her, reveled in it. The cool night air caressed her skin as his hot mouth landed on her ears, then her neck. He traveled down kissing and biting her skin until he found her breasts. Isabella thought for certain her heart would simply burst from her chest as his mouth closed around a nipple.

He sucked and bit at her until moisture gathered between her thighs. His rough, callused hand found her most tender parts and wild, elemental heat spread from his touch. She could not stop the moan that escaped from her throat. He had set her on fire and only he could extinguish the flames.

"You are mine."

She groped for her scattered intelligence but could not form the words to answer him so she simply groaned. He took her groan for assent and lifted her into his arms and deposited her on the bed. Her skin was still throbbing from his sensual assault.

Then he undressed.

He was magnificent.

His body was honed by years of hard labor, rippling with muscles, dusted with dark whorls of hair on his chest, which led down to his erection. His shaft stood straight, already engorged, nested in a cloud of dark hair.

Isabella quivered with anticipation as he approached the bed, her breath coming in short pants. His body was as hot as a cookstove when he covered her. He nudged her entrance.

"You are already wet for me."

Embarrassment surged through her, washing her cheeks with color. That was indeed true. Without ceremony, he thrust into her channel. His rhythm was not gentle. He pounded into her, immersing her in a whirlpool of sensations and pleasure. She clung to his back, hanging onto him as if she might blow away if she didn't. He nipped at her neck, surely leaving tooth marks, then at her breasts.

Isabella could hardly keep up with him so she allowed him to lead her into the maelstrom. He thrust faster and faster until she thought she might explode again in pleasure. Instead he buried himself so deep inside her, he touched her womb. As he shouted, she felt his seed spill within her.

It was done. She was truly his wife in name and in body.

As he rolled off her and the heat left her skin, a tear rolled down her cheek. It should have been perfect. It would have been perfect.

Yet he had called another's name when he found his release.

Catherine.

CHAPTER 24

OR TWO MONTHS the fugitives remained absent; in those two months, Mrs. Linton encountered and conquered the worst shock of what was denominated a brain fever. No mother could have nursed an only child more devotedly than Edgar tended her. Day and night he was watching, and patiently enduring all the annoyances that irritable nerves and a shaken reason could inflict.

Though Kenneth remarked that what he saved from the grave would only recompense his care by forming the source of constant future anxiety—in fact, that his health and strength were being sacrificed to preserve a mere ruin of humanity—he knew no limits in gratitude and joy when Catherine's life was declared out of danger. Hour after hour he would sit beside her, tracing the gradual return to bodily health, and flattering his too sanguine hopes with the illusion that her mind would settle back to its right balance also, and she would soon be entirely her former self.

The first time she left her chamber was at the commencement of the following March. Mr. Linton had put on her pillow, in the morning, a handful of golden crocuses, her eye, long stranger to any gleam of pleasure, caught them in waking, and shone delighted as she gathered them eagerly together.

"These are the earliest flowers at the Heights," she exclaimed. "They remind me of soft thaw winds, and warm sunshine, and nearly melted snow. Edgar, is there not a south wind, and is not the snow almost gone?"

"The snow is quite gone down here, darling," replied her husband, "and I only see two white spots on the whole range of moors. The sky is blue, and the larks are singing, and the becks and brooks are all brim full. Catherine, last spring at this time, I was longing to have you under this roof, now, I wish you were a mile or two up those hills. The air blows so sweetly, I feel that it would cure you."

"I shall never be there but once more," said the invalid, "and then you'll leave me, and I shall remain forever. Next spring you'll long again to have me under this roof, and you'll look back and think you were happy today."

Linton lavished on her the kindest caresses, and tried to cheer her by the fondest words, but, vaguely regarding the flowers, she let the tears collect on her lashes and stream down her cheeks unheeding.

We knew she was really better, and, therefore, decided that long confinement to a single place produced much of this despondency, and it might be partially removed by a change of scene.

The master told me to light a fire in the many-weeks' deserted parlor, and to set an easy chair in the sunshine by the window, and then he brought her down, and she sat a long while enjoying the genial heat, and, as we expected, revived by the objects round her, which, though familiar, were free from the dreary associations investing her hated sick chamber.

By evening she seemed greatly exhausted, yet no arguments could persuade her to return to that apartment, and I had to arrange the parlor sofa for her bed, till another room could be prepared.

To obviate the fatigue of mounting and descending the stairs, we fitted up this, where you lie at present, on the same floor with the parlor, and she was soon strong enough to move from one to the other, leaning on Edgar's arm.

Ah, I thought myself, she might recover, so waited on as she was. And there was double cause to desire it, for on her existence depended that of another. **Catherine was carrying a child.** We cherished the hope that in a little while Mr. Linton's heart would be gladdened, and his lands secured from a stranger's grip, by the birth of an heir.

I should mention that Isabella sent to her brother, some six weeks from her departure, a short note, announcing her marriage with Heathcliff. It appeared dry and cold, but at the bottom was dotted in with pencil an obscure apology, and an entreaty for kind remembrance and reconciliation, if her proceeding had offended him: asserting that she could not help it then, and being done, she had now no power to repeal it.

Linton did not reply to this, I believe, and, in a fortnight more, I got a long letter, which I considered odd, coming from the pen of a bride just out of the honeymoon. I'll read it, for I keep it yet. Any relic of the dead is precious, if they were valued living.

Dear Ellen, it begins.

I came last night to Wuthering Heights, and heard, for the first time, that Catherine has been, and is yet, very ill. I must not write to her, I suppose, and my brother is either too angry or too distressed to answer what I sent him. Still, I must write to somebody, and the only choice left me is you.

Inform Edgar that I'd give the world to see his face again—that my heart returned to Thrushcross Grange in twenty-four hours after I left it, and is there at this moment, full of warm feelings for him, and Catherine! I can't follow it though—(these words are underlined)— they need not expect me, and they may draw what conclusions they please, taking care, however, to lay nothing at the door of my weak will or deficient affection.

The remainder of the letter is for yourself alone. I want to ask you two questions. The first is, how did you contrive to preserve the common sympathies of human nature when you resided here? I cannot recognize any sentiment which those around share with me.

The second question I have great interest in, it is this—Is Mr. Heathcliff a man? If so, is he mad? And if not, is he a devil? I shan't tell my reasons for making this inquiry, but I beseech you to explain, if you can, what I have married. That is, when you call to see me, and you must call, Ellen, very soon. Don't write, but come, and bring me something from Edgar.

Now, you shall hear how I have been received in my new home, as I am led to imagine the Heights will be. It is to amuse myself that I dwell on such subjects as the lack of external comforts. They never occupy my thoughts, except at the moment when I miss them. I should laugh and dance for joy, if I found their absence was the total of my miseries, and the rest was an unnatural dream!

The sun set behind the Grange as we turned on to the moors, by that, I judged it to be six o'clock, and my companion halted half an hour, to inspect the park, and the gardens, and, probably, the place itself, as well as he could. It was dark when we dismounted in the paved yard of the farmhouse, and your old fellow-servant, Joseph, issued out to receive us by the light of a dip candle. He did it with a courtesy that redounded to his credit. His first act was to elevate his torch to a level with my face, squint malignantly, project his under lip, and turn away.

Then he took the two horses, and led them into the stables, reappearing for the purpose of locking the outer gate, as if we lived in an ancient castle.

Heathcliff stayed to speak to him, and I entered the kitchen—a dingy, untidy hole. I daresay you would not know it, it is so changed since it was in your charge. By the fire stood a ruffianly child, strong in limb and dirty in garb, with a look of Catherine in his eyes and about his mouth.

"This is Edgar's legal nephew," I reflected. "Mine in a manner, I must shake hands, and—yes—I must kiss him. It is right to establish a good understanding at the beginning."

I approached, and, attempting to take his chubby fist, said. "How do you do, my dear?"

He replied in a jargon I did not comprehend.

"Shall you and I be friends, Hareton?" was my next essay at conversation.

An oath, and a threat to set Throttler on me if I did not "frame off" rewarded my perseverance.

"Hey, Throttler, lad!" whispered the little wretch, rousing a half-bred bulldog from its lair in a corner. "Now, wilt thou be goring?" he asked authoritatively.

Love for my life urged a compliance; I stepped over the threshold to wait till the others should enter. Mr. Heathcliff was nowhere visible, and Joseph, whom I followed to the stables, and requested to accompany me in, after staring and muttering to himself, screwed up his nose and replied, "Mim! Mim! Mim! Did ever Christian body hear aught like it? Mincing un' munching! How can I tell whet ye say?"

"I say, I wish you to come with me into the house!" I cried, thinking him deaf, yet highly disgusted at his rudeness.

"None o' me! I getten summut else to do," he answered, and continued his work, moving his lantern jaws meanwhile, and surveying my dress and countenance (the former a great deal too fine, but the latter, I'm sure, as sad as he could desire) with sovereign contempt.

I walked round the yard, and through a wicket, to another door, at which I took the liberty of knocking, in hopes some more civil servant might show himself. After a short suspense, it was opened by a tall, gaunt man, without neckerchief, and otherwise extremely slovenly; his features were lost in masses of shaggy hair that hung on his shoulders, and his eyes, too, were like a ghostly Catherine's with all their beauty annihilated.

"What's your business here?" he demanded, grimly. "Who are you?"

"My name was Isabella Linton," I replied. "You've seen me before, sir. I'm lately married to Mr. Heathcliff, and he has brought me here—I suppose, by your permission."

"Is he come back, then?" asked the hermit, glaring like a hungry wolf.

"Yes—we came just now," I said, "but he left me by the kitchen door, and when I would have gone in, your little boy played sentinel over the place, and frightened me off by the help of a bulldog."

"It's well the hellish villain has kept his word!" growled my future host, searching the darkness beyond me in expectation of discovering Heathcliff, and then he indulged in a soliloquy of execrations, and threats of what he would have done had the "fiend" deceived him.

I repented having tried this second entrance, and was almost inclined to slip away before he finished cursing, but ere I could execute that intention, he ordered me in, and shut and re-fastened the door.

There was a great fire, and that was all the light in the huge apartment, whose floor had grown a uniform grey, and the once brilliant pewter-dishes, which used to attract my gaze when I was a girl, partook of a similar obscurity, created by tarnish and dust. I inquired whether I might call the maid, and be conducted to a bedroom? Mr. Earnshaw vouchsafed no answer. He walked up and down, with his hands in his pockets, apparently quite forgetting my presence, and his abstraction was evidently so deep, and his whole aspect so misanthropical, that I shrank from disturbing him again.

You'll not be surprised, Ellen, at my feeling particularly cheerless, seated in worse than solitude on that inhospitable hearth, and remembering that four miles distant lay my delightful home, containing the only people I loved on earth, and there might as well be the Atlantic to part us, instead of those four miles. I could not overpass them!

I questioned with myself—where must I turn for comfort? And—mind you don't tell Edgar, or Catherine—above every sorrow beside, this rose preeminent despair at finding nobody who could or would be my ally against Heathcliff!

I had sought shelter at Wuthering Heights, almost gladly, because I was secured by that arrangement from living alone with him, but he knew the people we were coming amongst, and he did not fear their intermeddling.

I sat and thought a doleful time. The clock struck eight, and nine, and still my companion paced to and fro, his head bent on his breast, and perfectly silent, unless a groan or a bitter ejaculation forced itself out at intervals.

I listened to detect a woman's voice in the house, and filled the interim with wild regrets and dismal anticipations, which, at last, spoke audibly in irrepressible sighing and weeping. I was not aware how openly I grieved, till Earnshaw halted opposite, in his measured walk, and gave me a stare of newly-awakened surprise. Taking advantage of his recovered attention, I exclaimed, "I'm tired with my journey, and I want to go to bed! Where is the maidservant? Direct me to her, as she won't come to me!"

"We have none," he answered, "you must wait on yourself!"

"Where must I sleep, then?" I sobbed. I was beyond regarding self-respect, weighed down by fatigue and wretchedness.

"Joseph will show you Heathcliff's chamber," said he, "open that door—he's in there."

I was going to obey, but he suddenly arrested me, and added in the strangest tone, "Be so good as to turn your lock, and draw your bolt—don't omit it!"

"Well!" I said. "But why, Mr. Earnshaw?" I did not relish the notion of deliberately fastening myself in with Heathcliff.

"Look here!" he replied, pulling from his waistcoat a curiously-constructed pistol, having a double-edged spring knife attached to the barrel. "That's a great tempter to a desperate man, is it not? I cannot resist going up with this every night, and trying his door. If once I find it open he's done for, I do it invariably, even though the minute before I have been recalling a hundred reasons that should make me refrain. It is some devil that urges me to thwart my own schemes by killing him. You fight against that devil for love as long as you may, when the time comes, not all the angels in heaven shall save him!"

I surveyed the weapon inquisitively. A hideous notion struck me. How powerful I should be possessing such an instrument! I took it from his hand, and touched the blade. He looked astonished at the expression my face assumed during a brief second. It was not horror, it was covetousness. He snatched the pistol back, jealously, shut the knife, and returned it to its concealment.

"I don't care if you tell him," said he. "Put him on his guard, and watch for him. You know the terms we are on, I see — his danger does not shock you."

"What has Heathcliff done to you?" I asked. "In what has he wronged you, to warrant this appalling hatred? Wouldn't it be wiser to bid him quit the house?"

"No!" thundered Earnshaw, "should he offer to leave me, he's a dead man. Persuade him to attempt it, and you are a murderess! Am I to lose all, without a chance of retrieval? Is Hareton to be a beggar? Oh, damnation! I will have it back, and I'll have his gold too, and then his blood, and hell shall have his soul! It will be ten times blacker with that guest than ever it was before!"

You've acquainted me, Ellen, with your old master's habits. He is clearly on the verge of madness. He was so last night at least. I shuddered to be near him, and thought on the servant's ill-bred moroseness as comparatively agreeable. He now recommenced his moody walk, and I raised the latch, and escaped into the kitchen. Joseph was bending over the fire, peering into a large pan that swung above it, and a wooden bowl of oatmeal stood on the settle close by.

The contents of the pan began to boil, and he turned to plunge his hand into the bowl, I conjectured that this preparation was probably for our supper, and, being hungry, I resolved it should be eatable, so, crying out sharply, "I'll make the porridge!"

I removed the vessel out of his reach, and proceeded to take off my hat and riding habit. "Mr. Earnshaw," I continued, "directs me to wait on myself. I will. I'm not going to act the lady among you, for fear I should starve."

"Good Lord!" he muttered, sitting down, and stroking his ribbed stockings from the knee to the ankle. "If there's to be fresh order-ings—just when I gotten used to two masters, if I mun have a mistress set o'er my head, it's like time to be flitting. I never did think to see t' day that I would leave th' old place—but I doubt it's nigh at hand!"

This lamentation drew no notice from me. I went briskly to work, sighing to remember a period when it would have been all merry fun, but compelled speedily to drive off the remembrance. It racked me to recall past happiness and the greater peril there was of conjuring up its apparition, the quicker the spoon ran round, and the faster the handfuls of meal fell into the water.

Joseph beheld my style of cookery with growing indignation.

"There!" he ejaculated. "Hareton, thou willn't sup thy porridge tonight, they'll be naught but lumps as big as my nose. There, again! I'd fling in bowl un' all, if I were ye! Have done with it. Bang, bang. It's a mercy t' bottom isn't heaved out!"

It was rather a rough mess, I own, when poured into the basins, four had been provided, and a gallon pitcher of new milk was brought from the dairy, which Hareton seized and commenced drinking and spilling from the expansive lip.

I expostulated, and desired that he should have his in a mug, affirming that I could not taste the liquid treated so dirtily. The old cynic chose to be vastly offended at this nicety, assuring me, repeat-edly, that "the bairn was every bit as good" as I, "and every bit as wholesome," and wondering how I could fashion to be so conceited. Meanwhile, the infant ruffian continued sucking, and glowered up at me defyingly, as he slavered into the jug.

"I shall have my supper in another room," I said. "Have you no place you call a parlor?"

"Parlor!" he echoed, sneeringly, "parlor! Nay, we've no parlors. If yah do not like our company, there's master's, and if yah do not like the master, there's us."

"Then I shall go upstairs," I answered. "Show me a chamber."

I put my basin on a tray, and went myself to fetch some more milk. With great grumblings, the fellow rose, and preceded me in my ascent. We mounted to the garrets, he opened a door, now and then, to look into the apartments we passed.

"Here's a room," he said, at last, flinging back a cranky board on hinges. "It's well enough to ate a few porridge in. There's a pack o' corn i' t' corner, there, nearly clean. If ye're feared o' mucking yer grand silk clothes, spread yer handkerchief on the top of it."

The room was a kind of lumber-hole smelling strong of malt and grain, various sacks of which articles were piled around, leaving a wide, bare space in the middle.

"Why, man," I exclaimed, facing him angrily, "this is not a place to sleep in. I wish to see my bedroom."

"Bedroom!" he repeated, in a tone of mockery. "Ye see all t' bedrooms there is—yon's mine."

He pointed into the second garret, only differing from the first in being more naked about the walls, and having a large, low, curtainless bed, with an indigo-colored quilt, at one end.

"What do I want with yours?" I retorted. "I suppose Mr. Heathcliff does not lodge at the top of the house, does he?"

"Oh! It's Master Heathcliff's ye're wanting?" cried he, as if making a new discovery. "Couldn't ye ha' said so, at first? And then, I would ha' told ye, about all this work, that that's just one ye cannot see—he always keeps it locked, and nobody ever sees it but himself."

"You've a nice house, Joseph," I could not refrain from observing, "and pleasant inmates, and I think the concentrated essence of all the madness in the world took up its abode in my brain the day I

linked my fate with theirs! However, that is not to the present purpose—there are other rooms. For heaven's sake be quick, and let me
settle somewhere!"

He made no reply to this adjuration, only plodding doggedly
down the wooden steps, and halting before an apartment, which,
from that halt and the superior quality of its furniture, I conjectured
to be the best one. There was a carpet—a good one, but the pattern
was obliterated by dust, a fireplace hung with cut-paper, dropping
to pieces, a handsome oak-bedstead with ample crimson curtains of
rather expensive material and modern make, but they had evidently
experienced rough usage.

The valances hung in festoons, wrenched from their rings, and
the iron rod supporting them bent in an arc on one side, causing the
drapery to trail upon the floor. The chairs were also damaged, many
of them severely, and deep indentations deformed the panels of the
walls.

I was endeavoring to gather resolution for entering and taking possession, when my fool of a guide announced, "This here is t'
master's."

My supper by this time was cold, my appetite gone, and my
patience exhausted. I insisted on being provided instantly with a place
of refuge, and means of repose.

"Where the devil?" began the religious elder. "The Lord bless
us! The Lord forgive us! Where the hell would ye going, ye marred,
wearisome ox! Ye've seen all but Hareton's bit of a chamber. There's
not another hole to lie down in in th' house!"

I was so vexed, I flung my tray and its contents on the ground,
and then seated myself at the stair head, hid my face in my hands, and
cried.

"Ech! Ech!" exclaimed Joseph. "Well done, Miss Cathy! Well
done, Miss Cathy! However, t' master shall just tumble over them
broken pots, and then we'll hear something. We'll hear how it's
going to be. Good for nothing madling! If ye deserve pining from

this to Christmas, flinging the precious gifts of God under foot in yer flaysome rages! But I'm mistaken if ye'll show yer spirit long. Will Heathcliff bide such bonny ways, think ye? I wish he may catch ye in that fit. I really wish he did."

And so he went on scolding to his den beneath, taking the candle with him, and I remained in the dark.

The period of reflection succeeding this silly action compelled me to admit the necessity of smothering my pride and choking my wrath, and bestirring myself to remove its effects.

An unexpected aid presently appeared in the shape of Throttler, whom I now recognized as a son of our old Skulker. It had spent its whelphood at the Grange, and was given by my father to Mr. Hindley. I fancy it knew me. It pushed its nose against mine by way of salute, and then hastened to devour the porridge, while I groped from step to step, collecting the shattered earthenware, and drying the spatters of milk from the banister with my pocket-handkerchief.

Our labors were scarcely over when I heard Earnshaw's tread in the passage. My assistant tucked in his tail, and pressed to the wall, I stole into the nearest doorway. The dog's endeavor to avoid him was unsuccessful, as I guessed by a scutter downstairs, and a prolonged, piteous yelping. I had better luck. He passed on, entered his chamber, and shut the door.

Directly after, Joseph came up with Hareton, to put him to bed. I had found shelter in Hareton's room, and the old man, on seeing me, said, "They's room for both ye un' yer pride, now, I should think in the house. It's empty, ye may hev' it all to yourself, and Him as always makes a third, i' such ill company!"

Gladly did I take advantage of this intimation, and the minute I flung myself into a chair, by the fire, I nodded, and slept. My slumber was deep and sweet, though over far too soon. Mr. Heathcliff awoke me, he had just come in, and demanded, in his loving manner, what I was doing there?

I told him the cause of my staying up so late—that he had the key of our room in his pocket. The adjective our gave mortal offence. He swore it was not, nor ever should be, mine, and he'd—but I'll not repeat his language, nor describe his habitual conduct. He is ingenious and unresting in seeking to gain my abhorrence! I sometimes wonder at him with an intensity that deadens my fear. Yet, I assure you, a tiger or a venomous serpent could not rouse terror in me equal to that which he wakens. He told me of Catherine's illness, and accused my brother of causing it, promising that I should be Edgar's proxy in suffering, till he could get hold of him.

I thought I loved him, Ellen, and I thought he might care for me. Now I know I was wrong. He pines for Catherine and another will never take her place in her heart. Yet it was done and now I cannot escape him.

I do hate him—I am wretched—I have been a fool! Beware of uttering one breath of this to any one at the Grange. I shall expect you every day—don't disappoint me!

—Isabella.

CHAPTER 25

*A*S SOON AS I HAD PERUSED this epistle I went to the master, and informed him that his sister had arrived at the Heights. I told him she had sent me a letter expressing her sorrow for Mrs. Linton's situation, and her ardent desire to see him with a wish that he would transmit to her, as early as possible, some token of forgiveness by me.

"Forgiveness!" said Linton. "I have nothing to forgive her, Ellen. You may call at Wuthering Heights this afternoon, if you like, and say that I am not angry, but I'm sorry to have lost her, especially as I can never think she'll be happy. It is out of the question my going to see her, however. We are eternally divided, and should she really wish to oblige me, let her persuade the villain she has married to leave the country."

"And you won't write her a little note, sir?" I asked imploringly.

"No," he answered. "It is needless. My communication with Heathcliff's family shall be as sparing as his with mine. It shall not exist!"

Mr. Edgar's coldness depressed me exceedingly, and all the way from the Grange I puzzled my brains how to put more heart into what he said, when I repeated it, and how to soften his refusal of even a few lines to console Isabella.

I daresay she had been on the watch for me since morning. I saw her looking through the lattice as I came up the garden causeway, and I nodded to her, but she drew back, as if afraid of being observed.

I entered without knocking. There never was such a dreary, dismal scene as the formerly cheerful house presented! I must confess, that if I had been in the young lady's place, I would, at least, have swept the hearth, and wiped the tables with a duster. But she already partook of the pervading spirit of neglect that encompassed her. Her pretty face was wan and listless, her hair uncurled. Some locks hanging lankly down, and some carelessly twisted round her head.

Probably she had not touched her dress since yester evening. Hindley was not there. Mr. Heathcliff sat at a table, turning over some papers in his pocket-book, but he rose when I appeared, asked me how I did, quite friendly, and offered me a chair.

He was the only thing there that seemed decent, and I thought he never looked better. So much had circumstances altered their positions, that he would certainly have struck a stranger as a born and bred gentleman, and his wife as a thorough little slattern!

She came forward eagerly to greet me, and held out one hand to take the expected letter.

I shook my head. She wouldn't understand the hint, but followed me to a sideboard, where I went to lay my bonnet, and importuned me in a whisper to give her directly what I had brought.

Heathcliff guessed the meaning of her maneuvers, and said, "If you have got anything for Isabella, as no doubt you have, Nelly, give it to her. You needn't make a secret of it. We have no secrets between us."

"Oh, I have nothing," I replied, thinking it best to speak the truth at once. "My master bid me tell his sister that she must not expect either a letter or a visit from him at present. He sends his love, ma'am, and his wishes for your happiness, and his pardon for the grief you have occasioned, but he thinks that after this time his household and the household here should drop intercommunication, as nothing could come of keeping it up."

Mrs. Heathcliff's lip quivered slightly, and she returned to her seat in the window. Her husband took his stand on the hearthstone, near me, and began to put questions concerning Catherine.

I told him as much as I thought proper of her illness, and he extorted from me, by cross-examination, most of the facts connected with its origin. I blamed her, as she deserved, for bringing it all on herself, and ended by hoping that he would follow Mr. Linton's example and avoid future interference with his family, for good or evil.

"Mrs. Linton is now just recovering," I said. "She'll never be like she was, but her life is spared, and if you really have a regard for her, you'll shun crossing her way again—nay, you'll move out of this country entirely. And that you may not regret it, I'll inform you Catherine Linton is as different now from your old friend Catherine Earnshaw, as that young lady is different from me. Her appearance is changed greatly, her character much more so; and the person who is compelled, of necessity, to be her companion, will only sustain his affection hereafter by the remembrance of what she once was, by common humanity, and a sense of duty!"

"That is quite possible," remarked Heathcliff, forcing himself to seem calm. "Quite possible that your master should have nothing but common humanity and a sense of duty to fall back upon. But do you imagine that I shall leave Catherine to his duty and humanity? And can you compare my feelings respecting Catherine to his? Before you leave this house, I must exact a promise from you that you'll get me an interview with her. Consent, or refuse, I will see her! What do you say?"

"I say, Mr. Heathcliff," I replied, "you must not. You never shall, through my means. Another encounter between you and the master would kill her altogether."

"With your aid that may be avoided," he continued, "and should there be danger of such an event—should he be the cause of adding a single trouble more to her existence—why, I think I shall be justified in going to extremes! I wish you had sincerity enough to tell me whether Catherine would suffer greatly from his loss. The fear that she would restrains me. And there you see the distinction between our feelings. Had he been in my place, and I in his, though I hated him with a hatred that turned my life to gall, I never would have raised a hand against him. You may look incredulous, if you please! I never would have banished him from her society as long as she desired his. The moment her regard ceased, I would have torn his heart out, and drunk his blood! But, till then—if you don't believe me, you don't know me—till then, I would have died by inches before I touched a single hair of his head!"

"And yet," I interrupted, "you have no scruples in completely ruining all hopes of her perfect restoration, by thrusting yourself into her remembrance now, when she has nearly forgotten you, and involving her in a new tumult of discord and distress."

"You suppose she has nearly forgotten me?" he said. "Oh, Nelly! You know she has not! You know as well as I do, that for every thought she spends on Linton she spends a thousand on me! At a most miserable period of my life, I had a notion of the kind. It haunted me on my return to the neighborhood last summer, but only her own assurance could make me admit the horrible idea again. And then, Linton would be nothing, nor Hindley, nor all the dreams that ever I dreamt. Two words would comprehend my future—death and hell. Existence, after losing her, would be hell. Yet I was a fool to fancy for a moment that she valued Edgar Linton's attachment more than mine. If he loved with all the powers of his puny being, he couldn't love as much in eighty years as I could in a day. And Catherine has a heart as deep as I have. The sea could be as readily contained in that horse-trough as her whole affection be monopolized by him. Tush! He is scarcely a degree dearer to her than her dog, or her horse. It is not in him to be loved like me. How can she love in him what he has not?"

"Catherine and Edgar are as fond of each other as any two people can be," cried Isabella, with sudden vivacity. "No one has a right to talk in that manner, and I won't hear my brother depreciated in silence!"

"Your brother is wondrous fond of you too, isn't he?" observed Heathcliff, scornfully. "He turns you adrift on the world with surprising alacrity."

"He is not aware of what I suffer," she replied. "I didn't tell him that."

"You have been telling him something, then. You have written, have you?"

"To say that I was married, I did write—you saw the note."

"And nothing since?"

"No."

"My young lady is looking sadly the worse for her change of condition," I remarked. "Somebody's love comes short in her case, obviously, whose, I may guess, but, perhaps, I shouldn't say."

"I should guess it was her own," said Heathcliff. "She degenerates into a mere slut! She is tired of trying to please me uncommonly early. You'd hardly credit it, but the very morrow of our wedding she was weeping to go home. However, she'll suit this house so much the better for not being over nice, and I'll take care she does not disgrace me by rambling abroad."

"Well, sir," returned I, "I hope you'll consider that Mrs. Heathcliff is accustomed to be looked after and waited on, and that she has been brought up like an only daughter, whom everyone was ready to serve. You must let her have a maid to keep things tidy about her, and you must treat her kindly. Whatever be your notion of Mr. Edgar, you cannot doubt that she has a capacity for strong attachments, or she wouldn't have abandoned the elegancies, and comforts, and friends of her former home, to fix contentedly, in such a wilderness as this, with you."

"She abandoned them under a delusion," he answered, "picturing in me a hero of romance, and expecting unlimited indulgences from my chivalrous devotion. I can hardly regard her in the light of a rational creature, so obstinately has she persisted in forming a fabulous notion of my character and acting on the false impressions she cherished. But, at last, I think she begins to know me. I don't perceive the silly smiles and grimaces that provoked me at first, and the senseless incapability of discerning that I was in earnest when I gave her my opinion of her infatuation and herself. It was a marvelous effort of perspicacity to discover that I did not love her. I believed, at one time, no lessons could teach her that! And yet it is poorly learnt, for this morning she announced, as a piece of appalling intelligence, that I had actually succeeded in making her hate me! A positive labor of Hercules, I assure you! If it be achieved, I have cause to return thanks. Can I trust your assertion, Isabella? Are you sure you hate me? If I let you alone for half a day, won't you come sighing and wheedling to me again? I daresay she would rather I had seemed all tenderness before you. It wounds her vanity to have the truth exposed. But I don't care who knows that the passion was wholly on one side. I never told her a lie about it.

"She cannot accuse me of showing one bit of deceitful softness. The first thing she saw me do, on coming out of the Grange, was to hang up her little dog, and when she pleaded for it, the first words I uttered were a wish that I had the hanging of every being belonging to her, except one. Possibly she took that exception for herself. But no brutality disgusted her. I suppose she has an innate admiration of it, if only her precious person were secure from injury! Now, was it not the depth of absurdity—of genuine idiocy, for that pitiful, slavish, mean-minded witch to dream that I could love her? Tell your master, Nelly, that I never, in all my life, met with such an abject thing as she is. She even disgraces the name of Linton, and I've sometimes relented, from pure lack of invention, in my experiments on what she could endure, and still creep shamefully cringing back! But tell him, also, to set his fraternal and magisterial heart at ease. That I keep strictly within the limits of the law. I have avoided, up to this period, giving her the slightest right to claim a separation, and, what's more, she'd thank nobody for dividing us. If she desired to go, she might. The nuisance of her presence outweighs the gratification to be derived from tormenting her!"

"Mr. Heathcliff," said I, "this is the talk of a madman. Your wife, most likely, is convinced you are mad, and, for that reason, she has borne with you hitherto. But now that you say she may go, she'll doubtless avail herself of the permission. You are not so bewitched, ma'am, are you, as to remain with him of your own accord?"

"Take care, Ellen!" answered Isabella, her eyes sparkling irefully, there was no misdoubting by their expression the full success of her partner's endeavors to make himself detested. "Don't put faith in a single word he speaks. He's a lying fiend! A monster, and not a human being! I've been told I might leave him before, and I've made the attempt, but I dare not repeat it! Only, Ellen, promise you'll not mention a syllable of his infamous conversation to my brother or Catherine. Whatever he may pretend, he wishes to provoke Edgar to desperation. He says he has married me on purpose to obtain power over him, and he shan't obtain it—I'll die first! I just hope, I pray, that he may forget his diabolical prudence and kill me! The single pleasure I can imagine is to die, or to see him dead!"

"There—that will do for the present!" said Heathcliff. "If you are called upon in a court of law, you'll remember her language, Nelly! And take a good look at that countenance. She's near the point that would suit me. No, you're not fit to be your own guardian, Isabella, now, and I, being your legal protector, must retain you in my custody, however distasteful the obligation may be. Go upstairs, I have something to say to Ellen Dean in private. That's not the way. Upstairs, I tell you! Why, this is the road upstairs, child!"

He seized, and thrust her from the room, and returned muttering, "I have no pity! I have no pity! The more the worms writhe, the more I yearn to crush out their entrails! It is a moral teething, and I grind with greater energy in proportion to the increase of pain."

"Do you understand what the word pity means?" I said, hastening to resume my bonnet. "Did you ever feel a touch of it in your life?"

"Put that down!" he interrupted, perceiving my intention to depart. "You are not going yet. Come here now, Nelly. I must either persuade or compel you to aid me in fulfilling my determination to see Catherine, and that without delay. I swear that I meditate no harm. I don't desire to cause any disturbance, or to exasperate or insult Mr. Linton, I only wish to hear from herself how she is, and why she has been ill, and to ask if anything that I could do would be of use to her." **His dark eyes were wild with need.**

"Last night I was in the Grange garden six hours, and I'll return there tonight, and every night I'll haunt the place, and every day, till I find an opportunity of entering. If Edgar Linton meets me, I shall not hesitate to knock him down, and give him enough to insure his quiescence while I stay. If his servants oppose me, I shall threaten them off with these pistols. But wouldn't it be better to prevent my coming in contact with them, or their master? And you could do it so easily. I'd warn you when I came, and then you might let me in unobserved, as soon as she was alone, and watch till I departed, your conscience quite calm. You would be hindering mischief."

I protested against playing that treacherous part in my employer's house. And, besides, I urged the cruelty and selfishness of his destroying Mrs. Linton's tranquility for his satisfaction.

"The commonest occurrence startles her painfully," I said. "She's all nerves, and she couldn't bear the surprise, I'm positive. Don't persist, sir! Or else I shall be obliged to inform my master of your designs, and he'll take measures to secure his house and its inmates from any such unwarrantable intrusions!"

"In that case I'll take measures to secure you, woman!" exclaimed Heathcliff. "You shall not leave Wuthering Heights till tomorrow morning. It is a foolish story to assert that Catherine could not bear to see me, and as to surprising her, I don't desire it. You must prepare her—ask her if I may come. You say she never mentions my name, and that I am never mentioned to her. To whom should she mention me if I am a forbidden topic in the house? She thinks you are all spies for her husband. Oh, I've no doubt she's in hell among you! I guess by her silence, as much as anything, what she feels. You say she is often restless, and anxious looking. Is that a proof of tranquility? You talk of her mind being unsettled. How the devil could it be otherwise in her frightful isolation? And that insipid, paltry creature attending her from duty and humanity! From pity and charity! He might as well plant an oak in a flower pot, and expect it to thrive, as imagine he can restore her to vigor in the soil of his shallow cares!" Spittle flew from his mouth as he postulated on Edgar's lack of husbandly love. "Let us settle it at once. Will you stay here, and am I to fight my way to Catherine over Linton and his footman? Or will you be my friend, as you have been hitherto, and do what I request? Decide! Because there is no reason for my lingering another minute, if you persist in your stubborn ill-nature!"

Well, Mr. Lockwood, I argued and complained, and flatly refused him fifty times, but in the long run, he forced me to an agreement. I engaged to carry a letter from him to my mistress, and should she consent, I promised to let him have intelligence of Linton's next absence from home, when he might come, and get in as he was able. I wouldn't be there, and my fellow servants should be equally out of the way.

Was it right or wrong? I fear it was wrong, though expedient. I thought I prevented another explosion by my compliance, and I thought, too, it might create a favorable crisis in Catherine's mental illness. Then I remembered Mr. Edgar's stern rebuke of my carrying tales, and I tried to smooth away all disquietude on the subject, by affirming, with frequent iteration, that that betrayal of trust, if it merited so harsh an appellation, should be the last. Notwithstanding, my journey homeward was sadder than my journey thither, and many misgivings I had, ere I could prevail on myself to put the missive into Mrs. Linton's hand.

But here is Kenneth, I'll go down, and tell him how much better you are. My history is dree, as we say, and will serve to while away another morning.

Dree, and dreary! I reflected as the good woman descended to receive the doctor. And not exactly of the kind which I should have chosen to amuse me. But never mind! I'll extract wholesome medicines from Mrs. Dean's bitter herbs, and firstly, let me beware of the fascination that lurks in Catherine Heathcliff's brilliant eyes. I should be in a curious taking if I surrendered my heart to that young person, and the daughter turned out a second edition of the mother.

That night when my hand closed around my member, I pictured the blonde young goddess who inhabited Wuthering Heights, and perhaps not surprising given the feverish nature of my illness, I also pictured her mother with her; and the two together pleasured me to heights I had never before achieved.

CHAPTER 26

*a*NOTHER WEEK OVER—and I am so many days nearer health, and spring! I have now heard all my neighbor's history, at different sittings, as the housekeeper could spare time from more important occupations. I'll continue it in her own words, only a little condensed. She is, on the whole, a very fair narrator, and I don't think I could improve her style.

In the evening, she said, the evening of my visit to the Heights, I knew, as well as if I saw him, that Mr. Heathcliff was about the place, and I shunned going out, because I still carried his letter in my pocket, and didn't want to be threatened or teased any more. I had made up my mind not to give it till my master went somewhere, as I could not guess how its receipt would affect Catherine. The consequence was, that it did not reach her before the lapse of three days. The fourth was Sunday, and I brought it into her room after the family were gone to church.

There was a manservant left to keep the house with me, and we generally made a practice of locking the doors during the hours of service. But on that occasion the weather was so warm and pleasant that

I set them wide open. To fulfill my engagement, as I knew who would be coming, I told my companion that the mistress wished very much for some oranges, and he must run over to the village and get a few, to be paid for on the morrow. He departed, and I went upstairs.

Mrs. Linton sat in a loose white dress, with a light shawl over her shoulders, in the recess of the open window, as usual. Her thick, long hair had been partly removed at the beginning of her illness, and now she wore it simply combed in its natural tresses over her temples and neck. Her appearance was altered, as I had told Heathcliff, but when she was calm, there seemed unearthly beauty in the change.

The flash of her eyes had been succeeded by a dreamy and melancholy softness, they no longer gave the impression of looking at the objects around her. They appeared always to gaze beyond, and far beyond—you would have said out of this world. Then, the paleness of her face—its haggard aspect having vanished as she recovered flesh— and the peculiar expression arising from her mental state, though painfully suggestive of their causes, added to the touching interest which she awakened. Invariably to me, I know, and to any person who saw her, I should think, refuted more tangible proofs of convalescence, and stamped her as one doomed to decay.

A book lay spread on the sill before her, and the scarcely perceptible wind fluttered its leaves at intervals. I believe Linton had laid it there for she never endeavored to divert herself with reading, or occupation of any kind. He would spend many an hour in trying to entice her attention to some subject which had formerly been her amusement.

She was conscious of his aim, and in her better moods endured his efforts placidly, only showing their uselessness by now and then suppressing a wearied sigh, and checking him at last with the saddest of smiles and kisses. At other times, she would turn petulantly away, and hide her face in her hands, or even push him off angrily, and then he took care to let her alone, for he was certain of doing no good.

Gimmerton chapel bells were still ringing, and the full, mellow flow of the beck in the valley came soothingly on the ear. It was a sweet substitute for the yet absent murmur of the summer foliage, which drowned that music about the Grange when the trees were in leaf. At Wuthering Heights it always sounded on quiet days following a great thaw or a season of steady rain. And of Wuthering Heights Catherine was thinking as she listened. That is, if she thought or listened at all, but she had the vague, distant look I mentioned before, which expressed no recognition of material things either by ear or eye.

"There's a letter for you, Mrs. Linton," I said, gently inserting it in one hand that rested on her knee. "You must read it immediately, because it wants an answer. Shall I break the seal?"

"Yes," she answered, without altering the direction of her eyes.

I opened it—it was very short. "Now," I continued, "read it."

She drew away her hand, and let it fall. I replaced it in her lap, and stood waiting till it should please her to glance down, but that movement was so long delayed that at last I resumed, "Must I read it, ma'am? It is from Mr. Heathcliff."

There was a start and a troubled gleam of recollection, and a struggle to arrange her ideas. She lifted the letter, and seemed to peruse it, and when she came to the signature she sighed. Yet still I found she had not gathered its import, for, upon my desiring to hear her reply, she merely pointed to the name, and gazed at me with mournful and questioning eagerness.

"Well, he wishes to see you," said I, guessing her need of an interpreter. "He's in the garden by this time, and impatient to know what answer I shall bring."

As I spoke, I observed a large dog lying on the sunny grass beneath raise its ears as if about to bark, and then smoothing them back, announce, by a wag of the tail, that someone approached whom it did not consider a stranger.

Mrs. Linton bent forward, and listened breathlessly. The minute after a step traversed the hall, the open house was too tempting for Heathcliff to resist walking in. Most likely he supposed that I was inclined to shirk my promise, and so resolved to trust to his own audacity.

With straining eagerness Catherine gazed towards the entrance of her chamber. He did not hit the right room directly. She motioned me to admit him, but he found it out ere I could reach the door, and in a stride or two was at her side, and had her grasped in his arms.

He neither spoke nor loosed his hold for some five minutes, during which period he bestowed more kisses than ever he gave in his life before, I daresay. But then my mistress had kissed him first, and I plainly saw that he could hardly bear, for downright agony, to look into her face! The same conviction had stricken him as me, from the instant he beheld her, that there was no prospect of ultimate recovery there—she was fated, sure to die.

"Oh, Cathy! Oh, my life! How can I bear it?" was the first sentence he uttered, in a tone that did not seek to disguise his despair. And now he stared at her so earnestly that I thought the very intensity of his gaze would bring tears into his eyes, but they burned with anguish. They did not melt.

"What now?" said Catherine, leaning back, and returning his look with a suddenly clouded brow. Her humor was a mere vane for constantly varying caprices. "You and Edgar have broken my heart, Heathcliff! And you both come to bewail the deed to me, as if you were the people to be pitied! I shall not pity you, not I. You have killed me—and thriven on it, I think. How strong you are! How many years do you mean to live after I am gone?"

Heathcliff had knelt on one knee to embrace her, he attempted to rise, but she seized his hair, and kept him down.

"I wish I could hold you," she continued, bitterly, "till we were both dead! I shouldn't care what you suffered. I care nothing for your sufferings. Why shouldn't you suffer? I do! Will you forget me? Will you be happy when I am in the earth? Will you say twenty years hence, 'That's the grave of Catherine Earnshaw? I loved her long ago, and was wretched to lose her, but it is past. I've loved many others since.

My children are dearer to me than she was, and, at death, I shall not rejoice that I am going to her. I shall be sorry that I must leave them!' Will you say so, Heathcliff?"

"Don't torture me till I'm as mad as yourself," cried he, wrenching his head free, and grinding his teeth.

The two, to a cool spectator, made a strange and fearful picture. Well might Catherine deem that heaven would be a land of exile to her, unless with her mortal body she cast away her moral character also. Her present countenance had a wild vindictiveness in its white cheek, and a bloodless lip and scintillating eye, and she retained in her closed fingers a portion of the locks she had been grasping. As to her companion, while raising himself with one hand, he had taken her arm with the other, and so inadequate was his stock of gentleness to the requirements of her condition, that on his letting go I saw four distinct impressions left blue in the colorless skin.

"Are you possessed with a devil," he pursued, savagely, "to talk in that manner to me when you are dying? Do you reflect that all those words will be branded in my memory, and eating deeper eternally after you have left me? You know you lie to say I have killed you and, Catherine, you know that I could as soon forget you as my existence! Is it not sufficient for your infernal selfishness, that while you are at peace I shall writhe in the torments of hell?"

"I shall not be at peace," moaned Catherine, recalled to a sense of physical weakness by the violent, unequal throbbing of her heart, which beat visibly and audibly under this excess of agitation.

She said nothing further till the paroxysm was over, then she continued, more kindly, "I'm not wishing you greater torment than I have, Heathcliff. I only wish us never to be parted. And should a word of mine distress you hereafter, think I feel the same distress underground, and for my own sake, forgive me! Come here and kneel down again! You never harmed me in your life. Nay, if you nurse anger that will be worse to remember than my harsh words! Won't you come here again? Do!"

Heathcliff went to the back of her chair, and leant over, but not so far as to let her see his face, which was livid with emotion. She bent round to look at him, he would not permit it. Turning abruptly, he walked to the fireplace, where he stood, silent, with his back towards us.

Mrs. Linton's glance followed him suspiciously. Every movement woke a new sentiment in her. After a pause and a prolonged gaze, she resumed, addressing me in accents of indignant disappointment.

"Oh, you see, Nelly, he would not relent a moment to keep me out of the grave. That is how I'm loved! Well, never mind. That is not my Heathcliff. I shall love mine yet, and take him with me. He's in my soul. And," added she musingly, "the thing that irks me most is this shattered prison, after all. I'm tired, tired of being enclosed here. I'm wearying to escape into that glorious world, and to be always there, not seeing it dimly through tears, and yearning for it through the walls of an aching heart, but really with it, and in it. Nelly, you think you are better and more fortunate than I, in full health and strength. You are sorry for me—very soon that will be altered. I shall be sorry for you. I shall be incomparably beyond and above you all. I wonder he won't be near me!" She went on to herself. "I thought he wished it. Heathcliff, dear! You should not be sullen now. Do come to me, Heathcliff."

In her eagerness she rose and supported herself on the arm of the chair. At that earnest appeal he turned to her, looking absolutely desperate. His eyes, wide and wet, at last flashed fiercely on her, his breast heaved convulsively. An instant they held asunder, and then how they met I hardly saw, but Catherine made a spring, and he caught her, and they were locked in an embrace from which I thought my mistress would never be released alive. In fact, to my eyes, she seemed directly insensible. He flung himself into the nearest seat, and on my approaching hurriedly to ascertain if she had fainted, he gnashed at me, and foamed like a mad dog, and gathered her to him with greedy jealousy. I did not feel as if I were in the company of a creature of my own species. It appeared that he would not understand, though I spoke to him, so I stood off, and held my tongue, in great perplexity.

A movement of Catherine's relieved me a little presently. She put up her hand to clasp his neck, and bring her cheek to his as he held her. While he, in return, covering her with frantic caresses, said wildly. "You teach me now how cruel you've been—cruel and false. Why did you despise me? Why did you betray your own heart, Cathy? I have not one word of comfort. You deserve this. You have killed yourself. Yes, you may kiss me, and cry, and wring out my kisses and tears. They'll blight you—they'll damn you. You loved me—then what right had you to leave me? What right—answer me—for the poor fancy you felt for Linton? Because misery and degradation, and death, and nothing that God or Satan could inflict would have parted us, you, of your own will, did it. I have not broken your heart—you have broken it, and in breaking it, you have broken mine. So much the worse for me that I am strong. Do I want to live? What kind of living will it be when you—oh, God! Would you like to live with your soul in the grave?"

"Let me alone. Let me alone," sobbed Catherine. "If I've done wrong, I'm dying for it. It is enough! You left me too, but I won't upbraid you! I forgive you. Forgive me!"

"It is hard to forgive, and to look at those eyes, and feel those wasted hands," he answered. "Kiss me again, and don't let me see your eyes! I forgive what you have done to me. I love my murderer—but yours! How can I?"

They were silent—their faces hid against each other, and washed by each other's tears. At least, I suppose the weeping was on both sides, as it seemed Heathcliff could weep on a great occasion like this.

I grew very uncomfortable, meanwhile, for the afternoon wore fast away, the man whom I had sent off returned from his errand, and I could distinguish, by the shine of the western sun up the valley, a concourse thickening outside Gimmerton chapel porch.

"Service is over," I announced. "My master will be here in half an hour."

Heathcliff groaned a curse, and strained Catherine closer. She never moved.

Ere long I perceived a group of the servants passing up the road towards the kitchen wing. Mr. Linton was not far behind, he opened the gate himself and sauntered slowly up, probably enjoying the lovely afternoon that breathed as soft as summer.

"Now he is here," I exclaimed. "For heaven's sake, hurry down! You'll not meet any one on the front stairs. Do be quick, and stay among the trees till he is fairly in."

"I must go, Cathy," said Heathcliff, seeking to extricate himself from his companion's arms. "But if I live, I'll see you again before you are asleep. I won't stray five yards from your window."

"You must not go!" she answered, holding him as firmly as her strength allowed. "You shall not, I tell you."

"For one hour," he pleaded earnestly.

"Not for one minute," she replied.

"I must—Linton will be up immediately," persisted the alarmed intruder.

He would have risen, and unfixed her fingers by the act—she clung fast, gasping. There was mad resolution in her face.

"No!" she shrieked. "Oh, don't, don't go. It is the last time! Edgar will not hurt us. Heathcliff, I shall die! I shall die!"

"Damn the fool! There he is," cried Heathcliff, sinking back into his seat. "Hush, my darling! Hush, hush, Catherine! I'll stay. If he shot me so, I'd expire with a blessing on my lips."

And there they were fast again. I heard my master mounting the stairs—the cold sweat ran from my forehead. I was horrified.

"Are you going to listen to her ravings?" I said, passionately. "She does not know what she says. Will you ruin her, because she has not wit to help herself? Get up! You could be free instantly. That is the most diabolical deed that ever you did. We are all done for—master, mistress, and servant."

I wrung my hands, and cried out, and Mr. Linton hastened his step at the noise. In the midst of my agitation, I was sincerely glad to observe that Catherine's arms had fallen relaxed, and her head hung down.

"She's fainted, or dead," I thought. "So much the better. Far better that she should be dead, than lingering a burden and a misery-maker to all about her."

Edgar sprang to his unbidden guest, blanched with astonishment and rage. What he meant to do I cannot tell, however, the other stopped all demonstrations, at once, by placing the lifeless-looking form in his arms.

"Look there!" he said. "Unless you be a fiend, help her first—then you shall speak to me!"

He walked into the parlor, and sat down. Mr. Linton summoned me, and with great difficulty, and after resorting to many means, we managed to restore her to sensation, but she was all bewildered, she sighed, and moaned, and knew nobody. Edgar, in his anxiety for her, forgot her hated friend. I did not. I went, at the earliest opportunity, and besought him to depart, affirming that Catherine was better, and he should hear from me in the morning how she passed the night.

"I shall not refuse to go out of doors," he answered, "but I shall stay in the garden. And, Nelly, mind you keep your word tomorrow. I shall be under those larch-trees. Mind! Or I pay another visit, whether Linton be in or not."

He sent a rapid glance through the half-open door of the chamber, and, ascertaining that what I stated was apparently true, delivered the house of his luckless presence.

CHAPTER 27

ABOUT TWELVE O'CLOCK that night was born the Catherine you saw at Wuthering Heights. A puny, seven-months' child, and two hours after the mother died, having never recovered sufficient consciousness to miss Heathcliff, or know Edgar.

The latter's distraction at his bereavement is a subject too painful to be dwelt on, its after-effects showed how deep the sorrow sunk.

A great addition, in my eyes, was his being left without an heir. I bemoaned that, as I gazed on the feeble orphan, and I mentally abused old Linton for (what was only natural partiality) the securing his estate to his own daughter, instead of his son's.

An unwelcomed infant it was, poor thing! It might have wailed out of life, and nobody cared a morsel, during those first hours of existence. We redeemed the neglect afterwards, but its beginning was as friendless as its end is likely to be.

Next morning—bright and cheerful out of doors—stole softened in through the blinds of the silent room, and suffused the couch and its occupant with a mellow, tender glow.

Edgar Linton had his head laid on the pillow, and his eyes shut. His young and fair features were almost as deathlike as those of the form beside him, and almost as fixed. But his was the hush of exhausted anguish, and hers of perfect peace. Her brow smooth, her lids closed, her lips wearing the expression of a smile, no angel in heaven could be more beautiful than she appeared. And I partook of the infinite calm in which she lay. My mind was never in a holier frame than while I gazed on that untroubled image of Divine rest.

I instinctively echoed the words she had uttered a few hours before. "Incomparably beyond and above us all! Whether still on earth or now in heaven, her spirit is at home with God!"

I don't know if it be a peculiarity in me, but I am seldom otherwise than happy while watching in the chamber of death, should no frenzied or despairing mourner share the duty with me. I see a repose that neither earth nor hell can break, and I feel an assurance of the endless and shadowless hereafter—the Eternity they have entered—where life is boundless in its duration, and love in its sympathy, and joy in its fullness.

I noticed on that occasion how much selfishness there is even in a love like Mr. Linton's, when he so regretted Catherine's blessed release! To be sure, one might have doubted, after the wayward and impatient existence she had led, whether she merited a haven of peace at last. One might doubt in seasons of cold reflection, but not then, in the presence of her corpse. It asserted its own tranquility, which seemed a pledge of equal quiet to its former inhabitant.

Do you believe such people are happy in the other world, sir? I'd give a great deal to know.

I declined answering Mrs. Dean's question, which struck me as something heterodox. She proceeded.

Retracing the course of Catherine Linton, I fear we have no right to think she is, but we'll leave her with her Maker.

The master looked asleep, and I ventured soon after sunrise to quit the room and steal out to the pure refreshing air. The servants thought me gone to shake off the drowsiness of my protracted watch, in reality, my chief motive was seeing Mr. Heathcliff. If he had remained among the larches all night, he would have heard nothing of the stir at the Grange, unless, perhaps, he might catch the gallop of the messenger going to Gimmerton. If he had come nearer, he would probably be aware, from the lights flitting to and fro, and the opening and shutting of the outer doors, that all was not right within.

I wished, yet feared, to find him. I felt the terrible news must be told, and I longed to get it over, but how to do it I did not know.

He was there—at least, a few yards further in the park, leant against an old ash-tree, his hat off, and his hair soaked with the dew that had gathered on the budded branches, and fell pattering round him. He had been standing a long time in that position, for I saw a pair of mice passing and repassing scarcely three feet from him, busy in building their nest, and regarding his proximity no more than that of a piece of timber. They flew off at my approach.

He raised his eyes and spoke. "She's dead!" he said. "I've not waited for you to learn that. Put your handkerchief away—don't snivel before me. Damn you all! She wants none of your tears!"

I was weeping as much for him as her. We do sometimes pity creatures that have none of the feeling either for themselves or others. When I first looked into his face, I perceived that he had got intelligence of the catastrophe, and a foolish notion struck me that his heart was quelled and he prayed, because his lips moved and his gaze was bent on the ground.

"Yes, she's dead!" I answered, checking my sobs and drying my cheeks. "Gone to heaven, I hope, where we may, every one, join her, if we take due warning and leave our evil ways to follow good!"

"Did she take due warning, then?" asked Heathcliff, attempting a sneer. "Did she die like a saint? Come, give me a true history of the event. How did—?"

He endeavored to pronounce the name, but could not manage it, and compressing his mouth he held a silent combat with his inward agony, defying, meanwhile, my sympathy with an unflinching, ferocious stare.

"How did she die?" he resumed, at last—fain, notwithstanding his hardihood, to have a support behind him, for, after the struggle, he trembled, in spite of himself, to his very finger-ends.

"Poor wretch!" I thought, "you have a heart and nerves the same as your brother men! Why should you be anxious to conceal them? Your pride cannot blind God! You tempt him to wring them, till he forces a cry of humiliation."

"Quietly as a lamb!" I answered, aloud. "She drew a sigh, and stretched herself, like a child reviving, and sinking again to sleep, and five minutes after I felt one little pulse at her heart, and nothing more!"

"And—did she ever mention me?" he asked, hesitating, as if he dreaded the answer to his question would introduce details that he could not bear to hear.

"Her senses never returned. She recognized nobody from the time you left her," I said. "She lies with a sweet smile on her face, and her latest ideas wandered back to pleasant early days. Her life closed in a gentle dream—may she wake as kindly in the other world!"

"May she wake in torment!" he cried, with frightful vehemence, stamping his foot, and groaning in a sudden paroxysm of ungovernable passion. "Why, she's a liar to the end! Where is she? Not there—not in heaven—not perished—where? Oh! you said you cared nothing for my sufferings! And I pray one prayer—I repeat it till my tongue stiffens—Catherine Earnshaw, may you not rest as long as I am living, you said I killed you—haunt me, then! The murdered do haunt their murderers, I believe. I know that ghosts have wandered on earth. Be with me always—take any form—drive me mad! only do not leave me in this abyss, where I cannot find you! Oh, God! It is unutterable! I cannot live without my life! I cannot live without my soul!"

He dashed his head against the knotted trunk, and, lifting up his eyes, howled, not like a man, but like a savage beast being goaded to death with knives and spears.

I observed several splashes of blood about the bark of the tree, and his hand and forehead were both stained, probably the scene I witnessed was a repetition of others acted during the night. It hardly moved my compassion—it appalled me. Still, I felt reluctant to quit him so. But the moment he recollected himself enough to notice me watching, he thundered a command for me to go, and I obeyed. He was beyond my skill to quiet or console!

Mrs. Linton's funeral was appointed to take place on the Friday following her decease, and till then her coffin remained uncovered, and strewn with flowers and scented leaves, in the great drawing-room. Linton spent his days and nights there, a sleepless guardian, and—a circumstance concealed from all but me—Heathcliff spent his nights, at least, outside, equally a stranger to repose.

I held no communication with him. Still, I was conscious of his design to enter, if he could, and on the Tuesday, a little after dark, when my master, from sheer fatigue, had been compelled to retire a couple of hours, I went and opened one of the windows, moved by his perseverance to give him a chance of bestowing on the faded image of his idol one final adieu.

He did not omit to avail himself of the opportunity, cautiously and briefly, too cautiously to betray his presence by the slightest noise.

I shouldn't have discovered that he had been there, except for the disarrangement of the drapery about the corpse's face, and for observing on the floor a curl of light hair, fastened with a silver thread, which, on examination, I ascertained to have been taken from a locket hung round Catherine's neck. Heathcliff had opened the trinket and cast out its contents, replacing them by a black lock of his own. I twisted the two, and enclosed them together.

Mr. Earnshaw was, of course, invited to attend the remains of his sister to the grave. He sent no excuse, but he never came, so that, besides her husband, the mourners were wholly composed of tenants and servants. Isabella was not asked.

The place of Catherine's interment, to the surprise of the villagers, was neither in the chapel under the carved monument of the

Lintons, nor yet by the tombs of her own relations, outside. It was dug on a green slope in a corner of the kirkyard, where the wall is so low that heath and bilberry plants have climbed over it from the moor, and peat mould almost buries it. Her husband lies in the same spot now, and they have each a simple headstone above, and a plain grey block at their feet, to mark the graves.

CHAPTER 28

*T*HAT FRIDAY MADE THE LAST of our fine days for a month. In the evening the weather broke. The wind shifted from south to north-east, and brought rain first, and then sleet and snow.

On the morrow one could hardly imagine that there had been three weeks of summer. The primroses and crocuses were hidden under wintry drifts, the larks were silent, the young leaves of the early trees smitten and blackened. And dreary, and chill, and dismal, that morrow did creep over!

My master kept his room, I took possession of the lonely parlor, converting it into a nursery. And there I was, sitting with the moaning doll of a child laid on my knee, rocking it to and fro, and watching, meanwhile, the still driving flakes build up the uncurtained window, when the door opened, and some person entered, out of breath and laughing!

My anger was greater than my astonishment for a minute. I supposed it one of the maids, and I cried, "Have done! How dare you show your giddiness here. What would Mr. Linton say if he heard you?"

"Excuse me!" answered a familiar voice, "but I know Edgar is in bed, and I cannot stop myself."

With that the speaker came forward to the fire, panting and holding her hand to her side.

"I have run the whole way from Wuthering Heights!" she continued, after a pause, "except where I've flown. I couldn't count the number of falls I've had. Oh, I'm aching all over! Don't be alarmed! There shall be an explanation as soon as I can give it, only just have the goodness to step out and order the carriage to take me on to Gimmerton, and tell a servant to seek up a few clothes in my wardrobe."

The intruder was Mrs. Heathcliff. She certainly seemed in no laughing predicament. Her hair streamed on her shoulders, dripping with snow and water, she was dressed in the girlish dress she commonly wore, befitting her age more than her position—a low frock with short sleeves, and nothing on either head or neck. The frock was of light silk, and clung to her with wet, **and betrayed her increase, which showed that whatever Heathcliff had promised to Catherine, he had not kept himself celibate.**

Her feet were protected merely by thin slippers. Add to this a deep cut under one ear, which only the cold prevented from bleeding profusely, a white face scratched and bruised, and a frame hardly able to support itself through fatigue, and you may fancy my first fright was not much allayed when I had had leisure to examine her.

"My dear young lady," I exclaimed, "I'll stir nowhere, and hear nothing, till you have removed every article of your clothes, and put on dry things, and certainly you shall not go to Gimmerton tonight, so it is needless to order the carriage."

"Certainly I shall," she said, "walking or riding. Yet I've no objection to dress myself decently. And—ah, see how it flows down my neck now! The fire does make it smart."

She insisted on my fulfilling her directions, before she would let me touch her, and not till after the coachman had been instructed to get ready, and a maid set to pack up some necessary attire, did I obtain her consent for binding the wound and helping to change her garments.

"Now, Ellen," she said, when my task was finished and she was seated in an easy chair on the hearth, with a cup of tea before her, "you sit down opposite me, and put poor Catherine's baby away. I don't like to see it! You mustn't think I care little for Catherine, because I behaved so foolishly on entering. I've cried, too, bitterly—yes, more than anyone else has reason to cry. We parted unreconciled, you remember, and I shan't forgive myself. But, for all that, I was not going to sympathies with him—the brute beast! Oh, give me the poker! This is the last thing of his I have about me." She slipped the gold ring from her third finger, and threw it on the floor. "I'll smash it!" she continued, striking it with childish spite, "and then I'll burn it!"

She took and dropped the misused article among the coals. "There! He shall buy another, if he gets me back again. He'd be capable of coming to seek me, to tease Edgar. I dare not stay, lest that notion should possess his wicked head! Besides, Edgar has not been kind, has he? And I won't come suing for his assistance, nor will I bring him into more trouble. Necessity compelled me to seek shelter here, though, if I had not learned he was out of the way, I'd have halted at the kitchen, washed my face, warmed myself, got you to bring what I wanted, and departed again to anywhere out of the reach of my accursed—of that incarnate goblin! Ah, he was in such a fury! If he had caught me! It's a pity Earnshaw is not his match in strength. I wouldn't have run till I'd seen him all but demolished, had Hindley been able to do it!"

"Well, don't talk so fast, Miss!" I interrupted, "you'll disorder the handkerchief I have tied round your face, and make the cut bleed again. Drink your tea, and take breath, and give over laughing. Laughter is sadly out of place under this roof, and in your condition!"

"An undeniable truth," she replied. "Listen to that child! It maintains a constant wail—send it out of my hearing for an hour, I shan't stay any longer."

I rang the bell, and committed it to a servant's care, and then I inquired what had urged her to escape from Wuthering Heights in such an unlikely plight, and where she meant to go, as she refused remaining with us.

"I ought, and I wish to remain," answered she, "to cheer Edgar and take care of the baby, for two things, and because the Grange is my right home. But I tell you Heathcliff wouldn't let me! Do you think he could bear to see me grow fat and merry—could bear to think that we were tranquil, and not resolve on poisoning our comfort? Now, I have the satisfaction of being sure that he detests me, to the point of its annoying him seriously to have me within earshot or eyesight. I notice, when I enter his presence, the muscles of his countenance are involuntarily distorted into an expression of hatred, partly arising from his knowledge of the good causes I have to feel that sentiment for him, and partly from original aversion. It is strong enough to make me feel pretty certain that he would not chase me over England, supposing I contrived a clear escape, and therefore I must get quite away. I've recovered from my first desire to be killed by him. I'd rather he'd kill himself! He has extinguished my love effectually, and so I'm at my ease. I can recollect yet how I loved him, and can dimly imagine that I could still be loving him, if—no, no! Even if he had doted on me, the devilish nature would have revealed its existence somehow. Catherine had an awfully perverted taste to esteem him so dearly, knowing him so well. Monster! Would that he could be blotted out of creation, and out of my memory!"

"Hush, hush! He's a human being," I said. "Be more charitable. There are worse men than he is yet!"

"He's not a human being," she retorted, "and he has no claim on my charity. I gave him my heart, and he took and pinched it to death, and flung it back to me. People feel with their hearts, Ellen, and since he has destroyed mine, I have not power to feel for him. I would not, though he groaned from this to his dying day, and wept tears of blood for Catherine! No, indeed, indeed, I wouldn't!" And here Isabella began to cry; but, immediately dashing the water from her lashes, she recommenced.

"You asked, what has driven me to flight at last? I was compelled to attempt it, because I had succeeded in rousing his rage a pitch above his malignity. Pulling out the nerves with red hot pincers requires more coolness than knocking on the head. He was worked up to forget the fiendish prudence he boasted of, and proceeded to murderous violence. I experienced pleasure in being able to exasperate him. The sense of pleasure woke my instinct of self-preservation, so I fairly broke free, and if ever I come into his hands again he is welcome to a signal revenge.

"Yesterday, you know, Mr. Earnshaw should have been at the funeral. He kept himself sober for the purpose—tolerably sober. Not going to bed mad at six o'clock and getting up drunk at twelve. Consequently, he rose, in suicidal low spirits, as fit for the church as for a dance, and instead, he sat down by the fire and swallowed gin or brandy by tumblerfuls."

"Heathcliff—I shudder to name him yet again—has been a stranger in the house from last Sunday till today. Whether the angels have fed him, or his kin beneath, I cannot tell, but he has not eaten a meal with us for nearly a week. He has just come home at dawn, and gone upstairs to his chamber, locking himself in—as if anybody dreamt of coveting his company! There he has continued, praying like a Methodist. Only the deity he implored is senseless dust and ashes, and God, when addressed, was curiously confounded with his own black father! After concluding these precious orisons—and they lasted generally till he grew hoarse and his voice was strangled in his throat—he would be off again, always straight down to the Grange! I wonder Edgar did not send for a constable, and give him into custody! For me, grieved as I was about Catherine, it was impossible to avoid regarding this season of deliverance from degrading oppression as a holiday.

"I recovered spirits sufficient to bear Joseph's eternal lectures without weeping, and to move up and down the house less with the foot of a frightened thief than formerly. You wouldn't think that

I should cry at anything Joseph could say, but he and Hareton are detestable companions. I'd rather sit with Hindley, and hear his awful talk, than with 't' little master' and his staunch supporter, that odious old man!

"When Heathcliff is in, I'm often obliged to seek the kitchen and their society, or starve among the damp uninhabited chambers. When he is not, as was the case this week. I establish a table and chair at one corner of the house fire, and never mind how Mr. Earnshaw may occupy himself, and he does not interfere with my arrangements. He is quieter now than he used to be, if no one provokes him—more sullen and depressed, and less furious. Joseph affirms he's sure he's an altered man, that the Lord has touched his heart, and he is saved 'so as by fire.' I'm puzzled to detect signs of the favorable change, but it is not my business.

"Yester-evening I sat in my nook reading some old books till late on towards twelve. It seemed so dismal to go upstairs, with the wild snow blowing outside, and my thoughts continually reverting to the kirkyard and the new-made grave! I dared hardly lift my eyes from the page before me, that melancholy scene so instantly usurped its place.

"Hindley sat opposite, his head leant on his hand, perhaps meditating on the same subject. He had ceased drinking at a point below irrationality, and had neither stirred nor spoken during two or three hours. There was no sound through the house but the moaning wind, which shook the windows every now and then, the faint crackling of the coals, and the click of my snuffers as I removed at intervals the long wick of the candle. Hareton and Joseph were probably fast asleep in bed. It was very, very sad. And while I read I sighed, for it seemed as if all joy had vanished from the world, never to be restored.

"The doleful silence was broken at length by the sound of the kitchen latch. Heathcliff had returned from his watch earlier than usual, owing, I suppose, to the sudden storm.

"That entrance was fastened, and we heard him coming round to get in by the other. I rose with an irrepressible expression of what I felt on my lips, which induced my companion, who had been staring towards the door, to turn and look at me."

"'I'll keep him out five minutes,' he exclaimed. 'You won't object?'

"'No, you may keep him out the whole night for me,' I answered. 'Do! Put the key in the look, and draw the bolts.'

"Earnshaw accomplished this ere his guest reached the front, he then came and brought his chair to the other side of my table, leaning over it, and searching in my eyes for a sympathy with the burning hate that gleamed from his. As he both looked and felt like an assassin, he couldn't exactly find that, but he discovered enough to encourage him to speak.

"'You, and I,' he said, 'have each a great debt to settle with the man out yonder! If we were neither of us cowards, we might combine to discharge it. Are you as soft as your brother? Are you willing to endure to the last, and not once attempt a repayment?'

"'I'm weary of enduring now,' I replied, 'and I'd be glad of a retaliation that wouldn't recoil on myself, but treachery and violence are spears pointed at both ends—they wound those who resort to them worse than their enemies.'

"'Treachery and violence are a just return for treachery and violence!' cried Hindley. 'Mrs. Heathcliff, I'll ask you to do nothing, but sit still and be dumb. Tell me now, can you? I'm sure you would have as much pleasure as I in witnessing the conclusion of the fiend's existence. He'll be your death unless you overreach him, and he'll be my ruin. Damn the hellish villain! He knocks at the door as if he were master here already! Promise to hold your tongue, and before that clock strikes—it wants three minutes of one—you're a free woman!'

"He took the implements which I described to you in my letter from his breast, and would have turned down the candle. I snatched it away, however, and seized his arm.

"'I'll not hold my tongue!' I said. 'You mustn't touch him. Let the door remain shut, and be quiet!'

"'No! I've formed my resolution, and by God I'll execute it!' cried the desperate being. 'I'll do you a kindness in spite of yourself, and Hareton justice! And you needn't trouble your head to screen me; Catherine is gone. Nobody alive would regret me, or be ashamed, though I cut my throat this minute—and it's time to make an end!'

"I might as well have struggled with a bear, or reasoned with a lunatic. The only resource left me was to run to a lattice and warn his intended victim of the fate that awaited him.

"'You'd better seek shelter somewhere else tonight!' I exclaimed, in rather a triumphant tone. 'Mr. Earnshaw has a mind to shoot you, if you persist in endeavoring to enter.'

"'You'd better open the door, you—' he answered, addressing me by some elegant term that I don't care to repeat.

"'I shall not meddle in the matter,' I retorted again. 'Come in and get shot, if you please. I've done my duty.'

"With that I shut the window and returned to my place by the fire, having too small a stock of hypocrisy at my command to pretend any anxiety for the danger that menaced him.

"Earnshaw swore passionately at me, affirming that I loved the villain yet, and calling me all sorts of names for the base spirit I evinced. And I, in my secret heart (and conscience never reproached me), thought what a blessing it would be for him should Heathcliff put him out of misery, and what a blessing for me should he send Heathcliff to his right abode! As I sat nursing these reflections, the casement behind me banged to the floor by a blow from the latter individual, and his black countenance looked blightingly through. The stanchions stood too close to suffer his shoulders to follow, and I smiled, exulting in my fancied security. His hair and clothes were whitened with snow, and his sharp cannibal teeth, revealed by cold and wrath, gleamed through the dark.

"'Isabella, let me in, or I'll make you repent!' he 'girned,' as Joseph calls it.

"'I cannot commit murder,' I replied. 'Mr. Hindley stands sentinel with a knife and loaded pistol.'

"'Let me in by the kitchen door,' he said.

"'Hindley will be there before me,' I answered. 'And that's a poor love of yours that cannot bear a shower of snow! We were left at peace in our beds as long as the summer moon shone, but the moment a blast of winter returns, you must run for shelter! Heathcliff, if I were you, I'd go stretch myself over her grave and die like a faithful dog. The world is surely not worth living in now, is it? You had distinctly impressed on me the idea that Catherine was the whole joy of your life. I can't imagine how you think of surviving her loss.'

"'He's there, is he?' exclaimed my companion, rushing to the gap. 'If I can get my arm out I can hit him!'

"I'm afraid, Ellen, you'll set me down as really wicked, but you don't know all, so don't judge. I wouldn't have aided or abetted an attempt on even his life for anything. Wish that he were dead, I must, and therefore I was fearfully disappointed, and unnerved by terror for the consequences of my taunting speech, when he flung himself on Earnshaw's weapon and wrenched it from his grasp.

"The charge exploded, and the knife, in springing back, closed into its owner's wrist. Heathcliff pulled it away by main force, slitting up the flesh as it passed on, and thrust it dripping into his pocket. He then took a stone, struck down the division between two windows, and sprang in. His adversary had fallen senseless with excessive pain and the flow of blood that gushed from an artery or a large vein.

"The ruffian kicked and trampled on him, and dashed his head repeatedly against the flags, holding me with one hand, meantime, to prevent me summoning Joseph.

"He exerted preter-human self-denial in abstaining from finishing him completely; but getting out of breath, he finally desisted, and dragged the apparently inanimate body on to the settle.

"There he tore off the sleeve of Earnshaw's coat, and bound up the wound with brutal roughness, spitting and cursing during the operation as energetically as he had kicked before. Being at liberty, I lost no time in seeking the old servant, who, having gathered by degrees the purport of my hasty tale, hurried below, gasping, as he descended the steps two at once.

"'What is there to do, now? What is there to do, now?'

"'There's this to do,' thundered Heathcliff, 'that your master's mad, and should he last another month, I'll have him to an asylum. And how the devil did you come to fasten me out, you toothless hound? Don't stand muttering and mumbling there. Come, I'm not going to nurse him. Wash that stuff away, and mind the sparks of your candle—it is more than half brandy!'

"'And so ye've been murdering on him?' exclaimed Joseph, lifting his hands and eyes in horror. 'If ever I seed a sight like this! May the Lord—'

"Heathcliff gave him a push on to his knees in the middle of the blood, and flung a towel to him; but instead of proceeding to dry it up, he joined his hands and began a prayer, which excited my laughter from its odd phraseology. I was in the condition of mind to be shocked at nothing. In fact, I was as reckless as some malefactors show themselves at the foot of the gallows.

"'Oh, I forgot you,' said the tyrant. 'You shall do that. Down with you. And you conspire with him against me, do you, viper? There, that is work fit for you!'

"He shook me till my teeth rattled, and pitched me beside Joseph, who steadily concluded his supplications, and then rose, vowing he would set off for the Grange directly. Mr. Linton was a magistrate, and though he had fifty wives dead, he should inquire into this.

"He was so obstinate in his resolution, that Heathcliff deemed it expedient to compel from my lips a recapitulation of what had taken place, standing over me, heaving with malevolence, as I reluctantly delivered the account in answer to his questions.

"It required a great deal of labor to satisfy the old man that Heathcliff was not the aggressor, especially with my hardly wrung replies. However, Mr. Earnshaw soon convinced him that he was alive still. Joseph hastened to administer a dose of spirits, and by their succor his master presently regained motion and consciousness.

"Heathcliff, aware that his opponent was ignorant of the treatment received while insensible, called him deliriously intoxicated, and said he should not notice his atrocious conduct further, but advised him to get to bed. To my joy, he left us, after giving this judicious counsel, and Hindley stretched himself on the hearthstone. I departed to my own room, marveling that I had escaped so easily.

"This morning, when I came down, about half an hour before noon, Mr. Earnshaw was sitting by the fire, deadly sick. His evil genius, almost as gaunt and ghastly, leant against the chimney. Neither appeared inclined to dine, and, having waited till all was cold on the table, I commenced alone.

"Nothing hindered me from eating heartily, and I experienced a certain sense of satisfaction and superiority, as, at intervals, I cast a look towards my silent companions, and felt the comfort of a quiet conscience within me.

"After I had done, I ventured on the unusual liberty of drawing near the fire, going round Earnshaw's seat, and kneeling in the corner beside him.

"Heathcliff did not glance my way, and I gazed up, and contemplated his features almost as confidently as if they had been turned to stone. His forehead, that I once thought so manly, and that I now think so diabolical, was shaded with a heavy cloud. His basilisk eyes were nearly quenched by sleeplessness, and weeping, perhaps, for the lashes were wet then; his lips devoid of their ferocious sneer, and sealed in an expression of unspeakable sadness. Had it been another, I would have covered my face in the presence of such profound grief. In his case, I was gratified, and, ignoble as it seems to insult a fallen enemy, I couldn't miss this chance of sticking in a dart. his weakness was the only time when I could taste the delight of paying wrong for wrong."

"Fie, fie, Miss!" I interrupted. "One might suppose you had never opened a Bible in your life. If God afflict your enemies, surely that ought to suffice you. It is both mean and presumptuous to add your torture to his!"

"In general I'll allow that it would be, Ellen," she continued. "But what misery laid on Heathcliff could content me, unless I have a hand in it? I'd rather he suffered less, if I might cause his sufferings and he might know that I was the cause. Oh, I owe him so much. On only one condition can I hope to forgive him. It is, if I may take an eye for an eye, a tooth for a tooth, for every wrench of agony return a wrench. Reduce him to my level. As he was the first to injure, make him the first to implore pardon, and then—why then, Ellen, I might show you some generosity. But it is utterly impossible I can ever be revenged, and therefore I cannot forgive him. Hindley wanted some water, and I handed him a glass, and asked him how he was.

"'Not as ill as I wish,' he replied. 'But leaving out my arm, every inch of me is as sore as if I had been fighting with a legion of imps!'

"'Yes, no wonder,' was my next remark. 'Catherine used to boast that she stood between you and bodily harm. She meant that certain persons would not hurt you for fear of offending her. It's well people don't really rise from their grave, or, last night, she might have witnessed a repulsive scene! Are not you bruised, and cut over your chest and shoulders?'

"'I can't say,' he answered, 'but what do you mean? Did he dare to strike me when I was down?'

"'He trampled on and kicked you, and dashed you on the ground,' I whispered. 'And his mouth watered to tear you with his teeth, because he's only half man, not so much, and the rest fiend.'

"Mr. Earnshaw looked up, like me, to the countenance of our mutual foe, who, absorbed in his anguish, seemed insensible to anything around him. The longer he stood, the plainer his reflections revealed their blackness through his features.

"'Oh, if God would but give me strength to strangle him in my last agony, I'd go to hell with joy,' groaned the impatient man, writhing to rise, and sinking back in despair, convinced of his inadequacy for the struggle.

"'Nay, it's enough that he has murdered one of you,' I observed aloud. 'At the Grange, everyone knows your sister would have been living now had it not been for Mr. Heathcliff. After all, it is preferable to be hated than loved by him. When I recollect how happy we were—how happy Catherine was before he came—I'm fit to curse the day.'

"Most likely, Heathcliff noticed more the truth of what was said, than the spirit of the person who said it. His attention was roused, I saw, for his eyes rained down tears among the ashes, and he drew his breath in suffocating sighs. I stared full at him, and laughed scornfully. The clouded windows of hell flashed a moment towards me, the fiend who usually looked out, however, was so dimmed and drowned that I did not fear to hazard another sound of derision.

"'Get up, and begone out of my sight,' said the mourner.

"I guessed he uttered those words, at least, though his voice was hardly intelligible.

"'I beg your pardon,' I replied. 'But I loved Catherine too; and her brother requires attendance, which, for her sake, I shall supply. Now, that she's dead, I see her in Hindley. Hindley has exactly her eyes, if you had not tried to gouge them out, and made them black and red, and he has her—'

"'Get up, wretched idiot, before I stamp you to death!' he cried, making a movement that caused me to make one also.

"'But then,' I continued, holding myself ready to flee, 'if poor Catherine had trusted you, and assumed the ridiculous, contemptible, degrading title of Mrs. Heathcliff, she would soon have presented a similar picture! She wouldn't have borne your abominable behavior quietly. Her detestation and disgust must have found voice.'

"The back of the settle and Earnshaw's person interposed between me and him, so instead of endeavoring to reach me, he snatched a dinner knife from the table and flung it at my head. It struck beneath my ear, and stopped the sentence I was uttering. But, pulling it out, I sprang to the door and delivered another, which I hope went a little deeper than his missile.

"The last glimpse I caught of him was a furious rush on his part, checked by the embrace of his host, and both fell locked together on the hearth. In my flight through the kitchen I bid Joseph speed to his master. I knocked over Hareton, who was hanging a litter of puppies from a chair-back in the doorway, and, blessed as a soul, escaped from purgatory, I bounded, leaped, and flew down the steep road; then, quitting its windings, shot direct across the moor, rolling over banks, and wading through marshes. Precipitating myself, in fact, towards the beacon light of the Grange. And far rather would I be condemned to a perpetual dwelling in the infernal regions than, even for one night, abide beneath the roof of Wuthering Heights again."

Isabella ceased speaking, and took a drink of tea, then she rose, and bidding me put on her bonnet, and a great shawl I had brought. She turned a deaf ear to my entreaties for her to remain another hour, and stepped on to a chair, kissed Edgar's and Catherine's portraits, bestowed a similar salute on me, and descended to the carriage, accompanied by Fanny, who yelped wild with joy at recovering her mistress. She was driven away, never to revisit this neighborhood. A regular correspondence was established between her and my master when things were more settled.

I believe her new abode was in the south, near London, there she had a son born a few months subsequent to her escape. He was christened Linton, and, from the first, she reported him to be an ailing, peevish creature.

Mr. Heathcliff, meeting me one day in the village, inquired where she lived. I refused to tell. He remarked that it was not of any moment, only she must beware of coming to her brother. She should not be with him, if he had to keep her himself.

Though I would give no information, he discovered, through some of the other servants, both her place of residence and the existence of the child. Still, he didn't molest her, for which forbearance she might thank his aversion, I suppose.

He often asked about the infant, when he saw me, and on

hearing its name, smiled grimly, and observed: "They wish me to hate it too, do they?"

"I don't think they wish you to know anything about it," I answered.

"But I'll have it," he said, "when I want it. They may reckon on that!"

Fortunately, Isabella died before Heathcliff was able to seize possession of their child. It was thirteen years after the decease of Catherine, when Linton was twelve, or a little more.

On the day succeeding Isabella's unexpected visit I had no opportunity of speaking to my master. He shunned conversation, and was fit for discussing nothing. When I could get him to listen, I saw it pleased him that his sister had left her husband, whom he abhorred with an intensity that the mildness of his nature would scarcely seem to allow. So deep and sensitive was his aversion, that he refrained from going anywhere where he was likely to see or hear of Heathcliff.

Grief, and that together, transformed him into a complete hermit. He threw up his office of magistrate, ceased even to attend church, avoided the village on all occasions. He spent a life of entire seclusion within the limits of his park and grounds, only varied by solitary rambles on the moors, and visits to the grave of his wife, mostly at evening, or early morning before other wanderers were abroad.

But he was too good to be thoroughly unhappy long. He didn't pray for Catherine's soul to haunt him. Time brought resignation, and a melancholy sweeter than common joy. He recalled her memory with ardent, tender love, and hopeful aspiring to the better world, where he doubted not she was gone.

And he had earthly consolation and affections also. For a few days, I said, he seemed regardless of the puny successor to the departed. That coldness melted as fast as snow in April, and ere the tiny thing could stammer a word or totter a step it wielded a despot's scepter in his heart.

It was named Catherine, but he never called it the name in full, as he had never called the first Catherine short—probably because

Heathcliff had a habit of doing so. The little one was always Cathy. It formed to him a distinction from the mother, and yet a connection with her, and his attachment sprang from its relation to her, far more than from its being his own.

I used to draw a comparison between him and Hindley Earnshaw, and perplex myself to explain satisfactorily why their conduct was so opposite in similar circumstances. They had both been fond husbands, and were both attached to their children, and I could not see how they shouldn't both have taken the same road, for good or evil. But, I thought in my mind, Hindley, with apparently the stronger head, has shown himself sadly the worse and the weaker man. When his ship struck, the captain abandoned his post, and the crew, instead of trying to save her, rushed into riot and confusion, leaving no hope for their luckless vessel.

Linton, on the contrary, displayed the true courage of a loyal and faithful soul. He trusted God, and God comforted him. One hoped, and the other despaired. They chose their own lots, and were righteously doomed to endure them.

But you'll not want to hear my moralizing, Mr. Lockwood, you'll judge, as well as I can, all these things. At least, you'll think you will, and that's the same.

The end of Earnshaw was what might have been expected. It followed fast on his sister's. There were scarcely six months between them. We, at the Grange, never got a very succinct account of his state preceding it. All that I did learn was on occasion of going to aid in the preparations for the funeral. Mr. Kenneth came to announce the event to my master.

"Well, Nelly," said he, riding into the yard one morning, too early not to alarm me with an instant presentiment of bad news. "It's yours and my turn to go into mourning at present. Who's given us the slip now, do you think?"

"Who?" I asked in a flurry.

"Why, guess!" he returned, dismounting, and slinging his bridle on a hook by the door. "And nip up the corner of your apron. I'm certain you'll need it."

"Not Mr. Heathcliff, surely?" I exclaimed.

"What! Would you have tears for him?" said the doctor. "No, Heathcliff's a tough young fellow. He looks blooming today. I've just seen him. He's rapidly regaining flesh since he lost his better half."

"Who is it, then, Mr. Kenneth?" I repeated impatiently.

"Hindley Earnshaw! Your old friend Hindley," he replied, "and my wicked gossip. Though he's been too wild for me this long while. There! I said we should draw water. But cheer up! He died true to his character, drunk as a lord. Poor lad! I'm sorry, too. One can't help missing an old companion. though he had the worst tricks with him that ever man imagined, and has done me many a rascally turn. He's barely twenty-seven, it seems, that's your own age. Who would have thought you were born in one year?"

I confess this blow was greater to me than the shock of Mrs. Linton's death. Ancient associations lingered round my heart. I sat down in the porch and wept as for a blood relation, desiring Kenneth to get another servant to introduce him to the master.

I could not hinder myself from pondering on the question, had he had fair play? Whatever I did, that idea would bother me. It was so tiresomely pertinacious that I resolved on requesting leave to go to Wuthering Heights, and assist in the last duties to the dead.

Mr. Linton was extremely reluctant to consent, but I pleaded eloquently for the friendless condition in which he lay, and I said my old master and foster-brother had a claim on my services as strong as his own. Besides, I reminded him that the child Hareton was his wife's nephew, and, in the absence of nearer kin, he ought to act as its guardian, and he ought to and must inquire how the property was left, and look over the concerns of his brother-in-law.

He was unfit for attending to such matters then, but he bid me speak to his lawyer, and at length permitted me to go. His lawyer had been Earnshaw's also. I called at the village, and asked him to accompany me. He shook his head, and advised that Heathcliff should be let alone, affirming, if the truth were known, Hareton would be found little else than a beggar.

"His father died in debt," he said, "the whole property is mortgaged, and the sole chance for the natural heir is to allow him an opportunity of creating some interest in the creditor's heart, that he may be inclined to deal leniently towards him."

When I reached the Heights, I explained that I had come to see everything carried on decently, and Joseph, who appeared in sufficient distress, expressed satisfaction at my presence. Mr. Heathcliff said he did not perceive that I was wanted, but I might stay and order the arrangements for the funeral, if I chose.

"Correctly," he remarked, "that fool's body should lie buried at the crossroads, without ceremony of any kind. I happened to leave him ten minutes yesterday afternoon, and in that interval he fastened the two doors of the house against me, and he has spent the night in drinking himself to death deliberately! We broke in this morning, for we heard him snorting like a horse, and there he was, laid over the settle. Flaying and scalping would not have wakened him. I sent for Kenneth, and he came, but not till the beast had changed into carrion. He was both dead and cold, and stark, and so you'll allow it was useless making more stir about him!"

The old servant confirmed this statement, but muttered, "I'd rather he'd gone himself for the doctor! I should have taken care of the master better nor him—and he wasn't dead when I left, naught o' t' sort!"

I insisted on the funeral being respectable. Mr. Heathcliff said I might have my own way there too. Only, he desired me to remember that the money for the whole affair came out of his pocket. He maintained a hard, careless deportment, indicative of neither joy nor sorrow. If anything, it expressed a flinty gratification at a piece of difficult work successfully executed. I observed once, indeed, something like exultation in his aspect. It was just when the people were bearing the coffin from the house. He had the hypocrisy to represent a mourner; and previous to following with Hareton, he lifted the unfortunate child on to the table and muttered, with peculiar gusto, "Now, my bonny lad, you are mine! And we'll see if one tree won't grow as crooked as another, with the same wind to twist it!"

The unsuspecting thing was pleased at this speech. He played with Heathcliff's whiskers, and stroked his cheek, but I divined its meaning, and observed tartly, "That boy must go back with me to Thrushcross Grange, sir. There is nothing in the world less yours than he is!"

"Does Linton say so?" he demanded.

"Of course—he has ordered me to take him," I replied.

"Well," said the scoundrel, "we'll not argue the subject now, but I have a fancy to try my hand at rearing a young one, so intimate to your master that I must supply the place of this with my own, if he attempt to remove it. I don't engage to let Hareton go undisputed, but I'll be pretty sure to make the other come! Remember to tell him."

This hint was enough to bind our hands. I repeated its substance on my return, and Edgar Linton, little interested at the commencement, spoke no more of interfering. I'm not aware that he could have done it to any purpose, had he been ever so willing.

The guest was now the master of Wuthering Heights. He held firm possession, and proved to the attorney—who, in his turn, proved it to Mr. Linton—that Earnshaw had mortgaged every yard of land he owned for cash to supply his mania for gaming, and he, Heathcliff, was the mortgagee.

In that manner Hareton, who should now be the first gentleman in the neighborhood, was reduced to a state of complete dependence on his father's inveterate enemy, and lives in his own house as a servant, deprived of the advantage of wages. Quite unable to right himself, because of his friendlessness, and his ignorance that he has been wronged.

CHAPTER 29

THE NARRATION OF THIS SAD TALE had inspired in me a kind of flagging of the spirits, which I meant to obviate by taking a ramble across the moors. The cold and snowy weather that had caused my illness had melted away, leaving behind a warmer, though still somewhat chill and damp, environment. Bundled up against the wind with an excess of shawls and scarves supplied by Mrs. Dean, I struck out from the Grange.

I had no direct intention of heading to the Heights, though I would not have minded catching a glimpse of young Cathy, should she be out for a walk herself, or a ride. Although I did not plan it such, my steps took me unfailingly toward the boundary between the properties, and thence to the stable where that other Catherine had spent so many passionate moments with Heathcliff.

I fancied I heard a low moan of pleasure, and stopped still in my tracks, wondering how my mind was deceiving me. Then I realized the sound was real, and human, and not the entreaties of a ghost, so I crept closer to the stable until I had reached the door, which was slightly ajar. It was the work of only a moment to ease the door open enough to admit the upper portion of my body so that I might perceive what went on. My jaw dropped at the astonishing spectacle before me: Cathy had taken up occupation of a bench, her skirt hiked above her hips, with Hareton looming above her. As I watched, he shoved his trousers down. His shaft throbbed in front of him, huge and hard, and he ground out something I could not hear. It must have been a command, for she pulled off and kicked aside her drawers. He knelt before her, his hands gripping her knees as she sat on the bench. Then he wrenched her thighs apart and applied his mouth to her with a vigorous lapping that made her moan and clutch his shoulders.

I leaned nearer to get a better view. Cathy threw her head back and encouraged him with hoarse cries. Before she could climax, Hareton lifted his mouth from her. Then, without a word, he reared up and plunged his engorged member deep inside her. She cried out and clutched him to her as he did so, and reached her completion almost immediately. That inflamed him to hammer harder at her, during which she enthusiastically beat on his back with her fists. His completion took a few moments longer, and it wrenched a cry from his throat.

When they were done, I wiped the sweat from my face and withdrew my head and shoulders from the doorway. I took a moment to adjust my own hard member in my trousers, then took off quickly down the road before one of them could take it in mind to come out and see me standing there, gaping.

My afternoon's ramble had sufficiently tired me to return to my bedroom and recommence listening to Mrs. Dean's tale, which I did as soon as I had applied my own fist to my shaft, and wrung it dry.

CHAPTER 30

HE TWELVE YEARS, continued Mrs. Dean, following that dismal period were the happiest of my life. My greatest troubles in their passage rose from our little lady's trifling illnesses, which she had to experience in common with all children, rich and poor.

For the rest, after the first six months, she grew like a larch, and could walk and talk too, in her own way, before the heath blossomed a second time over Mrs. Linton's dust.

She was the most winning thing that ever brought sunshine into a desolate house. A real beauty in face, with the Earnshaws' handsome dark eyes, but the Lintons' fair skin and small features, and yellow curling hair. Her spirit was high, though not rough, and qualified by a heart sensitive and lively to excess in its affections.

That capacity for intense attachments reminded me of her mother. Still, she did not resemble her, for she could be soft and mild as a dove, and she had a gentle voice and pensive expression. Her anger was never furious, her love never fierce. It was deep and tender.

However, it must be acknowledged, she had faults to foil her gifts. A propensity to be saucy was one, and a perverse will, that indulged children invariably acquire, whether they be good tempered or cross. If a servant chanced to vex her, it was always, "I shall tell papa!"

And if he reproved her, even by a look, you would have thought it a heart-breaking business. I don't believe he ever did speak a harsh word to her. He took her education entirely on himself, and made it an amusement. Fortunately, curiosity and a quick intellect made her an apt scholar. She learned rapidly and eagerly, and did honor to his teaching.

Till young Catherine reached the age of thirteen, she had not once been beyond the range of the park by herself. Mr. Linton would take her with him a mile or so outside, on rare occasions, but he trusted her to no one else. Gimmerton was an unsubstantial name in her ears, the chapel, the only building she had approached or entered, except her own home. Wuthering Heights and Mr. Heathcliff did not exist for her. She was a perfect recluse, and, apparently, perfectly contented.

Sometimes, indeed, while surveying the country from her nursery window, she would observe, "Ellen, how long will it be before I can walk to the top of those hills? I wonder what lies on the other side—is it the sea?"

"No, Miss Cathy," I would answer, "it is hills again, just like these."

"And what are those golden rocks like when you stand under them?" she once asked.

The abrupt descent of Peniston Crags particularly attracted her notice, especially when the setting sun shone on it and the topmost heights, and the whole extent of landscape besides lay in shadow.

I explained that they were bare masses of stone, with hardly enough earth in their clefts to nourish a stunted tree.

"And why are they bright so long after it is evening here?" she pursued.

"Because they are a great deal higher up than we are," replied I.

"You could not climb them. They are too high and steep. In winter, the frost is always there before it comes to us, and deep into summer I have found snow under that black hollow on the northeast side!"

"Oh, you have been on them!" she cried gleefully. "Then I can go, too, when I am a woman. Has Papa been, Ellen?"

"Papa would tell you, Miss," I answered, hastily, "that they are not worth the trouble of visiting. The moors, where you ramble with him, are much nicer, and Thrushcross park is the finest place in the world."

"But I know the park, and I don't know those," she murmured to herself. "And I should delight to look round me from the brow of that tallest point. My little pony Minny shall take me some time."

One of the maids mentioning the Fairy Cave quite turned her head with a desire to fulfill this project. She teased Mr. Linton about it, and he promised she should have the journey when she got older. But Miss Catherine measured her age by months, and, "Now, am I old enough to go to Peniston Crags?" was the constant question in her mouth.

The road thither wound close by Wuthering Heights. Edgar had not the heart to pass it, so she received as constantly the answer, "Not yet, love. Not yet."

I said Mrs. Heathcliff lived above a dozen years after quitting her husband. Her family was of a delicate constitution. She and Edgar both lacked the ruddy health that you will generally meet in these parts. What her last illness was, I am not certain. I conjecture, they died of the same thing, a kind of fever, slow at its commencement, but incurable, and rapidly consuming life towards the close.

She wrote to inform her brother of the probable conclusion of a four-months' indisposition under which she had suffered, and entreated him to come to her, if possible, for she had much to settle, and she wished to bid him adieu, and deliver Linton safely into his hands.

Her hope was that Linton might be left with him, as he had been with her. His father, she would fain convince herself, had no desire to assume the burden of his maintenance or education. My master hesitated not a moment in complying with her request. Reluctant as he was to leave home at ordinary calls, he flew to answer this. He commended Catherine to my peculiar vigilance, in his absence, with reiterated orders that she must not wander out of the park, even under my escort. He did not calculate on her going unaccompanied.

He was away three weeks. The first day or two, my charge sat in a corner of the library, too sad for either reading or playing. In that quiet state she caused me little trouble, but it was succeeded by an interval of impatient, fretful weariness, and being too busy, and too old then, to run up and down amusing her, I hit on a method by which she might entertain herself. I used to send her on her travels round the grounds—now on foot, and now on a pony, indulging her with a patient audience of all her real and imaginary adventures when she returned.

The summer shone in full prime, and she took such a taste for this solitary rambling that she often contrived to remain out from breakfast till tea, and then the evenings were spent in recounting her fanciful tales. I did not fear her breaking bounds, because the gates were generally locked, and I thought she would scarcely venture forth alone, if they had stood wide open.

Unluckily, my confidence proved misplaced. Catherine came to me, one morning, at eight o'clock, and said she was that day an Arabian merchant, going to cross the Desert with his caravan. I must give her plenty of provision for herself and beasts—a horse and three camels, personated by a large hound and a couple of pointers. I got together good store of dainties, and slung them in a basket on one side of the saddle, and she sprang up as gay as a fairy, sheltered by her wide-brimmed hat and gauze veil from the July sun, and trotted off with a merry laugh, mocking my cautious counsel to avoid galloping, and come back early.

The naughty thing never made her appearance at tea. One traveler, the hound, being an old dog and fond of its ease, returned, but neither Cathy, nor the pony, nor the two pointers were visible in any direction. I dispatched emissaries down this path, and that path, and at last went wandering in search of her myself.

There was a laborer working at a fence round a plantation, on the borders of the grounds. I inquired of him if he had seen our young lady.

"I saw her at morn," he replied. "She would have me to cut her a hazel switch, and then she leapt her Galloway over the hedge yonder, where it is lowest, and galloped out of sight."

You may guess how I felt at hearing this news. It struck me directly she must have started for Penistone Crags. "What will become of her?" I ejaculated, pushing through a gap which the man was repairing, and making straight to the highroad. I walked as if for a wager, mile after mile, till a turn brought me in view of the Heights, but no Catherine could I detect, far or near.

The Crags lie about a mile and a half beyond Mr. Heathcliff's place, and that is four from the Grange, so I began to fear night would fall ere I could reach them.

"And what if she should have slipped in clambering among them," I reflected, "and been killed, or broken some of her bones?"

My suspense was truly painful, and, at first, it gave me delightful relief to observe, in hurrying by the farmhouse, Charlie, the fiercest of the pointers, lying under a window, with swelled head and bleeding ear. I opened the wicket and ran to the door, knocking vehemently for admittance. A woman whom I knew, and who formerly lived at Gimmerton, answered. She had been servant there since the death of Mr. Earnshaw.

"Ah," said she, "you are come a-seeking your little mistress! Don't be frightened. She's here safe, but I'm glad it isn't the master."

"He is not at home then, is he?" I panted, quite breathless with quick walking and alarm.

"No, no," she replied. "Both he and Joseph are off, and I think they won't return this hour or more. Step in and rest you a bit."

I entered, and beheld my stray lamb seated on the hearth, rocking herself in a little chair that had been her mother's when a child.
Her hat was hung against the wall, and she seemed perfectly at home,
laughing and chattering, in the best spirits imaginable, to Hareton—
now a great, strong lad of eighteen—who stared at her with considerable curiosity and astonishment. He comprehended precious little
of the fluent succession of remarks and questions, which her tongue
never ceased pouring forth.

"Very well, Miss!" I exclaimed, concealing my joy under an
angry countenance. "This is your last ride till Papa comes back. I'll
not trust you over the threshold again, you naughty, naughty girl!"

"Aha, Ellen!" she cried, gaily, jumping up and running to my
side. "I shall have a pretty story to tell tonight, and so you've found me
out. Have you ever been here in your life before?"

"Put that hat on, and home at once," said I. "I'm dreadfully
grieved at you, Miss Cathy. You've done extremely wrong! It's no use
pouting and crying. That won't repay the trouble I've had, scouring
the country after you. To think how Mr. Linton charged me to keep
you in, and you stealing off so! It shows you are a cunning little fox,
and nobody will put faith in you anymore."

"What have I done?" sobbed she, instantly checked. "Papa
charged me nothing. He'll not scold me, Ellen—he's never cross, like
you!"

"Come, come!" I repeated. "I'll tie the ribbon. Now, let us
have no petulance. Oh, for shame! You thirteen years old, and such
a baby!"

This exclamation was caused by her pushing the hat from her
head, and retreating to the chimney out of my reach.

"Nay," said the servant, "don't be hard on the bonny lass, Mrs.
Dean. We made her stop. She'd fain have ridden forwards, afeard you
should be uneasy. Hareton offered to go with her, and I thought he
should. It's a wild road over the hills."

Hareton, during the discussion, stood with his hands in his

pockets, too awkward to speak, though he looked as if he did not relish my intrusion.

"How long am I to wait?" I continued, disregarding the woman's interference. "It will be dark in ten minutes. Where is the pony, Miss Cathy? And where is Phoenix? I shall leave you, unless you be quick, so please yourself."

"The pony is in the yard," she replied, "and Phoenix is shut in there. He's bitten—and so is Charlie. I was going to tell you all about it, but you are in a bad temper, and don't deserve to hear."

I picked up her hat, and approached to reinstate it, but perceiving that the people of the house took her part, she commenced capering round the room, and on my giving chase, ran like a mouse over and under and behind the furniture, rendering it ridiculous for me to pursue.

Hareton and the woman laughed, and she joined them, and waxed more impertinent still, till I cried, in great irritation, "Well, Miss Cathy, if you were aware whose house this is you'd be glad enough to get out."

"It's your father's, isn't it?" said she, turning to Hareton.

"Nay," he replied, looking down, and blushing bashfully.

He could not stand a steady gaze from her eyes, though they were just his own.

"Whose then—your master's?" she asked.

He colored deeper, with a different feeling, muttered an oath, and turned away.

"Who is his master?" continued the tiresome girl, appealing to me. "He talked about 'our house,' and 'our folk.' I thought he had been the owner's son. And he never said Miss. He should have done, shouldn't he, if he's a servant?"

Hareton grew black as a thundercloud at this childish speech. I silently shook my questioner, and at last succeeded in equipping her for departure.

"Now, get my horse," she said, addressing her unknown

kinsman as she would one of the stableboys at the Grange. "And you may come with me. I want to see where the goblin-hunter rises in the marsh, and to hear about the fairishes, as you call them. But make haste! What's the matter? Get my horse, I say."

"I'll see thee damned before I be thy servant!" growled the lad.

"You'll see me what!" asked Catherine in surprise.

"Damned—thou saucy witch!" he replied.

"There, Miss Cathy! You see you have got into pretty company," I interposed. "Nice words to be used to a young lady! Pray don't begin to dispute with him. Come, let us seek for Minny ourselves, and begone."

"But, Ellen," cried she, staring fixed in astonishment, "how dare he speak so to me? Mustn't he be made to do as I ask him? You wicked creature, I shall tell Papa what you said. Now, then!"

Hareton did not appear to feel this threat, so the tears sprang into her eyes with indignation. "You bring the pony," she exclaimed, turning to the woman, "and let my dog free this moment!"

"Softly, Miss," answered she addressed. "You'll lose nothing by being civil. Though Mr. Hareton, there, be not the master's son, he's your cousin. And I was never hired to serve you."

"He my cousin!" cried Cathy, with a scornful laugh.

"Yes, indeed," responded her reprover.

"Oh, Ellen! Don't let them say such things," she pursued in great trouble. "Papa is gone to fetch my cousin from London. My cousin is a gentleman's son. That my—" she stopped, and wept outright, upset at the bare notion of relationship with such a clown.

"Hush, hush!" I whispered. "People can have many cousins and of all sorts, Miss Cathy, without being any the worse for it, only they needn't keep their company, if they be disagreeable and bad."

"He's not—he's not my cousin, Ellen!" she went on, gathering fresh grief from reflection, and flinging herself into my arms for refuge from the idea.

I was much vexed at her and the servant for their mutual

revelations, having no doubt of Linton's approaching arrival, communicated by the former, being reported to Mr. Heathcliff; and feeling as confident that Catherine's first thought on her father's return would be to seek an explanation of the latter's assertion concerning her rude-bred kindred.

Hareton, recovering from his disgust at being taken for a servant, seemed moved by her distress, and, having fetched the pony round to the door, he took, to propitiate her, a fine crooked-legged terrier whelp from the kennel, and putting it into her hand, bid her whist! for he meant naught.

Pausing in her lamentations, she surveyed him with a glance of awe and horror, then burst forth anew.

I could scarcely refrain from smiling at this antipathy to the poor fellow, who was a well-made, athletic youth, good looking in features, and stout and healthy, but attired in garments befitting his daily occupations of working on the farm and lounging among the moors after rabbits and game. Still, I thought I could detect in his physiognomy a mind owning better qualities than his father ever possessed.

Good things lost amid a wilderness of weeds, to be sure, whose rankness far overtopped their neglected growth, yet, notwithstanding, evidence of a wealthy soil, that might yield luxuriant crops under other and favorable circumstances. Mr. Heathcliff, I believe, had not treated him physically ill, thanks to his fearless nature, which offered no temptation to that course of oppression. He had none of the timid susceptibility that would have given zest to ill-treatment, in Heathcliff's judgment.

He appeared to have bent his malevolence on making Hareton into a brute. He was never taught to read or write, never rebuked for any bad habit which did not annoy his keeper, never led a single step towards virtue, or guarded by a single precept against vice. And from what I heard, Joseph contributed much to his deterioration, by a narrow-minded partiality, which prompted him to flatter and pet him, as a boy, because he was the head of the old family. As he had been in the habit of accusing Catherine Earnshaw and Heathcliff, when children, of putting the master past his patience, and compelling him to seek solace in drink by what he termed their "offal ways," so at present he laid the whole burden of Hareton's faults on the shoulders of the usurper of his property.

If the lad swore, he wouldn't correct him, nor however culpably he behaved. It gave Joseph satisfaction, apparently, to watch him go the worst lengths. He allowed that the lad was ruined, that his soul was abandoned to perdition, but then, he reflected that Heathcliff must answer for it. Hareton's blood would be required at his hands, and there lay immense consolation in that thought.

Joseph had instilled into him a pride of name, and of his lineage, he would, had he dared, have fostered hate between him and the present owner of the Heights. But his dread of that owner amounted to superstition, and he confined his feelings regarding him to muttered innuendoes and private threats of God's punishments.

I don't pretend to be intimately acquainted with the mode of living customary in those days at Wuthering Heights. I only speak from hearsay, for I saw little. The villagers affirmed Mr. Heathcliff was tightfisted, and a cruel hard landlord to his tenants, but the house, inside, had regained its ancient aspect of comfort under female management, and the scenes of riot common in Hindley's time were not now enacted within its walls. The master was too gloomy to seek companionship with any people, good or bad, and he is yet.

This, however, is not making progress with my story. Miss Cathy rejected the peace-offering of the terrier, and demanded her own dogs, Charlie and Phoenix. They came limping and hanging their heads, and we set out for home, sadly out of sorts, every one of us.

I could not wring from my little lady how she had spent the day, except that, as I supposed, the goal of her pilgrimage was Peniston Crags. She'd arrived without adventure to the gate of the farmhouse, when Hareton happened to issue forth, attended by some canine followers, who attacked her train.

They had a smart battle, before their owners could separate them. That formed an introduction. Catherine told Hareton who she was, and where she was going, and asked him to show her the way, finally beguiling him to accompany her.

He opened the mysteries of the Fairy Cave, and twenty other queer places. But, being in disgrace, I was not favored with a description of the interesting objects she saw.

I could gather, however, that her guide had been a favorite till she hurt his feelings by addressing him as a servant, and Heathcliff's housekeeper hurt hers by calling him her cousin. Then the language he had held to her rankled in her heart, she who was always "love," and "darling," and "queen," and "angel," with everybody at the Grange, to be insulted so shockingly by a stranger! She did not comprehend it, and hard work I had to obtain a promise that she would not lay the grievance before her father. I explained how he objected to the whole household at the Heights, and how sorry he would be to find she had been there. I insisted most on the fact that if she revealed my negligence of his orders, he would perhaps be so angry that I should have to leave, and Cathy couldn't bear that prospect. She pledged her word, and kept it for my sake. After all, she was a sweet little girl.

CHAPTER 31

A LETTER, EDGED WITH BLACK, announced the day of my master's return. Isabella was dead, and he wrote to bid me get mourning for his daughter, and arrange a room, and other accommodations, for his youthful nephew.

Catherine ran wild with joy at the idea of welcoming her father back, and indulged most sanguine anticipations of the innumerable excellencies of her "real" cousin.

The evening of their expected arrival came. Since early morning she had been busy ordering her own small affairs, and now attired in her new black frock—poor thing! Her aunt's death impressed her with no definite sorrow—she obliged me, by constant worrying, to walk with her down through the grounds to meet them.

"Linton is just six months younger than I am," she chattered, as we strolled leisurely over the swells and hollows of mossy turf, under shadow of the trees. "How delightful it will be to have him for a playfellow! Aunt Isabella sent papa a beautiful lock of his hair. It was lighter than mine—more flaxen, and quite as fine. I have it carefully preserved in a little glass box, and I've often thought what a pleasure it would be to see its owner. Oh! I am happy—and Papa, dear, dear Papa! Come, Ellen, let us run! Come, run."

She ran, and returned and ran again, many times before my sober footsteps reached the gate, and then she seated herself on the grassy bank beside the path, and tried to wait patiently, but that was impossible. She couldn't be still a minute.

"How long they are!" she exclaimed. "Ah, I see, some dust on the road—they are coming! No! When will they be here? May we not go a little way—half a mile, Ellen, only just half a mile? Do say yes. To that clump of birches at the turn!"

I refused staunchly. At length, her suspense was ended. The traveling carriage rolled in sight. Miss Cathy shrieked and stretched out her arms as soon as she caught her father's face looking from the window. He descended, nearly as eager as herself, and a considerable interval elapsed ere they had a thought to spare for any but themselves.

While they exchanged caresses I took a peep in to see after Linton. He was asleep in a corner, wrapped in a warm, fur-lined cloak, as if it had been winter. A pale, delicate, effeminate boy, who might have been taken for my master's younger brother, so strong was the resemblance. But there was a sickly peevishness in his aspect that Edgar Linton never had.

The latter saw me looking, and having shaken hands, advised me to close the door, and leave him undisturbed, for the journey had fatigued him. Cathy would fain have taken one glance, but her father told her to come, and they walked together up the park, while I hastened before to prepare the servants.

"Now, darling," said Mr. Linton, addressing his daughter, as they halted at the bottom of the front steps. "Your cousin is not so strong or so merry as you are, and he has lost his mother, remember, a very short time since; therefore, don't expect him to play and run about with you directly. And don't harass him much by talking. Let him be quiet this evening, at least, will you?"

"Yes, yes, Papa," answered Catherine. "But I do want to see him, and he hasn't once looked out."

The carriage stopped, and the sleeper being roused, was lifted to the ground by his uncle.

"This is your cousin Cathy, Linton," he said, putting their little hands together. "She's fond of you already, and mind you don't grieve her by crying tonight. Try to be cheerful now, the travelling is at an end, and you have nothing to do but rest and amuse yourself as you please."

"Let me go to bed, then," answered the boy, shrinking from Catherine's salute, and he put his fingers to remove incipient tears.

"Come, come, there's a good child," I whispered, leading him in. "You'll make her weep too—see how sorry she is for you!"

I do not know whether it was sorrow for him, but his cousin put on as sad a countenance as himself, and returned to her father. All three entered, and mounted to the library, where tea laid ready.

I proceeded to remove Linton's cap and mantle, and placed him on a chair by the table, but he was no sooner seated than he began to cry afresh. My master inquired what was the matter.

"I can't sit on a chair," sobbed the boy.

"Go to the sofa, then, and Ellen shall bring you some tea," answered his uncle patiently.

He had been greatly tried during the journey, I felt convinced, by his fretful ailing charge. Linton slowly trailed himself off, and lay down. Cathy carried a footstool and her cup to his side.

At first she sat silent, but that could not last. She had resolved to make a pet of her little cousin, as she would have him to be, and she commenced stroking his curls, and kissing his cheek, and offering him tea in her saucer, like a baby. This pleased him, for he was not much better. He dried his eyes, and lightened into a faint smile.

"Oh, he'll do very well," said the master to me, after watching them a minute. "Very well, if we can keep him, Ellen. The company of a child of his own age will instill new spirit into him soon, and by wishing for strength he'll gain it."

"Ay, if we can keep him!" I mused to myself, and sore misgivings came over me that there was slight hope of that. And then, I thought, however will that weakling live at Wuthering Heights? Between his father and Hareton, what playmates and instructors they'll be.

Our doubts were presently decided—even earlier than I expected. I had just taken the children upstairs, after tea was finished, and seen Linton asleep. He would not suffer me to leave him till that was the case. I had come down, and was standing by the table in the hall, lighting a bedroom candle for Mr. Edgar, when a maid stepped out of the kitchen and informed me that Mr. Heathcliff's servant Joseph was at the door, and wished to speak with the master.

"I shall ask him what he wants first," I said, in considerable trepidation. "A very unlikely hour to be troubling people, and the instant they have returned from a long journey. I don't think the master can see him."

Joseph had advanced through the kitchen as I uttered these words, and now presented himself in the hall. He had donned in his Sunday garments, with his most sanctimonious and sourest face, and, holding his hat in one hand, and his stick in the other, he proceeded to clean his shoes on the mat.

"Good-evening, Joseph," I said, coldly. "What business brings you here tonight?"

"It's Master Linton I mun speak to," he answered, waving me disdainfully aside.

"Mr. Linton is going to bed, unless you have something particular to say, I'm sure he won't hear it now," I continued. "You had better sit down in there, and entrust your message to me."

"Which is his room?" pursued the fellow, surveying the range of closed doors.

I perceived he was bent on refusing my mediation, so very reluctantly I went up to the library, and announced the unseasonable visitor, advising that he should be dismissed till next day.

Mr. Linton had no time to empower me to do so, for Joseph mounted close at my heels, and, pushing into the apartment, planted himself at the far side of the table, with his two fists clapped on the head of his stick, and began in an elevated tone, as if anticipating opposition: "Heathcliff has sent me for his lad, and I mustn't go back without him."

Edgar Linton was silent a minute, an expression of exceeding sorrow overcast his features. He would have pitied the child on his own account, but, recalling Isabella's hopes and fears, and anxious wishes for her son, and her commendations of him to his care, he grieved bitterly at the prospect of yielding him up, and searched in his heart how it might be avoided. No plan offered itself. The very exhibition of any desire to keep him would have rendered the claimant more peremptory. There was nothing left but to resign him. However, he was not going to rouse him from his sleep.

"Tell Mr. Heathcliff," he answered calmly, "that his son shall come to Wuthering Heights tomorrow. He is in bed, and too tired to go the distance now. You may also tell him that the mother of Linton desired him to remain under my guardianship, and, at present, his health is very precarious."

"No!" said Joseph, giving a thud with his prop on the floor, and assuming an authoritative air. "No! That means naught. Heathcliff makes no account of the mother, nor ye neither, but he'll have his lad, and I mean to take him—so now ye know!"

"You shall not tonight!" answered Linton decisively. "Walk down stairs at once, and repeat to your master what I have said. Ellen, show him down. Go—"

And, aiding the indignant elder with a lift by the arm, he rid the room of him and closed the door.

"Very well!" shouted Joseph, as he slowly drew off. "Tomorrow morn, he's come himself, and thrust him out, if ye dare!"

CHAPTER 32

To OBVIATE THE DANGER of this threat being fulfilled, Mr. Linton commissioned me to take the boy home early, on Catherine's pony, and, said he, "As we shall now have no influence over his destiny, good or bad, you must say nothing of where he is gone to my daughter. She cannot associate with him hereafter, and it is better for her to remain in ignorance of his proximity, lest she should be restless, and anxious to visit the Heights. Merely tell her his father sent for him suddenly, and he has been obliged to leave us."

Linton was very reluctant to be roused from his bed at five o'clock, and astonished to be informed that he must prepare for further traveling. I softened off the matter by stating that he was going to spend some time with his father, Mr. Heathcliff, who wished to see him so much, he did not like to defer the pleasure till he should recover from his late journey.

"My father!" he cried, in strange perplexity. "Mamma never told me I had a father. Where does he live? I'd rather stay with Uncle."

"He lives a little distance from the Grange," I replied, "just beyond those hills—not so far, but you may walk over here when you get hearty.

And you should be glad to go home, and to see him. You must try to love him, as you did your mother, and then he will love you."

"But why have I not heard of him before?" asked Linton. "Why didn't Mamma and he live together, as other people do?"

"He had business to keep him in the north," I answered, "and your mother's health required her to reside in the south."

"And why didn't Mamma speak to me about him?" persevered the child. "She often talked of Uncle, and I learnt to love him long ago. How am I to love Papa? I don't know him."

"Oh, all children love their parents," I said. "Your mother, perhaps, thought you would want to be with him if she mentioned him often to you. Let us make haste. An early ride on such a beautiful morning is much preferable to an hour's more sleep."

"Is she to go with us," he demanded, "the little girl I saw yesterday?"

"Not now," replied I.

"Is Uncle?" he continued.

"No, I shall be your companion there," I said.

Linton sank back on his pillow and fell into a brown study.

"I won't go without Uncle," he cried at length. "I can't tell where you mean to take me."

I attempted to persuade him of the naughtiness of showing reluctance to meet his father; still he obstinately resisted any progress towards dressing, and I had to call for my master's assistance in coaxing him out of bed.

The poor thing was finally got off, with several delusive assurances that his absence should be short, that Mr. Edgar and Cathy would visit him, and other promises, equally ill-founded, which I invented and reiterated at intervals throughout the way.

The pure heather-scented air, the bright sunshine, and the gentle canter of Minny, relieved his despondency after a while. He began to put questions concerning his new home, and its inhabitants, with greater interest and liveliness.

"Is Wuthering Heights as pleasant a place as Thrushcross Grange?" he inquired, turning to take a last glance into the valley, whence a light mist mounted and formed a fleecy cloud on the skirts of the blue.

"It is not so buried in trees," I replied, "and it is not quite so large, but you can see the country beautifully all round, and the air is healthier for you—fresher and drier. You will, perhaps, think the building old and dark at first, though it is a respectable house, the next best in the neighborhood. And you will have such nice rambles on the moors. Hareton Earnshaw—that is, Miss Cathy's other cousin, and so yours in a manner—will show you all the sweetest spots, and you can bring a book in fine weather, and make a green hollow your study, and, now and then, your uncle may join you in a walk. He does, frequently, walk out on the hills."

"And what is my father like?" he asked. "Is he as young and handsome as Uncle?"

"He's as young," said I, "but he has black hair and eyes, and looks sterner, and he is taller and bigger altogether. He'll not seem to you so gentle and kind at first, perhaps, because it is not his way. Still, mind you, be frank and cordial with him, and naturally he'll be fonder of you than any uncle, for you are his own."

"Black hair and eyes!" mused Linton. "I can't fancy him. Then I am not like him, am I?"

"Not much," I answered. Not a morsel, I thought, surveying with regret the white complexion and slim frame of my companion, and his large languid eyes—his mother's eyes, save that, unless a morbid touchiness kindled them a moment, they had not a vestige of her sparkling spirit.

"How strange that he should never come to see Mamma and me!" he murmured. "Has he ever seen me? If he has, I must have been a baby. I remember not a single thing about him!"

"Why, Master Linton," said I, "three hundred miles is a great distance, and ten years seem very different in length to a grown-up person compared with what they do to you. It is probable Mr. Heathcliff proposed going from summer to summer, but never found a convenient opportunity, and now it is too late. Don't trouble him with questions on the subject. It will disturb him, for no good."

The boy was fully occupied with his own cogitations for the remainder of the ride, till we halted before the farmhouse garden gate. I watched to catch his impressions in his countenance. He surveyed the carved front and low-browed lattices, the straggling gooseberry bushes and crooked firs, with solemn intentness, and then shook his head. His private feelings entirely disapproved of the exterior of his new abode. But he had sense to postpone complaining. There might be compensation within.

Before he dismounted, I went and opened the door. It was half-past six, the family had just finished breakfast. The servant was clearing and wiping down the table. Joseph stood by his master's chair telling some tale concerning a lame horse, and Hareton was preparing for the hayfield.

"Hallo, Nelly!" said Mr. Heathcliff, when he saw me. "I feared I should have to come down and fetch my property myself. You've brought it, have you? Let us see what we can make of it."

He got up and strode to the door. Hareton and Joseph followed in gaping curiosity. Poor Linton ran a frightened eye over the faces of the three.

"Surely," said Joseph after a grave inspection, "he's swopped wi' ye, Master, an' yon's his lass!"

Heathcliff, having stared his son into an ague of confusion, uttered a scornful laugh.

"God! What a beauty! What a lovely, charming thing!" he exclaimed. "Haven't they reared it on snails and sour milk, Nelly? Oh, damn my soul! But that's worse than I expected—and the devil knows I was not sanguine!"

I bid the trembling and bewildered child get down, and enter. He did not thoroughly comprehend the meaning of his father's

WUTHERING HEIGHTS

speech, or whether it were intended for him. Indeed, he was not yet certain that the grim, sneering stranger was his father. But he clung to me with growing trepidation, and on Mr. Heathcliff's taking a seat and bidding him "come hither" he hid his face on my shoulder and wept.

"Tut, tut!" said Heathcliff, stretching out a hand and dragging him roughly between his knees, and then holding up his head by the chin. "None of that nonsense! We're not going to hurt thee, Linton— isn't that thy name? Thou art thy mother's child, entirely! Where is my share in thee, puling chicken?"

He took off the boy's cap and pushed back his thick flaxen curls, felt his slender arms and his small fingers, during which examination Linton ceased crying, and lifted his great blue eyes to inspect the inspector.

"Do you know me?" asked Heathcliff, having satisfied himself that the limbs were all equally frail and feeble.

"No," said Linton, with a gaze of vacant fear.

"You've heard of me, I daresay?"

"No," he replied again.

"No! What a shame of your mother, never to waken your filial regard for me! You are my son, then, I'll tell you, and your mother was a wicked slut to leave you in ignorance of the sort of father you possessed. Now, don't wince, and color up! Though it is something to see you have not white blood. Be a good lad, and I'll do for you. Nelly, if you be tired you may sit down; if not, get home again. I guess you'll report what you hear and see to the cipher at the Grange, and this thing won't be settled while you linger about it."

"Well," replied I, "I hope you'll be kind to the boy, Mr. Heathcliff, or you'll not keep him long, and he's all you have akin in the wide world, that you will ever know—remember."

"I'll be very kind to him, you needn't fear," he said, laughing. "Only nobody else must be kind to him. I'm jealous of monopolizing his affection. And, to begin my kindness, Joseph, bring the lad some breakfast. Hareton, you infernal calf, begone to your work. Yes, Nell," he added, when they had departed, "my son is prospective owner of your place, and I should not wish him to die till I was certain of being his successor. Besides, he's mine, and I want the triumph of seeing my descendant fairly lord of their estates, my child hiring their children to till their fathers' lands for wages. That is the sole consideration that can make me endure the whelp. I despise him for himself, and hate him for the memories he revives! But that consideration is sufficient. He's as safe with me, and shall be tended as carefully as your master tends his own. I have a room upstairs, furnished for him in handsome style. I've engaged a tutor to come three times a week, from twenty miles' distance to teach him what he pleases to learn. I've ordered Hareton to obey him. And in fact I've arranged everything with a view to preserve the superior and the gentleman in him, above his associates. I do regret, however, that he so little deserves the trouble. If I wished any blessing in the world, it was to find him a worthy object of pride, and I'm bitterly disappointed with the whey-faced, whining wretch!"

While he was speaking, Joseph returned bearing a basin of milk-porridge, and placed it before Linton. Who stirred round the homely mess with a look of aversion, and affirmed he could not eat it.

I saw the old man-servant shared largely in his master's scorn of the child, though he was compelled to retain the sentiment in his heart, because Heathcliff plainly meant his underlings to hold him in honor.

"Cannot ate it?" repeated he, peering in Linton's face, and subduing his voice to a whisper, for fear of being overheard. "But Master Hareton never ate naught else, when he were a little 'un, and what were good enough for him's good enough for ye, I's rather think!"

"I shan't eat it!" answered Linton, snappishly. "Take it away."

Joseph snatched up the food indignantly, and brought it to us.

"Is there aught ails th' victuals?" he asked, thrusting the tray under Heathcliff's nose.

"What should ail them?" he said.

"What!" answered Joseph, "yon dainty chap says he cannot ate 'em. But I guess it's aright! His mother were just same—we were almost too mucky to sow the corn for making her bread."

"Don't mention his mother to me," said the master, angrily. "Get him something that he can eat, that's all. What is his usual food, Nelly?"

I suggested boiled milk or tea, and the housekeeper received instructions to prepare some.

Come, I reflected, his father's selfishness may contribute to his comfort. He perceives his delicate constitution, and the necessity of treating him tolerably. I'll console Mr. Edgar by acquainting him with the turn Heathcliff's humor has taken. Having no excuse for lingering longer, I slipped out, while Linton was engaged in timidly rebuffing the advances of a friendly sheep dog. But he was too much on the alert to be cheated. As I closed the door, I heard a cry, and a frantic repetition of the words—"Don't leave me! I'll not stay here! I'll not stay here!"

Then the latch was raised and fell. They did not suffer him to come forth. I mounted Minny, and urged her to a trot, and so my brief guardianship ended.

CHAPTER 33

WE HAD SAD WORK with little Cathy that day. She rose in high glee, eager to join her cousin, and such passionate tears and lamentations followed the news of his departure that Edgar himself was obliged to soothe her, by affirming he should come back soon. He added, however, "if I can get him," and there were no hopes of that.

This promise poorly pacified her, but time was more potent, and though still at intervals she inquired of her father when Linton would return, before she did see him again his features had waxed so dim in her memory that she did not recognize him.

When I chanced to encounter the housekeeper of Wuthering Heights, in paying business visits to Gimmerton, I used to ask how the young master got on, for he lived almost as secluded as Catherine herself, and was never to be seen. I could gather from her that he continued in weak health, and was a tiresome inmate. She said Mr. Heathcliff seemed to dislike him ever longer and worse, though he took some trouble to conceal it. He had an antipathy to the sound of his voice, and could not do at all with his sitting in the same room with him many minutes together.

There seldom passed much talk between them. Linton learnt his lessons and spent his evenings in a small apartment they called the parlor or else lay in bed all day for he was constantly getting coughs, and colds, and aches, and pains of some sort.

"And I never know such a fainthearted creature," added the woman, "nor one so careful of himself. He will go on, if I leave the window open a bit late in the evening. Oh! It's killing, a breath of night air! He must have a fire in the middle of summer. Joseph's tobacco pipe is poison. He must always have sweets and dainties, and always milk, milk forever—heeding naught how the rest of us are pinched in winter. There he'll sit, wrapped in his furred cloak in his chair by the fire, with some toast and water or other slop on the hob to sip at. If Hareton, for pity, comes to amuse him—Hareton is not bad-natured, though he's rough—they're sure to part, one swearing and the other crying. I believe the master would relish Earnshaw's thrashing him to a mummy, if he were not his son, and I'm certain he would be fit to turn him out of doors, if he knew half the nursing he gives himself. But then he won't go into danger of temptation. He never enters the parlor, and should Linton show those ways in the house where he is, he sends him upstairs directly."

I divined, from this account, that utter lack of sympathy had rendered young Heathcliff selfish and disagreeable, if he were not so originally, and my interest in him, consequently, decayed—though still I was moved with a sense of grief at his lot, and a wish that he had been left with us.

Mr. Edgar encouraged me to gain information. He thought a great deal about him, I fancy, and would have run some risk to see him, and he told me once to ask the housekeeper whether he ever came into the village?

She said he had only been twice, on horseback, accompanying his father, and both times he pretended to be quite knocked up for three or four days afterwards. That housekeeper left, if I recollect rightly, two years after he came, and another, whom I did not know, was her successor. She lives there still.

Time wore on at the Grange in its former pleasant way, till Miss Cathy reached sixteen. On the anniversary of her birth we never manifested any signs of rejoicing, because it was also the anniversary of my late mistress's death. Her father invariably spent that day alone in the library, and walked, at dusk, as far as Gimmerton kirkyard, where he would frequently prolong his stay beyond midnight. Therefore Catherine was thrown on her own resources for amusement.

This twentieth of March was a beautiful spring day, and when her father had retired, my young lady came down dressed for going out, and said she asked to have a ramble on the edge of the moor with me. Mr. Linton had given her leave, if we went only a short distance and were back within the hour.

"So make haste, Ellen!" she cried. "I know where I wish to go, where a colony of moor-game are settled. I want to see whether they have made their nests yet."

"That must be a good distance up," I answered. "They don't breed on the edge of the moor."

"No, it's not," she said. "I've gone very near with Papa."

I put on my bonnet and sallied out, thinking nothing more of the matter. She bounded before me, and returned to my side, and was off again like a young greyhound. At first, I found plenty of entertainment in listening to the larks singing far and near, and enjoying the sweet, warm sunshine, and watching her, my pet, and my delight, with her golden ringlets flying loose behind, and her bright cheek, as soft and pure in its bloom as a wild rose, and her eyes radiant with cloudless pleasure. She was a happy creature, and an angel, in those days. It's a pity she could not be content.

"Well," said I, "where are your moor-game, Miss Cathy? We should be at them. The Grange park fence is a great way off now."

"Oh, a little further—only a little further, Ellen," was her answer, continually. "Climb to that hillock, pass that bank, and by the time you reach the other side I shall have raised the birds."

But there were so many hillocks and banks to climb and pass, that, at length, I began to be weary, and told her we must halt, and retrace our steps. I shouted to her, as she had outstripped me a long way. She either did not hear or did not regard, for she still sprang on, and I was compelled to follow. Finally, she dived into a hollow, and before I came in sight of her again, she was two miles nearer Wuthering Heights than her own home, and I beheld a couple of persons arrest her, one of whom I felt convinced was Mr. Heathcliff himself.

Cathy had been caught in the fact of plundering, or, at least, hunting out the nests of the grouse. The Heights were Heathcliff's land, and he was reproving the poacher.

"I've neither taken any nor found any," she said, as I toiled to them, expanding her hands in corroboration of the statement. "I didn't mean to take them, but Papa told me there were quantities up here, and I wished to see the eggs."

Heathcliff glanced at me with an ill-meaning smile, expressing his acquaintance with the party, and, consequently, his malevolence towards it, and demanded who "Papa" was?

"Mr. Linton of Thrushcross Grange," she replied. "I thought you did not know me, or you wouldn't have spoken in that way."

"You suppose Papa is highly esteemed and respected, then?" he said, sarcastically.

"And what are you?" inquired Catherine, gazing curiously on the speaker. "That man I've seen before. Is he your son?"

She pointed to Hareton, the other individual, who had gained nothing but increased bulk and strength by the addition of two years to his age. He seemed as awkward and rough as ever.

"Miss Cathy," I interrupted, "it will be three hours instead of one that we are out, presently. We really must go back."

"No, that man is not my son," answered Heathcliff, pushing me aside. "But I have one, and you have seen him before too. And, though your nurse is in a hurry, I think both you and she would be the better for a little rest. Will you just turn this nab of heath, and walk into my house? You'll get home earlier for the ease, and you shall receive a kind welcome."

I whispered Catherine that she mustn't, on any account, accede to the proposal. It was entirely out of the question.

"Why?" she asked, aloud. "I'm tired of running, and the ground is dewy. I can't sit here. Let us go, Ellen. Besides, he says I have seen his son. He's mistaken, I think, but I guess where he lives—at the farmhouse I visited in coming from Peniston Crags. Don't you?"

"I do. Come, Nelly, hold your tongue—it will be a treat for her to look in on us. Hareton, get forwards with the lass. You shall walk with me, Nelly."

"No, she's not going to any such place," I cried, struggling to release my arm, which he had seized, but she was almost at the door-stones already, scampering round the brow at full speed. Her appointed companion did not pretend to escort her. He shied off by the roadside, and vanished.

"Mr. Heathcliff, it's very wrong," I continued. "You know you mean no good. And there she'll see Linton, and all will be told as soon as ever we return, and I shall have the blame."

"I want her to see Linton," he answered. "He's looking better these few days—it's not often he's fit to be seen. And we'll soon persuade her to keep the visit secret. Where is the harm of it?"

"The harm of it is, that her father would hate me if he found I suffered her to enter your house, and I am convinced you have a bad design in encouraging her to do so," I replied.

"My design is as honest as possible. I'll inform you of its whole scope," he said. "That the two cousins may fall in love, and get married. I'm acting generously to your master. His young chit has no expectations, and should she second my wishes she'll be provided for at once as joint successor with Linton."

"If Linton died," I answered, "and his life is quite uncertain, Catherine would be the heir."

"No, she would not," he said. "There is no clause in the will to secure it so. His property would go to me, but, to prevent disputes, I desire their union, and am resolved to bring it about."

"And I'm resolved she shall never approach your house with me again," I returned, as we reached the gate, where Miss Cathy waited our coming.

Heathcliff bade me be quiet, and, preceding us up the path, hastened to open the door. My young lady gave him several looks, as if she could not exactly make up her mind what to think of him, but now he smiled when he met her eye, and softened his voice in addressing her. I was foolish enough to imagine the memory of her mother might disarm him from desiring her injury.

Linton stood on the hearth. He had been out walking in the fields, for his cap was on, and he was calling to Joseph to bring him dry shoes. He had grown tall of his age, still wanting some months of sixteen. His features were pretty yet, and his eye and complexion brighter than I remembered them, though with merely temporary luster borrowed from the salubrious air and genial sun.

"Now, who is that?" asked Mr. Heathcliff, turning to Cathy. "Can you tell?"

"Your son?" she said, having doubtfully surveyed, first one and then the other.

"Yes, yes," answered he. "But is this the only time you have beheld him? Think! Ah! You have a short memory. Linton, don't you recall your cousin, that you used to tease us so with wishing to see?"

"What, Linton!" cried Cathy, kindling into joyful surprise at the name. "Is that little Linton? He's taller than I am! Are you Linton?"

The youth stepped forward, and acknowledged himself. She kissed him fervently, and they gazed with wonder at the change time had wrought in the appearance of each.

Catherine had reached her full height, her figure was both plump and slender, elastic as steel, and her whole aspect sparkling with health and spirits. Linton's looks and movements were very languid, and his form extremely slight, but there was a grace in his manner that mitigated these defects, and rendered him not unpleasing.

After exchanging numerous marks of fondness with him, his

cousin went to Mr. Heathcliff, who lingered by the door, dividing his attention between the objects inside and those that lay without. Pretending, that is, to observe the latter, and really noting the former alone.

"And you are my uncle, then!" she cried, reaching up to salute him. "I thought I liked you, though you were cross at first. Why don't you visit at the Grange with Linton? To live all these years such close neighbors, and never see us, is odd. What have you done so for?"

"I visited it once or twice too often before you were born," he answered. "There—damn it! If you have any kisses to spare, give them to Linton. They are thrown away on me."

"Naughty Ellen!" exclaimed Catherine, flying to attack me next with her lavish caresses. "Wicked Ellen! To try to hinder me from entering. But I'll take this walk every morning in future. May I, Uncle? And sometimes bring Papa. Won't you be glad to see us?"

"Of course," replied the uncle, with a hardly suppressed grimace, resulting from his deep aversion to both the proposed visitors. "But stay," he continued, turning towards the young lady. "Now I think of it, I'd better tell you. Mr. Linton has a prejudice against me. We quarreled at one time of our lives, with unchristian ferocity, and, if you mention coming here to him, he'll put a veto on your visits altogether. Therefore, you must not mention it, unless you be careless of seeing your cousin hereafter. You may come, if you will, but you must not mention it."

"Why did you quarrel?" asked Catherine, considerably crestfallen.

"He thought me too poor to wed his sister," answered Heathcliff, "and was grieved that I got her. His pride was hurt, and he'll never forgive it."

"That's wrong!" said the young lady. "Sometime I'll tell him so. But Linton and I have no share in your quarrel. I'll not come here, then, he shall come to the Grange."

"It will be too far for me," murmured her cousin. "To walk four miles would kill me. No, come here, Miss Catherine, now and then. Not every morning, but once or twice a week."

The father launched towards his son a glance of bitter contempt.

"I am afraid, Nelly, I shall lose my labor," he muttered to me. "Miss Catherine, as the ninny calls her, will discover his value, and send him to the devil. Now, if it had been Hareton! Do you know that, twenty times a day, I covet Hareton, with all his degradation? I'd have loved the lad had he been someone else. But I think he's safe from her love. I'll pit him against that paltry creature, unless it bestir itself briskly. We calculate it will scarcely last till it is eighteen. Oh, confound the vapid thing! He's absorbed in drying his feet, and never looks at her. Linton!"

"Yes, Father," answered the boy.

"Have you nothing to show your cousin anywhere about, not even a rabbit or a weasel's nest? Take her into the garden, before you change your shoes, and into the stable to see your horse."

"Wouldn't you rather sit here?" asked Linton, addressing Cathy in a tone that expressed reluctance to move again.

"I don't know," she replied, casting a longing look to the door, and evidently eager to be active.

He kept his seat, and shrank closer to the fire. Heathcliff rose, and went into the kitchen, and from thence to the yard, calling out for Hareton. Hareton responded, and presently the two re-entered. The young man had been washing himself, as was visible by the glow on his cheeks and his wetted hair.

"Oh, I'll ask you, Uncle," cried Miss Cathy, recollecting the housekeeper's assertion. "That is not my cousin, is he?"

"Yes," he, replied, "your mother's nephew. Don't you like him!"

Catherine looked queer.

"Is he not a handsome lad?" he continued.

The uncivil little thing stood on tiptoe, and whispered a sentence in Heathcliff's ear. He laughed; Hareton darkened. I perceived he was very sensitive to suspected slights, and had obviously a dim notion of his inferiority.

But his master or guardian chased the frown by exclaiming, "You'll be the favorite among us, Hareton! She says you are a—what was it? Well, something very flattering. Here! You go with her round the farm. And behave like a gentleman, mind! Don't use any bad words, and don't stare when the young lady is not looking at you, and be ready to hide your face when she is, and, when you speak, say your words slowly, and keep your hands out of your pockets. Be off, and entertain her as nicely as you can."

He watched the couple walking past the window. Earnshaw had his countenance completely averted from his companion. He seemed studying the familiar landscape with a stranger's and an artist's interest. Catherine took a sly look at him, expressing small admiration. She then turned her attention to seeking out objects of amusement for herself, and tripped merrily on, lilting a tune to supply the lack of conversation.

"I've tied his tongue," observed Heathcliff. "He'll not venture a single syllable all the time! Nelly, you recollect me at his age— nay, some years younger. Did I ever look so stupid. So 'gaumless,' as Joseph calls it?"

"Worse," I replied, "because more sullen with it."

"I've a pleasure in him," he continued, reflecting aloud. "He has satisfied my expectations. If he were a born fool I should not enjoy it half so much. But he's no fool, and I can sympathize with all his feelings, having felt them myself. I know what he suffers now, for instance, exactly. It is merely a beginning of what he shall suffer, though. And he'll never be able to emerge from his bathos of coarseness and ignorance. I've got him faster than his scoundrel of a father secured me, and lower, for he takes a pride in his brutishness. I've taught him to scorn everything extra-animal as silly and weak. Don't you think Hindley would be proud of his son, if he could see him?

Almost as proud as I am of mine. But there's this difference: one is gold put to the use of paving-stones, and the other is tin polished to ape a service of silver. Mine has nothing valuable about it, yet I shall have the merit of making it go as far as such poor stuff can go. His had first-rate qualities, and they are lost, rendered worse than unavailing. I have nothing to regret; he would have more than any, but I, are aware of. And the best of it is, Hareton is damnably fond of me! You'll own that I've outmatched Hindley there. If the dead villain could rise from his grave to abuse me for his offspring's wrongs, I should have the fun of seeing the said offspring fight him back again, indignant that he should dare to rail at the one friend he has in the world!"

Heathcliff chuckled a fiendish laugh at the idea. I made no reply, because I saw that he expected none.

Meantime, our young companion, who sat too removed from us to hear what was said, began to evince symptoms of uneasiness, probably repenting that he had denied himself the treat of Catherine's society for fear of a little fatigue. His father remarked the restless glances wandering to the window, and the hand irresolutely extended towards his cap.

"Get up, you idle boy!" he exclaimed, with assumed heartiness. "Away after them! They are just at the corner, by the stand of hives."

Linton gathered his energies, and left the hearth. The lattice was open, and, as he stepped out, I heard Cathy inquiring of her unsociable attendant what was that inscription over the door? Hareton stared up, and scratched his head like a true clown.

"It's some damnable writing," he answered. "I cannot read it."

"Can't read it?" cried Catherine, "I can read it. It's English. But I want to know why it is there."

Linton giggled. The first appearance of mirth he had exhibited.

"He does not know his letters," he said to his cousin. "Could you believe in the existence of such a colossal dunce?"

"Is he all as he should be?" asked Miss Cathy, seriously. "Or is he simple—not right? I've questioned him twice now, and each time he looked so stupid I think he does not understand me. I can hardly understand him, I'm sure!"

Linton repeated his laugh, and glanced at Hareton tauntingly, who certainly did not seem quite clear of comprehension at that moment.

"There's nothing the matter but laziness, is there, Earnshaw?" he said. "My cousin fancies you are an idiot. There you experience the consequence of scorning 'book-learning,' as you would say. Have you noticed, Catherine, his frightful Yorkshire pronunciation?"

"Why, where the devil is the use on't?" growled Hareton, more ready in answering his daily companion. He was about to enlarge further, but the two youngsters broke into a noisy fit of merriment, my giddy miss being delighted to discover that she might turn his strange talk to matter of amusement.

"Where is the use of the devil in that sentence?" tittered Linton. "Papa told you not to say any bad words, and you can't open your mouth without one. Do try to behave like a gentleman, now do!"

"If thou weren't more a lass than a lad, I'd fell thee this minute, I would, pitiful lath of a crater!" retorted the angry boor, retreating, while his face burnt with mingled rage and mortification. He was conscious of being insulted, and embarrassed how to resent it.

Mr. Heathcliff having overheard the conversation, as well as I, smiled when he saw him go, but immediately afterwards cast a look of singular aversion on the flippant pair, who remained chattering in the doorway—the boy finding animation enough while discussing Hareton's faults and deficiencies, and relating anecdotes of his goings on, and the girl relishing his pert and spiteful sayings, without considering the ill-nature they evinced. I began to dislike, more than to compassionate, Linton, and to excuse his father in some measure for holding him cheap.

We stayed till afternoon. I could not tear Miss Cathy away sooner, but happily my master had not quitted his apartment, and remained ignorant of our prolonged absence.

As we walked home, I would fain have enlightened my charge on the characters of the people we had quitted, but she got it into her head that I was prejudiced against them.

"Aha!" she cried, "you take Papa's side, Ellen. You are partial, I know, or else you wouldn't have cheated me so many years into the notion that Linton lived a long way from here. I'm really extremely angry, only I'm so pleased I can't show it! But you must hold your tongue about my uncle, he's my uncle, remember, and I'll scold Papa for quarrelling with him."

And so she ran on, till I relinquished the endeavor to convince her of her mistake. She did not mention the visit that night, because she did not see Mr. Linton. Next day it all came out, sadly to my chagrin, and still I was not altogether sorry. I thought the burden of directing and warning would be more efficiently borne by him than me. But he was too timid in giving satisfactory reasons for his wish that she should shun connection with the household of the Heights, and Catherine liked good reasons for every restraint that harassed her petted will.

"Papa!" she exclaimed, after the morning's salutations, "guess whom I saw yesterday, in my walk on the moors. Ah, Papa, you started! You've not done right, have you, now? I saw—but listen, and you shall hear how I found you out, and Ellen, who is in league with you, and yet pretended to pity me so, when I kept hoping, and was always disappointed about Linton's coming back!"

She gave a faithful account of her excursion and its consequences, and my master, though he cast more than one reproachful look at me, said nothing till she had concluded. Then he drew her to him, and asked if she knew why he had concealed Linton's near neighborhood from her? Could she think it was to deny her a pleasure that she might harmlessly enjoy?

"It was because you disliked Mr. Heathcliff," she answered.

"Then you believe I care more for my own feelings than yours, Cathy?" he said. "No, it was not because I disliked Mr. Heathcliff, but because Mr. Heathcliff dislikes me. He is a most diabolical man, delighting to wrong and ruin those he hates, if they give him the slightest opportunity. I knew that you could not keep up an acquaintance with your cousin without being brought into contact with him, and I knew he would detest you on my account. So for your own good, and nothing else, I took precautions that you should not see Linton again. I meant to explain this some time as you grew older, and I'm sorry I delayed it."

"But Mr. Heathcliff was quite cordial, Papa," observed Catherine, not at all convinced, "and he didn't object to our seeing each other. He said I might come to his house when I pleased, only I must not tell you, because you had quarreled with him, and would not forgive him for marrying Aunt Isabella. And you won't. You are the one to be blamed. He is willing to let us be friends, at least, Linton and I, and you are not."

My master, perceiving that she would not take his word for her uncle-in-law's evil disposition, gave a hasty sketch of his conduct to Isabella, and the manner in which Wuthering Heights became his property. He could not bear to discourse long upon the topic, for though he spoke little of it, he still felt the same horror and detestation of his ancient enemy that had occupied his heart ever since Mrs. Linton's death. "She might have been living yet, if it had not been for him!" was his constant bitter reflection, and, in his eyes, Heathcliff seemed a murderer.

Miss Cathy—conversant with no bad deeds except her own slight acts of disobedience, injustice, and passion, arising from hot temper and thoughtlessness, and repented of on the day they were committed—was amazed at the blackness of spirit that could brood on and cover revenge for years, and deliberately prosecute its plans without a visitation of remorse. She appeared so deeply impressed and shocked at this new view of human nature—excluded from all her studies and all her ideas till now—that Mr. Edgar deemed it unnecessary to pursue the subject.

He merely added, "You will know hereafter, darling, why I wish you to avoid his house and family, now return to your old employments and amusements, and think no more about them."

Catherine kissed her father, and sat down quietly to her lessons for a couple of hours, according to custom, then she accompanied him into the grounds, and the whole day passed as usual. But in the evening, when she had retired to her room, and I went to help her to undress, I found her crying, on her knees by the bedside.

"Oh, fie, silly child!" I exclaimed. "If you had any real griefs you'd be ashamed to waste a tear on this little contrariety. You never had one shadow of substantial sorrow, Miss Catherine. Suppose, for a minute, that master and I were dead, and you were by yourself in the world. How would you feel, then? Compare the present occasion with such an affliction as that, and be thankful for the friends you have, instead of coveting more."

"I'm not crying for myself, Ellen," she answered, "it's for him. He expected to see me again tomorrow, and there he'll be so disappointed. And he'll wait for me, and I shan't come!"

"Nonsense!" said I, "do you imagine he has thought as much of you as you have of him? Hasn't he Hareton for a companion? Not one in a hundred would weep at losing a relation they had just seen twice, for two afternoons. Linton will conjecture how it is, and trouble himself no further about you."

"But may I not write a note to tell him why I cannot come?" she asked, rising to her feet. "And just send those books I promised to lend him? His books are not as nice as mine, and he wanted to have them extremely, when I told him how interesting they were. May I not, Ellen?"

"No, indeed! No, indeed!" replied I with decision. "Then he would write to you, and there'd never be an end of it. No, Miss Catherine, the acquaintance must be dropped entirely. So Papa expects, and I shall see that it is done."

"But how can one little note—?" she recommenced, putting on an imploring countenance.

"Silence!" I interrupted. "We'll not begin with your little notes. Get into bed."

She threw at me a very naughty look, so naughty that I would not kiss her good night at first. I covered her up, and shut her door, in great displeasure, but, repenting half-way, I returned softly, and lo! There was Miss standing at the table with a bit of blank paper before her and a pencil in her hand, which she guiltily slipped out of sight on my entrance.

"You'll get nobody to take that, Catherine," I said, "if you write it, and at present I shall put out your candle."

I set the extinguisher on the flame, receiving as I did so a slap on my hand and a petulant 'cross thing!' I then quitted her again, and she drew the bolt in one of her worst, most peevish humors.

The letter was finished and forwarded to its destination by a milk-fetcher who came from the village, but that I didn't learn till some time afterwards. Weeks passed on, and Cathy recovered her temper, though she grew wondrous fond of stealing off to corners by herself and often, if I came near her suddenly while reading, she would start and bend over the book, evidently desirous to hide it, and I detected edges of loose paper sticking out beyond the leaves.

She also got a trick of coming down early in the morning and lingering about the kitchen, as if she were expecting the arrival of something, and she had a small drawer in a cabinet in the library, which she would trifle over for hours, and whose key she took special care to remove when she left it.

One day, as she inspected this drawer, I observed that the play-things and trinkets, which recently formed its contents, were trans-muted into bits of folded paper. My curiosity and suspicions were roused; I determined to take a peep at her mysterious treasures. One night, as soon as she and my master were safe upstairs, I searched, and readily found among my house keys one that would fit the lock.

Having opened, I emptied the whole contents into my apron, and took them with me to examine at leisure in my own chamber.

Though I could not but suspect, I was still surprised to discover that they were a mass of correspondence—daily almost, it must have been—from Linton Heathcliff, answers to documents forwarded by her. The earlier dated were embarrassed and short; gradually, however, they expanded into copious love letters, foolish, as the age of the writer rendered natural, yet with touches here and there that I thought were borrowed from a more experienced source.

Some of them struck me as singularly odd compounds of ardor and flatness, commencing in strong feeling, and concluding in the affected, wordy style that a schoolboy might use to a fancied, incorporeal sweetheart. Whether they satisfied Cathy I don't know, but they appeared very worthless trash to me. After turning over as many as I thought proper, I tied them in a handkerchief and set them aside, relocking the vacant drawer.

Following her habit, my young lady descended early, and visited the kitchen. I watched her go to the door, on the arrival of a certain little boy, and, while the dairymaid filled his can, she tucked something into his jacket pocket, and plucked something out. I went round by the garden, and laid wait for the messenger, who fought valorously to defend his trust, and we spilt the milk between us, but I succeeded in abstracting the epistle, and, threatening serious consequences if he did not look sharp home.

I remained under the wall and perused Miss Cathy's affectionate composition. It was more simple and more eloquent than her cousin's—very pretty and very silly. I shook my head, and went meditating into the house. The day being wet, she could not divert herself with rambling about the park, so, at the conclusion of her morning studies, she resorted to the solace of the drawer. Her father sat reading at the table, and I, on purpose, had sought a bit of work in some unripped fringes of the window-curtain, keeping my eye steadily fixed on her proceedings.

Never did any bird flying back to a plundered nest, which it had left brimful of chirping young ones, express more complete despair, in its anguished cries and flutterings, than she by her single "Oh!" and the change that transfigured her late happy countenance. Mr. Linton looked up.

"What is the matter, love? Have you hurt yourself?" he said.

His tone and look assured her he had not been the discoverer of the hoard.

"No, Papa!" she gasped. "Ellen! Ellen! Come upstairs—I'm sick!"

I obeyed her summons, and accompanied her out.

"Oh, Ellen! You have got them," she commenced immediately, dropping on her knees, when we were enclosed alone. "Oh, give them to me, and I'll never, never do so again! Don't tell Papa. You have not told Papa, Ellen? Say you have not? I've been exceedingly naughty, but I won't do it anymore!"

With a grave severity in my manner I bade her stand up.

"So," I exclaimed, "Miss Catherine, you are tolerably far on, it seems. You may well be ashamed of them! A fine bundle of trash you study in your leisure hours, to be sure. Why, it's good enough to be printed! And what do you suppose the master will think when I display it before him? I haven't shown it yet, but you needn't imagine I shall keep your ridiculous secrets. For shame! And you must have led the way in writing such absurdities. He would not have thought of beginning, I'm certain."

"I didn't! I didn't!" sobbed Cathy, fit to break her heart. "I didn't once think of loving him till—"

"Loving!" cried I, as scornfully as I could utter the word. "Loving! Did anybody ever hear the like! I might just as well talk of loving the miller who comes once a year to buy our corn. Pretty loving, indeed! And both times together you have seen Linton hardly four hours in your life! Now here is the babyish trash. I'm going with it to the library, and we'll see what your father says to such loving."

She sprang at her precious epistles, but I hold them above my head, and then she poured out further frantic entreaties that I would burn them—do anything rather than show them. And being really fully as much inclined to laugh as scold—for I esteemed it all girlish vanity—I at length relented in a measure, and asked, "If I consent to burn them, will you promise faithfully neither to send nor receive a letter again, nor a book (for I perceive you have sent him books), nor locks of hair, nor rings, nor playthings?"

"We don't send playthings," cried Catherine, her pride overcoming her shame.

"Nor anything at all, then, my lady?" I said. "Unless you will, here I go."

"I promise, Ellen!" she cried, catching my dress. "Oh, put them in the fire, do, do!"

But when I proceeded to open a place with the poker the sacrifice was too painful to be borne. She earnestly supplicated that I would spare her one or two.

"One or two, Ellen, to keep for Linton's sake!"

I unknotted the handkerchief, and commenced dropping them in from an angle, and the flame curled up the chimney.

"I will have one, you cruel wretch!" she screamed, darting her hand into the fire, and drawing forth some half-consumed fragments, at the expense of her fingers.

"Very well—and I will have some to exhibit to Papa!" I answered, shaking back the rest into the bundle, and turning anew to the door.

She emptied her blackened pieces into the flames, and motioned me to finish the immolation. It was done, I stirred up the ashes, and interred them under a shovelful of coals, and she mutely, and with a sense of intense injury, retired to her private apartment. I descended to tell my master that the young lady's qualm of sickness was almost gone, but I judged it best for her to lie down a while.

She wouldn't dine, but she reappeared at tea, pale, and red about the eyes, and marvelously subdued in outward aspect.

Next morning I answered the letter by a slip of paper, inscribed, "Master Heathcliff is requested to send no more notes to Miss Linton, as she will not receive them." And, henceforth, the little boy came with vacant pockets.

CHAPTER 34

*S*UMMER DREW TO AN END, and early autumn. It was past Michaelmas, but the harvest was late that year, and a few of our fields were still uncleared.

Mr. Linton and his daughter would frequently walk out among the reapers. At the carrying of the last sheaves, they stayed till dusk, and the evening happening to be chill and damp, my master caught a bad cold, that settled obstinately on his lungs, and confined him indoors throughout the whole of the winter, nearly without intermission.

Poor Cathy, frightened from her little romance, had been considerably sadder and duller since its abandonment, and her father insisted on her reading less, and taking more exercise. She had his companionship no longer. I esteemed it a duty to supply its lack, as much as possible, with mine—an inefficient substitute, for I could only spare two or three hours, from my numerous diurnal occupations, to follow her footsteps, and then my society was obviously less desirable than his.

On a fresh watery afternoon in October, or the beginning of November, when the turf and paths were rustling with moist, withered leaves, and the cold blue sky was half hidden by clouds—dark grey streamers, rapidly mounting from the west, and boding abundant rain—I requested my young lady to forgo her ramble, because I was certain of showers. She refused, and I unwillingly donned a cloak, and took my umbrella to accompany her on a stroll to the bottom of the park, a formal walk which she generally affected if low-spirited—and that she invariably was when Mr. Edgar had been worse than ordinary, a thing never known from his confession, but guessed both by her and me from his increased silence and the melancholy of his countenance.

She went sadly on. There was no running or bounding now, though the chill wind might well have tempted her to race. And often, from the side of my eye, I could detect her raising a hand, and brushing something off her cheek.

I gazed round for a means of diverting her thoughts. On one side of the road rose a high, rough bank, where hazels and stunted oaks, with their roots half exposed, held uncertain tenure. The soil was too loose for the latter, and strong winds had blown some nearly horizontal. In summer Miss Catherine delighted to climb along these trunks, and sit in the branches, swinging twenty feet above the ground, and I, pleased with her agility and her light, childish heart, still considered it proper to scold every time I caught her at such an elevation, but so that she knew there was no necessity for descending. From dinner to tea she would lie in her breeze-rocked cradle, doing nothing except singing old songs—my nursery lore—to herself, or watching the birds, joint tenants, feed and entice their young ones to fly; or nestling with closed lids, half thinking, half dreaming, happier than words can express.

"Look, Miss!" I exclaimed, pointing to a nook under the roots of one twisted tree. "Winter is not here yet. There's a little flower up yonder, the last bud from the multitude of bluebells that clouded those turf steps in July with a lilac mist. Will you clamber up, and pluck it to show to Papa?"

Cathy stared a long time at the lonely blossom trembling in its earthy shelter, and replied, at length, "No, I'll not touch it. But it looks melancholy, does it not, Ellen?"

"Yes," I observed, "about as starved and sackless as you. Your cheeks are bloodless—let us take hold of hands and run. You're so low, I daresay I shall keep up with you."

"No," she repeated, and continued sauntering on, pausing at intervals to muse over a bit of moss, or a tuft of blanched grass, or a fungus spreading its bright orange among the heaps of brown foliage, and, ever and anon, her hand was lifted to her averted face.

"Catherine, why are you crying, love?" I asked, approaching and putting my arm over her shoulder. "You mustn't cry because Papa has a cold; be thankful it is nothing worse."

She now put no further restraint on her tears, her breath was stifled by sobs.

"Oh, it will be something worse," she said. "And what shall I do when Papa and you leave me, and I am by myself? I can't forget your words, Ellen; they are always in my ear. How life will be changed, how dreary the world will be, when Papa and you are dead."

"None can tell whether you won't die before us," I replied. "It's wrong to anticipate evil. We'll hope there are years and years to come before any of us go. Master is young, and I am strong, and hardly forty-five. My mother lived till eighty, a canty dame to the last. And suppose Mr. Linton were spared till he saw sixty, that would be more years than you have counted, Miss. And would it not be foolish to mourn a calamity above twenty years beforehand?"

"But Aunt Isabella was younger than Papa," she remarked, gazing up with timid hope to seek further consolation.

"Aunt Isabella had not you and me to nurse her," I replied. "She wasn't as happy as Master. She hadn't as much to live for. All you need do is to wait well on your father, and cheer him by letting him see you cheerful, and avoid giving him anxiety on any subject. Mind that, Cathy! I'll not disguise but you might kill him if you were wild and reckless, and cherished a foolish, fanciful affection for the son of a person who would be glad to have him in his grave, and allowed him to discover that you fretted over the separation he has judged it expedient to make."

"I fret about nothing on earth except Papa's illness," answered my companion. "I care for nothing in comparison with Papa. And I'll never—never—oh, never, while I have my senses, do an act or say a word to vex him. I love him better than myself, Ellen, and I know it by this. I pray every night that I may live after him, because I would rather be miserable than that he should be. That proves I love him better than myself."

"Good words," I replied. "But deeds must prove it also, and after he is well, remember you don't forget resolutions formed in the hour of fear."

As we talked, we neared a door that opened on the road, and my young lady, lightening into sunshine again, climbed up and seated herself on the top of the wall, reaching over to gather some hips that bloomed scarlet on the summit branches of the wild-rose trees shadowing the highway side. The lower fruit had disappeared, but only birds could touch the upper, except from Cathy's present station.

In stretching to pull them, her hat fell off, and as the door was locked, she proposed scrambling down to recover it. I bid her be cautious lest she got a fall, and she nimbly disappeared. But the return was no such easy matter. The stones were smooth and neatly cemented, and the rosebushes and blackberry stragglers could yield no assistance in reascending. I, like a fool, didn't recollect that, till I heard her laughing and exclaiming, "Ellen! You'll have to fetch the key, or else I must run round to the porter's lodge. I can't scale the ramparts on this side!"

"Stay where you are," I answered. "I have my bundle of keys in my pocket. Perhaps I may manage to open it. If not, I'll go."

Catherine amused herself with dancing to and fro before the door, while I tried all the large keys in succession. I had applied the last, and found that none would do. So, repeating my desire that she would remain there, I was about to hurry home as fast as I could, when an approaching sound arrested me. It was the trot of a horse. Cathy's dance stopped, and in a minute the horse stopped also.

"Who is that?" I whispered.

"Ellen, I wish you could open the door," whispered back my companion, anxiously.

"Ho, Miss Linton!" cried a deep voice (the rider's). "I'm glad to meet you. Don't be in haste to enter, for I have an explanation to ask and obtain."

"I shan't speak to you, Mr. Heathcliff," answered Catherine. "Papa says you are a wicked man, and you hate both him and me, and Ellen says the same."

"That is nothing to the purpose," said Heathcliff. (He it was.) "I don't hate my son, I suppose, and it is concerning him that I demand your attention. Yes, you have cause to blush. Two or three months since, were you not in the habit of writing to Linton? Making love in play, eh? You deserved, both of you, flogging for that! You especially, the elder, and less sensitive, as it turns out. I've got your letters, and if you give me any pertness I'll send them to your father. I presume you grew weary of the amusement and dropped it, didn't you? Well, you dropped Linton with it into a Slough of Despond. He was in earnest—in love, really. As true as I live, he's dying for you, breaking his heart at your fickleness. Not figuratively, but actually. Though Hareton has made him a standing jest for six weeks, and I have used more serious measures, and attempted to frighten him out of his idiocy, he gets worse daily, and he'll be under the sod before summer, unless you restore him!"

"How can you lie so glaringly to the poor child?" I called from the inside. "Pray ride on! How can you deliberately get up such paltry falsehoods? Miss Cathy, I'll knock the lock off with a stone. You won't believe that vile nonsense. You can feel in yourself it is impossible that a person should die for the love of a stranger."

"I was not aware there were eavesdroppers," muttered the

detected villain. "Worthy Mrs. Dean, I like you, but I don't like your double dealing," he added aloud. "How could you lie so glaringly as to affirm I hated the 'poor child'? And invent bugbear stories to terrify her from my door-stones? Catherine Linton (the very name warms me), my bonny lass, I shall be from home all this week. Go and see if have not spoken truth. Do, there's a darling! Just imagine your father in my place, and Linton in yours, then think how you would value your careless lover if he refused to stir a step to comfort you, when your father himself entreated him; and don't, from pure stupidity, fall into the same error. I swear, on my salvation, he's going to his grave, and none but you can save him!"

The lock gave way and I issued out.

"I swear Linton is dying," repeated Heathcliff, looking hard at me. "And grief and disappointment are hastening his death. Nelly, if you won't let her go, you can walk over yourself. But I shall not return till this time next week, and I think your master himself would scarcely object to her visiting her cousin."

"Come in," said I, taking Cathy by the arm and half forcing her to re-enter, for she lingered, viewing with troubled eyes the features of the speaker, too stern to express his inward deceit.

He pushed his horse close, and, bending down, observed, "Miss Catherine, I'll own to you that I have little patience with Linton, and Hareton and Joseph have less. I'll own that he's with a harsh set. He pines for kindness, as well as love, and a kind word from you would be his best medicine. Don't mind Mrs. Dean's cruel cautions, but be generous, and contrive to see him. He dreams of you day and night, and cannot be persuaded that you don't hate him, since you neither write nor call."

I closed the door, and rolled a stone to assist the loosened lock in holding it, and spreading my umbrella, I drew my charge underneath. The rain began to drive through the moaning branches of the trees, and warned us to avoid delay.

Our hurry prevented any comment on the encounter with

Heathcliff, as we stretched towards home, but I divined instinctively that Catherine's heart was clouded now in double darkness. Her features were so sad, they did not seem hers. She evidently regarded what she had heard as every syllable true.

The master had retired to rest before we came in. Cathy stole to his room to inquire how he was, but he had fallen asleep. She returned, and asked me to sit with her in the library. We took our tea together, and afterwards she lay down on the rug, and told me not to talk, for she was weary.

I got a book, and pretended to read. As soon as she supposed me absorbed in my occupation, she recommenced her silent weeping. It appeared, at present, her favorite diversion. I suffered her to enjoy it a while, then I expostulated, deriding and ridiculing all Mr. Heathcliff's assertions about his son, as if I were certain she would coincide. Alas! I hadn't skill to counteract the effect his account had produced. It was just what he intended.

"You may be right, Ellen," she answered, "but I shall never feel at ease till I know. And I must tell Linton it is not my fault that I don't write, and convince him that I shall not change."

What use were anger and protestations against her silly credulity? We parted that night—hostile; but next day beheld me on the road to Wuthering Heights, by the side of my willful young mistress's pony. I couldn't bear to witness her sorrow. To see her pale, dejected countenance, and heavy eyes and I yielded, in the faint hope that Linton himself might prove, by his reception of us, how little of the tale was founded on fact.

CHAPTER 35

*T*HE RAINY NIGHT had ushered in a misty morning—half frost, half drizzle—and temporary brooks crossed our path—gurgling from the uplands. My feet were thoroughly wetted; I was cross and low, exactly the humor suited for making the most of these disagreeable things.

We entered the farmhouse by the kitchen way, to ascertain whether Mr. Heathcliff were really absent, because I put slight faith in his own affirmation.

Joseph seemed sitting in a sort of Elysium alone, beside a roaring fire, a quart of ale on the table near him, bristling with large pieces of toasted oat-cake, and his black, short pipe in his mouth. Catherine ran to the hearth to warm herself. I asked if the master was in? My question remained so long unanswered, that I thought the old man had grown deaf, and repeated it louder.

"Na—ay!" he snarled, or rather screamed through his nose. "Na—ay! You must go back where yah come from."

"Joseph!" cried a peevish voice, simultaneously with me, from the inner room. "How often am I to call you? There are only a few red ashes now. Joseph! Come this moment."

Vigorous puffs, and a resolute stare into the grate, declared he had no ear for this appeal. The housekeeper and Hareton were invisible, one gone on an errand, and the other at his work, probably. We knew Linton's tones, and entered.

"Oh, I hope you'll die in a garret, starved to death!" said the boy, mistaking our approach for that of his negligent attendant.

He stopped on observing his error. His cousin flew to him.

"Is that you, Miss Linton?" he said, raising his head from the arm of the great chair, in which he reclined. "No—don't kiss me. It takes my breath. Dear me! Papa said you would call," continued he, after recovering a little from Catherine's embrace, while she stood by looking very contrite. "Will you shut the door, if you please? You left it open, and those—those detestable creatures won't bring coals to the fire. It's so cold!"

I stirred up the cinders, and fetched a scuttle full myself. The invalid complained of being covered with ashes, but he had a tiresome cough, and looked feverish and ill, so I did not rebuke his temper.

"Well, Linton," murmured Catherine, when his corrugated brow relaxed, "are you glad to see me? Can I do you any good?"

"Why didn't you come before?" he asked. "You should have come, instead of writing. It tired me dreadfully writing those long letters. I'd far rather have talked to you. Now, I can neither bear to talk, nor anything else. I wonder where Zillah is! Will you" (looking at me) "step into the kitchen and see?"

I had received no thanks for my other service, and being unwilling to run to and fro at his behest, I replied, "Nobody is out there but Joseph."

"I want to drink," he exclaimed fretfully, turning away. "Zillah is constantly gadding off to Gimmerton since Papa went. It's miserable! And I'm obliged to come down here—they resolved never to hear me upstairs."

"Is your father attentive to you, Master Heathcliff?" I asked, perceiving Catherine to be checked in her friendly advances.

"Attentive? He makes them a little more attentive at least," he cried. "The wretches! Do you know, Miss Linton, that brute Hareton laughs at me! I hate him! indeed, I hate them all. They are odious beings."

Cathy began searching for some water. She lighted on a pitcher in the dresser, filled a tumbler, and brought it. He bid her add a spoonful of wine from a bottle on the table, and having swallowed a small portion, appeared more tranquil, and said she was very kind.

"And are you glad to see me?" asked she, reiterating her former question and pleased to detect the faint dawn of a smile.

"Yes, I am. It's something new to hear a voice like yours!" he replied. "But I have been vexed, because you wouldn't come. And papa swore it was owing to me. He called me a pitiful, shuffling, worthless thing, and said you despised me, and if he had been in my place, he would be more the master of the Grange than your father by this time. But you don't despise me, do you, Miss—?"

"I wish you would say Catherine, or Cathy," interrupted my young lady. "Despise you? No! Next to papa and Ellen, I love you better than anybody living. I don't love Mr. Heathcliff, though, and I dare not come when he returns. Will he stay away many days?"

"Not many," answered Linton, "but he goes on to the moors frequently, since the shooting season commenced, and you might spend an hour or two with me in his absence. Do! Say you will! I think I should not be peevish with you. You'd not provoke me, and you'd always be ready to help me, wouldn't you?"

"Yes," said Catherine, stroking his long soft hair. "If I could only get Papa's consent, I'd spend half my time with you. Pretty Linton! I wish you were my brother."

"And then you would like me as well as your father?" observed he, more cheerfully. "But Papa says you would love me better than him and all the world, if you were my wife, so I'd rather you were that."

"No, I should never love anybody better than Papa," she returned gravely. "And people hate their wives, sometimes, but not their sisters and brothers. And if you were the latter, you would live with us, and Papa would be as fond of you as he is of me."

Linton denied that people ever hated their wives, but Cathy affirmed they did, and, in her wisdom, instanced his own father's aversion to her aunt. I endeavored to stop her thoughtless tongue. I couldn't succeed till everything she knew was out. Master Heathcliff, much irritated, asserted her relation was false.

"Papa told me, and Papa does not tell falsehoods," she answered pertly.

"My papa scorns yours!" cried Linton. "He calls him a sneaking fool."

"Yours is a wicked man," retorted Catherine, "and you are very naughty to dare to repeat what he says. He must be wicked to have made Aunt Isabella leave him as she did."

"She didn't leave him," said the boy. "You shan't contradict me."

"She did," cried my young lady.

"Well, I'll tell you something!" said Linton. "Your mother hated your father. Now then."

"Oh!" exclaimed Catherine, too enraged to continue.

"And she loved mine," added he.

"You little liar! I hate you now!" she panted, and her face grew red with passion.

"She did! She did!" sang Linton, sinking into the recess of his chair, and leaning back his head to enjoy the agitation of the other disputant, who stood behind.

"Hush, Master Heathcliff!" I said. "That's your father's tale, too, I suppose."

"It isn't. You hold your tongue!" he answered. "She did, she did, Catherine! She did, she did!"

Cathy, beside herself, gave the chair a violent push, and caused him to fall against one arm. He was immediately seized by a suffocating cough that soon ended his triumph.

It lasted so long that it frightened even me. As to his cousin, she wept with all her might, aghast at the mischief she had done, though she said nothing.

I held him till the fit exhausted itself. Then he thrust me away, and leant his head down silently. Catherine quelled her lamentations also, took a seat opposite, and looked solemnly into the fire.

"How do you feel now, Master Heathcliff?" I inquired, after waiting ten minutes.

"I wish she felt as I do," he replied. "Spiteful, cruel thing! Hareton never touches me. He never struck me in his life. And I was better today. And there—" his voice died in a whimper.

"I didn't strike you!" muttered Cathy, chewing her lip to prevent another burst of emotion.

He sighed and moaned like one under great suffering, and kept it up for a quarter of an hour—on purpose to distress his cousin, apparently, for whenever he caught a stifled sob from her he put renewed pain and pathos into the inflexions of his voice.

"I'm sorry I hurt you, Linton," she said at length, racked beyond endurance. "But I couldn't have been hurt by that little push, and I had no idea that you could, either. You're not much, are you, Linton? Don't let me go home thinking I've done you harm. Answer! Speak to me."

"I can't speak to you," he murmured. "You've hurt me so that I shall lie awake all night choking with this cough! If you had it you'd know what it was, but you'll be comfortably asleep while I'm in agony, and nobody near me! I wonder how you would like to pass those fearful nights!" And he began to wail aloud, for very pity of himself.

"Since you are in the habit of passing dreadful nights," I said, "it won't be Miss who spoils your ease. You'd be the same had she never come. However, she shall not disturb you again, and perhaps you'll get quieter when we leave you."

"Must I go?" asked Catherine dolefully, bending over him. "Do you want me to go, Linton?"

"You can't alter what you've done," he replied pettishly, shrinking from her, "unless you alter it for the worse by teasing me into a fever."

"Well, then, I must go?" she repeated.

"Let me alone, at least," said he. "I can't bear your talking."

She lingered, and resisted my persuasions to departure a tiresome while, but as he neither looked up nor spoke, she finally made a movement to the door, and I followed. We were recalled by a scream. Linton had slid from his seat on to the hearthstone, and lay writhing in the mere perverseness of an indulged plague of a child, determined to be as grievous and harassing as it can.

I thoroughly gauged his disposition from his behavior, and saw at once it would be folly to attempt humoring him. Not so my companion. She ran back in terror, knelt down, and cried, and soothed, and entreated, till he grew quiet from lack of breath, by no means from compunction at distressing her.

"I shall lift him on to the settle," I said, "and he may roll about as he pleases. We can't stop to watch him. I hope you are satisfied, Miss Cathy, that you are not the person to benefit him, and that his condition of health is not occasioned by attachment to you. Now, then, there he is! Come away. As soon as he knows there is nobody by to care for his nonsense, he'll be glad to lie still."

She placed a cushion under his head, and offered him some water, he rejected the latter, and tossed uneasily on the former, as if it were a stone or a block of wood. She tried to put it more comfortably.

"I can't do with that," he said, "it's not high enough."

Catherine brought another to lie above it.

"That's too high," murmured the provoking thing.

"How must I arrange it, then?" she asked despairingly.

He twined himself up to her, as she half knelt by the settle, and converted her shoulder into a support.

"No, that won't do," I said. "You'll be content with the cushion, Master Heathcliff. Miss has wasted too much time on you already. We cannot remain five minutes longer."

"Yes, yes, we can!" replied Cathy. "He's good and patient now. He's beginning to think I shall have far greater misery than he will tonight, if I believe he is the worse for my visit. And then I dare not come again. Tell the truth about it, Linton, for I mustn't come, if I have hurt you."

"You must come, to cure me," he answered. "You ought to come, because you have hurt me. You know you have extremely! I was not as ill when you entered as I am at present—was I?"

"But you've made yourself ill by crying and being in a passion— I didn't do it all," said his cousin. "However, we'll be friends now. And you want me—you would wish to see me sometimes, really?"

"I told you I did," he replied impatiently. "Sit on the settle and let me lean on your knee. That's as Mamma used to do, whole afternoons together. Sit quite still and don't talk. But you may sing a song, if you can sing, or you may say a nice long interesting ballad—one of those you promised to teach me, or a story. I'd rather have a ballad, though. Begin."

Catherine repeated the longest she could remember. The employment pleased both mightily. Linton would have another, and after that another, notwithstanding my strenuous objections, and so they went on until the clock struck twelve, and we heard Hareton in the court, returning for his dinner.

"And tomorrow, Catherine, will you be here tomorrow?" asked young Heathcliff, holding her frock as she rose reluctantly.

"No," I answered, "nor next day neither."

She, however, gave a different response evidently, for his forehead cleared as she stooped and whispered in his ear.

"You won't go tomorrow, recollect, Miss!" I commenced, when we were out of the house. "You are not dreaming of it, are you?"

She smiled.

"Oh, I'll take good care," I continued. "I'll have that lock mended, and you can escape by no way else."

"I can get over the wall," she said, laughing. "The Grange is not a prison, Ellen, and you are not my jailer. And besides, I'm almost seventeen. I'm a woman. And I'm certain Linton would recover quickly if he had me to look after him. I'm older than he is, you know, and wiser. Less childish, am I not? And he'll soon do as I direct him, with some slight coaxing. He's a pretty little darling when he's good. I'd make such a pet of him, if he were mine. We should never quarrel, should we, after we were used to each other? Don't you like him, Ellen?"

"Like him!" I exclaimed. "The worst-tempered bit of a sickly slip that ever struggled into its teens. Happily, as Mr. Heathcliff conjectured, he'll not win twenty. I doubt whether he'll see spring, indeed. And small loss to his family whenever he drops off. And lucky it is for us that his father took him. The kinder he was treated, the more tedious and selfish he'd be. I'm glad you have no chance of having him for a husband, Miss Catherine."

My companion waxed serious at hearing this speech. To speak of his death so regardlessly wounded her feelings.

"He's younger than I," she answered, after a protracted pause of meditation, "and he ought to live the longest. He will—he must live as long as I do. He's as strong now as when he first came into the north, I'm positive of that. It's only a cold that ails him, the same as Papa has. You say Papa will get better, and why shouldn't he?"

"Well, well," I cried, "after all, we needn't trouble ourselves, for listen, Miss—and mind, I'll keep my word—if you attempt going to Wuthering Heights again, with or without me, I shall inform Mr. Linton, and, unless he allow it, the intimacy with your cousin must not be revived."

"It has been revived," muttered Cathy, sulkily.

"Must not be continued, then!" I said.

"We'll see," was her reply, and she set off at a gallop, leaving me to toil in the rear.

We both reached home before our dinnertime, my master supposed we had been wandering through the park, and therefore he demanded no explanation of our absence. As soon as I entered, I hastened to change my soaked shoes and stockings, but sitting such awhile at the Heights had done the mischief. On the succeeding morning I was laid up, and during three weeks I remained incapacitated for attending to my duties—a calamity never experienced prior to that period, and never, I am thankful to say, since.

My little mistress behaved like an angel in coming to wait on me, and cheer my solitude—the confinement brought me exceedingly low. It is wearisome, to a stirring active body, but few have slighter reasons for complaint than I had. The moment Catherine left Mr. Linton's room, she appeared at my bedside. Her day was divided between us; no amusement usurped a minute. She neglected her meals, her studies, and her play, and she was the fondest nurse that ever watched. She must have had a warm heart, when she loved her father so, to give so much to me. I said her days were divided between us, but the master retired early, and I generally needed nothing after six o'clock, thus the evening was her own.

Poor thing! I never considered what she did with herself after tea. And though frequently, when she looked in to bid me goodnight, I remarked a fresh color in her cheeks and a pinkness over her slender fingers, instead of fancying the line borrowed from a cold ride across the moors, I laid it to the charge of a hot fire in the library.

CHAPTER 36

*A*T THE CLOSE OF THREE WEEKS I was able to quit my chamber and move about the house. And on the first occasion of my sitting up in the evening I asked Catherine to read to me, because my eyes were weak. We were in the library, the master having gone to bed. She consented, rather unwillingly, I fancied, and imagining my sort of books did not suit her, I bid her please herself in the choice of what she perused.

She selected one of her own favorites, and got forward steadily about an hour; then came frequent questions.

"Ellen, are not you tired? Hadn't you better lie down now? You'll be sick, keeping up so long, Ellen."

"No, no, dear, I'm not tired," I returned, continually.

Perceiving me immovable, she essayed another method of showing her dis-relish for her occupation. It changed to yawning, and stretching, and then, "Ellen, I'm tired."

"Give over then and talk," I answered.

That was worse. She fretted and sighed, and looked at her watch till eight, and finally went to her room, completely overdone with sleep, judging by her peevish, heavy look, and the constant rubbing she inflicted on her eyes. The following night she seemed more impatient still, and on the third from recovering my company, she complained of a headache, and left me.

I thought her conduct odd, and having remained alone a long while, I resolved on going and inquiring whether she were better, and asking her to come and lie on the sofa, instead of upstairs in the dark.

No Catherine could I discover upstairs, and none below. The servants affirmed they had not seen her. I listened at Mr. Edgar's door, all was silence. I returned to her apartment, extinguished my candle, and seated myself in the window.

The moon shone bright, a sprinkling of snow covered the ground, and I reflected that she might, possibly, have taken it into her head to walk about the garden, for refreshment. I did detect a figure creeping along the inner fence of the park, but it was not my young mistress. On its emerging into the light, I recognized one of the grooms.

He stood a considerable period, viewing the carriage-road through the grounds, then started off at a brisk pace, as if he had detected something, and reappeared presently, leading Miss's pony, and there she was, just dismounted, and walking by its side.

The man took his charge stealthily across the grass towards the stable. Cathy entered by the casement window of the drawing-room, and glided noiselessly up to where I awaited her. She put the door gently too, slipped off her snowy shoes, untied her hat, and was proceeding, unconscious of my espionage, to lay aside her mantle, when I suddenly rose and revealed myself. The surprise petrified her an instant. She uttered an inarticulate exclamation, and stood fixed.

"My dear Miss Catherine," I began, too vividly impressed by her recent kindness to break into a scold, "where have you been riding out at this hour? And why should you try to deceive me by telling a tale? Where have you been? Speak!"

"To the bottom of the park," she stammered. "I didn't tell a tale."

"And nowhere else?" I demanded.

"No," was the muttered reply.

"Oh, Catherine!" I cried, sorrowfully. "You know you have been doing wrong, or you wouldn't be driven to uttering an untruth to me. That does grieve me. I'd rather be three months ill, than hear you frame a deliberate lie."

She sprang forward, and bursting into tears, threw her arms round my neck.

"Well, Ellen, I'm so afraid of you being angry," she said. "Promise not to be angry, and you shall know the very truth. I hate to hide it."

We sat down in the window-seat. I assured her I would not scold, whatever her secret might be, and I guessed it, of course, so she commenced: "I've been to Wuthering Heights, Ellen, and I've never missed going a day since you fell ill, except thrice before, and twice after you left your room. I gave Michael books and pictures to prepare Minny every evening, and to put her back in the stable. You mustn't scold him either, mind. I was at the Heights by half-past six, and generally stayed till half-past eight, and then galloped home. It was not to amuse myself that I went. I was often wretched all the time. Now and then I was happy. Once in a week perhaps.

"At first, I expected there would be sad work persuading you to let me keep my word to Linton. For I had engaged to call again next day, when we quitted him, but, as you stayed upstairs on the morrow, I escaped that trouble. While Michael was refastening the lock of the park door in the afternoon, I got possession of the key, and told him how my cousin wished me to visit him, because he was sick, and couldn't come to the Grange, and how Papa would object to my going. Then I negotiated with him about the pony. He is fond of reading, and he thinks of leaving soon to get married, so he offered, if I would lend him books out of the library, to do what I wished. But I preferred giving him my own, and that satisfied him better.

"On my second visit Linton seemed in lively spirits, and Zillah (that is their housekeeper) made us a clean room and a good fire, and told us that, as Joseph was out at a prayer-meeting and Hareton Earnshaw was off with his dogs—robbing our woods of pheasants, as I heard afterwards—we might do what we liked.

"She brought me some warm wine and gingerbread, and appeared exceedingly good-natured, and Linton sat in the armchair, and I in the little rocking chair on the hearth-stone, and we laughed and talked so merrily, and found so much to say. We planned where we would go, and what we would do in summer. I needn't repeat that, because you would call it silly.

"One time, however, we were near quarrelling. He said the pleasantest manner of spending a hot July day was lying from morning till evening on a bank of heath in the middle of the moors, with the bees humming dreamily about among the bloom, and the larks singing high up overhead, and the blue sky and bright sun shining steadily and cloudlessly. That was his most perfect idea of heaven's happiness. Mine was rocking in a rustling green tree, with a west wind blowing, and bright white clouds flitting rapidly above, and not only larks, but throstles, and blackbirds, and linnets, and cuckoos pouring out music on every side. And the moors seen at a distance, broken into cool dusky dells, but close by great swells of long grass undulating in waves to the breeze, and woods and sounding water, and the whole world awake and wild with joy. He wanted all to lie in an ecstasy of peace, I wanted all to sparkle and dance in a glorious jubilee.

"I said his heaven would be only half-alive, and he said mine would be drunk. I said I should fall asleep in his, and he said he could not breathe in mine, and began to grow very snappish. At last, we agreed to try both, as soon as the right weather came, and then we kissed each other and were friends.

"After sitting still an hour, I looked at the great room with its smooth uncarpeted floor, and thought how nice it would be to play in, if we removed the table, and I asked Linton to call Zillah in to help us, and we'd have a game at blindman's buff; she should try to catch us. You used to, you know, Ellen. He wouldn't. There was no pleasure in it, he said, but he consented to play at ball with me. We found two in a cupboard, among a heap of old toys, tops, and hoops, and battledores and shuttlecocks. One was marked C and the other H. I wished to have the C because that stood for Catherine, and the H might be for Heathcliff, his name, but the bran came out of H and Linton didn't like it.

"I beat him constantly and he got cross again, and coughed, and returned to his chair. That night, though, he easily recovered his good humor. He was charmed with two or three pretty songs—your songs, Ellen, and when I was obliged to go, he begged and entreated me to come the following evening, and I promised. Minny and I went flying home as light as air, and I dreamt of Wuthering Heights and my sweet, darling cousin, till morning.

"On the morrow I was sad, partly because you were poorly, and partly that I wished my father knew, and approved of my excursions. But it was beautiful moonlight after tea, and, as I rode on, the gloom cleared. I shall have another happy evening, I thought to myself, and what delights me more, my pretty Linton will.

"I trotted up their garden, and was turning round to the back, when that fellow Earnshaw met me, took my bridle, and bid me go in by the front entrance. He patted Minny's neck, and said she was a bonny beast, and appeared as if he wanted me to speak to him. I only told him to leave my horse alone, or else it would kick him.

"He answered in his vulgar accent, 'It wouldn't do much hurt if it did,' and surveyed its legs with a smile.

"I was half inclined to make it try. However, he moved off to open the door, and, as he raised the latch, he looked up to the inscription above, and said, with a stupid mixture of awkwardness and elation, 'Miss Catherine! I can read yon, now.'

"'Wonderful,' I exclaimed. 'Pray let us hear you—you are grown clever!'

"He spelt, and drawled over by syllables, the name—'Hareton Earnshaw.'

"'And the figures?' I cried, encouragingly, perceiving that he came to a dead halt.

"'I cannot tell them yet,' he answered.

"'Oh, you dunce!' I said, laughing heartily at his failure.

"The fool stared, with a grin hovering about his lips, and a scowl gathering over his eyes, as if uncertain whether he might not join in my mirth—whether it were not pleasant familiarity, or what it really was, contempt.

"I settled his doubts, by suddenly retrieving my gravity and desiring him to walk away, for I came to see Linton, not him. He reddened—I saw that by the moonlight—dropped his hand from the latch, and skulked off, a picture of mortified vanity. He imagined himself to be as accomplished as Linton, I suppose, because he could spell his own name, and was marvelously discomfited that I didn't think the same."

"Stop, Miss Catherine, dear!" I interrupted. "I shall not scold, but I don't like your conduct there. If you had remembered that Hareton was your cousin as much as Master Heathcliff, you would have felt how improper it was to behave in that way. At least, it was praiseworthy ambition for him to desire to be as accomplished as Linton, and probably he did not learn merely to show off. You had made him ashamed of his ignorance before, I have no doubt, and he wished to remedy it and please you. To sneer at his imperfect attempt was very bad breeding. Had you been brought up in his circumstances, would you be less rude? He was as quick and as intelligent a child as ever you were, and I'm hurt that he should be despised now, because that base Heathcliff has treated him so unjustly."

"Well, Ellen, you won't cry about it, will you?" she exclaimed, surprised at my earnestness. "But wait, and you shall hear if he conned his A B C to please me, and if it were worth while being civil to him. I entered, Linton was lying on the settle, and half got up to welcome me.

"'I'm ill tonight, Catherine, love,' he said, 'and you must have all the talk, and let me listen. Come, and sit by me. I was sure you wouldn't break your word, and I'll make you promise again, before you go.'

"I knew now that I mustn't tease him, as he was ill, and I spoke softly and put no questions, and avoided irritating him in any way. I had brought some of my nicest books for him. He asked me to read a little of one, and I was about to comply, when Earnshaw burst the door open, having gathered venom with reflection. He advanced direct to us, seized Linton by the arm, and swung him off the seat.

"'Get to thy own room!' he said, in a voice almost inarticulate with passion, and his face looked swelled and furious. 'Take her there if she comes to see thee. Thou shan't keep me out of this. Begone wi' ye both!'

"He swore at us, and left Linton no time to answer, nearly throwing him into the kitchen, and he clenched his fist as I followed, seemingly longing to knock me down. I was afraid for a moment, and I let one volume fall, he kicked it after me, and shut us out. I heard a malignant, crackly laugh by the fire, and turning, beheld that odious Joseph standing rubbing his bony hands, and quivering.

"'I were sure he'd shove ye out! He's a grand lad! He's gotten the right spirit in him! He knows—ay, he knows, as well as I do, who should be t' master yonder! Ech, ech, ech! He made ye skift properly! Ech, ech, ech!'

"'Where must we go?' I asked of my cousin, disregarding the old wretch's mockery.

"Linton was white and trembling. He was not pretty then, Ellen. Oh, no! He looked frightful, for his thin face and large eyes were wrought into an expression of frantic, powerless fury. He grasped the handle of the door, and shook it. It was fastened inside.

"'If you don't let me in, I'll kill you! If you don't let me in, I'll kill you!' he rather shrieked than said. 'Devil! devil! I'll kill you—I'll kill you!'

"Joseph uttered his croaking laugh again.

"'There, that's t' father!' he cried. 'That's father! We've always something o' either side in us. Never heed, Hareton, lad—do not be afraid—he cannot get at thee!'

"I took hold of Linton's hands, and tried to pull him away, but he shrieked so shockingly that I dared not proceed. At last his cries were choked by a dreadful fit of coughing, blood gushed from his mouth, and he fell on the ground.

"I ran into the yard, sick with terror, and called for Zillah, as loud as I could. She soon heard me. She was milking the cows in a shed behind the barn, and hurrying from her work, she inquired what there was to do?

"I hadn't breath to explain. Dragging her in, I looked about for Linton. Earnshaw had come out to examine the mischief he had caused, and he was then conveying the poor thing upstairs. Zillah and I ascended after him, but he stopped me at the top of the steps, and said I shouldn't go in. I must go home. I exclaimed that he had killed Linton, and I would enter. Joseph locked the door, and declared I should do 'no such stuff,' and asked me whether I were 'bound to be as mad as him.' I stood crying till the housekeeper reappeared. She affirmed he would be better in a bit, but he couldn't do with that shrieking and din, and she took me, and nearly carried me into the house.

"Ellen, I was ready to tear my hair off my head! I sobbed and wept so that my eyes were almost blind, and the ruffian you have such sympathy with stood opposite. Presuming every now and then to bid me 'wisht,' and denying that it was his fault. And, finally, frightened by my assertions that I would tell Papa, and that he should be put in prison and hanged, he commenced blubbering himself, and hurried out to hide his cowardly agitation.

"Still, I was not rid of him. When at length they compelled me to depart, and I had got some hundred yards off the premises, he suddenly issued from the shadow of the roadside, and checked Minny and took hold of me.

"'Miss Catherine, I'm ill grieved,' he began, 'but it's rather too bad—'

"I gave him a cut with my whip, thinking perhaps he would murder me. He let go, thundering one of his horrid curses, and I galloped home more than half out of my senses.

"I didn't bid you good night that evening, and I didn't go to Wuthering Heights the next. I wished to go exceedingly, but I was strangely excited, and dreaded to hear that Linton was dead, sometimes, and sometimes shivered at the thought of encountering Hareton.

"On the third day I took courage. At least, I couldn't bear longer suspense, and stole off once more. I went at five o'clock, and walked, fancying I might manage to creep into the house, and up to Linton's room, unobserved. However, the dogs gave notice of my approach.

"Zillah received me, and saying 'the lad was mending nicely,' showed me into a small, tidy, carpeted apartment, where, to my inexpressible joy, I beheld Linton laid on a little sofa, reading one of my books. But he would neither speak to me nor look at me, through a whole hour, Ellen. He has such an unhappy temper. And what quite confounded me, when he did open his mouth, it was to utter the falsehood that I had occasioned the uproar, and Hareton was not to blame!

"Unable to reply, except passionately, I got up and walked from the room. He sent after me a faint 'Catherine!' He did not reckon on being answered so, but I wouldn't turn back, and the morrow was the second day on which I stayed at home, nearly determined to visit him no more.

"But it was so miserable going to bed and getting up, and never hearing anything about him, that my resolution melted into air before it was properly formed. It had appeared wrong to take the journey once, now it seemed wrong to refrain. Michael came to ask if he must saddle Minny. I said 'Yes,' and considered myself doing a duty as she bore me over the hills. I was forced to pass the front windows to get to the court. It was no use trying to conceal my presence.

"'Young master is in the house,' said Zillah, as she saw me

making for the parlor. I went in, Earnshaw was there also, but he quitted the room directly, but not before his gaze settled on mine. There was much to say without speaking. Linton sat in the great armchair half asleep, walking up to the fire, I began in a serious tone, partly meaning it to be true, 'As you don't like me, Linton, and as you think I come on purpose to hurt you, and pretend that I do so every time, this is our last meeting. Let us say good-bye. Tell Mr. Heathcliff that you have no wish to see me, and that he mustn't invent any more falsehoods on the subject.'"

"'Sit down and take your hat off, Catherine,' he answered. 'You are so much happier than I am, you ought to be better. Papa talks enough of my defects, and shows enough scorn of me, to make it natural I should doubt myself. I doubt whether I am not altogether as worthless as he calls me, frequently, and then I feel so cross and bitter, I hate everybody! I am worthless and bad in temper, bad in spirit, almost always, and, if you choose, you may say good-bye. You'll get rid of an annoyance. Only, Catherine, do me this justice. Believe that if I might be as sweet, and as kind, and as good as you are, I would be, as willingly, and more so, than as happy and as healthy. And believe that your kindness has made me love you deeper than if I deserved your love. Though I couldn't, and cannot help showing my nature to you, I regret it and repent it, and shall regret and repent it till I die!'

"I felt he spoke the truth, and I felt I must forgive him. And, though we should quarrel the next moment, I must forgive him again. We were reconciled, but we cried, both of us, the whole time I stayed—not entirely for sorrow, yet I was sorry Linton had that distorted nature. He'll never let his friends be at ease, and he'll never be at ease himself!

"I have always gone to his little parlor, since that night, because his father returned the day after. About three times, I think, we have been merry and hopeful, as we were the first evening. The rest of my visits were dreary and troubled, now with his selfishness and spite, and now with his sufferings. But I've learned to endure the former

WUTHERING HEIGHTS

with nearly as little resentment as the latter.

"Mr. Heathcliff purposely avoids me. I have hardly seen him at all. Last Sunday, indeed, coming earlier than usual, I heard him abusing poor Linton cruelly for his conduct of the night before. I can't tell how he knew of it, unless he listened. Linton had certainly behaved provokingly. However, it was the business of nobody but me, and I interrupted Mr. Heathcliff's lecture by entering and telling him so. He burst into a laugh, and went away, saying he was glad I took that view of the matter. Since then, I've told Linton he must whisper his bitter things. Now, Ellen, you have heard all."

When she uttered the last, she raised her chin in such a determined way that I knew I had not heard all. I gave her a sharp look, and saw that a flush was making its way up her throat and to her cheeks, and I said, scandalized, "Have you allowed your cousin any liberties?" It had not occurred to me, considering my judgment of his weak nature, that he would be able to perform any act of a carnal variety. Now I realized that young Linton would not be above working on her tenderness for him to achieve that object which so many men set such store by.

Catherine shook her head, but would not look at me, and twisted her hands together in her lap. Then she whispered, "He is so very pretty when he is not complaining."

Then it all came out. During one of their arguments, Catherine tried to stop his complaining by kissing him. Astonished, he made a petulant cry and pushed her away, but doing so, his hand found her breast, and immediately he stopped fussing at her. Catherine slapped his hand away, but he proved more determined then than he had ever been before.

"Let me touch you," he said, and when Catherine shook her head, he let out such a wailing that she was afraid Mr. Heathcliff would storm into the room, demanding to know what had caused the ruckus. Shushing him, she let Linton put his hand on her breast, and knead it in his fingers, and he sighed and said how soft

it was. Then he discovered how he could pluck her nipple, and make her gasp. He did not care if she liked it or not; he merely enjoyed making her gasp. He touched her through her dress at first, and then insisted that she bare herself to him, so that he could see her breasts, and touch her skin.

She tried to object at first, but he began to set up such a commotion that she quickly undid her dress so that he could put his hands on her. Now his hands were sensitive and gentle, and she leaned into him, enjoying the sensation. She had never experienced anything quite like it.

He drew her down onto the settle beside him, then took her hand and guided it to his groin. "You see how hard you have made me, Catherine? You must rectify the situation."

Catherine sprang up, denying that she would do anything of the sort.

"Look what you have done, you miserable tease!" he cried out. "You have made me want you, and now you deny me the sweet pleasure you promised! You are a wicked woman! I hate you!"

At that Catherine began to cry, and told him that she had never promised him anything of the sort, and that if he hated her, that was his own fault, and if he wanted her to, she would leave and never return.

Then he retreated into one of his sulky silences. Catherine could never resist that challenge, so she went to him, and petted him, and got him to admit that he wanted her to stay, and then before she could quite understand what was happening, he had talked her out of her undergarments—"Just so I can touch, Catherine!" and then he had her climb on top—"Just to relieve the ache a little, Catherine!" and then he was inside of her, and she cried out as his penetration breached her maidenhood, and he shrieked, too, then pushed her off, saying she was suffocating him.

She retreated, and he gasped at the sight of her blood on his member, now limp and shrinking, and set up a shrieking fit until she had cleaned him up and restored his clothing, and her own, to order. Then he demanded that the fire be built higher, which she did, before creeping away home.

Well, Mr. Lockwood, you can imagine that on hearing that tale, I told her she should never visit that pathetic creature again. I even threatened to tell her father what had transpired. She said, "I can't be prevented from going to Wuthering Heights, except by inflicting misery on two people, whereas, if you'll only not tell Papa, my going need disturb the tranquility of none. You'll not tell, will you? It will be very heartless, if you do."

"I'll make up my mind on that point by tomorrow, Miss Catherine," I replied. "It requires some study, and so I'll leave you to your rest, and go think it over."

I thought it over aloud, in my master's presence, walking straight from her room to his, and relating the whole story, with the exception of her conversations with her cousin, and any mention of Hareton. Mr. Linton was alarmed and distressed, more than he would acknowledge to me. In the morning, Catherine learnt my betrayal of her confidence, and she learnt also that her secret visits were to end.

In vain she wept and writhed against the interdict, and implored her father to have pity on Linton. All she got to comfort her was a promise that he would write and give him leave to come to the Grange when he pleased, but explaining that he must no longer expect to see Catherine at Wuthering Heights. Perhaps, had he been aware of his nephew's disposition and state of health, he would have seen fit to withhold even that slight consolation.

CHAPTER 37

"THESE THINGS HAPPENED LAST WINTER, sir," said Mrs. Dean, "hardly more than a year ago. Last winter, I did not think, at another twelve months' end, I should be amusing a stranger to the family with relating them! Yet, who knows how long you'll be a stranger? You're too young to rest always contented, living by yourself, and I some way fancy no one could see Catherine Linton and not love her. You smile, but why do you look so lively and interested when I talk about her? And why have you asked me to hang her picture over your fireplace? And why—?"

"Stop, my good friend!" I cried. **Mrs. Dean was sailing quite near the truth. Cathy dominated my dreams and my waking. But I was hardly bold enough to claim her, and I did not want Mrs. Dean trying to arrange a match, and clucking like a hen over the twists and turns of a love relationship. For all I knew, she'd be telling my story to another stranger, at twelve months' end!**

"It may be very possible that I should love her, but would she love me? I doubt it too much to venture my tranquility by running into temptation," I lied, then added for good measure, "And then my home is not here. I'm of the busy world, and to its arms I must return. Go on. Was Catherine obedient to her father's commands?"

"She was," continued the housekeeper. "Her affection for him was still the chief sentiment in her heart, and he spoke without anger. He spoke in the deep tenderness of one about to leave his treasure amid perils and foes, where his remembered words would be the only aid that he could bequeath to guide her. He said to me, a few days afterwards, 'I wish my nephew would write, Ellen, or call. Tell me, sincerely, what you think of him. Is he changed for the better, or is there a prospect of improvement, as he grows a man?'

"'He's very delicate, sir,' I replied, 'and scarcely likely to reach manhood. But this I can say, he does not resemble his father, and if Miss Catherine had the misfortune to marry him, he would not be beyond her control, unless she were extremely and foolishly indulgent. However, master, you'll have plenty of time to get acquainted with him and see whether he would suit her—it wants four years and more to his being of age.'"

Edgar sighed, and, walking to the window, looked out towards Gimmerton Kirk. It was a misty afternoon, but the February sun shone dimly, and we could just distinguish the two fir trees in the yard, and the sparely scattered gravestones.

"I've prayed often," he half soliloquized, "for the approach of what is coming, and now I begin to shrink, and fear it. I thought the memory of the hour I came down that glen a bridegroom would be less sweet than the anticipation that I was soon, in a few months, or, possibly, weeks, to be carried up, and laid in its lonely hollow! Ellen, I've been very happy with my little Cathy. Through winter nights and summer days she was a living hope at my side. But I've been as happy musing by myself among those stones, under that old church, lying, through the long June evenings, on the green mound of her mother's grave, and wishing—yearning for the time when I might lie beneath it. What can I do for Cathy? How must I quit her? I'd not care one moment for Linton being Heathcliff's son, nor for his taking her from me, if he could console her for my loss. I'd not care that Heathcliff gained his ends, and triumphed in robbing me of my last blessing! But should Linton be unworthy—only a feeble tool to his father—I cannot abandon her to him! And, hard though it be to crush her buoyant spirit, I must persevere in making her sad while I live, and leaving her solitary when I die. Darling! I'd rather resign her to God, and lay her in the earth before me."

"Resign her to God as it is, sir," I answered, "and if we should lose you—which may He forbid—under His providence, I'll stand her friend and counselor to the last. Miss Catherine is a good girl. I don't fear that she will go willfully wrong, and people who do their duty are always finally rewarded."

Spring advanced, yet my master gathered no real strength, though he resumed his walks in the grounds with his daughter. To her inexperienced notions, this itself was a sign of convalescence, and then his cheek was often flushed, and his eyes were bright—she felt sure of his recovering. On her seventeenth birthday, he did not visit the churchyard. It was raining, and I observed, "You'll surely not go out tonight, sir?"

He answered, "'No, I'll defer it this year a little longer.'"

He wrote again to Linton, expressing his great desire to see him, and, had the invalid been presentable, I've no doubt his father would have permitted him to come. As it was, being instructed, he returned an answer, intimating that Mr. Heathcliff objected to his calling at the Grange, but his uncle's kind remembrance delighted him, and he hoped to meet him sometimes in his rambles, and personally to petition that his cousin and he might not remain long so utterly divided.

That part of his letter was simple, and probably his own. Heathcliff knew he could plead eloquently for Catherine's company. Then he added: "I do not ask that she may visit here, but am I never to see her, because my father forbids me to go to her home, and you forbid her to come to mine? Do, now and then, ride with her towards the Heights, and let us exchange a few words, in your presence! We have done nothing to deserve this separation, and you are not angry with me. You have no reason to dislike me, you allow, yourself. Dear uncle! Send me a kind note tomorrow, and leave to join you anywhere you please, except at Thrushcross Grange. I believe an interview would convince you that my father's character is not mine. He affirms I am more your nephew than his son, and though I have faults which render me unworthy of Catherine, she has excused them, and, for her sake, you should also. You inquire after my health—it is better, but while I remain cut off from all hope, and doomed to solitude, or the society of those who never did and never will like me, how can I be cheerful and well?"

Edgar, though he felt for the boy, could not consent to grant his request, because he could not accompany Catherine. He said, in summer, perhaps, they might meet. Meantime, he wished him to continue writing at intervals, and engaged to give him what advice and comfort he was able by letter, being well aware of his hard position in his family.

Linton complied, and had he been unrestrained, would probably have spoiled all by filling his epistles with complaints and lamentations. But his father kept a sharp watch over him, and, of course, insisted on every line that my master sent being shown. So, instead of penning his peculiar personal sufferings and distresses, the themes constantly uppermost in his thoughts, he harped on the cruel obligation of being held asunder from his friend and love, and gently intimated that Mr. Linton must allow an interview soon, or he should fear he was purposely deceiving him with empty promises.

Cathy was a powerful ally at home, and between them they at length persuaded my master to acquiesce in their having a ride or a walk together about once a week, under my guardianship, and on the moors nearest the Grange, for June found him still declining. Though he had set aside yearly a portion of his income for my young lady's fortune, he had a natural desire that she might retain—or at least return in a short time to—the house of her ancestors, and he considered her only prospect of doing that was by a union with his heir.

He had no idea that the latter was failing almost as fast as himself, nor had any one, I believe. No doctor visited the Heights, and no one saw Master Heathcliff to make report of his condition among us. I, for my part, began to fancy my forebodings were false, and that he must be actually rallying, when he mentioned riding and walking on the moors, and seemed so earnest in pursuing his object.

I could not picture a father treating a dying child as tyrannically and wickedly as I afterwards learned Heathcliff had treated him, to compel this apparent eagerness. His efforts redoubling the more imminently his avaricious and unfeeling plans were threatened with defeat by death.

CHAPTER 38

*S*UMMER WAS ALREADY PAST its prime, when Edgar reluctantly yielded his assent to their entreaties, and Catherine and I set out on our first ride to join her cousin. It was a close, sultry day, devoid of sunshine, but with a sky too dappled and hazy to threaten rain. Our place of meeting had been fixed at the guide-stone, by the crossroads. On arriving there, however, a little herd-boy, dispatched as a messenger, told us that, "Maister Linton were just o' this side th' Heights and he'd be much obliged to us to gang on a bit further."

"Then Master Linton has forgot the first injunction of his uncle," I observed. "He bid us keep on the Grange land, and here we are off at once."

"Well, we'll turn our horses' heads round when we reach him," answered my companion, "our excursion shall lie towards home."

But when we reached him, and that was scarcely a quarter of a mile from his own door, we found he had no horse, and we were forced to dismount, and leave ours to graze.

He lay on the heath, awaiting our approach, and did not rise till we came within a few yards. Then he walked so feebly, and looked so pale, that I immediately exclaimed, "Why, Master Heathcliff, you are not fit for enjoying a ramble this morning. How ill you do look!"

Catherine surveyed him with grief and astonishment. She changed the ejaculation of joy on her lips to one of alarm, and the congratulation on their long-postponed meeting to an anxious inquiry, whether he were worse than usual.

"No—better—better!" he panted, trembling, and retaining her hand as if he needed its support, while his large blue eyes wandered timidly over her, the hollowness round them transforming to haggard wildness the languid expression they once possessed.

"But you have been worse," persisted his cousin, "worse than when I saw you last, you are thinner, and—"

"I'm tired," he interrupted, hurriedly. "It is too hot for walking, let us rest here. And, in the morning, I often feel sick—Papa says I grow so fast."

Badly satisfied, Cathy sat down, and he reclined beside her.

"This is something like your paradise," said she, making an effort at cheerfulness. "You recollect the two days we agreed to spend in the place and way each thought pleasantest? This is nearly yours, only there are clouds, but then they are so soft and mellow, it is nicer than sunshine. Next week, if you can, we'll ride down to the Grange Park, and try mine."

Linton did not appear to remember what she talked of and he had evidently great difficulty in sustaining any kind of conversation. His lack of interest in the subjects she started, and his equal incapacity to contribute to her entertainment, were so obvious that she could not conceal her disappointment. An indefinite alteration had come over his whole person and manner. The pettishness that might be caressed into fondness, had yielded to a listless apathy there was less of the peevish temper of a child which frets and teases on purpose to be soothed, and more of the self-absorbed moroseness of a confirmed invalid, repelling consolation, and ready to regard the good-humored mirth of others as an insult.

Catherine perceived, as well as I did, that he held it rather a punishment, than a gratification, to endure our company, and she made no scruple of proposing, presently, to depart.

That proposal, unexpectedly, roused Linton from his lethargy, and threw him into a strange state of agitation. He glanced fearfully towards the Heights, begging she would remain another half-hour, at least.

"But I think," said Cathy, "you'd be more comfortable at home than sitting here, and I cannot amuse you today, I see, by my tales, and songs, and chatter. You have grown wiser than I, in these six months, you have little taste for my diversions now or else, if I could amuse you, I'd willingly stay."

"Stay to rest yourself," he replied. "And, Catherine, don't think or say that I'm very unwell. It is the heavy weather and heat that make me dull, and I walked about, before you came, a great deal for me. Tell Uncle I'm in tolerable health, will you?"

"I'll tell him that you say so, Linton. I couldn't affirm that you are," observed my young lady, wondering at his stubborn assertion of what was evidently an untruth.

"And be here again next Thursday," continued he, shunning her puzzled gaze. "And give him my thanks for permitting you to come— my best thanks, Catherine. And—and, if you did meet my father, and he asked you about me, don't lead him to suppose that I've been extremely silent and stupid. Don't look sad and downcast, as you are doing—he'll be angry."

"I care nothing for his anger," exclaimed Cathy, imagining she would be its object.

"But I do," said her cousin, shuddering. "Don't provoke him against me, Catherine, for he is very hard."

"Is he severe to you, Master Heathcliff?" I inquired. "Has he grown weary of indulgence, and passed from passive to active hatred?"

Linton looked at me, but did not answer. After keeping her seat by his side another ten minutes, during which his head fell drowsily on his breast, he uttered nothing except suppressed moans of exhaustion or pain. Cathy began to seek solace in looking for bilberries, and sharing the produce of her researches with me. She did not offer them to him, for she saw further notice would only weary and annoy.

"Is it half-an-hour now, Ellen?" she whispered in my ear, at last. "I can't tell why we should stay. He's asleep, and Papa will be wanting us back."

"Well, we must not leave him asleep," I answered. "Wait till he wakes, and be patient. You were mighty eager to set off, but your longing to see poor Linton has soon evaporated!"

"Why did he wish to see me?" returned Catherine. "In his crossest humors, formerly, I liked him better than I do in his present curious mood. It's just as if it were a task he was compelled to perform—this interview—for fear his father should scold him. But I'm hardly going to come to give Mr. Heathcliff pleasure, whatever reason he may have for ordering Linton to undergo this penance. And, though I'm glad he's better in health, I'm sorry he's so much less pleasant, and so much less affectionate to me."

"You think he is better in health, then?" I said.

"Yes," she answered, "because he always made such a great deal of his sufferings, you know. He is not tolerably well, as he told me to tell Papa, but he's better, very likely."

"There you differ with me, Miss Cathy," I remarked. "I should conjecture him to be far worse."

Linton here started from his slumber in bewildered terror, and asked if anyone had called his name.

"No," said Catherine, "unless in dreams. I cannot conceive how you manage to doze out of doors, in the morning."

"I thought I heard my father," he gasped, glancing up to the frowning nab above us. "You are sure nobody spoke?"

"Quite sure," replied his cousin. "Only Ellen and I were disputing concerning your health. Are you truly stronger, Linton, than when we separated in winter? If you be, I'm certain one thing is not stronger—your regard for me. Speak,—are you?"

The tears gushed from Linton's eyes as he answered, "Yes, yes, I am!" And, still under the spell of the imaginary voice, his gaze wandered up and down to detect its owner.

Cathy rose. "For today we must part," she said. "And I won't conceal that I have been sadly disappointed with our meeting, though I'll mention it to nobody but you—not that I stand in awe of Mr. Heathcliff!"

"Hush," murmured Linton, "for God's sake, hush! He's coming." And he clung to Catherine's arm, striving to detain her, but at that announcement she hastily disengaged herself, and whistled to Minny, who obeyed her like a dog.

"I'll be here next Thursday," she cried, springing to the saddle. "Good-bye. Quick, Ellen!"

And so we left him, scarcely conscious of our departure, so absorbed was he in anticipating his father's approach.

Before we reached home, Catherine's displeasure softened into a perplexed sensation of pity and regret, largely blended with vague, uneasy doubts about Linton's actual circumstances, physical and social. In which I partook, though I counseled her not to say much, for a second journey would make us better judges.

My master requested an account of our goings on. His nephew's offering of thanks was duly delivered, Miss Cathy gently touching on the rest. I also threw little light on his inquiries, for I hardly knew what to hide and what to reveal.

CHAPTER 39

*S*EVEN DAYS GLIDED AWAY, every one marking its course by the rapid alteration of Edgar Linton's state. The havoc that months had previously wrought was now emulated by the inroads of hours.

Catherine we would fain have deluded yet, but her own quick spirit refused to delude her. It divined in secret, and brooded on the dreadful probability, gradually ripening into certainty.

She had not the heart to mention her ride, when Thursday came round. I mentioned it for her, and obtained permission to order her out of doors, for the library, where her father stopped a short time daily—the brief period he could bear to sit up—and his chamber, had become her whole world. She grudged each moment that did not find her bending over his pillow, or seated by his side. Her countenance grew wan with watching and sorrow, and my master gladly dismissed her to what he flattered himself would be a happy change of scene and society, drawing comfort from the hope that she would not now be left entirely alone after his death.

He had a fixed idea, I guessed by several observations he let fall, that, as his nephew resembled him in person, he would resemble him in mind, for Linton's letters bore few or no indications of his defective character. And I, through pardonable weakness, refrained from correcting the error, asking myself what good there would be in disturbing his last moments with information that he had neither power nor opportunity to turn to account.

We deferred our excursion till the afternoon, a golden afternoon of August—every breath from the hills so full of life, that it seemed whoever respired it, though dying, might revive.

Catherine's face was just like the landscape—shadows and sunshine flitting over it in rapid succession, but the shadows rested longer, and the sunshine was more transient, and her poor little heart reproached itself for even that passing forgetfulness of its cares.

We discerned Linton watching at the same spot he had selected before. My young mistress alighted, and told me that, as she was resolved to stay a very little while, I had better hold the pony and remain on horseback, but I dissented. I wouldn't risk losing sight of the charge committed to me a minute, so we climbed the slope of heath together.

Master Heathcliff received us with greater animation on this occasion—not the animation of high spirits though, nor yet of joy. It looked more like fear.

"It is late!" he said, speaking short and with difficulty. "Is not your father very ill? I thought you wouldn't come."

"Why won't you be candid?" cried Catherine, swallowing her greeting. "Why cannot you say at once you don't want me? It is strange, Linton, that for the second time you have brought me here on purpose, apparently to distress us both, and for no reason besides!"

Linton shivered, and glanced at her, half-supplicating, half-ashamed, but his cousin's patience was not sufficient to endure this enigmatical behavior.

"My father is very ill," she said, "and why am I called from his bedside? Why didn't you send to absolve me from my promise, when you wished I wouldn't keep it? Come! I desire an explanation. Playing and trifling are completely banished out of my mind, and I can't dance attendance on your affectations now!"

"My affectations!" he murmured, "what are they? For heaven's sake, Catherine, don't look so angry! Despise me as much as you please, I am a worthless, cowardly wretch. I can't be scorned enough! But I'm too mean for your anger. Hate my father, and spare me, for contempt."

"Nonsense!" cried Catherine in a passion. "Foolish, silly boy! And there! He trembles as if I were really going to touch him! You needn't bespeak contempt, Linton. Anybody will have it spontaneously at your service. Get off! I shall return home. It is folly dragging you from the hearthstone, and pretending—what do we pretend? Let go my frock! If I pitied you for crying and looking so very frightened, you should spurn such pity. Ellen, tell him how disgraceful this conduct is. Rise, and don't degrade yourself into an abject reptile—don't!"

With streaming face and an expression of agony, Linton had thrown his nerveless frame along the ground. He seemed convulsed with exquisite terror.

"Oh!" he sobbed, "I cannot bear it! Catherine, Catherine, I'm a traitor, too, and I dare not tell you! But leave me, and I shall be killed! Dear Catherine, my life is in your hands, and you have said you loved me—and if you did, it wouldn't harm you. You'll not go, then? Kind, sweet, good Catherine! And perhaps you will consent—and he'll let me die with you!"

My young lady, on witnessing his intense anguish, stooped to raise him. The old feeling of indulgent tenderness overcame her vexation, and she grew thoroughly moved and alarmed.

"Consent to what?" she asked. "To stay? Tell me the meaning of this strange talk, and I will. You contradict your own words, and distract me! Be calm and frank, and confess at once all that weighs on your heart. You wouldn't injure me, Linton, would you? You wouldn't let any enemy hurt me, if you could prevent it? I'll believe you are a coward for yourself, but not a cowardly betrayer of your best friend."

"But my father threatened me," gasped the boy, clasping his attenuated fingers, "and I dread him—I dread him! I dare not tell!"

"Oh, well!" said Catherine, with scornful compassion, "keep your secret and save yourself. I'm no coward. I'm not afraid!"

Her magnanimity provoked his tears. He wept wildly, kissing her supporting hands, and yet could not summon courage to speak out. I was cogitating what the mystery might be, and determined Catherine should never suffer to benefit him or anyone else, by my good will, when, hearing a rustle among the ling, I looked up and saw Mr. Heathcliff almost close upon us, descending the Heights. He didn't cast a glance towards my companions, though they were sufficiently near for Linton's sobs to be audible, but hailing me in the almost hearty tone he assumed to none besides, and the sincerity of which I couldn't avoid doubting, he said:

"It is something to see you so near to my house, Nelly. How are you at the Grange? Let us hear. The rumor goes," he added, in a lower tone, "that Edgar Linton is on his deathbed. Perhaps they exaggerate his illness?"

"No, my master is dying," I replied. "It is true enough. A sad thing it will be for us all, but a blessing for him!"

"How long will he last, do you think?" he asked.

"I don't know," I said.

"Because," he continued, looking at the two young people, who were fixed under his eye—Linton appeared as if he could not venture to stir or raise his head, and Catherine could not move, on his account, "because that lad yonder seems determined to beat me, and I'd thank his uncle to be quick, and go before him! Hallo! Has the whelp been playing that game long? I did give him some lessons about sniveling. Is he pretty lively with Miss Linton generally?"

"Lively? No—he has shown the greatest distress," I answered. "To see him, I should say, that instead of rambling with his sweetheart on the hills, he ought to be in bed, under the hands of a doctor."

"He shall be, in a day or two," muttered Heathcliff. "But first—get up, Linton! Get up!" he shouted. "Don't grovel on the ground there—up, this moment!"

Linton had sunk prostrate again in another paroxysm of helpless fear, caused by his father's glance towards him, I suppose. There was nothing else to produce such humiliation. He made several efforts to obey, but his little strength was annihilated for the time, and he fell back again with a moan. Mr. Heathcliff advanced, and lifted him to lean against a ridge of turf.

"Now," said he, with curbed ferocity, "I'm getting angry and if you don't command that paltry spirit of yours—damn you! Get up directly!"

"I will, father," he panted. "Only, let me alone, or I shall faint. I've done as you wished, I'm sure. Catherine will tell you that I—that I—have been cheerful. Ah! Keep by me, Catherine, give me your hand."

"Take mine," said his father. "Stand on your feet. There now—she'll lend you her arm. That's right, look at her. You would imagine I was the devil himself, Miss Linton, to excite such horror. Be so kind as to walk home with him, will you? He shudders if I touch him."

"Linton dear!" whispered Catherine, "I can't go to Wuthering Heights. Papa has forbidden me. He'll not harm you. Why are you so afraid?"

"I can never re-enter that house," he answered. "I'm not to re-enter it without you!"

"Stop!" cried his father. "We'll respect Catherine's filial scruples. Nelly, take him in, and I'll follow your advice concerning the doctor, without delay."

"You'll do well," replied I. "But I must remain with my mistress. To mind your son is not my business."

"You are very stiff," said Heathcliff, "I know that, but you'll force me to pinch the baby and make it scream before it moves your charity. Come, then, my hero. Are you willing to return, escorted by me?"

He approached once more, and made as if he would seize the fragile being, but shrinking back, Linton clung to his cousin, and implored her to accompany him, with a frantic importunity that admitted no denial.

However I disapproved, I couldn't hinder her. Indeed, how could she have refused him herself? What was filling him with dread we had no means of discerning, but there he was, powerless under its grip, and any addition seemed capable of shocking him into idiocy.

We reached the threshold. Catherine walked in, and I stood waiting till she had conducted the invalid to a chair, expecting her out immediately, when Mr. Heathcliff, pushing me forward, exclaimed, "My house is not stricken with the plague, Nelly, and I have a mind to be hospitable today. Sit down, and allow me to shut the door."

He shut and locked it. I started.

"You shall have tea before you go home," he added. "I am by myself. Hareton is gone with some cattle to the Lees, and Zillah and Joseph are off on a journey of pleasure, and, though I'm used to being alone, I'd rather have some interesting company, if I can get it. Miss Linton, take your seat by him. I give you what I have. The present is hardly worth accepting, but I have nothing else to offer. It is Linton, I mean. How she does stare! It's odd what a savage feeling I have to anything that seems afraid of me! Had I been born where laws are less strict and tastes less dainty, I should treat myself to a slow vivisection of those two, as an evening's amusement."

Heathcliff drew in his breath, struck the table, and swore to himself, "By hell! I hate them."

"I am not afraid of you!" exclaimed Catherine, who could not hear the latter part of his speech. She stepped close up, her black eyes flashing with passion and resolution. "Give me that key. I will have it!" she said. "I wouldn't eat or drink here, if I were starving."

Heathcliff had the key in his hand that remained on the table. He looked up, seized with a sort of surprise at her boldness, or, possibly, reminded, by her voice and glance, of the person from whom she inherited it.

She snatched at the instrument, and half succeeded in getting it out of his loosened fingers, but her action recalled him to the present, he recovered it speedily.

"Now, Catherine Linton," he said, "stand off, or I shall knock you down, and, that will make Mrs. Dean mad."

Regardless of this warning, she captured his closed hand and its contents again. "We will go!" she repeated, exerting her utmost efforts to cause the iron muscles to relax, and finding that her nails made no impression, she applied her teeth pretty sharply.

Heathcliff glanced at me a glance that kept me from interfering a moment. Catherine was too intent on his fingers to notice his face. He opened them suddenly, and resigned the object of dispute, but, ere she had well secured it, he seized her with the liberated hand, and, pulling her on his knee, administered with the other a shower of terrific slaps on both sides of the head, each sufficient to have fulfilled his threat, had she been able to fall.

At this diabolical violence I rushed on him furiously. "You villain!" I began to cry, "you villain!" A touch on the chest silenced me. I am stout, and soon put out of breath, and, what with that and the rage, I staggered dizzily back and felt ready to suffocate, or to burst a blood-vessel.

The scene was over in two minutes, Catherine, released, put her two hands to her temples, and looked just as if she were not sure whether her ears were off or on. She trembled like a reed, poor thing, and leant against the table perfectly bewildered.

"I know how to chastise children, you see," said the scoundrel, grimly, as he stooped to repossess himself of the key, which had dropped to the floor. "Go to Linton now, as I told you, and cry at your ease! I shall be your father, tomorrow—all the father you'll have in a few days—and you shall have plenty of that. You can bear plenty. You're no weakling. You shall have a daily taste, if I catch such a devil of a temper in your eyes again!"

Cathy ran to me instead of Linton, and knelt down and put her burning cheek on my lap, weeping aloud. Her cousin had shrunk into a corner of the settle, as quiet as a mouse, congratulating himself, I dare say, that the correction had alighted on another than him.

Mr. Heathcliff, perceiving us all confounded, rose, and expeditiously made the tea himself. The cups and saucers were laid ready. He poured it out, and handed me a cup.

"Wash away your spleen," he said. "And help your own naughty pet and mine. It is not poisoned, though I prepared it. I'm going out to seek your horses."

Our first thought, on his departure, was to force an exit somewhere. We tried the kitchen door, but that was fastened outside. We looked at the windows—they were too narrow for even Cathy's little figure.

"Master Linton," I cried, seeing we were regularly imprisoned, "you know what your diabolical father is after, and you shall tell us, or I'll box your ears, as he has done your cousin's."

"Yes, Linton, you must tell," said Catherine. "It was for your sake I came, and it will be wickedly ungrateful if you refuse."

"Give me some tea, I'm thirsty, and then I'll tell you," he answered. "Mrs. Dean, go away. I don't like you standing over me. Now, Catherine, you are letting your tears fall into my cup. I won't drink that. Give me another."

Catherine pushed another to him, and wiped her face. I felt disgusted at the little wretch's composure, since he was no longer in terror for himself. The anguish he had exhibited on the moor subsided as soon as ever he entered Wuthering Heights, so I guessed he had been menaced with an awful visitation of wrath if he failed in decoying us there, and, that accomplished, he had no further immediate fears.

"Papa wants us to be married," he continued, after sipping some of the liquid. "And he knows your papa wouldn't let us marry now, and he's afraid of my dying if we wait, so we are to be married in the morning. You are to stay here all night, and, if you do as he wishes, you shall return home next day, and take me with you."

"Take you with her, pitiful changeling!" I exclaimed. "You marry? Why, the man is mad! Or he thinks us fools, every one. And do you imagine that beautiful young lady, that healthy, hearty girl, will tie herself to a little perishing monkey like you? Are you cherishing the notion that anybody, let alone Miss Catherine Linton, would have you for a husband? You want whipping for bringing us in here at all, with your dastardly puling tricks. Don't look so silly, now! I've a very good mind to shake you severely, for your contemptible treachery, and your imbecile conceit."

I did give him a slight shaking, but it brought on the cough, and he took to his ordinary resource of moaning and weeping, and Catherine rebuked me.

"Stay all night? No!" she said, looking slowly round. "Ellen, I'll burn that door down but I'll get out."

And she would have commenced the execution of her threat directly, but Linton was up in alarm for his dear self again. He clasped her in his two feeble arms sobbing.

"Won't you have me, and save me? Not let me come to the Grange? Oh, darling Catherine! You mustn't go and leave, after all. You must obey my father—you must!"

"I must obey my own," she replied, "and relieve him from this cruel suspense. The whole night! What would he think? He'll be distressed already. I'll either break or burn a way out of the house. Be quiet! You're in no danger, but if you hinder me—Linton, I love Papa better than you!"

The mortal terror he felt of Mr. Heathcliff's anger restored to the boy his coward's eloquence. Catherine was near distraught. Still, she persisted that she must go home, and tried entreaty in her turn, persuading him to subdue his selfish agony. While they were thus occupied, our jailer reentered.

"Your beasts have trotted off," he said, "and—now, Linton! Sniveling again? What has she been doing to you? Come, come— have done, and get to bed. In a month or two, my lad, you'll be able to pay her back her present tyrannies with a vigorous hand. You're pining for pure love, are you not? Nothing else in the world, and she shall have you! There, to bed! Zillah won't be here tonight, you must undress yourself. Hush! Hold your noise! Once in your own room, I'll not come near you. You needn't fear. By chance, you've managed tolerably. I'll look to the rest."

He spoke these words, holding the door open for his son to pass, and the latter achieved his exit exactly as a spaniel might which suspected the person who attended on it of designing a spiteful squeeze. The lock was re-secured. Heathcliff approached the fire, where my mistress and I stood silent. Catherine looked up, and instinctively raised her hand to her cheek. His nearness revived a painful sensation.

Anybody else would have been incapable of regarding the childish act with sternness, but he scowled on her and muttered, "Oh! You are not afraid of me? Your courage is well disguised. You seem damnably afraid!"

"I am afraid now," she replied, "because, if I stay, Papa will be miserable. How can I endure making him miserable—when he—when he—Mr. Heathcliff, let me go home! I promise to marry Linton. Papa would like me to, and I love him. Why should you wish to force me to do what I'll willingly do of myself?"

"Let him dare to force you," I cried. "There's law in the land, thank God! There is, though we be in an out-of-the-way place. I'd inform if he were my own son and it's felony without benefit of clergy!"

"Silence!" said the ruffian. "To the devil with your clamor! I don't want you to speak. Miss Linton, I shall enjoy myself remarkably in thinking your father will be miserable. I shall not sleep for satisfaction. You could have hit on no surer way of fixing your residence under my roof for the next twenty-four hours than informing me that such an event would follow. As to your promise to marry Linton, I'll take care you shall keep it, for you shall not quit this place till it is fulfilled."

"Send Ellen, then, to let Papa know I'm safe!" exclaimed Catherine, weeping bitterly. "Or marry me now. Poor Papa! Ellen, he'll think we're lost. What shall we do?"

"Not he! He'll think you are tired of waiting on him, and run off for a little amusement," answered Heathcliff. "You cannot deny that you entered my house of your own accord, in contempt of his injunctions to the contrary. And it is quite natural that you should desire amusement at your age, and that you would weary of nursing a sick man, and that man only your father. Catherine, his happiest days were over when your days began. He cursed you, I dare say, for coming into the world (I did, at least). And it would just do if he cursed you as he went out of it. I'd join him. I don't love you! How could I? Weep away. As far as I can see, it will be your chief diversion hereafter, unless Linton make amends for other losses. And your provident parent appears to fancy he may. His letters of advice and consolation entertained me vastly. In his last he recommended my jewel to be careful of his, and kind to her when he got her. Careful and kind— that's paternal. But Linton requires his whole stock of care and kindness for himself. Linton can play the little tyrant well. He'll undertake to torture any number of cats, if their teeth be drawn and their claws pared. You'll be able to tell his uncle fine tales of his kindness, when you get home again, I assure you."

"You're right there!" I said. "Explain your son's character. Show his resemblance to yourself, and then, I hope, Miss Cathy will think twice before she believes what she sees and hears!"

"I don't much mind speaking of his amiable qualities now," he answered, "because she must either accept him or remain a prisoner, and you along with her, till your master dies. I can detain you both, quite concealed, here. If you doubt, encourage her to retract her word, and you'll have an opportunity of judging!"

"I'll not retract my word," said Catherine. "I'll marry him within this hour, if I may go to Thrushcross Grange afterwards. Mr. Heathcliff, you're a cruel man, but you're not a fiend, and you won't, from mere malice, destroy irrevocably all my happiness. If Papa thought I had left him on purpose, and if he died before I returned, could I bear to live? I've given over crying. But I'm going to kneel here, at your knee, and I'll not get up, and I'll not take my eyes from your face till you look back at me! No, don't turn away! Do look! You'll see nothing to provoke you. I don't hate you. I'm not angry that you struck me. Have you never loved anybody in all your life, Uncle? Never? Ah! You must look once. I'm so wretched, you can't help being sorry and pitying me."

"Keep your fingers off, and move, or I'll kick you!" cried Heathcliff, brutally repulsing her. "I'd rather be hugged by a snake. How the devil can you dream of fawning on me? I detest you!"

He shrugged his shoulders—shook himself, indeed, as if his flesh crept with aversion, and thrust back his chair, while I got up, and opened my mouth, to commence a downright torrent of abuse. But I was rendered dumb in the middle of the first sentence, by a threat that I should be shown into a room by myself the very next syllable I uttered.

It was growing dark—we heard a sound of voices at the garden gate. Our host hurried out instantly. He had his wits about him; we had not. There was a talk of two or three minutes, and he returned alone.

"I thought it had been your cousin Hareton," I observed to Catherine. "I wish he would arrive! Who knows but he might take our part?"

"It was three servants sent to seek you from the Grange," said Heathcliff, overhearing me. "You should have opened a lattice and called out, but I could swear that chit is glad you didn't. She's glad to be obliged to stay, I'm certain."

At learning the chance we had missed, we both gave vent to our grief without control, and he allowed us to wail on till nine o'clock. Then he bid us go upstairs, through the kitchen, to Zillah's chamber, and I whispered my companion to obey. Perhaps we might contrive to get through the window there, or into a garret, and out by its skylight. The window, however, was narrow, like those below, and the garret trap was safe from our attempts, for we were fastened in as before.

Neither of us lay down. Catherine took her station by the lattice, and watched anxiously for morning, a deep sigh being the only answer I could obtain to my frequent entreaties that she would try to rest.

I seated myself in a chair, and rocked to and fro, passing harsh judgment on my many derelictions of duty, from which, it struck me then, all the misfortunes of my employers sprang. It was not the case, in reality, I am aware, but it was, in my imagination, that dismal night, and I thought Heathcliff himself less guilty than I.

At seven o'clock he came, and inquired if Miss Linton had risen. She ran to the door immediately, and answered, "Yes."

"Here, then," he said, opening it, and pulling her out. I rose to follow, but he turned the lock again. I demanded my release.

"Be patient," he replied. "I'll send up your breakfast in a while."

I thumped on the panels, and rattled the latch angrily and Catherine asked why I was still shut up? He answered, I must try to endure it another hour, and they went away. I endured it two or three hours. At length, I heard a footstep, not Heathcliff's.

"I've brought you something to eat," said a voice, "open t' door!"

Complying eagerly, I beheld Hareton, laden with food enough to last me all day.

"Take it," he added, thrusting the tray into my hand.

"Stay one minute," I began.

"Nay," cried he, and retired, regardless of any prayers I could pour forth to detain him.

And there I remained enclosed the whole day, and the whole of the next night, and another, and another. Five nights and four days I remained, altogether, seeing nobody but Hareton once every morning, and he was a model of a jailer—surly, and dumb, and deaf to every attempt at moving his sense of justice or compassion.

At length, I finally came to recognize that the impetus for the increase in his surly manner was that he coveted Catherine for himself. I thought that perhaps stirring his sense of grievance and injustice would move him to my side, so on the next morning, I resolved to encourage his frustration with the situation.

When he brought the meal, I said, "I suppose the wedding has been accomplished. Heathcliff no doubt bribed the curate."

The only response was a grunt.

I sighed. "I wish I could have been there for her. She could have used some instruction for her wedding night." I did not want Hareton to know she hadn't gone to her husband a virgin; I wanted him to think about what a prize he had lost.

He stiffened, but said nothing.

I plucked up my courage and went on. "Perhaps he's too unwell to consummate their marriage. Perhaps that's why Mr. Heathcliff is forcing us to stay—"

"They've done it!" Hareton yelled, probably as much to drown out my words as to answer my unstated question. "Mr. Heathcliff made them, or the marriage could be set aside."

My heart gave a queer lurch. "Made them?" I repeated.

"He said Miss couldn't go home to Thrushcross Grange until she did it, no matter how much she cried. So then they said they had, but he wouldn't believe it, so he set me to watch."

I gasped. The exquisite cruelty of the demand was immediately apparent to me. I sorrowed that Heathcliff could think of it. How impossible it would be for Linton to sustain the effort required with another man watching, especially Hareton, who despised him; and how humiliating for Catherine, on all counts; and how devastating to Hareton, who cherished a tenderness for Catherine himself. Heathcliff could not have devised a more vicious plan had he twenty years to develop it.

"He cried the whole time," Hareton said in disgust. "And Catherine despised him."

I did not see how that could result in the successful consummation of their marriage, and said so. He grunted, but I pushed, and at length he gave over and said, "I was watching from the door, and I saw they weren't getting anywhere, so I came in. And I bade Cathy take off her clothes, because a naked woman concentrates a man's mind wonderfully."

Then he told his story. Cathy flatly refused at first to take off her clothes, but Hareton said it was the only way, and then Linton started bawling and finally, in an excess of frustration, she stripped off her dress and stood naked and glorious in front of the two men.

Annoyed, she marched over to the bed, where Linton lay, and stripped off his trousers. Her rough handling did nothing to arouse him, and he begged her to stop.

Finally Hareton grasped her arm, and, bending near, uttered provocative and naughty words. "Pretend you're doing it with me," he suggested.

She gasped and pulled her arm away. "Linton is my husband!" she cried, as if greatly affronted. But Hareton knew she was thinking about what he'd said, because this time when she reached out to touch her husband, it was with a gentle caress.

"Oh, Linton," she whispered. "You know I'm very pleased to be your wife."

Linton made a mewling sound, and she petted him and kissed him until he had settled down again and had stopped crying. He closed his eyes and murmured that she must do what she had to do. Then she began to stroke him, her fingers caressing over his thighs and his shaft.

Hareton had his own shaft in hand, watching every movement she made. Catherine looked up and saw him. He didn't try to hide his arousal or what he was doing about it. Instead of crying out or objecting, Catherine began stroking Linton the way Hareton was stroking himself.

Hareton stepped a little closer to the bed, so he could see her naked body better. The firelight cast a glow on her skin, and he fancied that she might prefer to have his shaft inside her, instead of her husband's.

He glanced between her legs and when he met her gaze again, he swallowed hard, desire in his eyes. Cathy's hand crept down to that secret place. She rubbed herself as she watched him do the same. It was a silent ballet, two people pleasuring each other without touch.

She didn't know what she was searching for, but when it arrived, she was caught up in a whirlwind of sensation. Waves of pleasure washed over her as she watched Hareton find his own. He kept his gaze on her as well. When it was done, she settled herself over Linton, whose eyes flew open at her touch. With a convulsion, he emptied himself inside her with one cry.

Cathy rolled off him and cleaned up, then put her clothes back on. She crept into the chair to sleep, unwilling to share a bed with Linton. Hareton went to report what he'd seen to Heathcliff, and hoped her sleep was troubled with dreams of him.

CHAPTER 40

ON THE FIFTH MORNING, or rather afternoon, a different step approached—lighter and shorter, and, this time, the person entered the room. It was Zillah, donned in her scarlet shawl, with a black silk bonnet on her head, and a willow-basket swung to her arm.

"Eh, dear! Mrs. Dean!" she exclaimed. "Well! There is a talk about you at Gimmerton. I never thought but you were sunk in the Blackhorse marsh, and missy with you, till master told me you'd been found, and he'd lodged you here! What! And you must have got on an island, sure? And how long were you in the hole? Did master save you, Mrs. Dean? But you're not so thin—you've not been so poorly, have you?"

"Your master is a true scoundrel!" I replied. "But he shall answer for it. He needn't have raised that tale. It shall all be laid bare!"

"What do you mean?" asked Zillah. "It's not his tale. They tell that in the village—about your being lost in the marsh, and I calls to Earnshaw, when I come in—'Eh, they's queer things, Mr. Hareton, happened since I went off. It's a sad pity of that likely young lass, and cant Nelly Dean.' He stared. I thought he had not heard aught, so I told him the rumor.

"The master listened, and he just smiled to himself, and said, 'If they have been in the marsh, they are out now, Zillah. Nelly Dean is lodged, at this minute, in your room. You can tell her to flit, when you go up, here is the key. The bog-water got into her head, and she would have run home quite flighty, but I fixed her till she came round to her senses. You can bid her go to the Grange at once, if she be able, and carry a message from me, that her young lady will follow in time to attend the squire's funeral.'"

"Mr. Edgar is not dead?" I gasped. "Oh! Zillah, Zillah!"

"No, no, sit you down, my good mistress," she replied. "You're right sickly yet. He's not dead. Doctor Kenneth thinks he may last another day. I met him on the road and asked."

Instead of sitting down, I snatched my outdoor things, and hastened below, for the way was free. On entering the house, I looked about for someone to give information of Catherine. The place was filled with sunshine, and the door stood wide open, but nobody seemed at hand.

As I hesitated whether to go off at once, or return and seek my mistress, a slight cough drew my attention to the hearth. Linton lay on the settle, sole tenant, sucking a stick of sugar-candy, and pursuing my movements with apathetic eyes.

"Where is Miss Catherine?" I demanded sternly, supposing I could frighten him into giving intelligence, by catching him thus, alone. He sucked on like an innocent.

"Is she gone?" I said.

"No," he replied. "She's upstairs. She's not to go. We won't let her."

"You won't let her, little idiot!" I exclaimed. "Direct me to her room immediately, or I'll make you sing out sharply."

"Papa would make you sing out, if you attempted to get there," he answered. "He says I'm not to be soft with Catherine. She's my wife, and it's shameful that she should wish to leave me. He says she hates me and wants me to die, that she may have my money, but she shan't have it. And she shan't go home! She never shall! She may cry, and be sick as much as she pleases!"

He resumed his former occupation, closing his lids, as if he meant to drop asleep.

"Master Heathcliff," I resumed, "have you forgotten all Catherine's kindness to you last winter, when you affirmed you loved her, and when she brought you books and sung you songs, and came many a time through wind and snow to see you? She wept to miss one evening, because you would be disappointed, and you felt then that she was a hundred times too good to you. Now you believe the lies your father tells, though you know he detests you both. And you join him against her. That's fine gratitude, is it not?"

The corner of Linton's mouth fell, and he took the sugar-candy from his lips.

"Did she come to Wuthering Heights because she hated you?" I continued. "Think for yourself! As to your money, she does not even know that you will have any. And you say she's sick, and yet you leave her alone, up there in a strange house! You who have felt what it is to be so neglected! You could pity your own sufferings, and she pitied them, too, but you won't pity hers! I shed tears, Master Heathcliff, you see—an elderly woman, and a servant merely—and you, after pretending such affection, and having reason to worship her almost, store every tear you have for yourself, and lie there quite at ease. Ah! You're a heartless, selfish boy!"

"I can't stay with her," he answered crossly. "I'll not stay by myself. She cries so I can't bear it. And she won't give over and consent to stay, though I say I'll call my father. I did call him once, and he threatened to strangle her if she was not quiet, but she began again the instant he left the room, moaning and grieving all night long, though I screamed for vexation that I couldn't sleep."

"Is Mr. Heathcliff out?" I inquired, perceiving that the wretched creature had no power to sympathize with his cousin's mental tortures.

"He's in the court," he replied, "talking to Doctor Kenneth, who says Uncle is dying, truly, at last. I'm glad, for I shall be master of the Grange after him. Catherine always spoke of it as her house. It isn't hers! It's mine. Papa says everything she has is mine. All her nice books are mine. She offered to give me them, and her pretty birds, and her pony Minny, if I would get the key of our room, and let her out, but I told her she had nothing to give, they were all, all mine. And then she cried, and took a little picture from her neck, and said I should have that, two pictures in a gold case, on one side her mother, and on the other Uncle, when they were young. That was yesterday— I said they were mine, too, and tried to get them from her. The spiteful thing wouldn't let me. She pushed me off, and hurt me. I shrieked out—that frightens her—she heard Papa coming, and she broke the hinges and divided the case, and gave me her mother's portrait, the other she attempted to hide. But Papa asked what was the matter, and I explained it. He took the one I had away, and ordered her to resign hers to me, she refused, and he—he struck her down, and wrenched it off the chain, and crushed it with his foot."

"And were you pleased to see her struck?" I asked, having my designs in encouraging his talk.

"I winked," he answered. "I wink to see my father strike a dog or a horse, he does it so hard. Yet I was glad at first—she deserved punishing for pushing me. But when Papa was gone, she made me come to the window and showed me her cheek cut on the inside, against her teeth, and her mouth filling with blood, and then she gathered up the bits of the picture, and went and sat down with her face to the wall, and she has never spoken to me since. I sometimes think she can't speak for pain. I don't like to think so, but she's a naughty thing for crying continually, and she looks so pale and wild, I'm afraid of her."

"And you can get the key if you choose?" I said.

"Yes, when I am upstairs," he answered. "But I can't walk upstairs now."

"In what apartment is it?" I asked.

"Oh," he cried, "I shan't tell you where it is. It is our secret. Nobody, neither Hareton nor Zillah, is to know. There! You've tired me—go away, go away!" And he turned his face on to his arm, and shut his eyes again.

I considered it best to depart without seeing Mr. Heathcliff, and bring a rescue for my young lady from the Grange.

On reaching it, the astonishment of my fellow servants to see me, and their joy also, was intense, and when they heard that their little mistress was safe, two or three were about to hurry up and shout the news at Mr. Edgar's door. But I bespoke the announcement of it myself.

How changed I found him, even in those few days! He lay an image of sadness and resignation awaiting his death. Very young he looked. Though his actual age was thirty-nine, one would have called him ten years younger, at least. He thought of Catherine, for he murmured her name. I touched his hand, and spoke.

"Catherine is coming, dear master!" I whispered. "She is alive and well, and will be here, I hope, tonight."

I trembled at the first effects of this intelligence. He half rose up, looked eagerly round the apartment, and then sank back in a swoon.

As soon as he recovered, I related our compulsory visit, and detention at the Heights. I said Heathcliff forced me to go in, which was not quite true. I uttered as little as possible against Linton, nor did I describe all his father's brutal conduct—my intentions being to add no bitterness, if I could help it, to his already overflowing cup.

He divined that one of his enemy's purposes was to secure the personal property, as well as the estate, to his son, or rather himself. Yet why he did not wait till his decease was a puzzle to my master, because ignorant how nearly he and his nephew would quit the world together.

However, he felt that his will had better be altered. Instead of leaving Catherine's fortune at her own disposal, he determined to put it in the hands of trustees for her use during life, and for her children, if she had any, after her. By that means, it could not fall to Mr. Heathcliff should Linton die.

Having received his orders, I dispatched a man to fetch the attorney, and four more, provided with serviceable weapons, to demand my young lady of her jailer. Both parties were delayed very late. The single servant returned first.

He said Mr. Green, the lawyer, was out when he arrived at his house, and he had to wait two hours for his re-entrance, and then Mr. Green told him he had a little business in the village that must be done, but he would be at Thrushcross Grange before morning.

The four men came back unaccompanied also. They brought word that Catherine was ill—too ill to quit her room, and Heathcliff would not suffer them to see her. I scolded the stupid fellows well, for listening to that tale, which I would not carry to my master, resolving to take a whole bevy up to the Heights, at daylight, and storm it literally, unless the prisoner were quietly surrendered to us.

Her father shall see her, I vowed, and vowed again, if that devil be killed on his own door-stones in trying to prevent it!

Happily, I was spared the journey and the trouble.

I had gone downstairs at three o'clock to fetch a jug of water, and was passing through the hall with it in my hand, when a sharp knock at the front door made me jump.

"Oh! It is Green," I said, recollecting myself. "Only Green," and I went on, intending to send somebody else to open it, but the knock was repeated. Not loud, and still importunately.

I put the jug on the banister and hastened to admit him myself. The harvest moon shone clear outside. It was not the attorney. My own sweet little mistress sprang on my neck sobbing, "Ellen, Ellen! Is Papa alive?"

"Yes," I cried. "Yes, my angel, he is, God be thanked, you are safe with us again!"

She wanted to run, breathless as she was, upstairs to Mr. Linton's room, but I compelled her to sit down on a chair, and made her drink, and washed her pale face, chafing it into a faint color with my apron. Then I said I must go first, and tell of her arrival, imploring her to say, she should be happy with young Heathcliff. She stared, but soon comprehending why I counseled her to utter the falsehood, she assured me she would not complain.

I couldn't abide to be present at their meeting. I stood outside the chamber door a quarter of an hour, and hardly ventured near the bed, then. All was composed, however. Catherine's despair was as silent as her father's joy. She supported him calmly, in appearance, and he fixed on her features his raised eyes that seemed dilating with ecstasy.

He died blissfully, Mr. Lockwood. He died so. Kissing her cheek, he murmured, "I am going to her, and you, darling child, shall come to us!" and never stirred or spoke again, but continued that rapt, radiant gaze, till his pulse imperceptibly stopped and his soul departed. None could have noticed the exact minute of his death, it was so entirely without a struggle.

Whether Catherine had spent her tears, or whether the grief was too weighty to let them flow, she sat there dry-eyed till the sun rose. She sat till noon, and would still have remained brooding over that deathbed, but I insisted on her coming away and taking some repose.

It was well I succeeded in removing her, for at dinnertime appeared the lawyer, having called at Wuthering Heights to get his instructions how to behave. He had sold himself to Mr. Heathcliff. That was the cause of his delay in obeying my master's summons. Fortunately, no thought of worldly affairs crossed the latter's mind, to disturb him, after his daughter's arrival.

Mr. Green took upon himself to order everything and everybody about the place. He gave all the servants but me, notice to quit. He would have carried his delegated authority to the point of insisting that Edgar Linton should not be buried beside his wife, but in the chapel, with his family. There was the will, however, to hinder that, and my loud protestations against any infringement of its directions.

The funeral was hurried over. Catherine, Mrs. Linton Heathcliff now, was suffered to stay at the Grange till her father's corpse had quitted it.

She told me that her anguish had at last spurred Linton to incur the risk of liberating her. She heard the men I sent disputing at the door, and she gathered the sense of Heathcliff's answer. It drove her desperate. Linton, who had been conveyed up to the little parlor soon after I left, was terrified into fetching the key before his father reascended. He had the cunning to unlock and re-lock the door, without shutting it, and when he should have gone to bed, he begged to sleep with Hareton, and his petition was granted for once.

Catherine stole out before break of day. She dared not try the doors lest the dogs should raise an alarm, she visited the empty chambers and examined their windows, and, luckily, lighting on her mother's, she got easily out of its lattice, and on to the ground, by means of the fir tree close by. Her accomplice suffered for his share in the escape, notwithstanding his timid contrivances.

CHAPTER 41

*T*HE EVENING AFTER THE FUNERAL, my young lady
and I were seated in the library, now musing mournfully—one
of us despairingly—on our loss, now venturing conjectures as to the
gloomy future.

We had just agreed the best destiny that could await Catherine
would be a permission to continue resident at the Grange, at least during Linton's life, he being allowed to join her there, and I to remain as
housekeeper. That seemed rather too favorable an arrangement to be
hoped for, and yet I did hope, and began to cheer up under the prospect of retaining my home and my employment, and above all, my
beloved young mistress. A servant—one of the discarded ones, not
yet departed—rushed hastily in, and said "that devil Heathcliff" was
coming through the court. Should he fasten the door in his face?

If we had been mad enough to order that proceeding, we had
not time. He made no ceremony of knocking or announcing his
name. He was master, and availed himself of the master's privilege to
walk straight in, without saying a word.

The sound of our informant's voice directed him to the library.

He entered and, motioning him out, shut the door.

It was the same room into which he had been ushered, as a guest, eighteen years before. The same moon shone through the window, and the same autumn landscape lay outside. We had not yet lighted a candle, but all the apartment was visible, even to the portraits on the wall—the splendid head of Mrs. Linton, and the graceful one of her husband. Heathcliff advanced to the hearth. Time had little altered his person either. There was the same man, his dark face rather sallower and more composed, his frame a stone or two heavier, perhaps, and no other difference.

Catherine had risen with an impulse to dash out, when she saw him.

"Stop!" he said, arresting her by the arm. "No more runnings away! Where would you go? I'm come to fetch you home, and I hope you'll be a dutiful daughter and not encourage my son to further disobedience. I was embarrassed how to punish him when I discovered his part in the business. He's such a cobweb, a pinch would annihilate him, but you'll see by his look that he has received his due! I brought him down one evening, the day before yesterday, and just set him in a chair, and never touched him afterwards. I sent Hareton out, and we had the room to ourselves. In two hours, I called Joseph to carry him up again, and since then my presence is as potent on his nerves as a ghost. I fancy he sees me often, though I am not near. Hareton says he wakes and shrieks in the night by the hour together, and calls you to protect him from me, and, whether you like your precious mate, or not, you must come. He's your concern now. I yield all my interest in him to you."

"Why not let Catherine continue here," I pleaded, "and send Master Linton to her? As you hate them both, you'd not miss them. They can only be a daily plague to your unnatural heart."

"I'm seeking a tenant for the Grange," he answered, "and I want my children about me, to be sure. Besides, that lass owes me her services for her bread. I'm not going to nurture her in luxury and idleness after Linton is gone. Make haste and get ready, now, and don't oblige me to compel you."

"I shall," said Catherine. "Linton is all I have to love in the world, and though you have done what you could to make him hateful to me, and me to him, you cannot make us hate each other. And I defy you to hurt him when I am by, and I defy you to frighten me!"

"You are a boastful champion," replied Heathcliff, "but I don't like you well enough to hurt him. You shall get the full benefit of the torment, as long as it lasts. It is not I who will make him hateful to you—it is his own sweet spirit. He's as bitter as gall at your desertion and its consequences. Don't expect thanks for this noble devotion. I heard him draw a pleasant picture to Zillah of what he would do if he were as strong as I. The inclination is there, and his very weakness will sharpen his wits to find a substitute for strength."

"I know he has a bad nature," said Catherine. "He's your son. But I'm glad I've a better, to forgive it, and I know he loves me, and for that reason I love him. Mr. Heathcliff you have nobody to love you, and, however miserable you make us, we shall still have the revenge of thinking that your cruelty arises from your greater misery. You are miserable, are you not? Lonely, like the devil, and envious like him? Nobody loves you—nobody will cry for you when you die! I wouldn't be you!"

Catherine spoke with a kind of dreary triumph. She seemed to have made up her mind to enter into the spirit of her future family, and draw pleasure from the griefs of her enemies.

"You shall be sorry to be yourself presently," said her father-in-law, "if you stand there another minute. Begone, witch, and get your things!"

She scornfully withdrew.

In her absence, I began to beg for Zillah's place at the Heights, offering to resign mine to her, but he would suffer it on no account. He bid me be silent, and then, for the first time, allowed himself a glance round the room and a look at the pictures. Having studied

Mrs. Linton's, he said, "I shall have that home. Not because I need it, but—"

He turned abruptly to the fire, and continued, with what, for lack of a better word, I must call a smile. "I'll tell you what I did yesterday! I got the sexton, who was digging Linton's grave, to remove the earth off her coffin lid, and I opened it. I thought, once, I would have stayed there. When I saw her face again—it is hers yet!—he had hard work to stir me, but he said it would change if the air blew on it, and so I struck one side of the coffin loose, and covered it up. Not Linton's side, damn him! I wish he'd been soldered in lead. And I bribed the sexton to pull it away when I'm laid there, and slide mine out too, I'll have it made so. And then by the time Linton gets to us he'll not know which is which!"

"You were very wicked, Mr. Heathcliff!" I exclaimed. "Were you not ashamed to disturb the dead?"

"I disturbed nobody, Nelly," he replied, "and I gave some ease to myself. I shall be a great deal more comfortable now, and you'll have a better chance of keeping me underground, when I get there. Disturbed her? No! She has disturbed me, night and day, through eighteen years—incessantly—remorselessly—till yesternight, and yesternight I was tranquil. I dreamt I was sleeping the last sleep by that sleeper, with my heart stopped and my cheek frozen against hers."

"And if she had been dissolved into earth, or worse, what would you have dreamt of then?" I said.

"Of dissolving with her, and being more happy still!" he answered. "Do you suppose I dread any change of that sort? I expected such a transformation on raising the lid—but I'm better pleased that it should not commence till I share it. Besides, unless I had received a distinct impression of her passionless features that strange feeling would hardly have been removed. It began oddly. You know I was wild after she died, and eternally, from dawn to dawn, praying her to return to me—her spirit—I have a strong faith in ghosts. I have a conviction that they can, and do, exist among us!

"The day she was buried, there came a fall of snow. In the evening I went to the churchyard. It blew bleak as winter—all round was solitary. I didn't fear that her fool of a husband would wander up the glen so late, and no one else had business to bring them there. Being alone, and conscious two yards of loose earth was the sole barrier between us, I said to myself, 'I'll have her in my arms again! If she be cold, I'll think it is this north wind that chills me, and if she be motionless, it is sleep.' I got a spade from the tool house, and began to delve with all my might—it scraped the coffin, I fell to work with my hands, the wood commenced cracking about the screws.

"I was on the point of attaining my object, when it seemed that I heard a sigh from someone above, close at the edge of the grave, and bending down. 'If I can only get this off,' I muttered. 'I wish they may shovel in the earth over us both!' I wrenched at it more desperately still. There was another sigh, close at my ear. I appeared to feel the warm breath of it displacing the sleet-laden wind. I knew no living thing in flesh and blood was by, but, as certainly as you perceive the approach to some substantial body in the dark, though it cannot be discerned, so certainly I felt that Cathy was there. Not under me, but on the earth.

"A sudden sense of relief flowed from my heart through every limb. I relinquished my labor of agony, and turned consoled at once, unspeakably consoled. Her presence was with me. It remained while I refilled the grave, and led me home. You may laugh, if you will, but I was sure I should see her there. I was sure she was with me, and I could not help talking to her.

"Having reached the Heights, I rushed eagerly to the door. It was fastened, and, I remember, that accursed Earnshaw and my wife opposed my entrance. I remember stopping to kick the breath out of him, and then hurrying upstairs, to my room and hers. I looked round impatiently—I felt her by me—I could almost see her, and yet I could not! I ought to have sweat blood then, from the anguish of my yearning—from the fervor of my supplications to have but one glimpse! I had not one.

"She showed herself, as she often was in life, a devil to me! And, since then, sometimes more and sometimes less, I've been the sport of that intolerable torture! Infernal! Keeping my nerves at such a stretch that, if they had not resembled catgut, they would long ago have relaxed to the feebleness of Linton's. When I sat in the house with Hareton, it seemed that on going out I should meet her, when I walked on the moors I should meet her coming in. When I went from home I hastened to return, she must be somewhere at the Heights, I was certain! And when I slept in her chamber—I was beaten out of that—I couldn't lie there, for the moment I closed my eyes, she was either outside the window, or sliding back the panels, or entering the room, or even resting her darling head on the same pillow as she did when a child, and I must open my lids to see. And so I opened and closed them a hundred times a night—to be always disappointed! It racked me! I've often groaned aloud, till that old rascal Joseph no doubt believed that my conscience was playing the fiend inside of me.

"Now, since I've seen her, I'm pacified—a little. It was a strange way of killing. Not by inches, but by fractions of hairbreadths, to beguile me with the specter of a hope through eighteen years!"

Mr. Heathcliff paused and wiped his forehead, his hair clung to it, wet with perspiration, his eyes fixed on the red embers of the fire, the brows not contracted, but raised next the temples, diminishing the grim aspect of his countenance, but imparting a peculiar look of trouble, and a painful appearance of mental tension towards one absorbing subject. He only half addressed me, and I maintained silence. I didn't like to hear him talk!

After a short period, he resumed his meditation on the picture, took it down and leant it against the sofa to contemplate it at better advantage, and while so occupied Catherine entered, announcing that she was ready, and her pony should be saddled.

"Send that over tomorrow," said Heathcliff to me, then turning to her, he added. "You may do without your pony. It is a fine evening, and you'll need no ponies at Wuthering Heights, for what journeys you take, your own feet will serve you. Come along."

"Good-bye, Ellen!" whispered my dear little mistress. As she kissed me, her lips felt like ice. "Come and see me, Ellen, don't forget."

"Take care you do no such thing, Mrs. Dean!" said her new father. "When I wish to speak to you I'll come here. I want none of your prying at my house!"

He signed her to precede him, and casting back a look that cut my heart, she obeyed. I watched them, from the window, walk down the garden. Heathcliff fixed Catherine's arm under his. Though she disputed the act at first evidently, and with rapid strides he hurried her into the alley, whose trees concealed them.

CHAPTER 42

I HAVE PAID A VISIT TO THE HEIGHTS, but I have not seen her since she left. Joseph held the door in his hand when I called to ask after her, and wouldn't let me pass. He said Mrs. Linton was "thrang," and the master was not in. Zillah has told me something of the way they go on, otherwise I should hardly know who was dead and who living. She thinks Catherine haughty, and does not like her, I can guess by her talk.

My young lady asked some aid of her when she first came, but Mr. Heathcliff told her to follow her own business, and let his daughter-in-law look after herself, and Zillah willingly acquiesced, being a narrow-minded, selfish woman. **I think she was quite jealous of my young mistress. Although Zillah is a hearty attractive woman, there is no comparison between the two.** Catherine evinced a child's annoyance at the other's neglect, repaid it with contempt, and thus enlisted my informant among her enemies, as securely as if she had done her some great wrong.

I had a long talk with Zillah about six weeks ago, a little before you came, one day when we foregathered on the moor, and this is what she told me.

"The first thing Mrs. Linton did," she said, "on her arrival at the Heights, was to run upstairs, without even wishing good evening to me and Joseph. She shut herself into Linton's room, and remained till morning. Then, while the master and Earnshaw were at breakfast, she entered the house, and asked all in a quiver if the doctor might be sent for? Her cousin was very ill.

"'We know that!' answered Heathcliff, 'but his life is not worth a farthing, and I won't spend a farthing on him.'

"'But I cannot tell how to do,' she said, 'and if nobody will help me, he'll die!'

"'Walk out of the room,' cried the master, 'and let me never hear a word more about him! None here care what becomes of him, if you do, act the nurse, if you do not, lock him up and leave him.'

"Then she began to bother me, and I said I'd had enough plague with the tiresome thing. We each had our tasks, and hers was to wait on Linton. Mr. Heathcliff bid me leave that labor to her.

"How they managed together, I can't tell. I fancy he fretted a great deal, and moaned himself night and day, and she had precious little rest. One could guess by her white face and heavy eyes. She sometimes came into the kitchen all wildered like, and looked as if she would fain beg assistance, but I was not going to disobey the master. I never dare disobey him, Mrs. Dean, and, though I thought it wrong that Kenneth should not be sent for, it was no concern of mine either to advise or complain, and I always refused to meddle.

"Once or twice, after we had gone to bed, I've happened to open my door again and seen her sitting crying on the stairs' top, and then I've shut myself in quick, for fear of being moved to interfere. I did pity her then, I'm sure. Still I didn't wish to lose my place, you know.

"At last, one night she came boldly into my chamber, and frightened me out of my wits, by saying, 'Tell Mr. Heathcliff that his son is dying—I'm sure he is, this time. Get up, instantly, and tell him.'

"Having uttered this speech, she vanished again. I lay a quarter of an hour listening and trembling. Nothing stirred—the house was quiet.

"'She's mistaken,' I said to myself. 'He's got over it. I needn't disturb them.' And I began to doze. But my sleep was marred a second time by a sharp ringing of the bell—the only bell we have, put up on purpose for Linton, and the master called to me to see what was the matter, and inform them that he wouldn't have that noise repeated.

"I delivered Catherine's message. He cursed to himself, and in a few minutes came out with a lighted candle, and proceeded to their room. I followed. Mrs. Heathcliff was seated by the bedside, with her hands folded on her knees. Her father-in-law went up, held the light to Linton's face, looked at him, and touched him, afterwards he turned to her.

"'Now—Catherine,' he said, 'How do you feel?'

"She was dumb.

"'How do you feel, Catherine?' he repeated.

"'He's safe, and I'm free,' she answered. 'I should feel well—but,' she continued, with a bitterness she couldn't conceal, 'you have left me so long to struggle against death alone, that I feel and see only death! I feel like death!'

"And she looked like it, too! I gave her a little wine. Hareton and Joseph, who had been wakened by the ringing and the sound of feet, and heard our talk from outside, now entered. Joseph was fain, I believe, of the lad's removal. Hareton seemed a thought bothered—though he was more taken up with staring at Catherine than thinking of Linton. But the master bid him get off to bed again. We didn't want his help. He afterwards made Joseph remove the body to his chamber, and told me to return to mine, and Mrs. Heathcliff remained by herself.

"In the morning, he sent me to tell her she must come down to breakfast. She had undressed, and appeared going to sleep, and said she was ill, at which I hardly wondered. I informed Mr. Heathcliff, and he replied—'Well, let her be till after the funeral, and go up now and then to get her what is needful, and, as soon as she seems better, tell me.'

Cathy stayed upstairs a fortnight, according to Zillah, who visited her twice a day, and would have been rather more friendly, but her attempts at increasing kindness were proudly and promptly repelled.

Heathcliff went up once, to show her Linton's will. He had bequeathed the whole of his, and what had been her, moveable property, to his father. The poor creature was threatened, or coaxed, into that act during her week's absence, when his uncle died. The lands, being a minor, he could not meddle with. However, Mr. Heathcliff has claimed and kept them in his wife's right and his also. I suppose legally, at any rate, Catherine, destitute of cash and friends, cannot disturb his possession.

"Nobody," said Zillah, "ever approached her door, except that once, but I, and nobody asked anything about her. The first occasion of her coming down into the house was on a Sunday afternoon. She had cried out, when I carried up her dinner, that she couldn't bear any longer being in the cold. I told her the master was going to Thrushcross Grange, and Earnshaw and I needn't hinder her from descending. As soon as she heard Heathcliff's horse trot off, she made her appearance, donned in black, and her yellow curls combed back behind her ears as plain as a Quaker. She couldn't comb them out.

"Joseph and I generally go to chapel on Sundays." (The kirk, you know, has no minister now, explained Mrs. Dean; and they call the Methodists' or Baptists' place, I can't say which it is at Gimmerton, a chapel.)

"Joseph had gone," she continued, "but I thought proper to bide at home. Young folks are always the better for an elder's over-looking, and Hareton, with all his bashfulness, isn't a model of nice behavior. I let him know that his cousin would very likely sit with us, and she had been always used to see the Sabbath respected, so he had as good leave his guns and bits of indoor work alone, while she stayed.

"He colored up at the news, and cast his eyes over his hands and clothes. The train oil and gunpowder were shoved out of sight in a minute. I saw he meant to give her his company, and I guessed, by his way, he wanted to be presentable, so, laughing, as I durst not laugh when the master is by, I offered to help him, if he would, and joked at his confusion. He grew sullen, and began to swear.

"Now, Mrs. Dean," Zillah went on, seeing me not pleased by her manner, "you happen think your young lady too fine for Mr. Hareton, and happen you're right. But I own I should love well to bring her pride a peg lower. And what will all her learning and her daintiness do for her, now? She's as poor as you or I. Poorer, I'll be bound. You're saving, and I'm doing my little all, that road."

Hareton allowed Zillah to give him her aid, and she flattered him into a good humor, so, when Catherine came, half forgetting her former insults, he tried to make himself agreeable, by the house-keeper's account.

"Missis walked in," she said, "as chill as an icicle, and as high as a princess. I got up and offered her my seat in the armchair. No, she turned up her nose at my civility. Earnshaw rose, too, and bid her come to the settle, and sit close by the fire. He was sure she was starved.

"'I've been starved a month and more,' she answered, resting on the word as scornful as she could.

"And she got a chair for herself, and placed it at a distance from both of us. Having sat till she was warm, she began to look round, and discovered a number of books on the dresser. She was instantly upon her feet again, stretching to reach them, but they were too high up. Her cousin, after watching her endeavors a while, at last summoned courage to help her. She held her frock, and he filled it with the first that came to hand.

"That was a great advance for the lad. She didn't thank him, still, he felt gratified that she had accepted his assistance, and ventured to stand behind as she examined them, and even to stoop and point out what struck his fancy in certain old pictures that they contained, nor was he daunted by the saucy style in which she jerked the page from his finger. He contented himself with going a bit farther back and looking at her instead of the book.

"She continued reading, or seeking for something to read. His attention became, by degrees, quite centered in the study of her thick silky curls. Her face he couldn't see, and she couldn't see him. And, perhaps, not quite awake to what he did, but attracted like a child to a candle, at last he proceeded from staring to touching, he put out his hand and stroked one curl, as gently as if it were a bird. He might have stuck a knife into her neck, she started round in such a taking.

"'Get away this moment! How dare you touch me? Why are you stopping there?' she cried, in a tone of disgust. 'I can't endure you! I'll go upstairs again, if you come near me.'

"Mr. Hareton recoiled, looking as foolish as he could do. He sat down in the settle very quiet, and she continued turning over her volumes another half hour, finally, Earnshaw crossed over, and whispered to me.

"'Will you ask her to read to us, Zillah? I'm stalled of doing naught, and I do like—I could like to hear her! Do not say I wanted it, but ask of yourself.'

"'Mr. Hareton wishes you would read to us, ma'am,' I said, immediately. 'He'd take it very kind—he'd be much obliged.'

"She frowned, and looking up, answered. 'Mr. Hareton, and the whole set of you, will be good enough to understand that I reject any pretense at kindness you have the hypocrisy to offer! I despise you, and will have nothing to say to any of you! When I would have given my life for one kind word, even to see one of your faces, you all kept off. But I won't complain to you! I'm driven down here by the cold, not either to amuse you or enjoy your society.'

"'What could I ha' done?' began Earnshaw. 'How was I to blame?'"

"'Oh! You are an exception,' answered Mrs. Heathcliff. 'I never missed such a concern as you.'

"'But I offered more than once, and asked,' he said, kindling up at her pertness, 'I asked Mr. Heathcliff to let me wake for you—'

"'Be silent! I'll go out of doors, or anywhere, rather than have your disagreeable voice in my ear!' said my lady.

"Hareton muttered she might go to hell, for him! And unslinging his gun, restrained himself from his Sunday occupations no longer. He talked now, freely enough, and she presently saw fit to retreat to her solitude. But the frost had set in, and, in spite of her pride, she was forced to condescend to our company, more and more. However, I took care there should be no further scorning at my good nature. Ever since, I've been as stiff as herself, and she has no lover or liker among us. And she does not deserve one, for, let them say the least word to her, and she'll curl back without respect of any one. She'll snap at the master himself, and as good as dares him to thrash her, and the more hurt she gets, the more venomous she grows."

At first, on hearing this account from Zillah, I determined to leave my situation, take a cottage, and get Catherine to come and live with me. But Mr. Heathcliff would as soon permit that as he would set up Hareton in an independent house, and I can see no remedy, at present, unless she could marry again, and that scheme it does not come within my province to arrange.

Thus ended Mrs. Dean's story. Notwithstanding the doctor's prophecy, I am rapidly recovering strength. Though it be only the second week in January, I propose getting out on horseback in a day or two, and riding over to Wuthering Heights, to inform my landlord that I shall spend the next six months in London, and, if he likes, he may look out for another tenant to take the place after October. I would not pass another winter here for much.

CHAPTER 43

*Y*ESTERDAY WAS BRIGHT, calm, and frosty. I went to
the Heights as I proposed. My housekeeper entreated
me to bear a little note from her to her young lady, and I
did not refuse, for the worthy woman was not conscious of anything
odd in her request.

The front door stood open, but the jealous gate was fastened, as
at my last visit. I knocked and invoked Earnshaw from among the garden beds. He unchained it, and I entered. The fellow is as handsome
a rustic as need be seen. I took particular notice of him this time, but
then he does his best apparently to make the least of his advantages.

I asked if Mr. Heathcliff were at home. He answered, no, but he
would be in at dinnertime. It was eleven o'clock, and I announced my
intention of going in and waiting for him, at which he immediately
flung down his tools and accompanied me, in the office of watchdog,
not as a substitute for the host.

We entered together. Catherine was there, making herself useful
in preparing some vegetables for the approaching meal. She looked
more sulky and less spirited than when I had seen her first. She hardly

raised her eyes to notice me, and continued her employment with the same disregard to common forms of politeness as before, never returning my bow and good-morning by the slightest acknowledgment.

"She does not seem so amiable," I thought, "as Mrs. Dean would persuade me to believe. She's a beauty, it is true, but not an angel." **Still, her rudeness did not prevent me from indulging in a pleasantly erotic daydream at the sight of her splendid form, though her dress and manner were slovenly, and her person off-putting.**

Earnshaw surlily bid her remove her things to the kitchen. "Remove them yourself," she said, pushing them from her as soon as she had done, and retiring to a stool by the window, where she began to carve figures of birds and beasts out of the turnip-parings in her lap.

I approached her, pretending to desire a view of the garden, and, as I fancied, adroitly dropped Mrs. Dean's note on to her knee, unnoticed by Hareton—but she asked aloud, "What is that?" And chucked it off.

"A letter from your old acquaintance, the housekeeper at the Grange," I answered, annoyed at her exposing my kind deed, and fearful lest it should be imagined a missive of my own.

She would gladly have gathered it up at this information, but Hareton beat her, he seized and put it in his waistcoat, saying Mr. Heathcliff should look at it first. Thereat, Catherine silently turned her face from us, and, very stealthily, drew out her pocket-handkerchief and applied it to her eyes. Her cousin, after struggling a while to keep down his softer feelings, pulled out the letter and flung it on the floor beside her, as ungraciously as he could.

I did not wonder at their treatment of each other, despite my inadvertent knowledge that they were lovers. The atmosphere at the Heights was such that no one was likely to attain happiness there, or to treasure one another's company.

Catherine caught the missive and perused it eagerly, then she put a few questions to me concerning the inmates, rational and irrational, of her former home, and gazing towards the hills, murmured in solil-oquy, "I should like to be riding Minny down there! I should like to be climbing up there! Oh! I'm tired—I'm stalled, Hareton!"

And she leant her pretty head back against the sill, with half a yawn and half a sigh, and lapsed into an aspect of abstracted sadness, neither caring nor knowing whether we remarked her.

"Mrs. Heathcliff," I said, after sitting some time mute, "you are not aware that I am an acquaintance of yours? So intimate that I think it strange you won't come and speak to me. **I thought perhaps we could spend some time together.** My housekeeper never wearies of talking about and praising you, and she'll be greatly disappointed if I return with no news of or from you, except that you received her letter and said nothing!"

She appeared to wonder at this speech, and asked, "Does Ellen like you?"

"Yes, very well," I replied, hesitatingly.

"You must tell her," she continued, "that I would answer her letter, but I have no materials for writing. Not even a book from which I might tear a leaf."

"No books!" I exclaimed. "How do you contrive to live here without them? If I may take the liberty to inquire. Though provided with a large library, I'm frequently very dull at the Grange, take my books away, and I should be desperate!"

"I was always reading, when I had them," said Catherine, "and Mr. Heathcliff never reads, so he took it into his head to destroy my books. I have not had a glimpse of one for weeks. Only once, I searched through Joseph's store of theology, to his great irritation, and once, Hareton, I came upon a secret stock in your room—some Latin and Greek, and some tales and poetry. All old friends. I brought the last here—and you gathered them, as a magpie gathers silver spoons, for the mere love of stealing! They are of no use to you, or else you concealed them in the bad spirit that, as you cannot enjoy them, nobody else shall. Perhaps your envy counseled Mr. Heathcliff to rob me of my treasures? But I've most of them written on my brain and printed in my heart, and you cannot deprive me of those!"

Earnshaw blushed crimson when his cousin made this revelation of his private literary accumulations, and stammered an indignant denial of her accusations.

"Mr. Hareton is desirous of increasing his amount of knowledge," I said, coming to his rescue. "He is not envious, but emulous of your attainments. He'll be a clever scholar in a few years."

"And he wants me to sink into a dunce, meantime," answered Catherine. "Yes, I hear him trying to spell and read to himself, and pretty blunders he makes! I wish you would repeat Chevy Chase as you did yesterday. It was extremely funny. I heard you, and I heard you turning over the dictionary to seek out the hard words, and then cursing because you couldn't read their explanations!"

The young man evidently thought it too bad that he should be laughed at for his ignorance, and then laughed at for trying to remove it. I had a similar notion, and, remembered Mrs. Dean's anecdote of his first attempt at enlightening the darkness in which he had been reared.

I observed, "But, Mrs. Heathcliff, we have each had a commencement, and each stumbled and tottered on the threshold. Had our teachers scorned instead of aiding us, we should stumble and totter yet."

"Oh!" she replied, "I don't wish to limit his acquirements. Still, he has no right to appropriate what is mine, and make it ridiculous to me with his vile mistakes and mispronunciations! Those books, both prose and verse, were consecrated to me by other associations, and I hate to have them debased and profaned in his mouth! Besides, of all, he has selected my favorite pieces that I love the most to repeat, as if out of deliberate malice."

Harleton's chest heaved in silence a minute. He labored under a severe sense of mortification and wrath, which it was no easy task to suppress. I rose, and, from a gentlemanly idea of relieving his embarrassment, took up my station in the doorway, surveying the external prospect as I stood. He followed my example, and left the room, but presently reappeared, bearing half a dozen volumes in his hands, which he threw into Catherine's lap, exclaiming, "Take them! I never want to hear, or read, or think of them again!"

"I won't have them now," she answered. "I shall connect them with you, and dislike them. **You pretend to have feelings for me, then turn your back at the first word from your master.**"

She opened one that had obviously been often turned over, and read a portion in the drawling tone of a beginner, then laughed, and threw it from her. "And listen," she continued, provokingly, commencing a verse of an old ballad in the same fashion.

But his self-love would endure no further torment. I heard, and not altogether disapprovingly, a manual check given to her saucy tongue. The little wretch had done her utmost to hurt her cousin's sensitive though uncultivated feelings, and a physical argument was the only mode he had of balancing the account, and repaying its effects on the inflictor.

He afterwards gathered the books and hurled them on the fire. I read in his countenance what anguish it was to offer that sacrifice to spleen. I fancied that as they were consumed, he recalled the pleasure they had already imparted, and the triumph and ever-increasing pleasure he had anticipated from them. I guessed the incitement to his secret studies, also. He had been content with daily labor and rough animal enjoyments, till Catherine crossed his path. Shame at her scorn, and hope of her approval, were his first prompters to higher pursuits, and instead of guarding him from one and winning him to the other, his endeavors to raise himself had produced just the contrary result.

"Yes that's all the good that such a brute as you can get from them!" cried Catherine, sucking her damaged lip, and watching the conflagration with indignant eyes.

"You'd better hold your tongue, now!" he answered fiercely.

And his agitation precluded further speech, he advanced hastily to the entrance, where I made way for him to pass. **For a moment, I entertained the notion of expressing my attraction to her, and offering myself as an alternative to that rude brute. I fancied that my tender kisses on her poor bruised mouth would open her heart to me, that she might see how well-suited we were to one another.**

I moved from my position by the door, and was about to offer her my handkerchief, preparatory to embarking on a soliloquy about how well we might fit together, when I heard voices outside. Mr. Heathcliff, coming up the causeway, encountered Hareton, and laying hold of his shoulder asked, "What's to do now, my lad?"

"Naught, naught," he said, and broke away to enjoy his grief and anger in solitude.

Heathcliff stepped into the house and sighed. I drew away from Catherine, even if my body, notably my shaft straining in my trousers, protested the movement. I hoped Heathcliff would not notice the immediate cause of my discomfiture.

"It will be odd if I thwart myself," he muttered, unconscious that I was behind him. "But when I look for his father in his face, I find her every day more! How the devil is he so like? I can hardly bear to see him."

He bent his eyes to the ground, and walked moodily in. There was a restless, anxious expression in his countenance I had never remarked there before, and he looked sparer in person. His daughter-in-law, on perceiving him through the window, immediately escaped to the kitchen, so that I remained alone.

"I'm glad to see you out of doors again, Mr. Lockwood," he said, in reply to my greeting, "from selfish motives partly. I don't think I could readily supply your loss in this desolation. I've wondered, more than once, what brought you here."

"An idle whim, I fear, sir," was my answer, "or else an idle whim is going to spirit me away. I shall set out for London next week, and I must give you warning that I feel no disposition to retain Thrushcross

Grange beyond the twelve months I agreed to rent it. I believe I shall not live there anymore."

"Oh, indeed, you're tired of being banished from the world, are you?" he said. "But if you be coming to plead off paying for a place you won't occupy, your journey is useless. I never relent in exacting my due from any one."

"I'm coming to plead off nothing about it," I exclaimed, considerably irritated. "Should you wish it, I'll settle with you now," and I drew my notebook from my pocket.

"No, no," he replied, coolly, "you'll leave sufficient behind to cover your debts, if you fail to return. I'm not in such a hurry. Sit down and take your dinner with us, a guest that is safe from repeating his visit can generally be made welcome. Catherine! Bring the things in. Where are you?"

Catherine reappeared, bearing a tray of knives and forks.

"You may get your dinner with Joseph," muttered Heathcliff, aside, "and remain in the kitchen till he is gone."

She obeyed his directions very punctually. Perhaps she had no temptation to transgress. Living among clowns and misanthropists, she probably cannot appreciate a better class of people when she meets them.

With Mr. Heathcliff, grim and saturnine, on the one hand, and Hareton, absolutely silent, on the other, I made a somewhat cheerless meal, and bade adieu early. I would have departed by the back way, to get a last glimpse of Catherine and annoy old Joseph, but Hareton received orders to lead up my horse, and my host himself escorted me to the door, so I could not fulfill my wish.

"How dreary life gets over in that house!" I reflected, while riding down the road. "What a realization of something more romantic than a fairy tale it would have been for Mrs. Linton Heathcliff, had she and I struck up an attachment, as her good nurse desired, and migrated together into the stirring atmosphere of the town!"

CHAPTER 44

1802

*T*HIS SEPTEMBER I was invited to devastate the moors of a friend in the north, and on my journey to his abode, I unexpectedly came within fifteen miles of Gimmerton. The hostler at a roadside public-house was holding a pail of water to refresh my horses, when a cart of very green oats, newly reaped, passed by, and he remarked, "Yon's from Gimmerton, nah! They're always three weeks after other folk wi' their harvest."

"Gimmerton?" I repeated—my residence in that locality had already grown dim and dreamy. "Ah! I know. How far is it from this?"

"Happen fourteen mile o'er th' hills, and a rough road," he answered.

A sudden impulse seized me to visit Thrushcross Grange. It was scarcely noon, and I conceived that I might as well pass the night under my own roof as in an inn. Besides, I could spare a day easily to arrange matters with my landlord, and thus save myself the trouble of invading the neighborhood again. Having rested awhile, I directed my servant to inquire the way to the village, and, with great fatigue to our beasts, we managed the distance in some three hours.

I left him there, and proceeded down the valley alone. The grey church looked greyer, and the lonely churchyard lonelier. I distinguished a moor sheep cropping the short turf on the graves. It was sweet, warm weather—too warm for travelling, but the heat did not hinder me from enjoying the delightful scenery above and below. Had I seen it nearer August, I'm sure it would have tempted me to waste a month among its solitudes. In winter nothing more dreary, in summer nothing more divine, than those glens shut in by hills, and those bluff, bold swells of heath.

I reached the Grange before sunset, and knocked for admittance, but the family had retreated into the back premises, I judged, by one thin, blue wreath, curling from the kitchen chimney, and they did not hear. I rode into the court. Under the porch, a girl of nine or ten sat knitting, and an old woman reclined on the house steps, smoking a meditative pipe.

"Is Mrs. Dean within?" I demanded of the dame.

"Mistress Dean? Nay!" she answered. "She doesn't bide here. She's up at th' Heights."

"Are you the housekeeper, then?" I continued.

"Yeah, I keep the house," she replied.

"Well, I'm Mr. Lockwood, the master. Are there any rooms to lodge me in, I wonder? I wish to stay all night."

"T' maister!" she cried in astonishment. "What, whoever knew yah were coming? Yah should ha' send word. They's now nothing dry nor proper about t' place. No there isn't!"

She threw down her pipe and bustled in, the girl followed, and I entered too, soon perceiving that her report was true, and, moreover, that I had almost upset her wits by my unwelcome apparition. I bade her be composed. I would go out for a walk, and, meantime she must try to prepare a corner of a sitting room for me to sup in, and a bedroom to sleep in. No sweeping and dusting, only good fire and dry sheets were necessary.

She seemed willing to do her best, though she thrust the hearth-brush into the grates in mistake for the poker, and malappropriated several other articles of her craft. But I retired, confiding in her energy for a resting-place against my return. Wuthering Heights was the goal of my proposed excursion. An afterthought brought me back, when I had quitted the court.

"All well at the Heights?" I inquired of the woman.

"Yea, for all I know!" she answered, scurrying away with a pan of hot cinders.

I would have asked why Mrs. Dean had deserted the Grange, but it was impossible to delay her at such a crisis. I turned away and made my exit, rambling leisurely along, with the glow of a sinking sun behind, and the mild glory of a rising moon in front—one fading, and the other brightening—as I quitted the park, and climbed the stony by-road branching off to Mr. Heathcliff's dwelling. **I thought of Catherine often, both awake and in dreams, and wondered what life would be like if she had joined me in London as I had frequently wished her to do.**

Before I arrived in sight of the Heights, all that remained of day was a beamless amber light along the west, but I could see every pebble on the path, and every blade of grass, by that splendid moon.

I had neither to climb the gate nor to knock—it yielded to my hand. That is an improvement, I thought. And I noticed another, by the aid of my nostrils—a fragrance of stocks and wallflowers wafted on the air from amongst the homely fruit-trees.

Both doors and lattices were open, and yet, as is usually the case in a coal district, a fine red fire illumined the chimney. The comfort the eye derives from it renders the extra heat endurable. But the house of Wuthering Heights is so large that the inmates have plenty of space for withdrawing out of its influence, and accordingly what inmates there were had stationed themselves not far from one of the windows. I could both see them and hear them talk before I entered, and looked and listened in consequence, being moved thereto by a mingled sense of curiosity and envy, that grew as I lingered.

"Con-trary!" said a voice as sweet as a silver bell. "That for the third time, you dunce! I'm not going to tell you again. Recollect, or I'll pull your hair!"

"Contrary, then," answered another, in deep but softened tones. "And now, kiss me, for minding so well."

"No, read it over first correctly, without a single mistake."

The male speaker began to read. He was a young man, respectably dressed and seated at a table, having a book before him. His handsome features glowed with pleasure, and his eyes kept impatiently wandering from the page to a small white hand over his shoulder, which recalled him by a smart slap on the cheek, whenever its owner detected such signs of inattention. Its owner stood behind, her light, shining ringlets blending, at intervals, with his brown looks, as she bent to superintend his studies, and her face—it was lucky he could not see her face, or he would never have been so steady. I could, and I bit my lip in spite, at having thrown away the chance I might have had of doing something besides staring at its smiting beauty.

The task was done, not free from further blunders, but the pupil claimed a reward, and received at least five kisses, which, however, he generously returned. Then they came to the door, and from their conversation I judged they were about to issue out and have a walk on the moors. I supposed I should be condemned in Hareton Earnshaw's heart, if not by his mouth, to the lowest pit in the infernal regions if I showed my unfortunate person in his neighborhood then. Feeling very mean and malignant, I skulked round to seek refuge in the kitchen. There was unobstructed admittance on that side also, and at the door sat my old friend Nelly Dean, sewing and singing a song, which was often interrupted from within by harsh words of scorn and intolerance, uttered in far from musical accents.

"I'd rather, by th' half, hev' 'em swearing i' my lugs from morn to night, nor hearken ye hahsiver!" said the tenant of the kitchen, in answer to an unheard speech of Nelly's. "It's a blazing shame, that I cannot open t' blessed Book, but ye set up them glories to Satan, and all t' flaysome wickednesses that ever were born into th' world! Oh! You're a right ox, and she's another, and that poor lad will be lost atween ye. Poor lad!" he added, with a groan, "he's witched. I'm certain on't. Oh, Lord, judge 'em, for there's neither law nor justice among were rulers!"

"No! Or we should be sitting in flaming sticks, I suppose," retorted the singer. "But wisht, old man, and read your Bible like a Christian, and never mind me. This is 'Fairy Annie's Wedding'—a bonny tune—it goes to a dance."

Mrs. Dean was about to recommence, when I advanced, and recognizing me directly, she jumped to her feet, crying, "Why, bless you, Mr. Lockwood! How could you think of returning in this way? All's shut up at Thrushcross Grange. You should have given us notice!"

"I've arranged to be accommodated there, for as long as I shall stay," I answered. "I depart again tomorrow. And how are you transplanted here, Mrs. Dean? Tell me that."

"Zillah left, and Mr. Heathcliff wished me to come, soon after you went to London, and stay till you returned. But, step in, pray! Have you walked from Gimmerton this evening?"

"From the Grange," I replied, "and while they make me lodging room there, I want to finish my business with your master, because I don't think of having another opportunity in a hurry."

"What business, sir?" said Nelly, conducting me into the house. "He's gone out at present, and won't return soon."

"About the rent," I answered.

"Oh! Then it is with Mrs. Heathcliff you must settle," she observed, "or rather with me. She has not learnt to manage her affairs yet, and I act for her. There's nobody else."

I looked surprised.

"Ah! You have not heard of Heathcliff's death, I see," she continued.

"Heathcliff dead!" I exclaimed, astonished. "How long ago?"

"Three months since. But sit down, and let me take your hat, and I'll tell you all about it. Stop, you have had nothing to eat, have you?"

"I want nothing. I have ordered supper at home. You sit down too. I never dreamt of his dying! Let me hear how it came to pass. You say you don't expect them back for some time—the young people?"

"No—I have to scold them every evening for their late rambles, but they don't care for me. At least, have a drink of our old ale. It will do you good. You seem weary."

She hastened to fetch it before I could refuse, and I heard Joseph asking whether "it wasn't a crying scandal that she should have followers at her time of life? And then, to get them jocks out o' t' master's cellar! He fair shamed to 'bide still and see it."

She did not stay to retaliate, but re-entered in a minute, bearing a reaming silver pint, whose contents I lauded with becoming earnestness. And afterwards she furnished me with the sequel of Heathcliff's history. He had a "queer" end, as she expressed it.

I was summoned to Wuthering Heights, within a fortnight of your leaving us, she said, and I obeyed joyfully, for Catherine's sake. My first interview with her grieved and shocked me. She had altered so much since our separation. Mr. Heathcliff did not explain his reasons for taking a new mind about my coming here, he only told me he wanted me, and he was tired of seeing Catherine. I must make the little parlor my sitting-room, and keep her with me. It was enough if he were obliged to see her once or twice a day.

She seemed pleased at this arrangement, and, by degrees, I smuggled over a great number of books, and other articles, that had formed her amusement at the Grange, and flattered myself we should get on in tolerable comfort.

The delusion did not last long. Catherine, contented at first, in a brief space grew irritable and restless. For one thing, she was forbidden to move out of the garden, and it fretted her sadly to be confined to its narrow bounds as spring drew on, for another, in following the house, I was forced to quit her frequently, and she complained of loneliness. She preferred quarrelling with Joseph in the kitchen to sitting at peace in her solitude.

I did not mind their skirmishes, but Hareton was often obliged to seek the kitchen also, when the master wanted to have the house to himself. And though in the beginning she either left it at his approach, or quietly joined in my occupations, and shunned remarking or addressing him—and though he was always as sullen and silent as possible—after a while, she changed her behavior, and became incapable of letting him alone. Talking at him, commenting on his stupidity and idleness, expressing her wonder how he could endure the life he lived—how he could sit a whole evening staring into the fire, and dozing.

"He's just like a dog, is he not, Ellen?" she once observed, "or a cart-horse? He does his work, eats his food, and sleeps, eternally! What a blank, dreary mind he must have! Do you ever dream, Hareton? And, if you do, what is it about? But you can't speak to me!"

Then she looked at him, but he would neither open his mouth nor look again.

"He's, perhaps, dreaming now," she continued. "He twitched his shoulder as Juno twitches hers. Ask him, Ellen."

"Mr. Hareton will ask the master to send you upstairs, if you don't behave!" I said. He had not only twitched his shoulder but clenched his fist, as if tempted to use it.

"I know why Hareton never speaks, when I am in the kitchen," she exclaimed, on another occasion. "He is afraid I shall laugh at him. Ellen, what do you think? He began to teach himself to read once, and, because I laughed, he burned his books, and dropped it. Was he not a fool?"

"Were not you naughty?" I said. "Answer me that."

"Perhaps I was," she went on, "but I did not expect him to be so silly. Hareton, if I gave you a book, would you take it now? I'll try!"

She placed one she had been perusing on his hand, he flung it off, and muttered, if she did not give over, he would break her neck.

"Well, I shall put it here," she said, "in the table drawer. I'm going to bed."

Then she whispered me to watch whether he touched it, and departed. But he would not come near it, and so I informed her in the morning, to her great disappointment. I saw she was sorry for his persevering sulkiness and indolence. Her conscience reproved her for frightening him off improving himself—she had done it effectually.

But her ingenuity was at work to remedy the injury. While I ironed, or pursued other such stationary employments as I could not well do in the parlor, she would bring some pleasant volume and read it aloud to me. When Hareton was there, she generally paused in an interesting part, and left the book lying about. That she did repeatedly, but he was as obstinate as a mule, and, instead of snatching at her bait, in wet weather he took to smoking with Joseph.

They sat like automatons, one on each side of the fire, the elder happily too deaf to understand her wicked nonsense, as he would have called it, the younger doing his best to seem to disregard it. On fine evenings the latter followed his shooting expeditions, and Catherine yawned and sighed, and teased me to talk to her, and ran off into the court or garden the moment I began, and, as a last resource, cried, and said she was tired of living—her life was useless.

Mr. Heathcliff, who grew more and more disinclined to society, had almost banished Earnshaw from his apartment. Owing to an accident at the commencement of March, he became for some days a fixture in the kitchen. His gun burst while out on the hills by himself, a splinter cut his arm, and he lost a good deal of blood before he could reach home. The consequence was that, perforce, he was condemned to the fireside and tranquility, till he made it up again.

It suited Catherine to have him there. At any rate, it made her hate her room upstairs more than ever, and she would compel me to find out business below, that she might accompany me.

On Easter Monday, Joseph went to Gimmerton fair with some cattle, and, in the afternoon, I was busy getting up linen in the kitchen. Earnshaw sat, morose as usual, at the chimney corner, and my little mistress was beguiling an idle hour with drawing pictures on the window-panes, varying her amusement by smothered bursts of songs, and whispered ejaculations, and quick glances of annoyance and impatience in the direction of her cousin, who steadfastly smoked, and looked into the grate.

At a notice that I could do with her no longer intercepting my light, she removed to the hearthstone. I bestowed little attention on her proceedings, but, presently, I heard her begin, "I've found out, Hareton, that I want—that I'm glad—that I should like you to be my cousin now, if you had not grown so cross to me, and so rough."

Hareton returned no answer.

"Hareton, Hareton, Hareton! Do you hear?" she continued.

"Get off wi' ye!" he growled, with uncompromising gruffness.

"Let me take that pipe," she said, cautiously advancing her hand and abstracting it from his mouth.

Before he could attempt to recover it, it was broken, and behind the fire. He swore at her and seized another.

"Stop," she cried, "you must listen to me first, and I can't speak while those clouds are floating in my face."

"Will you go to the devil!" he exclaimed, ferociously, "and let me be!"

"No," she persisted, "I won't. I can't tell what to do to make you talk to me, and you are determined not to understand. When I call you stupid, I don't mean anything. I don't mean that I despise you. Come, you shall take notice of me, Hareton. You are my cousin, and you shall own me."

"I shall have naught to do wi' you and your mucky pride, and your damned mocking tricks!" he answered. "I'll go to hell, body and soul, before I look sideways after you again. Side out o' t' gate, now, this minute!"

Catherine frowned, and retreated to the window-seat chewing her lip, and endeavoring, by humming an eccentric tune, to conceal a growing tendency to sob.

"You should be friends with your cousin, Mr. Hareton," I interrupted, "since she repents of her sauciness. It would do you a great deal of good. It would make you another man to have her for a companion."

"A companion!" he cried. "When she hates me, and does not think me fit to wipe her shoes! Nay, if it made me a king, I'd not be scorned for seeking her good will anymore."

"It is not I who hate you, it is you who hate me!" wept Cathy, no longer disguising her trouble. "You hate me as much as Mr. Heathcliff does, and more."

"You're a damned liar," began Earnshaw. "Why have I made him angry, by taking your part, then, a hundred times? And that when you sneered at and despised me, and—Go on plaguing me, and I'll step in yonder, and say you worried me out of the kitchen!"

"I didn't know you took my part," she answered, drying her eyes, "and I was miserable and bitter at everybody, but now I thank you, and beg you to forgive me. What can I do besides?"

She returned to the hearth, and frankly extended her hand. He blackened and scowled like a thundercloud, and kept his fists resolutely clenched, and his gaze fixed on the ground. Catherine, by instinct, must have divined it was obdurate perversity, and not dislike, that prompted this dogged conduct, for, after remaining an instant undecided, she stooped and impressed on his cheek a gentle kiss.

The little rogue thought I had not seen her, and, drawing back, she took her former station by the window, quite demurely. I shook my head reprovingly, and then she blushed and whispered, "Well! What should I have done, Ellen? He wouldn't shake hands, and he wouldn't look. I must show him some way that I like him—that I want to be friends."

Whether the kiss convinced Hareton, I cannot tell. He was very careful, for some minutes, that his face should not be seen, and when he did raise it, he was sadly puzzled where to turn his eyes.

Catherine employed herself in wrapping a handsome book neatly in white paper, and having tied it with a bit of ribbon, and addressed it to "Mr. Hareton Earnshaw," she desired me to be her ambassadress, and convey the present to its destined recipient.

"And tell him, if he'll take it, I'll come and teach him to read it right," she said, "and, if he refuse it, I'll go upstairs, and never tease him again."

I carried it, and repeated the message, anxiously watched by my employer. Hareton would not open his fingers, so I laid it on his knee. He did not strike it off, either. I returned to my work. Catherine leaned her head and arms on the table, till she heard the slight rustle of the covering being removed, then she stole away, and quietly seated herself beside her cousin. He trembled, and his face glowed. All his rudeness and all his surly harshness had deserted him. He could not summon courage, at first, to utter a syllable in reply to her questioning look, and her murmured petition.

"Say you forgive me, Hareton, do. You can make me so happy by speaking that little word."

He muttered something inaudible.

"And you'll be my friend?" added Catherine, interrogatively.

"Nay, you'll be ashamed of me every day of your life," he answered. "And the more ashamed the more you know me, and I cannot bide it."

"So you won't be my friend?" she said, smiling as sweet as honey, and creeping close up.

I overheard no further distinguishable talk, but, on looking round again, I perceived two such radiant countenances bent over the page of the accepted book, that I did not doubt the treaty had been ratified on both sides, and the enemies were, thenceforth, sworn allies.

The work they studied was full of costly pictures, and those and their position had charm enough to keep them unmoved till Joseph came home. He, poor man, was perfectly aghast at the spectacle of Catherine seated on the same bench with Hareton Earnshaw, leaning her hand on his shoulder, and confounded at his favorite's endurance of her proximity. It affected him too deeply to allow an observation on the subject that night. His emotion was only revealed by the immense sighs he drew, as he solemnly spread his large Bible on the table, and overlaid it with dirty bank-notes from his pocket-book, the produce of the day's transactions. At length he summoned Hareton from his seat.

"Take these in to t' master, lad," he said, "and bide there. I's gang up to my own room. This hole's neither manful nor seemly for us. We must side out and search another."

"Come, Catherine," I said, "we must 'side out' too. I've done my ironing. Are you ready to go?"

"It is not eight o'clock!" she answered, rising unwillingly. "Hareton, I'll leave this book upon the chimney-piece, and I'll bring some more tomorrow."

"Any books that ye leave, I shall tak' into th' house," said Joseph, "and it'll be miracle if ye find 'em again, sure, ye may please yourself!"

Cathy threatened that his library should pay for hers, and, smiling as she passed Hareton, went singing upstairs, lighter of heart, I venture to say, than ever she had been under that roof before, except, perhaps, during her earliest visits to Linton.

The intimacy thus commenced grew rapidly, though it encountered temporary interruptions. Earnshaw was not to be civilized with a wish, and my young lady was no philosopher, and no paragon of patience, but both their minds tending to the same point—one loving and desiring to esteem, and the other loving and desiring to be esteemed—they contrived in the end to reach it.

You see, Mr. Lockwood, it was easy enough to win Mrs. Heathcliff's heart. But now, I'm glad you did not try. The crown of all my wishes will be the union of those two. I shall envy no one on their wedding day. There won't be a happier woman than myself in England!

As Mrs. Dean smiled over her story, I rose, a bit unhappy in mind. I had had a chance to make that delectable creature my own, and then I did not seize the opportunity. I walked restlessly to the window, where I saw that Catherine and Hareton had not ventured out for a ramble on the moors. Instead, they had stopped beneath an oak tree. I could see their figures, illuminated by the light of the moon, and I fancied they were declaring their love beneath its limbs as Heathcliff and Catherine had so many years before.

I sighed, sentimental, when Hareton captured Catherine's face in his rough hands, then leaned down to kiss her. She pressed against him, the picture of young, happy love. Then, as I watched, the sweetness of the kiss transformed into something more powerful and passionate.

I must have made a sound, because before I knew it, Mrs. Dean had joined me at the window. The sight of Hareton stripping off his shirt apparently rendered her mute, because she said not a word to me. She stood beside me and we watched as Hareton undid his trousers and presented himself, in all of his aroused male glory, to Catherine.

She did not shy away from his offering, but speedily stepped out of her dress. When they embraced, Mrs. Dean gave a little moan.

I swallowed hard, and of its own accord, my hand crept across the distance between us to rest on the pleasantly broad expanse of her buttocks. She made a little start, but did not round on me as I half expected her to.

She leaned a little nearer the window, where the two lovers were caressing each other. Hareton had his hand on Catherine's breast, flicking the nipple, then squeezing it until she threw her head back in escstasy. She kissed him with everything she was, her tongue dueling with his as their bodies readied for the joining.

Soon Catherine had shed all of her clothes and stood naked as nature intended. I let out a little sigh of pleasure at the sight of her lithe young body revealed so temptingly in the moonlight. Their bodies rasped and slid against each other until one could scarcely make out where Catherine left off and Hareton began.

Then it was finally time. His staff slid into her waiting channel as easily as a key into a lock—they were made to fit together.

He moved slowly, making me nearly shout with impatience. Fortunately, he could not contain his passion much longer, and his pace increased. Catherine kept his rhythm, thrusting up as he thrust in. I let out a tiny sound of pleasure that could not have gone much further than my companion's ears.

In the next moment, I felt Mrs. Dean's sturdy hand on the front of my trousers. I knew implicitly that for once she did not wish to engage in conversation. I believe I was fully incapable of it at the moment, at any rate.

Before I could venture to assay a responding caress, she had bent herself over the table. I seized her skirts and threw them over her head, then shoved my trousers down. In a moment, my probing arrow had found its target, and my shaft sank deep inside her soft, wet center.

That was enough to start her off again. "Oh, Mr. Lockwood!" she cried. "Yes! Yes!" Her exhortations and demands varied in nature, tone, and pitch, but I needed no further goad to continue my action. I pumped into her, thrusting my hips against hers over and over, my head reeling from the sensual pleasures I had so long denied myself.

I did, in a fit of ungentlemanly fantasy, pretend that she was that bonny lass Catherine, despite their differences in stoutness, but I held back from calling her any other name but her own.

We reached our completion in the moment the young lovers did. That night, Wuthering Heights found all of its inmates fully satisfied—excluding the sour old man Joseph, whose lover Zillah

had quitted the premises some months previously. Yet I scarcely
bore a thought for him as Mrs. Dean showed me what she had
learned from witnessing all of those escapades she should never
have watched over the years.

CHAPTER 45

WHEN MRS. DEAN CONSENTED to take a break in her carnal labors later that night, she continued the story of Catherine and Hareton.

On the morrow of that Monday, Earnshaw being still unable to follow his ordinary employments, and therefore remaining about the house, I speedily found it would be impracticable to retain my charge beside me, as heretofore.

She got downstairs before me, and out into the garden, where she had seen her cousin performing some easy work. When I went to bid them come to breakfast, I saw she had persuaded him to clear a large space of ground from currant and gooseberry bushes, and they were busy planning together an importation of plants from the Grange.

I was terrified at the devastation that had been accomplished in a brief half-hour. The black-currant trees were the apple of Joseph's eye, and she had just fixed her choice of a flower bed in the midst of them.

"There! That will be all shown to the master," I exclaimed, "the minute it is discovered. And what excuse have you to offer for taking such liberties with the garden? We shall have a fine explosion on the head of it. See if we don't! Mr. Hareton, I wonder you should have no more wit than to go and make that mess at her bidding!"

"I'd forgotten they were Joseph's," answered Earnshaw, rather puzzled, "but I'll tell him I did it."

We always ate our meals with Mr. Heathcliff. I held the mistress's post in making tea and carving, so I was indispensable at table. Catherine usually sat by me, but today she stole nearer to Hareton, and I presently saw she would have no more discretion in her friendship than she had in her hostility.

"Now, mind you don't talk with and notice your cousin too much," were my whispered instructions as we entered the room. "It will certainly annoy Mr. Heathcliff, and he'll be mad at you both."

"I'm not going to," she answered.

The minute after, she had sidled to Hareton, and was sticking primroses in his plate of porridge.

He dared not speak to her there. He dared hardly look, and yet she went on teasing, till he was twice on the point of being provoked to laugh. I frowned, and then she glanced towards the master, whose mind was occupied on other subjects than his company, as his countenance evinced, and she grew serious for an instant, scrutinizing him with deep gravity. Afterwards she turned, and recommenced her nonsense; at last, Hareton uttered a smothered laugh. Mr. Heathcliff started. His eye rapidly surveyed our faces. Catherine met it with her accustomed look of nervousness and yet defiance, which he abhorred.

"It is well you are out of my reach," he exclaimed. "What fiend possesses you to stare back at me, continually, with those infernal eyes? Down with them! And don't remind me of your existence again. I thought I had cured you of laughing."

"It was me," muttered Hareton.

"What do you say?" demanded the master.

Hareton looked at his plate, and did not repeat the confession.

Mr. Heathcliff looked at him a bit, and then silently resumed his breakfast and his interrupted musing. We had nearly finished, and the two young people prudently shifted wider asunder, so I anticipated no further disturbance during that sitting, when Joseph appeared at the door, revealing by his quivering lip and furious eyes that the outrage committed on his precious shrubs was detected.

He must have seen Cathy and her cousin about the spot before he examined it, for while his jaws worked like those of a cow chewing its cud, and rendered his speech difficult to understand, he began: "I mun hev' my wage, and I mun go! I had aimed to die where I'd served fur sixty year, and I thought I'd lug my books up into t' garret, and all my bits o' stuff, and they should have t' kitchen to theirselves, for t' sake o' quietness. It was hard to give up my awn hearthstone, but I thought I could do that! But nah, she's taken my garden fro' me, and by th' heart, master, I cannot stand it! Ye may bend to th' yoke an ye will—I'm not used to 't, and an old man doesn't soon get used to new things. I'd rather earn my bite an' my sup wi' a hammer in th' road!"

"Now, now, idiot!" interrupted Heathcliff, "cut it short! What's your grievance? I'll interfere in no quarrels between you and Nelly. She may thrust you into the coal-hole for anything I care."

"It's not Nelly!" answered Joseph. "I shouldn't shift for Nelly—nasty ill ox as she is. Thank God! She cannot steal the soul of nob'dy! She were never so handsome, but what a body must look at her 'bout winking. It's yon flaysome, graceless queen, what's bewitched our lad, wi' her bold looks and her forward ways—till—Nay! It fair bursts my heart! He's forgotten all I done for him, and made on him, and gone and ripped up a whole row o' t' grandest currant-trees i' t' garden!" And here he lamented outright, unmanned by a sense of his bitter injuries, and Earnshaw's ingratitude and dangerous condition.

"Is the fool drunk?" asked Mr. Heathcliff. "Hareton, is it you he's finding fault with?"

"I've pulled up two or three bushes," replied the young man, "but I'm going to set 'em again."

"And why have you pulled them up?" said the master.

Catherine wisely put in her tongue. "We wanted to plant some flowers there," she cried. "I'm the only person to blame, for I wished him to do it."

"And who the devil gave you leave to touch a stick about the place?" demanded her father-in-law, much surprised. "And who ordered you to obey her?" he added, turning to Hareton.

The latter was speechless. Catherine replied, "You shouldn't grudge a few yards of earth for me to ornament, when you have taken all my land!"

"Your land, insolent slut! You never had any," said Heathcliff.

"And my money," she continued, returning his angry glare, and meantime biting a piece of crust, the remnant of her breakfast.

"Silence!" he exclaimed. "Get done, and begone!"

"And Hareton's land, and his money," pursued the reckless thing. "Hareton and I are friends now, and I shall tell him all about you!"

The master seemed confounded a moment. He grew pale, and rose up, eyeing her all the while, with an expression of mortal hate.

"If you strike me, Hareton will strike you," she said. "So you may as well sit down."

"If Hareton does not turn you out of the room, I'll strike him to hell," thundered Heathcliff. "Damnable witch! Dare you pretend to rouse him against me? Off with her! Do you hear? Fling her into the kitchen! I'll kill her, Ellen Dean, if you let her come into my sight again!"

Hareton tried, under his breath, to persuade her to go.

"Drag her away!" Heathcliff cried, savagely. "Are you staying to talk?" And he approached to execute his own command.

"He'll not obey you, wicked man, any more," said Catherine. "And he'll soon detest you as much as I do."

"Wisht! Wisht!" muttered the young man, reproachfully, "I will not hear you speak so to him. Have done."

"But you won't let him strike me?" she cried.

"Come, then," he whispered earnestly.

It was too late. Heathcliff had caught hold of her.

"Now, you go!" he said to Earnshaw. "Accursed witch! This time she has provoked me when I could not bear it, and I'll make her repent it forever!"

He had his hand in her hair, Hareton attempted to release her locks, entreating him not to hurt her that once. Heathcliff's black eyes flashed. He seemed ready to tear Catherine in pieces, and I was just worked up to risk coming to the rescue, when of a sudden his fingers relaxed, he shifted his grasp from her head to her arm, and gazed intently in her face.

Then he drew his hand over his eyes, stood a moment to collect himself apparently, and turning anew to Catherine, said, with assumed calmness, "You must learn to avoid putting me in a passion, or I shall really murder you some time! Go with Mrs. Dean, and keep with her, and confine your insolence to her ears. As to Hareton Earnshaw, if I see him listen to you, I'll send him seeking his bread where he can get it! Your love will make him an outcast and a beggar. Nelly, take her, and leave me, all of you! Leave me!"

I led my young lady out. She was too glad of her escape to resist. The other followed, and Mr. Heathcliff had the room to himself till dinner. I had counseled Catherine to dine upstairs, but, as soon as he perceived her vacant seat, he sent me to call her. He spoke to none of us, ate very little, and went out directly afterwards, intimating that he should not return before evening.

The two new friends established themselves in the house during his absence, where I heard Hareton sternly check his cousin, on her offering a revelation of her father-in-law's conduct to his father. He said he wouldn't suffer a word to be uttered in his disparagement. If he were the devil, it didn't signify, he would stand by him, and he'd rather she would abuse himself, as she used to, than begin on Mr. Heathcliff.

Catherine was waxing cross at this, but he found means to make her hold her tongue, by asking how she would like him to speak ill of her father? Then she comprehended that Earnshaw took the master's reputation home to himself, and was attached by ties stronger than reason could break—chains, forged by habit, which it would be cruel to attempt to loosen.

She showed a good heart, thenceforth, in avoiding both complaints and expressions of antipathy concerning Heathcliff, and confessed to me her sorrow that she had endeavored to raise a bad spirit between him and Hareton. Indeed, I don't believe she has ever breathed a syllable, in the latter's hearing, against her oppressor, since.

When this slight disagreement was over, they were friends again, and as busy as possible in their several occupations of pupil and teacher. I came in to sit with them, after I had done my work, and I felt so soothed and comforted to watch them, that I did not notice how time got on. You know, they both appeared in a measure my children. I had long been proud of one, and now, I was sure, the other would be a source of equal satisfaction. His honest, warm, and intelligent nature shook off rapidly the clouds of ignorance and degradation in which it had been bred, and Catherine's sincere commendations acted as a spur to his industry. His brightening mind brightened his features, and added spirit and nobility to their aspect. I could hardly fancy it the same individual I had beheld on the day I discovered my little lady at Wuthering Heights, after her expedition to the Crags.

While I admired and they labored, dusk drew on, and with it returned the master. He came upon us quite unexpectedly, entering by the front way, and had a full view of the whole three, ere we could raise our heads to glance at him.

Well, I reflected, there was never a pleasanter, or more harmless sight, and it will be a burning shame to scold them. The red fire-light glowed on their two bonny heads, and revealed their faces animated with the eager interest of children, for, though he was twenty-three and she eighteen, each had so much of novelty to feel and learn, that neither experienced nor evinced the sentiments of sober disenchanted maturity.

They lifted their eyes together, to encounter Mr. Heathcliff. Perhaps you have never remarked that their eyes are precisely similar, and they are those of Catherine Earnshaw. The present Catherine has no other likeness to her, except a breadth of forehead, and a certain arch of the nostril that makes her appear rather haughty, whether she will or not. With Hareton the resemblance is carried farther. It is singular at all times; then it was particularly striking, because his senses were alert, and his mental faculties wakened to unwonted activity.

I suppose this resemblance disarmed Mr. Heathcliff. He walked to the hearth in evident agitation, but it quickly subsided as he looked at the young man. Or, I should say, altered its character, for it was there yet.

He took the book from his hand, and glanced at the open page, then returned it without any observation, merely signing Catherine away. Her companion lingered very little behind her, and I was about to depart also, but he bid me sit still.

"It is a poor conclusion, is it not?" Heathcliff observed, having brooded awhile on the scene he had just witnessed. "An absurd termination to my violent exertions? I get levers and mattocks to demolish the two houses, and train myself to be capable of working like Hercules, and when everything is ready and in my power, I find the will to lift a slate off either roof has vanished! My old enemies have not beaten me, now would be the precise time to revenge myself on their representatives. I could do it, and none could hinder me. But where is the use? I don't care for striking. I can't take the trouble to raise my hand! That sounds as if I had been laboring the whole time, only to exhibit a fine trait of magnanimity. It is far from being the case. I have lost the faculty of enjoying their destruction, and I am too idle to destroy for nothing.

"Nelly, there is a strange change approaching, I'm in its shadow at present. I take so little interest in my daily life that I hardly remember to eat and drink. Those two who have left the room are the only objects that retain a distinct material appearance to me, and that appearance causes me pain, amounting to agony. About her I won't speak, and I don't desire to think, but I earnestly wish she were invisible. Her presence invokes only maddening sensations. He moves me differently. And yet if I could do it without seeming insane, I'd never see him again! You'll perhaps think me rather inclined to become so," he added, making an effort to smile, "if I try to describe the thousand forms of past associations and ideas he awakens or embodies. But you'll not talk of what I tell you, and my mind is so eternally secluded in itself, it is tempting at last to turn it out to another.

"Five minutes ago Hareton seemed a personification of my youth, not a human being. I felt to him in such a variety of ways, that it would have been impossible to have accosted him rationally. In the first place, his startling likeness to Catherine connected him fearfully with her. That, however, which you may suppose the most potent to arrest my imagination, is actually the least. For what is not connected with her to me? And what does not recall her? I cannot look down to this floor, but her features are shaped in the flags!

"In every cloud, in every tree—filling the air at night, and caught by glimpses in every object by day—I am surrounded with her image! The most ordinary faces of men and women—my own features— mock me with a resemblance. The entire world is a dreadful collection of memoranda that she did exist, and that I have lost her!

"Well, Harleton's aspect was the ghost of my immortal love, of my wild endeavors to hold my right, my degradation, my pride, my happiness, and my anguish—but it is frenzy to repeat these thoughts to you. Only it will let you know why, with a reluctance to be always alone, his society is no benefit, rather an aggravation of the constant torment I suffer. And it partly contributes to render me regardless how he and his cousin go on together. I can give them no attention anymore."

"But what do you mean by a change, Mr. Heathcliff?" I said, alarmed at his manner, though he was neither in danger of losing his senses, nor dying. According to my judgment, he was quite strong and healthy, and, as to his reason, from childhood he had a delight in dwelling on dark things, and entertaining odd fancies. He might have had a singular obsession with his departed lover, but on every other point his wits were as sound as mine.

"I shall not know that till it comes," he said. "I'm only half conscious of it now."

"You have no feeling of illness, have you?" I asked.

"No, Nelly, I have not," he answered.

"Then you are not afraid of death?" I pursued.

"Afraid? No!" he replied. "I have neither a fear, nor a presentiment, nor a hope of death. Why should I? With my hard constitution and temperate mode of living, and unperilous occupations, I ought to, and probably shall, remain above ground till there is scarcely a black hair on my head. And yet I cannot continue in this condition! I have to remind myself to breathe—almost to remind my heart to beat! And it is like bending back a stiff spring. It is by compulsion that I do the slightest act not prompted by one thought, and by compulsion that I notice anything alive or dead, which is not associated with one universal idea. I have a single wish, and my whole being and faculties are yearning to attain it. They have yearned towards it so long, and so unwaveringly, that I'm convinced it will be reached—and soon— because it has devoured my existence. I am swallowed up in the anticipation of its fulfillment. My confessions have not relieved me, but they may account for some otherwise unaccountable phases of humor which I show. O God! It is a long fight, I wish it were over!"

He began to pace the room, muttering terrible things to himself, till I was inclined to believe, as he said Joseph did, that conscience had turned his heart to an earthly hell. I wondered greatly how it would end.

Though he seldom before had revealed this state of mind, even by looks, it was his habitual mood, I had no doubt. He asserted it himself, but not a soul, from his general bearing, would have conjectured the fact. You did not when you saw him, Mr. Lockwood. And at the period of which I speak, he was just the same as then, only fonder of continued solitude, and perhaps still more laconic in company.

CHAPTER 46

$\mathscr{F}$OR SOME DAYS AFTER that evening Mr. Heathcliff shunned meeting us at meals, yet he would not consent formally to exclude Hareton and Cathy. He had an aversion to yielding so completely to his feelings, choosing rather to absent himself, and eating once in twenty-four hours seemed sufficient sustenance for him.

One night, after the family were in bed, I heard him go downstairs, and out at the front door. I did not hear him reenter, and in the morning I found he was still away. We were in April then. The weather was sweet and warm, the grass as green as showers and sun could make it, and the two dwarf apple trees near the southern wall in full bloom. After breakfast, Catherine insisted on my bringing a chair and sitting with my work under the fir-trees at the end of the house, and she beguiled Hareton, who had perfectly recovered from his accident, to dig and arrange her little garden, which was shifted to that corner by the influence of Joseph's complaints.

I was comfortably reveling in the spring fragrance around, and the beautiful soft blue overhead, when my young lady, who had run down near the gate to procure some primrose roots for a border, returned only half laden, and informed us that Mr. Heathcliff was coming in. "And he spoke to me," she added, with a perplexed countenance.

"What did he say?" asked Hareton.

"He told me to begone as fast as I could," she answered. "But he looked so different from his usual look that I stopped a moment to stare at him."

"How?" he inquired.

"Why, almost bright and cheerful. No, almost nothing—very much excited, and wild, and glad!" she replied.

"Night-walking amuses him, then," I remarked, affecting a careless manner—in reality as surprised as she was. Anxious to ascertain the truth of her statement, for to see the master looking glad would not be an everyday spectacle, I framed an excuse to go in.

Heathcliff stood at the open door. He was pale, and he trembled. Yet, certainly, he had a strange joyful glitter in his eyes that altered the aspect of his whole face.

"Will you have some breakfast?" I said. "You must be hungry, rambling about all night!" I wanted to discover where he had been, but I did not like to ask directly.

"No, I'm not hungry," he answered, averting his head, and speaking rather contemptuously, as if he guessed I was trying to divine the occasion of his good humor.

I felt perplexed. I didn't know whether it were not a proper opportunity to offer a bit of admonition.

"I don't think it right to wander out of doors," I observed, "instead of being in bed. It is not wise, at any rate this moist season. I daresay you'll catch a bad cold or a fever. You have something the matter with you now!"

"Nothing but what I can bear," he replied, "and with the greatest pleasure, provided you'll leave me alone. Get in, and don't annoy me."

I obeyed and, in passing, I noticed he breathed as fast as a cat.

"Yes!" I reflected to myself, "we shall have a fit of illness. I cannot conceive what he has been doing."

That noon he sat down to dinner with us, and received a heaped-up plate from my hands, as if he intended to make amends for previous fasting.

"I've neither cold nor fever, Nelly," he remarked, in allusion to my morning's speech, "and I'm ready to do justice to the food you give me."

He took his knife and fork, and was going to commence eating, when the inclination appeared to become suddenly extinct. He laid them on the table, looked eagerly towards the window, then rose and went out. We saw him walking to and fro in the garden while we concluded our meal, and Earnshaw said he'd go and ask why he would not dine. He thought we had grieved him some way.

"Well, is he coming?" cried Catherine, when her cousin returned.

"Nay," he answered, "but he's not angry. He seemed rarely pleased indeed, only I made him impatient by speaking to him twice, and then he bid me be off to you. He wondered how I could want the company of anybody else."

I set his plate to keep warm on the fender, and after an hour or two he reentered, when the room was clear, in no degree calmer. The same unnatural—it was unnatural—appearance of joy under his black brows, the same bloodless hue, and his teeth visible, now and then, in a kind of smile, his frame shivering, not as one shivers with chill or weakness, but as a tight-stretched cord vibrates—a strong thrilling, rather than trembling.

I will ask what is the matter, I thought, or who should? And I exclaimed, "Have you heard any good news, Mr. Heathcliff? You look uncommonly animated."

"Where should good news come from to me?" he said. "I'm animated with hunger, and, seemingly, I must not eat."

"Your dinner is here," I returned. "Why won't you get it?"

"I don't want it now," he muttered, hastily. "I'll wait till supper. And, Nelly, once for all, let me beg you to warn Hareton and the other away from me. I wish to be troubled by nobody. I wish to have this place to myself."

"Is there some new reason for this banishment?" I inquired. "Tell me why you are so queer, Mr. Heathcliff? Where were you last night? I'm not putting the question through idle curiosity—"

"You are putting the question through very idle curiosity," he interrupted, with a laugh. "Yet I'll answer it. Last night I was on the threshold of hell. Today, I am within sight of my heaven. I have my eyes on it. Hardly three feet to sever me! And now you'd better go! You'll neither see nor hear anything to frighten you, if you refrain from prying."

Having swept the hearth and wiped the table, I departed, more perplexed than ever.

He did not quit the house again that afternoon, and no one intruded on his solitude, till, at eight o'clock, I deemed it proper, though unsummoned, to carry a candle and his supper to him.

He was leaning against the ledge of an open lattice, but not looking out. His face was turned to the interior gloom. The fire had smoldered to ashes. The room was filled with the damp, mild air of the cloudy evening, and so still, that not only the murmur of the beck down Gimmerton was distinguishable, but its ripples and its gurgling over the pebbles, or through the large stones which it could not cover.

I uttered an ejaculation of discontent at seeing the dismal grate, and commenced shutting the casements, one after another, till I came to his.

"Must I close this?" I asked, in order to rouse him, for he would not stir.

The light flashed on his features as I spoke. Oh, Mr. Lockwood, I cannot express what a terrible start I got by the momentary view!

Those deep black eyes! That smile, and ghastly paleness! It appeared to me, not Mr. Heathcliff, but a goblin. In my terror, I let the candle bend towards the wall, and it left me in darkness.

"Yes, close it," he replied, in his familiar voice. "There, that is pure awkwardness! Why did you hold the candle horizontally? Be quick, and bring another."

I hurried out in a foolish state of dread, and said to Joseph, "The master wishes you to take him a light and rekindle the fire." For I dared not go in myself again just then.

Joseph rattled some fire into the shovel, and went, but he brought it back immediately, with the supper-tray in his other hand, explaining that Mr. Heathcliff was going to bed, and he wanted nothing to eat till morning.

We heard him mount the stairs directly, he did not proceed to his ordinary chamber, but turned into that with the paneled bed. Its window, as I mentioned before, is wide enough for anybody to get through, and it struck me that he plotted another midnight excursion, of which he had rather we had no suspicion.

"Is he a ghoul or a vampire?" I mused. I had read of such hideous, incarnate demons. And then I set myself to reflect how I had tended him in infancy, and watched him grow to youth, and followed him almost through his whole course, and what absurd nonsense it was to yield to that sense of horror. "But where did he come from, the little dark thing, harbored by a good man to his bane?" muttered Superstition, as I dozed into unconsciousness.

I began, half dreaming, to weary myself with imagining some fit parentage for him, and, repeating my waking meditations, I tracked his existence over again, with grim variations, at last, picturing his death and funeral; of which, all I can remember is, being exceedingly vexed at having the task of dictating an inscription for his monument, and consulting the sexton about it, and, as he had no surname, and we could not tell his age, we were obliged to content ourselves with the single word, "Heathcliff." That came true—we were. If you enter the kirkyard, you'll read, on his headstone, only that, and the date of his death.

Dawn restored me to common sense. I rose, and went into the garden, as soon as I could see, to ascertain if there were any footmarks under his window. There were none. "He has stayed at home," I thought, "and he'll be all right today."

I prepared breakfast for the household, as was my usual custom, but told Hareton and Catherine to get theirs ere the master came down, for he lay late. They preferred taking it out of doors, under the trees, and I set a little table to accommodate them.

On my reentrance, I found Mr. Heathcliff below. He and Joseph were conversing about some farming business. He gave clear, minute directions concerning the matter discussed, but he spoke rapidly, and turned his head continually aside, and had the same excited expression, even more exaggerated.

When Joseph quitted the room he took his seat in the place he generally chose, and I put a basin of coffee before him. He drew it nearer, and then rested his arms on the table, and looked at the opposite wall, as I supposed, surveying one particular portion, up and down, with glittering, restless eyes, and with such eager interest that he stopped breathing during half a minute together.

"Come now," I exclaimed, pushing some bread against his hand. "Eat and drink that, while it is hot. It has been waiting near an hour."

He didn't notice me, and yet he smiled. I'd rather have seen him gnash his teeth than smile so.

"Mr. Heathcliff! Master!" I cried. "Don't, for God's sake, stare as if you saw an unearthly vision."

"Don't, for God's sake, shout so loud," he replied. "Turn round, and tell me, are we by ourselves?"

"Of course," was my answer. "Of course we are."

Still, I involuntarily obeyed him, as if I was not quite sure. With a sweep of his hand he cleared a vacant space in front among the breakfast things, and leant forward to gaze more at his ease.

Now, I perceived he was not looking at the wall, for when I regarded him alone, it seemed exactly that he gazed at something within two yards' distance. And whatever it was, it communicated, apparently, both pleasure and pain in exquisite extremes—at least the anguished, yet raptured, expression of his countenance suggested that idea.

The fancied object was not fixed, either. His eyes pursued it with unwearied diligence, and, even in speaking to me, were never weaned away. I vainly reminded him of his protracted abstinence from food. If he stirred to touch anything in compliance with my entreaties, if he stretched his hand out to get a piece of bread, his fingers clenched before they reached it, and remained on the table, forgetful of their aim.

I sat, a model of patience, trying to attract his absorbed attention from its engrossing speculation, till he grew irritable, and got up, asking why I would not allow him to have his own time in taking his meals? And saying that on the next occasion I needn't wait. I might set the things down and go. Having uttered these words he left the house, slowly sauntered down the garden path, and disappeared through the gate.

The hours crept anxiously by. Another evening came. I did not retire to rest till late, and when I did, I could not sleep. He returned after midnight, and, instead of going to bed, shut himself into the room beneath. I listened, and tossed about, and, finally, dressed and descended. It was too irksome to lie there, harassing my brain with a hundred idle misgivings.

I distinguished Mr. Heathcliff's step, restlessly measuring the floor, and he frequently broke the silence by a deep inspiration, resembling a groan. He muttered detached words also. The only one I could catch was the name of Catherine, coupled with some wild term of endearment or suffering, and spoken as one would speak to a person present, low and earnest, and wrung from the depth of his soul.

I had not courage to walk straight into the apartment, but I desired to divert him from his reverie, and therefore fell afoul of the kitchen fire, stirred it, and began to scrape the cinders. It drew him forth sooner than I expected.

He opened the door immediately, and said, "Nelly, come here— is it morning? Come in with your light."

"It is striking four," I answered. "You want a candle to take upstairs——you might have lit one at this fire."

"No, I don't wish to go upstairs," he said. "Come in, and kindle me a fire, and do anything there is to do about the room."

"I must blow the coals red first, before I can carry any," I replied, getting a chair and the bellows.

He roamed to and fro, meantime, in a state approaching distraction, his heavy sighs succeeding each other so thick as to leave no space for common breathing between.

"When day breaks I'll send for Green," he said. "I wish to make some legal inquiries of him while I can bestow a thought on those matters, and while I can act calmly. I have not written my will yet, and how to leave my property I cannot determine. I wish I could annihilate it from the face of the earth."

"I would not talk so, Mr. Heathcliff," I interposed. "Let your will be a while. You'll be spared to repent of your many injustices yet! I never expected that your nerves would be disordered. They are, at present, marvelously so, however, and almost entirely through your own fault. The way you've passed these three last days might knock up a Titan. Do take some food, and some repose. You need only look at yourself in a glass to see how you require both. Your cheeks are hollow, and your eyes bloodshot, like a person starving with hunger and going blind with loss of sleep."

"It is not my fault that I cannot eat or rest," he replied. "I assure you it is through no settled designs. I'll do both, as soon as I possibly can. But you might as well bid a man struggling in the water rest within arm's length of the shore! I must reach it first, and then I'll rest. Well, never mind Mr. Green. As to repenting of my injustices, I've done no injustice, and I repent of nothing. I'm too happy, and yet I'm not happy enough. My soul's bliss kills my body, but does not satisfy itself."

"Happy, master?" I cried. "Strange happiness! If you would hear me without being angry, I might offer some advice that would make you happier."

"What is that?" he asked. "Give it."

"You are aware, Mr. Heathcliff," I said, "that from the time you were thirteen years old you have lived a selfish, unchristian life, and probably hardly had a Bible in your hands during all that period. You must have forgotten the contents of the book, and you may not have space to search it now. Could it be hurtful to send for some one— some minister of any denomination, it does not matter which—to explain it, and show you how very far you have erred from its precepts, and how unfit you will be for its heaven, unless a change takes place before you die?"

"I'm rather obliged than angry, Nelly," he said, "for you remind me of the manner in which I desire to be buried. It is to be carried to the churchyard in the evening. You and Hareton may, if you please, accompany me. And mind, particularly, to notice that the sexton obeys my directions concerning the two coffins! No minister need come, nor need anything be said over me. I tell you I have nearly attained my heaven, and that of others is altogether unvalued and uncoveted by me."

"And supposing you persevered in your obstinate fast, and died by that means, and they refused to bury you in the precincts of the kirk?" I said, shocked at his godless indifference. "How would you like it?"

"They won't do that," he replied. "If they did, you must have me removed secretly, and if you neglect it you shall prove, practically, that the dead are not annihilated!"

As soon as he heard the other members of the family stirring, he retired to his den, and I breathed freer. But in the afternoon, while Joseph and Hareton were at their work, he came into the kitchen again, and, with a wild look, bid me come and sit in the house. He wanted somebody with him. I declined, telling him plainly that his strange talk and manner frightened me, and I had neither the nerve nor the will to be his companion alone.

"I believe you think me a fiend," he said, with his dismal laugh. "Something too horrible to live under a decent roof."

Then turning to Catherine, who was there, and who drew behind me at his approach, he added, half sneeringly, "Will you come, chuck? I'll not hurt you. No! To you I've made myself worse than the devil. Well, there is one who won't shrink from my company! By God! She's relentless. Oh, damn it! It's unutterably too much for flesh and blood to bear—even mine."

He solicited the society of no one more. At dusk he went into his chamber. Through the whole night, and far into the morning, we heard him groaning and murmuring to himself. Hareton was anxious to enter, but I bid him fetch Mr. Kenneth, and he should go in and see him. When he came, and I requested admittance and tried to open the door, I found it locked, and Heathcliff bid us be damned. He was better, and would be left alone, so the doctor went away.

The following evening was very wet. Indeed, it poured down till day-dawn, and, as I took my morning walk round the house, I observed the master's window swinging open, and the rain driving straight in. He cannot be in bed, I thought. Those showers would drench him through! He must either be up or out. But I'll make no more ado, I'll go boldly and look.

Having succeeded in obtaining entrance with another key, I ran to unclose the panels, for the chamber was vacant. Quickly pushing them aside, I peeped in. Mr. Heathcliff was there—laid on his back. His eyes met mine so keen and fierce, I started, and then he seemed to smile. I could not think him dead, but his face and throat were washed with rain, the bed-clothes dripped, and he was perfectly still. The lattice, flapping to and fro, had grazed one hand that rested on the sill, no blood trickled from the broken skin, and when I put my fingers to it, I could doubt no more. He was dead and stark!

I hasped the window. I combed his black long hair from his forehead, and I tried to close his eyes, to extinguish, if possible, that frightful, lifelike gaze of exultation before anyone else beheld it. They would not shut. They seemed to sneer at my attempts, and his parted lips and sharp white teeth sneered too! Taken with another fit of cowardice, I cried out for Joseph. Joseph shuffled up and made a noise, but resolutely refused to meddle with him.

"The devil's harried off his soul," he cried, "and he may have his carcass into t' bargain, for aught I care! Ech! What a wicked 'un he looks, grinning at death!" and the old sinner grinned in mockery. I thought he intended to cut a caper round the bed, but suddenly composing himself, he fell on his knees, and raised his hands, and returned thanks that the lawful master and the ancient stock were restored to their rights.

I felt stunned by the awful event, and my memory unavoidably recurred to former times with a sort of oppressive sadness. But poor Hareton, the most wronged, was the only one who really suffered much. He sat by the corpse all night, weeping in bitter earnest. He pressed its hand, and kissed the sarcastic, savage face that everyone else shrank from contemplating, and bemoaned him with that strong grief which springs naturally from a generous heart, though it be tough as tempered steel.

Mr. Kenneth was perplexed to pronounce of what disorder the master died. I concealed the fact of his having swallowed nothing for four days, fearing it might lead to trouble. I am persuaded he did not abstain on purpose. It was the consequence of his strange illness, not the cause.

We buried him, to the scandal of the whole neighborhood, as he wished. Earnshaw and I, the sexton, and six men to carry the coffin, comprehended the whole attendance. The six men departed when they had let it down into the grave. We stayed to see it covered. Hareton, with a streaming face, dug green sods, and laid them over the brown mould himself. At present it is as smooth and verdant as its companion mounds—and I hope its tenant sleeps as soundly. But the country folks, if you ask them, would swear on the Bible that he walks.

There are those who speak to having met him near the church, and on the moor, and even within this house. Idle tales, you'll say, and so say I. Yet that old man by the kitchen fire affirms he has seen two on 'em looking out of his chamber window on every rainy night since his death—and an odd thing happened to me about a month ago.

I was going to the Grange one evening—a dark evening, threatening thunder—and, just at the turn of the Heights, I encountered a little boy with a sheep and two lambs before him. He was crying terribly, and I supposed the lambs were skittish, and would not be guided.

"What is the matter, my little man?" I asked.

"There's Heathcliff and a woman yonder, under t' nab," he blubbered, "un' I dare not pass 'em."

I saw nothing, but neither the sheep nor he would go on so I bid him take the road lower down. He probably raised the phantoms from thinking, as he traversed the moors alone, on the nonsense he had heard his parents and companions repeat. Yet, still, I don't like being out in the dark now, and I don't like being left by myself in this grim house. I cannot help it, I shall be glad when they leave it, and shift to the Grange.

"They are going to the Grange, then?" I said.

"Yes," answered Mrs. Dean, "as soon as they are married, and that will be on New Year's Day."

"And who will live here then?"

"Why, Joseph will take care of the house, and, perhaps, a lad to keep him company. They will live in the kitchen, and the rest will be shut up."

"For the use of such ghosts as choose to inhabit it?" I observed.

"No, Mr. Lockwood," said Nelly, shaking her head. "I believe the dead are at peace, but it is not right to speak of them with levity."

At that moment the garden gate swung to. The ramblers were returning, their faces suffused with the happiness that comes from being satisfied in all respects.

"They are afraid of nothing," I grumbled, watching their approach through the window. "Together, they would brave Satan and all his legions."

As they stepped on to the door stones, and halted to take a last look at the moon—or, more correctly, at each other by her light—I felt irresistibly impelled to escape them again. Pressing a remembrance into the hand of Mrs. Dean, and disregarding her expostulations at my rudeness, I vanished through the kitchen as they opened the house door. So should have confirmed Joseph in his opinion of his fellow servant's gay indiscretions, had he not fortunately recognized me for a respectable character by the sweet ring of a sovereign at his feet.

My walk home was lengthened by a diversion in the direction of the kirk. When beneath its walls, I perceived decay had made progress, even in seven months. Many a window showed black gaps deprived of glass, and slates jutted off here and there, beyond the right line of the roof, to be gradually worked off in coming autumn storms.

I sought, and soon discovered, the three headstones on the slope next the moor. The middle one grey, and half-buried in the heath, Edgar Linton's only harmonized by the turf and moss creeping up its foot, Heathcliff's still bare.

I lingered round for a bit, under that benign sky, watched the moths fluttering among the heath and harebells, listened to the soft wind breathing through the grass, and wondered how anyone could ever imagine unquiet slumbers for the sleepers in that quiet earth.